THE
PASS

This book is dedicated to my loving wife, DeeDee, and our daughter, Brittany, who gave me encouragement and support throughout the writing process. Also to my son, Chris; my father; and the rest of my family for putting up with me.

It is also dedicated to those on the Mississippi Gulf Coast and elsewhere who were lost in Hurricane Katrina.

THE
PASS

FRANK WILEM

DeepBlue Press
Gulfport, MS

First Edition

ISBN # 978-0-615-66726-3

Printed in the
United States of America

Also by Frank Wilem:

The Keys

Summary

Ever considered just getting into the car and heading to parts unknown? Most people have—few actually do. Quint not only considers ditching his cheating wife and dead-end job for a tropical escape, he does it—and heads for the Keys.

After finishing two tours of duty as a Navy SEAL, Quint had longed for an ordinary life away from death and brutality. However, his post-service American dream becomes nothing more than a deep sleep, and he finds himself longing for a sense of purpose, a mission. He begins his new life tamely enough—as a charter boat captain in pursuit of the legal limits for his clients. But soon events converge to thrust Quint into a race to find the world's most valuable treasure while extracting himself from a shipwreck, rogue naval forces, and from the pursuit of a vile cadre of pirates and thieves, who are also committed to snatching the treasure from the grasp of ancient history or from anyone who gets in their way.

This fast-paced adventure starts in Mississippi then moves to the Keys. Soon Quint finds himself in Cay Sal looking for a lost Spanish galleon bearing the secret to an even bigger treasure. This leads him to South America where he searches for the most valuable and unusual treasure in the history of the world. It could also be the most dangerous if it falls into the wrong hands. Join Quint and Dawson in the adventure of their lives.

Acknowledgements

I would like to acknowledge the encouragement and support of my wife, DeeDee, for her editing assistance and advice. Karen Slade Bryant made a considerable contribution in editing the final manuscript and formatting it for publishing.

Also thanks to Linda Parker, Andy Chapman, and Marshall Lynch for their contributions during the novel development and The Gibbes Company for the dust jacket art work.

PROLOGUE

All day long Lt. Clark fought his upset stomach, terrified of his pending flight with a nuclear bomb on board, a bomb 100 times more powerful than the one dropped on Hiroshima. *Conventional bombs were one thing; that's what bombers were supposed to carry—not this abomination,* he thought.

Clark worried because the bomb was armed and fully operational. But with six built-in failsafe gates on the bomb, his buddies claimed it didn't matter. "What's your problem? You could hit it with a hammer or shoot it with a .45 without detonating it," they argued as if he were about to test their theory.

He took another slug of Pepto-Bismol straight from the bottle, tossed it into his flight bag, and headed for the aircrew briefing hut. The room, nearly filled with Air Force flight crews, was hazy with a blue cloud of cigarette smoke. Clark walked down a row of battered metal chairs and grabbed a seat beside his pilot. A minute later, he heard the briefing officer's voice—barely audible over the din of two dozen conversations—calling the airmen to order.

A chorus of squeaking chairs marked the end of the briefing as the flight crews departed the meeting, eager to get under way. Clark joined his crew headed for their plane, his rumbling stomach forgotten in the excitement over their flight. He took a deep breath of the crisp night air, admiring the clear skies over Barksdale Air Force Base, and stepped up to the plane to begin the preflight inspection.

He was proud of their new B-47 as he affectionately ran his hand along its shiny-smooth skin. In production since the early 1950s, its six powerful GE jet engines hung from revolutionary-designed swept wings. After completing the inspection, the three-man crew climbed the ladder and entered the plane through the hatch on the underside of the nose. Clark sat next to the pilot behind the long fighter-style canopy, glad he was not relegated to the bombardier's miniscule nose compartment. A few minutes later, they were climbing smoothly, and he heard the bump of the bicycle landing gear folding snugly inside the plane's body.

As Clark's thoughts shifted back to the mammoth 7,600-pound

nuclear weapon they carried, his nausea returned and sent him fumbling through his flight bag for his pink medicine. Silently, he prayed they would never drop the bomb—a prayer that would not be granted.

After taking off from Belle Chasse Naval Air Station, Dennis Feltzer was in a steep climb in his F-86 Sabre jet fighter on his first solo nighttime training mission. Below, he could see the lights of New Orleans' French Quarter, its streets filled with Mardi Gras revelers. With numerous nighttime missions in trainers and what seemed like a million daytime hours flying the F-86, he was relaxed—at least as much as anyone could be flying such a powerful jet at night.

The flight was perfect so far with the exception of the radar, which had stopped transmitting shortly after takeoff. But with hardly any nearby air traffic, he was not about to scrub his training mission over a balky radar.

The B-47 reached altitude, and the crew commenced its simulated bombing exercise, with mission protocol requiring both radio and radar silence. "Boy, it's weird flying totally blind at night," Clark said. "I guess it's good experience—just hope we never need it." The pilot nodded silently as Clark reached into his flight bag to remove the pink bottle for another "hit."

"Stomach acting up?"

"Yeah, all day."

"Probably a touch of that stomach flu going around. Half the squadron is down with it. We've got a couple of days of down time before we fly again. Get it cleared up."

"Roger," Clark promised without admitting the real problem was that he was scared of their payload. He wished he were back in sick bay with the flu rather than flying their simulated attack mission on the Soviet Union with that "thing" on board. Clark wiped his sweaty hands, lit a smoke, and inhaled deeply.

Though it seemed much longer, a few hours later they finally began the last leg of their mission, and Clark relaxed knowing they were headed home.

Dennis made a series of maneuvers in his F-86 per his training protocol for the night flight. After completing two rolls, he executed a three-second dive before initiating a climb to 37,000 feet. He finished his climb and started to dive again when a massive shape filled his windscreen. His plane shuddered violently as the left wing was sheared off, and he immediately lost control. After radioing a quick mayday, he prepared to eject.

Following the emergency procedure he learned in training but hoped never to use, he actuated the emergency oxygen bottle with shaking hands, lowered his head, and pulled up on the right handgrip to jettison the canopy. As it slid away, he sat upright and locked his harness with his feet in the footrests and his arms braced on the armrests. Tucking his chin, he squeezed the ejection trigger beneath the handgrip and felt the G's as he was rocketed out of the plane still strapped to his seat.

Clear of the plane, Dennis separated from the seat with the parachute strapped to his back. He pulled the ripcord, and the parachute deployed, but something was wrong. The chute's canopy was fouled in the rigging and would not inflate. His stomach knotted as he plummeted toward the shark-filled waters below. Frantically, he worked the control lines, trying to fill the canopy. The last thing he saw was his plane exploding in an enormous fireball as it slammed into the ocean, witnessed by only him and two fishermen a few miles away.

The big bomber was shaken by the impact of the unseen plane. "What the hell was that?" Clark screamed in fear, pink liquid spilling over the front of his flight suit from his third slug of Pepto-Bismol. While the pilot struggled to control of the aircraft, Clark scanned the panel.

"We must have been hit. Left wing's okay; check the right one; we're handling funny," the pilot said calmly.

Clark looked out the right side. Below he saw the F-86 fireball, and directly behind him, their badly damaged wing. "Mid-air collision. Number six engine's dangling, and we're losing fuel. I'm shutting her down," he said, as he scanned the instrument panel. "Rest of the engines seem okay."

"Maybe, but there's a problem with the control surfaces on your side. I can keep us level but don't know for how long. I'm dropping to a lower altitude," the pilot said, struggling to fly the violently shaking aircraft.

"Can we land her?"

"We'll land her; the question is, 'Will we walk away?' Radio base and request permission to jettison our payload."

"Sir, are... are you sure? We're under radio silence and... well... we're carrying a *nuclear* weapon, sir," Clark said in a shaky voice.

"No shit. Clark, the damn weapon is safed. Unless you're looking to go down with it, get me that authorization. Now!"

Clark swallowed hard to choke down the bile while switching the radio to the emergency military frequency. "Mayday, mayday. This is flight T149. We've had a mid-air collision and have a potential broken arrow situation. We've lost our number six engine and sustained control surface damage to our right wing. Request permission for a safe drop."

"Copy. Stand by." After what seemed like an eternity, the radio popped alive again. "Flight T149, this is base. Permission to jettison is granted. Repeat. Permission to jettison is granted. Mark position. Say again: Mark Position. Cleared to divert to Belle Chasse Naval Air Station for emergency landing."

Clark echoed the command before calling the bombardier over the intercom, "Bombardier, Flight Deck. Drop load."

"Flight, Bombardier, say again?"

"Bombardier, drop load and mark drop location coordinates."

A long pause followed after which he heard the reply, "This is Navigation, confirming that you wish me to *drop load.*"

"Yes, damn it all! Drop it right the hell now! Or do I have to come down there and do it myself?" Clark snapped back.

"No sir. Roger," the bombardier replied while opening the bomb bay doors. A moment later, the twelve-foot-long bomb slid out of the plane falling at 200 knots. The bomb bay doors closed, and the plane banked toward Belle Chasse Air Field to attempt a landing.

Meanwhile, the bomb continued its 7,200-foot fall into the shallow ocean water below. It came to rest with only a fin showing above the soft mud bottom between the Chandeleur Islands off the Louisiana coast and the Mississippi Sound where it would sit undisturbed for the next 50 years.

CHAPTER 1

Somewhere in the Middle East
Present Day

The red numbers on the timer's digital display relentlessly counted down toward zero with fewer than 30 seconds remaining. Concealed within the bowels of the high-rise office building's basement, it would have been impossible to remove or defuse the nuclear bomb in time even if its presence had been detected—which it had not.

When the display reached zero, a blinding light emanated from the device, accompanying a force seldom unleashed above ground since the Hiroshima and Nagasaki explosions marked the end of World War II. The energy vaporized the entire building, sending a shock wave racing from the epicenter, followed closely by a wall of searing heat that turned those in its path into ash-shadows against the few remaining partial walls. As the blast radius steadily increased, the temperatures fell, bringing the cruelest stage in which the flash fire only seared its victims, melting away their skin but leaving them alive.

Hordes of the horribly burned walked zombie-like, arms outstretched to avoid touching their bodies. A little girl in pitiful agony, the skin dropping away from her face and arms to leave only the raw flesh beneath, clutched her scorched doll and screamed, "Mommy!" crying through lidless eyes. As her image faded, the applause began amongst the crowd gathered to watch the video depicting the sick vision of their leader.

It was 2 a.m. as Abu Rashid Muhammad walked along the back of the darkened outdoor stage. The sheer rock wall rose above the giant entrance to the cave behind him, creating a horseshoe-shaped natural amphitheater. The technology supporting his event stood in stark contrast to the primitive cave-camp where they were gathered, hidden in a remote terrorist training camp in Syria. His breath formed a cloud, and he shivered in the cool desert night air. He struggled not to favor his chronically aching knee; he could show no weakness—he was their leader.

The world's landscape was changing, and he sometimes found it difficult to comprehend how far they had come. Progress with the recruitment of terrorists in the U.S—home-grown from within the Great Satan—was going well. It was now hard to justify returning to maintain the zeal of his followers with even this visit deemed a needless risk by Rashid's counsel. But it was good to be back. That this might be his last visit made him savor it all the more as he gazed out at the cheering throng.

Rashid relished being treated as a hero, championing the fight against unjust forces that kept his people impoverished. He enjoyed being viewed as their savior, a man with power so great as to risk Allah's displeasure.

Sheltered as the son of a wealthy family, Rashid often witnessed the hungry dressed in rags. While being chauffeured to his private school, he would throw them scraps smuggled from his own bountiful breakfast table. Though as a young boy he felt guilt for his life of plenty, he now seldom chose to share his own considerable fortune with the needy. He saw no irony in the fact that he lived in luxury while those before him were condemned to live in squalor. He was the anointed one—come to liberate his "children," as he saw the peasants gathered before him.

He approached the polished teak lectern, brightly illuminated by a spotlight. Above and slightly behind him, his huge image replaced the nuclear holocaust scene on the massive screen as it did on two others flanking the rock-walled, open-air stage.

Except for a few grey streaks, his otherwise dyed-black hair shone in the spotlight, and his teeth glowed bright white, as did his long robe. Rashid calmly surveyed the crowd standing before him, waiting for the applause to die away. The long pause served to establish him as their leader, lest there be any doubt—which there was not. The crowd sat in silent obedience as he leaned slightly forward to the microphone and spoke in a low voice, confident that they would remain silent to catch his every word.

"A new day dawns for us. This new day will come with unimaginable swiftness for those who sleep even as we work. Some will join us on this new day. Sadly, others will not. For them will soon come their last day. The computer-generated video you just witnessed illustrates what *will* come to pass." He paused while his adoring followers applauded.

"The Great Satan is a formidable adversary to be sure. Stealth, one of our key weapons, prevents me from unveiling our plan in all its wondrous glory as I might wish. But trust me when I tell you enormous effort has been expended in its conception, and even more will be required for its execution.

"I can tell you that we will follow the Chinese strategy of 'death by a thousand cuts.' Some will be minor paper cuts, while others will be deep gashes—overwhelming the Great Satan with waves of attacks. We will strike them in their big cities and their small villages, in their workplaces and homes, where they shop and where they play, shaking the very foundation of western decadence, causing it to crumble then collapse upon itself.

"This is our sacred mission, our calling, our legacy, our finest moment. Though some of us will be martyred, all will receive eternal reward. I know you stand ready to make the supreme sacrifice without a moment's hesitation, as do I. From this instant on, our entire reason for existence lies in the realization of this plan. That is why you train each day. It is why you study and pray.

"Now I bid you: go with Allah. May He protect you as you prepare to serve Him."

With the slightest bow of his head, Rashid stood. Then as choreographed, the screen behind him rose and two massive doors leading into the cave opened, unleashing an intense blinding light from within. He appeared supernatural, a shadowed figure illuminated by a light that seemed to consume him. The meeting had ended, but the chaos was just beginning.

"Omar, your actions sicken me. You are not driven by devotion to the cause; you simply yield to desires of the flesh," Akmed said, referring to the recent death of a young French reporter Omar had captured while opposing the American occupiers.

"But Akmed, the Holy Quran says: *'If a woman becomes captive in a war, her Muslim master is allowed to rape her 33:50.'* Were we not at war? And was she not my captive—making me her master?" Omar replied with a grin.

"Don't you dare lecture me about the Quran. Unlike you, I study and obey it rather than use it as cover to satisfy perverse appetites." Their conversation was interrupted by Rashid's entry into the expansive conference room. He made note of the ongoing argument, electing not to comment. Rashid did not view men through a prism of good and evil. Rather, he observed their capabilities and focused on applying their strengths and weaknesses to his task.

Rashid was pleased with his performance, confident that his fanatical followers were properly motivated. He gestured toward the waiting servant to begin tea service as he assumed his position at the head of the dark mahogany table in a chair that was, by design, several inches higher than the rest.

Rashid plucked lint off of one pin-striped sleeve of the finely tailored, Western-style suit for which he had traded his robe after leaving the stage. With his lieutenants similarly dressed in Western business attire, this could have easily passed for a Fortune 500 company board meeting.

"Sorry for the delay caused by my presentation to rally martyrs. We must ensure a steady supply of grist for our mill of terrorism against the Great Satan," he began while continuing to compulsively search for microscopic pieces of lint on his suit. "Once they leave here, they will operate as closed cells, and we no longer have the opportunity to meet with them to imbue them with the fervor needed to sustain their commitment. Thus, it is important that we leave them fully motivated. With the great strides we have made in recruiting home-grown followers in the U.S., we no longer need to groom large numbers here. They are already ready and waiting where we need them most.

"Our success requires immersing ourselves in the Western world so that we appear as one of them. But I called one last meeting here because I felt it useful to renew our own faith and commitment to our *one* cause, lest we become seduced by the temptations of the infidels."

Rashid paused as the servant set the tea service before him and tasted the strong brew, savoring its warmth before proceeding. "I am ready for a briefing on our project's status."

Rashid's deputy, Akmed, stood, his slight body elegant in a tailored dark suit. Rashid found Akmed's cunning mind more than offset his slight physical appearance. Unlike Omar, who lacked the religious fanaticism imbued in many of his followers, Akmed truly was a believer, though no blind follower.

"Preparations for the first of your 'thousand cuts' is proceeding on schedule. It was child's play to smuggle the teams into the U.S."

"Excellent. So there have been no problems?"

Akmed hesitated. "A minor one. An arms shipment appears to have been confiscated."

"Appears?"

"Our 'supplier' may have set us up after being paid for the weapons. The cache was definitely raided by the police, but we suspect they were paid by our supplier, who ended up with the shipment back in his possession."

Rashid frowned, and Akmed glanced at Talib, whose massive bulk rested like a coiled spring in the chair opposite him. While Rashid was to be feared, the men knew that it was his "hammer," Talib, who was to be watched. Those who had witnessed Talib's fury unleashed hoped never to be its recipient.

Omar sought the safety of Talib's shadow, lavishing praise on him whenever the opportunity presented itself. "So, we have nothing to show for the considerable sum paid for the weapons?" Omar said with a sly grin, scratching his thin beard. Akmed nodded, his eyes shooting back daggers.

Rashid noted the tension between the two men. "Such things are to be expected when dealing with men whose only god is money. These men must be punished to send the message that we are not fools."

Finished with his tea, he withdrew a stick of chewing gum—his weapon du jour in his ongoing battle to defeat the nicotine addiction he had acquired as a student in the U.S. He set the foil wrapper to one side and began to toy with a paper clip, bending it into different shapes as he turned to Omar. "Make sure Akmed has whatever support he requires. Keep me posted."

"By all means," Omar replied, inferring that Akmed was certain to need his help.

For the next two hours, they discussed business. "Anything else?" Rashid finally asked. No one replied. "Well, I have one more item," he announced, pausing for effect. He set aside his paper clip work of art now wrapped with the foil from his gum wrapper and focused on what he was about to say.

"For some time, I have sought a nuclear weapon for our special project to achieve the dream depicted in our video to provide a... shall we say... dramatic finale to our 'thousandth cut.' It's best that I not reveal much detail at this time, but I can say it could make Osama's 9/11 show look like a child's attempt to impress his parents. Perhaps I may have more to tell you at our next meeting."

Rashid rose and returned to his private room for the evening prayer. In the morning, he would return to the U.S., where he would resume his identity as a successful businessman.

CHAPTER
2

"Yes, I realize you've already delivered roses to her a dozen times this week, but since *I'm* paying, why do you care?" Quint asked, running his fingers through his unruly shaggy blond hair then down the side of his face. One finger traced the wicked scar traversing his left cheek, souvenir from a knife cut during a SEAL mission. He sat in his kitchen wearing a threadbare t-shirt yellowed with sweat and a matching pair of boxers, both overdue for the trash.

"I suppose I don't, it's just... well... unusual," the flower lady replied.

"So, consider me an unusual kind of guy."

"Well, the other thing... " the lady stammered before blurting out, "you should know that the garbage can beside her house is filled with flowers—she's throwing them out as fast as we deliver them."

"And?" Quint asked, his bright green eyes wrinkling in a grin.

"And, I thought that if you knew, maybe you'd want to stop sending them."

"Well, you thought wrong. Make sure they're fresh, and please try to have them delivered before lunch," he said before hanging up. His grin was short lived as he recalled the reason for his floral onslaught. The image of Evie laughing over her shoulder as he chased her down the beach flashed through his mind.

Between his share of the *Almiranta* treasure and payments he received from their find in Venezuela, Quint was wealthy beyond his wildest dreams. While he could now afford to do most anything or go most anywhere he chose, he found life was not so simple. His budding relationship with Evie, for example, had fallen victim to his newfound fortune.

As his new financial status became common knowledge, courtesy of several television and newspaper stories, along with the money had come fame. Not a crazy Hollywood-type fame but more of a local notoriety where everyone in town seemed to know him. And along with the fame had come beautiful women, establishing Quint as the most desirable bachelor in town.

At first he found it difficult to resist the gorgeous women who seemed to pop up everywhere, fawning over him, proclaiming him to be the most handsome and witty man they had ever met. Blinded by the glitz, he hardly noticed when Evie faded away. But by the time he awoke to the realization that the gold diggers were mainly in love with his bank account, he found her distanced.

How he wished he could trade the whole lot of them dressed in their latest designer fashions for a Saturday afternoon working on one of her never-ending house repair projects. He loved her dressed in faded jeans, silky brown hair gathered in a loose pony tail. He even loved the *real feel* of her broken nails and bandaged fingers, which stood in stark contrast to the painted women frequenting his life of late.

His campaign to send flowers twice a day until Evie relented was not working. *Maybe I should try calling her again,* Quint thought to himself, though he had called, written, and sent flowers, as well as a small fortune in expensive gifts, all to no avail. Finally, he decided he would muster the courage to try calling once more—tomorrow.

Quint downed a slug of coffee from his chipped mug and set it back on the scarred laminate-covered table that had served him well in the two years since finding it at a garage sale. Though in desperate need of replacement—like the television that worked only half the time and the cracked carafe on the coffee maker—it went ignored. To Quint, the value of his new-found prosperity lay in the freedom it afforded, not the "stuff," which, for the most part, held little interest to him.

At 40, Quint's face was weathered by years of sun and sea. Of average height but powerfully built, he accepted himself as he was rather than what he wished he could be. He found his personality rather than his looks to be his greatest asset.

It was peaceful living in the Keys—or maybe he was just at peace. Either way, life was good. Even the nightmares of his abusive father beating his mother—memories that had tormented Quint since he was a small child—no longer haunted him.

While adjusting to his wealth, Quint had shifted his focus toward finding a new direction in life. On the wall hung a framed photo of his charter boat *Mojito,* destroyed by a storm in Venezuela. Though he had considered replacing the boat, he was not sure about running fishing charters again. And getting the team back together to "save the world" was not on his short list.

What do I want to do? Quint wondered aloud. Once again the embryonic idea of starting a company with his old team reared its head, as it frequently had over the past week. Lost in thought, he was lazily stirring vanilla creamer into his second cup of coffee when the ringing phone interrupted his musings.

Halfway expecting a telemarketer, he considered letting the call go to voicemail before his curiosity got the better of him, and he grabbed his cell phone off the table while simultaneously muting the television news. As he set the remote back on the table, his hand caught the spoon in his coffee, sending a deluge of steaming, tawny-colored liquid into his lap.

"Quint," he answered brusquely while bobbling the phone as he jumped to his feet and pulled his boxers away from his smoldering groin.

"Hello Quint, my name is Rogers. A mutual acquaintance suggested I call. I've read about your remarkable recent adventures and am in need of someone with your, shall we say, 'special' expertise."

"You're referring to my Special Forces days?" Quint asked, regretting he had taken the call as he pulled a stack of napkins from the holder to blot up coffee, first from his lap and then from the table and chair. He managed to catch the phone—that had slipped from between his ear and shoulder—before it hit the floor.

"Yes, though I'm equally impressed with your more recent adventures. I believe you met a Colonel Botz?"

Quint remembered Botz, an American "spook" who had popped up at the Incan temple in the middle of the Venezuelan jungle. "Yeah, I remember being underwhelmed by him after he used us for bait and then tried to commandeer our chopper carrying a woman on our team in desperate need of medical attention."

"Evidently, he was a lot more impressed with you than you were with him. Would it be possible to meet in Miami this Friday evening?"

"That's a long way to go for a chat. Why Miami and why this Friday?" Quint asked, reseated after dealing with the coffee mishap.

"I'm flying in from Brazil for my daughter's twenty-first birthday party at our house in the Grove. Next week I'm speaking at a conference in Italy. I'll send my private jet to pick you up, and you're welcome to spend the night at my house, or I can have you flown back to the Keys later that night."

"Okay, you've addressed the logistics, and I suppose I could alter my plans," Quint replied, his stomach knotting as he remembered his Friday night date, "but you still haven't said why we need to talk."

"I'm sorry, but at the risk of sounding melodramatic, it really is something best not discussed over the phone—too many ears. Please, Quint, I believe you'll find the meeting quite interesting, and the party alone should make it worth your trouble."

Quint wasn't interested in the party, but his curiosity now piqued, he decided his date would just have to understand. And if not, that was okay too; he missed Evie. "Okay, I'll come. What time will your plane arrive?"

"As soon as we land and clear customs, they'll head your way. They should pick you up at the Key West airport's fixed-base operator terminal by 7 p.m. I'll kick off my daughter's party, then slip away to meet with you shortly after you arrive."

"That'll work. Given the small size of our FBO, I shouldn't have trouble linking up with your flight crew. If my partner, Dawson, is back in town, I'd like to include him as well."

"Splendid. I'll look forward to meeting both of you."

"By the way, how did you get my cell number?"

"You'd be surprised what I know about you," he said cryptically.

Roger, Rogers, Quint said sarcastically to himself as he hung up the phone, wondering what he might be getting himself into and hoping he wasn't wasting his time as he dialed Dawson.

CHAPTER 3

Returning from a month's vacation in the Med, Dawson hopped the New York subway for a late dinner in SoHo on his overnight layover. He returned close to midnight, his lonely steps echoing off the deserted underground subway station's stained concrete deck littered with cigarette butts. Papers skittered past a pile of crushed soft drink cans disgorged from an overturned trash can festooned with spray-painted graffiti. With his dark blue jacket collar turned up against the evening chill, Dawson's hands sought the warmth deep in the pockets of his khaki slacks.

His spicy dinner fare had not agreed with him. Already he could feel the onset of serious heartburn and looked forward to returning to his room for a dose of antacid. Across the platform he noticed three men in their twenties sauntering toward him, their cocky demeanor projecting an air of trouble. Choosing not to slip into the restroom on his right, he continued walking.

The leader wore a Yankee baseball cap with the bill turned sideways. Dawson smiled remembering Quint's saying, *You lose one point off your IQ for every degree your hat is turned to the side.*

Yankee's rotund buddy sported a too-large Knicks hat and an oversized red shirt, only partially covering a pair of baggy shorts hanging well below his knees. An enormous pair of untied sneakers completed his ensemble. Dawson wondered if they were long shorts or short pants. *At least they have the courage to look stupid,* Dawson thought. The third man had a shaved head and wore sunglasses.

"Hey, my man. I need a little cash. You help me out?" Yankee asked. Too late, Dawson noticed a fourth man inching along the platform behind him—he was trapped.

"Sorry, I'm tapped out," Dawson replied. Though eager to help those truly in need, he abhorred panhandlers feeding off the misplaced sympathy of others and hustlers who profited through intimidation.

"Well then, you see we got us a little problem."

"How's that?" Dawson asked.

"You got to pay the toll to pass by," Yankee said with a smile, running his tongue over a shiny gold tooth.

"Really?" Dawson asked as he spotted three more men approaching from the far side of the platform. *Uh-oh,* he thought. *If they're more of Yankee's buddies, I've got real trouble.*

"Yeah, really," the gold-toothed leader responded. "You see, I think you do got cash, and if you don't give it up well, then maybe we just got to take it."

"Gosh, wouldn't that be kinda' like stealing?" Dawson responded in a feigned shaky voice, relieved to see the other three men continue down the platform, oblivious to the ongoing drama between Dawson and the four men.

"It just might be," Yankee answered with a grin, the gold tooth glinting in the subway light.

"Guys, you really don't want to do this," Dawson said, moving to skirt the men in hopes of avoiding a conflict. Yankee resembled someone who brought back bad memories, and Dawson struggled not to let his mind go there. As Dawson passed, the bald one grabbed his arm, and Dawson's foot shot out with blinding speed, nailing the man in the groin, dropping him to the ground.

A heavy blow to the back of his head stunned Dawson for a moment. He took two steps forward, buying a moment to gather his wits. He knew that if he went down, it was over; the best he could hope for was that someone would find his battered body still alive.

Dawson spun and, with two fingers extended, jabbed the man behind him near the base of his neck. The man's hands flew to his crushed trachea and he fell to the concrete coughing and gasping.

As Knicks turned to run, his sagging pants slid to his ankles, tripping him. Eyes wide in horror, he fell toward the train tracks where his body came to rest on the high-voltage rail, his legs completing the circuit. A shower of sparks accompanied his dying screams and the stench of burning flesh wafting away from his lifeless body. In seconds, only the gold-toothed leader remained standing.

As Dawson stared into Yankee's eyes, memories flooded back of the night he had finally caught up with the drug addict responsible for his wife's and daughter's deaths, and he again felt the hatred. A look of fear crossed Yankee's face as he stared into Dawson's menacing blue eyes and saw his rage. He noticed the nose, broken more than once over the years, and realized that he had misjudged this victim.

Yankee's hesitation proved costly as Dawson delivered three hard blows to his torso. The two men sparred briefly, with Yankee landing a couple of glancing blows before Dawson nailed him in the solar plexus, forcing the air from his lungs. An upper cut to the man's chin collapsed him onto the pavement and had him writhing in pain. Dawson plucked the gold tooth from the ground beside its former owner, and with a chuckle he tossed it into the sewer grate.

"Next time get a regular tooth. Maybe you won't look like such a dumb ass," Dawson said, allowing his anger to fade. He climbed the stairs to the street above, pulled his jacket collar up against the misty rain, and whistled as he strolled down the street. He could still catch a few hours of sleep before his early morning flight to Miami.

Dawson answered the phone on the third ring, rubbing his eyes. His dark hair stood at wild angles, and the mid-morning sun high-lighted a ragged scar on his forearm. "Hello," he croaked, struggling to clear the cobwebs.

"Have a good night's sleep?" Quint asked.

"Until you woke me."

"When did your sorry ass get back from the Med?"

"Drove in from Miami at three this morning."

"Have a good trip?"

"Yeah, except for a little episode in the New York subway on the way back," he said, rubbing the back of his head where it still ached from the episode. "So are we playing 20 questions or is there a point to your call?"

"Yes, Mr. Grumpy. I called to see if you're ready to live a mean-ingful life again."

"I'd love to, but I'm polishing door knobs today. Tomorrow I clean toilets. Quint, what the hell are you talking about?"

"Tell you what, my buddy down at the Half-Shell Raw Bar just got a fresh sack of Apalachicola oysters and promised to save me a few dozen. Come on down, and I'll fill you in over oysters and beer, my treat."

"Deal. See you at one," Dawson replied.

Quint was about to hang up when the image of Lefty's worn face flashed through his mind. "Wait, let's make that a little later. I've got... uh... an errand to run."

"What's her name?"

"Ha, ha. See you at three," Quint said as he hung up. He had nearly forgotten it was the first Wednesday of the month, the day he always took Lefty for dialysis. He would have to get moving to avoid one of Lefty's sermons on the sanctity of punctuality.

After a quick shower, Quint threw on a threadbare t-shirt and a pair of shorts in only slightly better shape. While tying a knot on his ragged left sneaker, he broke the shoelace for the third time. "Damn," he swore, as he struggled to tie a knot in the short pieces before angrily ripping the shoe from his foot and flinging it across the room.

Quint stormed into the kitchen, snatched a garbage bag from the pantry, and proceeded to throw in the offending sneaker, along with a half-dozen pairs of worn out deck shoes. Next, he threw away a drawer full of socks and a pile of old underwear, all riddled with holes.

Realizing his overzealousness had left him barefoot, he scrounged a pair of flip flops from the bottom of his closet. He would make a trip to the boating store to restock while waiting on Lefty. Grabbing his keys, he headed down the stairs of his modest Key West garage apartment, located behind a small matching frame house— both painted white with garish green trim.

Quint spotted Lefty sitting astride his regular perch at the base of the Key West Bight Marina's memorial statue across from the Conch Republic restaurant. "Thought you'd forgotten about me," Lefty said, as he slid inside the pickup truck. Quint had splurged on the truck so he could reserve his restored 1970 Plymouth Road Runner for Sunday cruising.

"Have I ever forgotten you?" Quint asked, relieved that Lefty seemed clear-minded but not so pleased with his odor—he was long overdue for a date with soap and hot water. Lefty wore a new t-shirt emblazoned with "Breast Cancer Awareness Month" in bright pink letters and matching flip flops, a gift, Quint imagined, from some soft-hearted tourist. A pair of ragged shorts matched his filthy face, the right half of which seemed to have been partially cleaned and bore only streaks of dirt. His thinning shoulder-length hair was wrapped with a scrap of brightly colored bandana.

"God bless you, Quint. You're a decent man. I love you for it. Did I ever tell you about that lieutenant that saved my life in 'Nam?"

Lefty asked, before launching off on one of his monologues. Because of his rambling chants and bizarre appearance, Quint had avoided him at first until hints about Lefty's sad story surfaced during one of his rare, lucid moments. By asking around, Quint managed to piece together the rest of the story and chose to befriend him.

By the time they reached the dialysis clinic, Lefty had stopped speaking and drifted off into "Lefty-land." Not trusting him to make it the 200 feet to the clinic, Quint decided to park and walk with him. As he emerged from his truck, he noticed a familiar car heading toward him and found himself looking straight at Evie. Their eyes locked for only an instant before she looked off and continued driving past.

Quint watched until her car disappeared from view, before accompanying Lefty into the clinic where they waited until the dialysis was under way. "Lefty, I'll be back before you're finished to take you wherever you need to go," Quint said, hoping the vacant stare signified understanding.

Quint left the clinic hoping to catch up with Evie, but by the time he arrived, she had already parked and gone inside her house. Lacking the desire to engage in an awkward confrontation, he continued past her house, craning his neck to catch another glimpse of her.

Quint then embarked on a mini-shopping spree, stopping at the boating supply store for deck shoes and at K-Mart to replenish his underwear and sock drawer. By the time he returned to the clinic, Lefty had just finished and seemed to be normal, at least as normal as he ever was.

As he saw Quint approach, Lefty called out, "Quint! Looking great. Where you been?" as if he had no recollection of having been together only hours before.

"Ready to go?"

"Does the sun rise in the morning?" Lefty replied, following Quint out to the car, limping.

"Leg bothering you?"

"No, it's my right foot. When I walk much it starts hurting. Been doing it ever since I lost my shoes and started wearing these girly-looking flip flops." Quint nodded without replying and slipped into the driver's seat. As he pulled out of the parking spot, Lefty launched off on another tale and maintained a running dialogue until they reached Mallory Square. "You can let me out here."

Quint passed a group of Mopeds and pulled over to the curb before reaching into his pocket to withdraw all his cash. "Here, go buy another pair of shoes and grab a burger." Lefty started to shake his head. "Don't argue with me. You owe it to me after that dialysis trip." With a solemn nod, Lefty accepted the cash and limped off without questioning why he was obligated to take cash after Quint had done *him* a favor.

As Quint pulled away from the curb to go meet Dawson, he winced at the realization that he had just given away all of his remaining cash and had left his wallet at home.

Dawson forced himself out of bed in time for a quick workout and shower. He scrounged a twice-worn pair of cargo shorts from the chair beside his dresser and a freshly laundered Marty Wilson-designed t-shirt from his closet to dress for his meeting. He found Quint perched on a barstool beside a pitcher of icy beer and two platters of raw oysters displayed on the ancient wooden bar. A slight odor of fish mixed with the smell of diesel drifted in off the harbor.

After stirring extra horseradish into a plastic cup filled with cocktail sauce, Dawson impaled an oyster on his seafood fork, plunged it into the fiery sauce, and ceremoniously placed it atop a crisp cracker. "Mmmmm, ice cold and plenty salty—just like I love 'em," he mumbled through a mouth filled with oyster and cracker crumbs as he set to work on the rest of his dozen.

"How's life up north?"

"Quiet," Dawson replied. He had bought a house with deep water access conveniently located near his favorite bar on Big Pine Key, 30 miles away from the Key West craziness. Noticing Quint point to his left cheek, he wiped away a large glob of cocktail sauce.

"Since we're on your tab, I'm goin' for number two," he said holding up two fingers to the waitress. After jointly consuming six dozen oysters and as many crackers, they tossed their forks onto the platters filled with empty shells and eased back on their bar stools.

Dawson studied the tourists strolling down the dock, gaping at the large fish hung above the charter boat cleaning station while the crew cleaned the smaller ones. "Always clean the biggest last," Quint said.

"Oysters aside, why are we here?"

"Dawson, my whole life I longed for the financial freedom we now enjoy. While it's great, I never thought past this point. Now that I have the luxury to do whatever I want, I've been struggling with what to do next."

"You complaining?"

"No, I'm not looking for sympathy—just purpose. I've been thinking about the two of us setting up a for-profit limited liability company to pursue some new projects. I figured our former team members could be shareholders and serve on the LLC board. We'd favor profitable projects, but might also try to achieve something for the greater good, so to speak."

"What type of projects?"

"Been struggling with that question, but fate may have offered an answer." He recounted his conversation with Rogers.

Uncharacteristically, Dawson had no sarcastic come-back and pondered the idea before breaking the silence. "I owe you a lot."

"You don't owe me anything. I just…"

"No, I do. Not just for those times with the SEALS, but for pulling me out of the bottle after I lost Cathy and our daughter," Dawson said, pausing to look away with moist eyes. He tried not to recall the tragic automobile fire that killed his family and launched his self-destructive rampage to find the fuel truck driver responsible. "I'd probably still be lying in that hammock with my liver half-eaten from the rum if you hadn't found me.

"I enjoyed my trip to the Med—a lot. But I, too, began to wonder what I want to be when I grow up. I must say, you've made a whole lot more progress than I have addressing that question. I like your idea. You bounce it off of any of the others?"

"No, I wanted to get your reaction first."

"Let's go see what Rogers has in mind. The jet ride alone will be worth it." Dawson said as the waitress placed their check on the bar.

"Uh… by the way, I'm short on cash and forgot my wallet. You mind picking this one up?" Quint asked.

"What happened to, 'My treat?' *You* invite *me* for oysters and beer and then stick me with the tab. Now *that's* cheap. You really are a piece of work."

Quint's only reply was to smile, preferring not to explain the reason for his lack of cash.

CHAPTER
4

Rogers' jet was waiting when Quint and Dawson arrived at the Key West FBO Friday evening. Dressed in dark suits, the two men settled into the buttery, beige leather seats amidst a forest of rich walnut trim while the engines spooled up.

"Damn! I guess we're somebody now," Dawson exclaimed.

"Yeah, I could get used to this," Quint replied. A few minutes later the pilot banked in a long sweeping turn toward Miami over the pristine ocean waters, beneath which lay miles of coral reefs interspersed with the encrusted remains of centuries worth of shipwrecks.

Quint's thoughts drifted to charter fishing aboard *Mojito* and how he loved fishing these same waters. While he didn't miss the pressure of producing catches every day, he did miss spending time out on the ocean aboard his own boat.

After the brief flight to Miami, an impossibly long black limo waited on the tarmac to whisk them to Rogers' place in Coconut Grove. Dawson raided the well-stocked bar while Quint played with the lighting and music controls.

Quint was impressed as the driver maneuvered the mile-long Mercedes into a narrow driveway, actually more of a tunnel through thick vegetation. After winding through the perfectly manicured grounds, they stopped in front of a sprawling mansion, reminiscent of nearby Viscaya—the old James Deering estate on Biscayne Bay.

"Damn! Whatever this guy does, he must be good at it," Dawson commented, admiring the mansion and its grounds as the limo came to a halt.

"Welcome to the Rogers estate," a valet greeted them in a crisp tuxedo. "Gentlemen, please follow me," he said, guiding them past an impressive array of European luxury and sports cars.

The soft night breeze carried the scent of tropical flowers and rustled the fronds on a row of royal palms, their concrete-gray trunks and bright green tops illuminated by perfectly spaced landscape lighting. A row of stone columns lined the front steps and framed a pair of gargantuan wooden doors that Quint figured must weigh a ton.

A butler greeted them in the foyer holding a polished silver tray filled with drinks including a single Mojito, which he handed to Quint. "I believe you prefer your Mojito with Añejo rum and fresh Kentucky Colonel mint." Quint nodded and took a sip, the butler looking on expectantly.

"Excellent," Quint replied affirming his drink preference, impressed with the care Rogers had taken to accommodate his tastes, including procuring the special mint introduced to him by his buddy Leo.

"And for you," the butler said to Dawson, "a Jack and soda. Or we can swap this for a Cuba Libre with Diet Coke and extra lime if that's more to your liking this evening."

"Jack is perfect," Dawson said, sampling the sour mash drink, "and perfectly done as well," he added with a smile. Glowing with pride, the butler excused himself to continue delivering drinks. Dawson cut his Jack with water or soda more in the interests of the next morning than his health. Although he preferred Cuba Libres made with dark Bacardi and Coke, his waistline had forced a switch to Diet Coke, but he still found the caffeine exacted a price on his night's sleep.

Only minutes after arriving, Dawson met a potential conquest, introduced as Rachel, and they migrated out to the terrace to admire the moonlight over Biscayne Bay. Quint shook his head, impressed with Dawson's prowess, but mostly pleased to see him put the loss of his wife and daughter behind him—as well as the more recent death of Dr. Margaux Desmarais, with whom Dawson had a brief romance during their Incan adventure.

It was half past eight, and the party was in full swing, with the guests obviously competing to look the most posh. *A sizable family could retire on the money spent on wardrobes for this party,* Quint imagined. He hated this sort of affair and already wished it was over. He was always told, "Once you get there you'll have a great time; you'll be glad you went," but he never was.

His drink refreshed by the ever-vigilant butler, Quint now focused on the tie that was choking him. *The suit is bad enough—but this damn tie,* he thought to himself. Desperate to end his misery, he turned to a well-endowed young lady standing nearby dressed in a chic black cocktail dress that oozed understated elegance, "Would you please hold this for a moment?" he asked, handing her his drink.

"Certainly," she replied. He drew back the tie and loosened his collar button, instantly feeling the blood flow to his head increase. Though now appearing somewhat sloppy, he decided it was a small price to pay for comfort.

"That's better; be thankful you don't have to wear one of these," he said, pointing to his tie as he retrieved his drink.

"Look, I'm wearing pantyhose and high heels. Don't expect sympathy from me."

"Touché," Quint chuckled, noticing she seemed totally unlike the gold diggers he frequently encountered these days. Taken with her genuine friendly manner, he introduced himself.

"So you're the famous Quint! Tales of your adventures and marvelous good fortune precede you. That *Almiranta* story was fascinating, but the Venezuelan temple episode sounded even more intriguing," she remarked.

"Yeah, slow news day," he replied.

"Recovering treasure from the wreck of a Spanish galleon while fighting off pirates and the Cuban Navy hardly qualifies as a slow news day story. Should I look for you to be on '*Lifestyles of the Rich and Famous?*'"

"More like the '*Dumb and Lucky,*'" Quint laughed.

"I'll take luck over smart any day," she replied with a grin. "Okay, I see you're uncomfortable. Let's change the subject. How do you know Rogers?"

Quint hesitated, not quite sure how to best answer her question, given the seemingly confidential nature of the project Rogers wished to discuss. "Business," Quint replied, struggling not to stare at her assets.

"Hellllloooooo!" she said.

Quint blushed and realizing his gaze had lingered too long, stammered, "Sorry, but it's not my fault. It's gravity's," he said attempting to smooth things over with humor.

"Excuse me!" she responded, confused.

"It's well documented that large spheres maintain their own gravitational field, attracting men's eyes in an involuntary response, much like the earth and moon."

It took a second before she caught on, "I've got to hand it to you, that's good, that's really good," she said with a laugh.

Quint was about to change the subject when a drunken man stumbled up beside them. Unable to contain himself, the man pointed in the general direction of the pearls—and her chest—as he slurred, "My God those are big! Are they real?"

Already overly sensitized to this subject by Quint's antics, she slapped the drunk, sending him lurching backwards, spilling his drink, and nearly knocking him to the ground before Quint could catch him.

"Damn sensitive about her jewelry," the man slurred, heading off in search of another drink.

"Enjoy the party," Quint said, laughing at the man and at her red face over misinterpreting the man's innocent comment.

"You shouldn't be embarrassed. I accept full blame for my crude humor over-sensitizing you to the subject. So, how do you know Rogers?"

"I got to know some of the folks at Rogers' company while dating one of his employees. Though I had never before heard of Vector, as I learned more I became quite impressed. When a position for which I was qualified opened up, I jumped at the chance to be part of the company."

"I see, so where is this... employee tonight?"

"Long gone—looking for greener pastures. When we split, I kept the job. Overall, I got the best end of that deal. I love working for Rogers. So, you're here alone? I'm surprised to find you without some glitzy, blonde blood-sucker attached at the hip, given your recent notoriety."

Quint nodded. "Well... I'm in... that is—"

"It's complicated?" she asked, struggling to hide a smile at his awkward attempt to define his relationship status.

Quint hesitated and took a deep breath. He liked this woman, but he was determined to focus on fixing things with Evie. "Not really, just stupid. Having my head turned by a few of those bloodsuckers cost me the woman I love. I'm trying to fix it."

"Well, you get points for loyalty... and directness," she replied with a forced grin and changed the subject. "So what brought you to south Florida; you don't strike me as a native."

"No, I'm not. A few years ago, I was in a job I hated, and both my career and marriage seemed to be dead ends. I guess discovering that my wife was cheating on me was the final straw. A few days later, I just got up from my desk, quit my job, and headed for the Keys. No plan, not much money, just the feeling that it was time for a change. Never regretted it either."

Quint looked up to see a member of Rogers' security detail, who would have easily passed for Secret Service-type—dressed in a dark suit and wearing a small earpiece with a coiled cord—approaching. "It looks like I'm about to be granted an audience. Would you mind if I called you later with a few questions? I'd like to know more about Rogers."

"Not at all," she said, retrieving a business card from her purse. "And if you don't get back with her, and you still want to stay away from the vampires, give me a call."

"I'll do that," Quint smiled.

"Mr. Quint?" the Secret Service-type asked.

Quint nodded, "Just Quint."

"Very well, Quint, Mr. Rogers will meet with you," he said. As the two men headed down a dark paneled hallway, Quint stifled a laugh as he pictured the late kid's TV personality, wearing a button-up sweater and changing his shoes while singing, "It's a beautiful day in the neighborhood…"

They joined Dawson already waiting outside of a set of lavish oiled, wooden doors, which opened moments later. An older man emerged bidding Rogers goodbye. Quint had visions of the "Godfather" receiving a string of men to discuss their problems.

Dawson caught Rogers' eye. "Well, you must be the Quint I have heard so much about."

"No, I'm the Dawson you've heard very little about. This," he said, pointing to Quint, "would be the media star to whom you were referring."

Rogers chuckled, apologizing for his error. "Please come in. Forgive me for being unforgivably late but I hope you have enjoyed the party."

"Yes, thank you," Quint lied. Rogers was fiftyish but kept himself in shape. Had it not been for the thick gray hair he wore combed straight back, he might have been mistaken for a man ten years younger. One eye was slightly lower than the other as if his honest nature demanded he advertise that he was less than perfect.

"Personally, I find these parties boring, but on occasions such as family birthdays, I suppose one must make sacrifices," Rogers replied. He had a strong jaw and clear eyes that gave the impression he was about to laugh at an inside joke—sort of like Ronald Reagan without the dyed hair. Neat and well groomed, he was the type whose dinner jacket, though no doubt pricey, could have come from Walmart and still looked like an expensive custom-tailored Italian garment. Right away Quint warmed to the man's candor and unassuming manner.

"Quite an impressive affair," Dawson said.

"I think he was most impressed with one of your guests in particular," Quint added.

"Really, who?"

"Rachel," Dawson replied. "She seems nice. Said she works for you."

"That she does." Quint caught a glimpse of an odd smile before Rogers changed the subject. "Would you care for a drink?" he asked, guiding them to a sitting area near a coral stone fireplace in front of his desk.

"No thank you, we've imbibed plenty. So what can we do for you?" Quint asked, hoping to move things along as he took a seat in one of the fashionably worn, bomber-jacket brown leather chairs.

"We're going to get along fine; I value directness," Rogers smiled. "Now to the point: I need you to help save the world!"

Quint sat staring at Rogers in disbelief before replying dryly, "Well Rogers, I regret to inform you that you have the wrong superheros."

"Yeah," Dawson chimed in, "we're booked up moving mountains, plugging up nuisance volcanoes, and deflecting huge asteroids. Try one of the other defender-of-mankind types. Maybe Superman. Or perhaps Batman?"

Ignoring the sarcastic comments, Rogers continued, "The use of hyperbole was to get your attention. While an obvious exaggeration, it's actually true to some degree. Please allow me to explain.

"My company, Vector, is involved in a wide array of projects for the U.S. Government, most of which I am not at liberty to discuss. One thing we do is develop classified surveillance and intelligence gathering systems for the military. Several months ago, while we were beta testing a new eavesdropping package, our sophisticated algorithms detected Internet chatter related to a nuclear weapons threat."

"Here in the U.S.?" Dawson asked, incredulous.

"Yes."

"And how do you think they plan to get the weapon into the country?" Quint asked.

"It's already here." Rogers said, reaching for a classified briefing file in the drawer of his burled walnut desk. He proceeded to elaborate on the 1950s nuclear incident while Quint and Dawson listened, spellbound.

"So you're telling me that a bomb, a nuclear bomb, has just been lying in the shallow waters right off the coast of Mississippi for the past half a century? Come on," Quint replied, shaking his head in disbelief.

"It's not as uncommon as you might think," Rogers continued. "Over 50 nuclear weapons are known to have been lost over the last half century. The Russians seem to be the clumsiest—only 20 percent of them were U.S. mistakes, though seven of the U.S.'s 11 are lost here in the States.

"You're probably familiar with the loss of the Scorpion submarine, since it's one of the more famous. But you might not know that the Air Force jettisoned a bomb into the Pacific Ocean from a B-36 when it lost three of its engines en route from Alaska to Texas. Yet another nuclear weapon was lost in a B-52 crash and is still somewhere in a swamp near Goldsboro, North Carolina.

"Eighty miles off the coast of Japan, a 4E Skyhawk loaded with a nuclear weapon rolled off the Ticonderoga's number-two elevator and sank in 16,000 feet of water with the pilot still on board. These are only a few incidents that come to mind, and, of course this doesn't count the accidents where bombs were destroyed in mishaps or those that disappeared after the fall of the Soviet empire. So losing bombs is really not all that uncommon," Rogers concluded.

"While I appreciate your concern over a missing nuclear weapon, how does that involve us? You simply want us to be well informed, or are you trying to scare the crap out of us?" Quint asked.

"Neither, we want you to find it before the terrorists do," Rogers replied calmly.

"Oh, I see; well why didn't you just say so? We're kinda' tied up this week, but can pop up there early next week. Shouldn't take long to locate it so maybe we'll schedule in some fishing and a game of golf. By the way, what's the proper expression when you lose an atomic bomb, 'Sorry—my bad?'"

"I'm guessing it's probably more like, 'Oh, shit!'" Dawson replied.

The three men sat in silence for a few moments while Quint digested Rogers' proposition. "Well, this is all really scary and, assuming that it's true, the need to do something is certainly obvious. But at the risk of being equally obvious, why not call on someone like, oh I don't know, the U.S. military?"

"At the risk of sounding flippant, this is not the only crisis facing the U.S. At any one point in time there are literally dozens of crises ranging from biological or chemical weapons scares, to political coups that must be derailed, to assassination plots, and on and on. The U.S. Government has a wide array of tools to address each of these threat classes, but believe it or not, their assets are finite. Though the skills of many governmental teams far outstrip those of your group, few possess the search and recovery skills demonstrated by your team."

"What about the Navy?" Dawson challenged.

"Though the Navy certainly has those skills, their involvement raises other issues. The government sometimes needs to remain at arm's length since the press no longer exercises discretion and would delight in making this public.

"You may not realize that 'outsourcing,' as the government operatives love to call it, is quite common and one of the things with which we frequently assist them. In this case, a cover story of searching for a Spanish galleon would perfectly match your reputation and would be credible if the media were to catch wind of what you were up to. By finding the *Almiranta* your team demonstrated an ability to conduct effective search operations. Plus, you fared well in defensive mode while in Venezuela."

"Tell that to Dr. Margaux Desmarais," Dawson said acidly, as the memory of her death in Venezuela flashed through his mind.

"While you flatter us," Quint said, changing the subject, "couldn't one of your experienced Navy teams operating under cover achieve the same result?"

"Sure, they do it all the time and probably will if you wish not to get involved. But there are risks with that approach too. If one of the men were to get hurt or killed or blab over a beer, we'd have to explain why active duty Navy personnel were operating under cover in the U.S. probably tipping off the terrorists in the process. On the other hand, in the unlikely event your true activities were to become public knowledge, you would simply be private citizens acting independently out of a sense of patriotism based on information you pieced together from various public sources."

"Yeah, yeah, I watched *Mission Impossible*. And you'll deny any knowledge of our existence, blah, blah, blah. And we want to do this... why?" Quint asked sarcastically.

"Your strong sense of duty and patriotism coupled with the fact that the bomb is capable of vaporizing everything within a five-mile radius," Rogers replied. "Plus, I'm authorized to negotiate an eight-figure fee plus expenses and, by the way, the Spanish galleon wreck, providing your cover really does exist."

Quint blinked in surprise.

"In addition, assuming this were to work out to our mutual satisfaction, there would almost certainly be future... opportunities."

"Assuming we take the job and find the bomb, you expect us to recover it too?"

"Not hardly. In addition to the concern of its detonating, there is the issue of experiencing a radiation leak. Recovering a nuclear weapon submerged for half a century, likely to be badly corroded and possibly unstable, requires skills well beyond the capabilities of your team. That *is* a job that the Navy is best equipped to handle in short order.

"So, you interested in taking on this challenge?" Rogers asked, waiting silently while Quint considered the offer for a minute.

"We'll need some time to think it over."

"No can do—I need your answer now," Rogers responded firmly.

Quint glanced at Dawson. "Then it's no," Quint replied, rising to leave.

Rogers recoiled. "Well... uh... okay. Tell you what, how about you give me an answer within a week?"

"That we can do," Quint replied, as Dawson nodded.

"Good. Forgive me if I pushed too hard, but you must appreciate the dire nature of this situation. If detonated in Washington D.C., for instance, this bomb would take out the White House, the Capitol, the Supreme Court, the Smithsonian, and all the surrounding monuments, to say nothing of the thousands upon thousands of deaths it would cause," Rogers paused, reflecting on his own words.

"Do you really think it could still be detonated after all this time?"

"We can't afford to assume otherwise," Rogers replied. "Now, with that resolved, care to rejoin the party and accept my offer to stay the night?"

"I appreciate it, but we best be on our way," Quint replied, despite Dawson's obvious concern about abandoning his new love interest. "I believe you offered to fly us back tonight."

"Certainly. Have the limo driver take you back to the airport; I'll have the jet ready."

CHAPTER
5

Quint plopped back down in the plush seat of Rogers' private jet, reclining it to a more comfortable position. "What do you think?" he asked Dawson.

"Let's go for it. Seems like a big payout for a relatively simple job," Dawson replied while pouring them each an aged scotch from the decanter then returning it to its rich, walnut cradle. "Of course, if it sounds too good to be true..."

Quint nodded and asked, "Should we handle this as part of the grander LLC scheme?"

Dawson handed Quint a glass of liquor while searching for a napkin to mop up the few drops he had spilled. "Sure, make it the LLC's first project. It'll help us to define our future direction while developing our first customer at the same time."

"Makes sense," Quint agreed. "I'll do some due diligence on the Internet, and assuming there aren't any red flags, we'll do it, contingent upon the team's signing on. Maybe we can consummate the deal before Rogers leaves for Italy."

Quint searched his suit pockets the next morning and found the business card for the woman he had met at Roger's party. "Hey, this is Quint. We met at—"

"Rogers' party," she said, seeming pleased to hear from him.

"As I mentioned, we're considering a business venture with Rogers and hoped you might answer a few questions. How well do you know Rogers?"

"Been knowing him for nearly five years. The man's a saint and has done well for himself, building Vector from a half dozen employees into quite an operation."

"He called me out of the blue and invited me to that party for a meeting regarding a sensitive project. Obviously, he's got money. I just wanted to make sure he's legit and not a Columbian drug czar or something."

"Lord no," she laughed. "Don't worry about that. While I can't say much about our work since it involves 'spook' stuff for the government, I can say Rogers is connected. I'm sure whatever he has in mind for you is real."

"Thanks, that helps a lot," Quint said, managing to disengage before the conversation turned personal. He was determined to fix things with Evie and needed no distractions.

Quint's Internet search revealed no problems, and he was confident of Rogers' credibility as he dialed him the next day. "We're in, assuming the rest of our team signs up, which I don't expect to be a problem," Quint said.

"Splendid. I'd hoped you'd accept the offer."

"But there are conditions," Quint continued.

"Uh-oh, the devil is always in the details."

"We'll need a written agreement."

"Quint, we can't document much of this."

"I get that, but we don't move forward until the details are worked out to our satisfaction, and the basic terms are in an executed agreement as insurance. We'll also have a list of pricey equipment. I'll be honest; we may not need it all for the mission, but we get to keep it, nonetheless. As for the Spanish shipwreck cover, we'll need everything you have on it. We'll also need an agreement granting us rights to search for it, work it, and keep whatever we recover—tax free. The same goes for our eight-figured fee. Speaking of which, I'd like to agree on the eight figures."

"I'll see what I can do and get back with you this afternoon on the draft agreement. Send me your equipment list when you have it together. And the eight figures were a one followed by seven zeroes; don't get greedy."

"Roger," Quint said, immediately wishing he had not used that particular expression.

"How'd it go?" Dawson asked.

"We're on. Any luck contacting the rest of the team?"

"No, I hated to stir everyone up until we had the go ahead from

Rogers. I'll get started."

"Could you also work up an equipment list for Rogers?"

"Will do," Dawson agreed, as he hung up and dialed Leo.

"Dawson, you're back from the Med already?" Leo asked, his black tongue snaking across his lips.

"Yeah, and hit the ground with my feet running. You busy?"

"I always have time for you. I'm at my favorite sushi restaurant just finishing a jellyfish salad with their signature 'ocean roll.' The uni was fresh with a delightfully sweet taste but a slightly greasy texture," Leo replied as he leaned back in his chair and eased his ample stomach away from the table.

"What's uni?" Dawson asked hesitantly.

"It's Japanese for sea urchin gonads, though many people will tell you it's roe. It's served here with an unequaled squid ink dipping sauce. It's worth having my mouth dyed black until it wears off."

"Mmmm yummy," Dawson replied sarcastically.

Leo caught his reflection in the rusted chrome napkin holder, smoothed a renegade curl back in place, and brushed a grain of rice from his shrub-like beard. Not only was Leo physically large, everything he did was on an extra-large scale. And he took enormous pleasure in celebrating his considerable appetites—be they eating, drinking, fishing, sex, or, in his younger days, even drugs.

"You doing okay?"

"To tell you the truth, while I am enjoying the fruits of our success, things have been getting a little—"

"Boring?"

"Yeah. Sounds stupid, doesn't it?" Leo asked while munching on the last, tiny piece of ginger.

"No, in fact, I understand perfectly. That's why I'm calling. Quint and I are forming a for-profit LLC to pursue projects similar to our little adventure in Venezuela. We're offering each team member the option to buy in to whatever extent they feel comfortable, using the proceeds from our earlier escapades.

"FYI, we've already identified our first project, and it will yield a handsome profit, indeed. Unless otherwise agreed, each project will be expected to make money. Each partner will have a seat on the Board and a vote on the projects we accept. What do you think?"

"It's never dull with you two around. What about the non-financial risk, to my considerable hide, that is?"

"While some projects may involve risk, it's not likely to be much of an issue with this first one, at least not for our guys."

"I hear you," Leo replied shifting his considerable bulk in the rickety café-style chair, "but we've found things have a funny way of going to shit despite the best-laid plans."

"True. So, you in?"

"While I may later regret it, yeah, I'm in."

"Great. I'll get back to you once we work out the details, then things are going to move pretty quickly."

Dawson continued calling the former team members and was pleased when most of them jumped at the offer. He drafted an equipment list and e-mailed it to Quint before calling it a night.

"I forwarded your equipment list to Rogers. How's your recruiting effort going?" Quint asked, as he popped the last bite of bacon into his mouth.

"Leo, Kira, Colin, and Willy agreed to buy in to varying degrees. I haven't heard back from Dakota and a couple of the others. Only LaRue passed. Any word from Rogers?" Dawson asked.

Before Quint could reply, a second call came in on his cell phone. "It's Rogers. Let me get back to you."

"We've got a deal. I've drafted a written agreement, and your equipment list has been approved," Rogers began. "We need to meet at my office in Miami to finalize things. If I send the jet back down, can you be here for lunch?"

"You can count on it."

The person emerged from the building, walked rapidly past the smoker's area and once out of earshot, nervously dialed a number on a disposable phone. "Yes?" came Parvez's reply.

"Look, m-maybe I made a mistake agreeing to do this. I d-don't want to end up dead or in jail."

"We've been over all of this. Trust me, nobody will get hurt. Just do your job, and you'll get the money you need for your little project."

"Okay, I've been poking around as you asked and confirmed that your guy has competition. Rogers has hired a team to search for the bomb. They'll arrive within two days to survey the area. Their names are Quint and Dawson. I couldn't get their flight information, but I'm sure you can. I also managed to steal the Air Force's 1958 incident file, which I'll forward to you."

"Excellent. I'll wire your first payment." Then the line went dead.

Rogers sat looking out his office window at the Miami skyline. With the windows freshly cleaned, it seemed like he was standing outside. Had he been, he would have seen a slender black box, no larger than a stick of gum, stuck to the window frame.

Earlier that morning, a window washer began work early. After peering into Rogers' office to confirm it was empty, he peeled off the adhesive backing on a small electronics pack and placed the device. He then mounted a microphone, slightly larger than a pencil eraser and connected with a hair-thin wire to the device, at the corner of the glass. Whenever it detected conversations inside Rogers' office, the bug would record vibrations from the voices and transmit the results. After activating it, a tiny blinking green light confirmed that the window washer's job was done. This 10-minute job earned him twice his regular weekly income.

One of dozens of such electronics "bugs" already installed, it transmitted via a repeater to an innocuous Washington, D.C., office suite filled with sophisticated electronics equipment. Upon receipt of the new device's activation signal, a technician logged it into the system with a few key strokes. Now its transmissions would be recorded as they were received.

Mountains of information were recorded each day from a legion of such devices. Though there was far too much data to be analyzed without a huge staff, searches could easily be performed for key words over any given timeframe of interest. The results would then be e-mailed for the customer's review. The system was programmed to search the data from this device daily for the words: nuclear, bomb, Quint, and Dawson.

CHAPTER 6

Back in the U.S.- present day

Rashid ignored the television, tuned to a 24-hour news channel, as he reviewed a stack of reports. He looked up as mention of Osama bin Laden caught his attention. "Osama, you fool," he said, shaking his head at the screen in disgust. Smoothing the crease in his pinstriped suit pants and plucking a tiny piece of lint from his cuff, he leaned back in his high-tech black leather chair behind the glass desk in his sterile-looking office and thought about the man who had once been a close friend.

Like Osama, Rashid had a wealthy father who was preoccupied with running his businesses. As a young boy, Rashid was always trying to impress his father. Even now, Rashid felt a stab in his gut remembering the night he worked all evening coloring a special picture and maintained a lonely vigil in his chair by the front door waiting for his father's return. Eventually, sleep overcame the young lad, and the picture slipped from his clutch. He awoke early the next morning still in the chair, his picture lying on the floor bearing his father's footprint—it was the last time he could recall crying.

Rashid's teacher at the madrasas comforted him the next day, providing the praise he had sought from his father. This radical teacher was only too happy to fill Rashid's desperate need for a mentor, converting him into a militant Islamic extremist in the process.

Born only a few months apart, Rashid and Osama met as children at the Al-Thager Model School. They grew up together, both becoming devout Wahhabi Muslims. By the time Osama took his first wife at 17, he and Rashid had pledged their lives to fighting against what they perceived as Western imperialism.

While Rashid was committed to the cause, Osama became singularly obsessed and left school for Peshawar to join Abdullah Azzam in his fight against the Soviets in Afghanistan. Though somewhat envious of Osama's radical decision, Rashid chose a different course.

Unable or unwilling to spend much time with Rashid, his father assuaged his guilty conscience by eagerly funding his son's every whim, requiring steadily larger sums of money as he grew older. When Rashid decided to enter the belly of the beast and move to the United States in pursuit of his engineering studies, his father was only too happy to foot the bill.

Rashid attended LSU's College of Engineering to be near the oil drilling action in southern Louisiana. Taking full advantage of his father's largesse, he indulged himself with a Porsche Carrera and a plush apartment near the campus, immersing himself in the culture to better understand the Great Satan.

Over six feet tall with dark, exotic good looks and immaculate grooming, he was popular with the steady string of co-eds and was happy to entertain. He often found favor with his male peers by sharing his good fortune, frequently hooking them up with women as well. This generosity helped him build a network of loyal contacts through which he secured a summer co-op job.

A tap on the door announced Rashid's assistant, who entered dressed in an emerald business suit. Standing in front of his desk, she carefully placed an overnight envelope on the desk before him. She smiled as she noticed the collection of foil-wrapped paper clip figures that lined his desk. He must have spent much of the morning deep in thought to have so quickly replaced the previous day's collection, which now lay in the trash. "This was just delivered. I felt you might wish to see it immediately."

"Thank you. Please bring me some tea," he replied, plucking a piece of lint from his pants leg. Though she nodded her consent, Rashid was aware it offended her to be relegated to the status of a servant by a man who viewed all women as chattel; he hardly cared. He watched her walk away, undressing her with his eyes as he frequently did, before forcing his attention back to the matter at hand.

He ripped open the cardboard envelope and from within withdrew a smaller envelope with his name and a larger envelope marked "attachment." It was from Parvez, whom Rashid had hired for his spotless reputation in getting illicit things done efficiently. Wondering if his considerable investment was about to prove worthwhile, Rashid slid an oiled teak letter opener along the top edge of the smaller envelope and removed the one-page letter.

Rashid,

Though it has taken longer than I had hoped, we have finally succeeded. Here is the information you desired regarding the location of your "package." I have also included a transcript of a conversation we intercepted through our network of electronic bugs. I trust that you will be pleased with the result.

Please call me at the number written at the bottom of this note. I may have some further information of value.

Parvez

Rashid's eyes widened as he opened the second envelope. His assistant set the cup of tea on his desk, then retreated. Rashid was so engrossed that he did not bother to look up. After tapping out a quick e-mail to schedule a meeting with his associates for later in the week, he eagerly dialed Parvez.

"I take it you received my package and are pleased."

"Very much so."

"Regarding the transcript I sent, my team has done some further research. As the transcript indicated, the government, acting through a man by the name of Rogers, has employed a team of mercenary contractors to find the bomb and prevent you from getting your hands on it. The leaders of this group go by the names Quint and Dawson and should be arriving shortly in Gulfport, Mississippi. I will e-mail you their flight information.

"The copy of the Air Force's incident file involving the bomb, which I included is, as far as we know, the only copy, so it may give you an important edge. In it, you will find that a witness saw the plane collision. If he is still alive and you can find him, he could provide clues to the bomb's location."

"Parvez, you are truly amazing. How do you do it, or is that a trade secret?"

"My methods are not secret, but my track record supports my fee, which I assume you are eager to pay given our success."

"Absolutely."

"As for how I do it, I use eavesdropping electronics to develop leads initially. Whenever I stumble upon a situation of particular interest, I invest in the placement of a mole to get more detailed information. Over the years, I've inserted numerous such moles. While many produce nothing of interest, the occasional hit makes it all worthwhile.

"I believe you will find my mole in Rogers' office to be of further use, so as part of my service, I'll provide you with their contact information. Deal with them directly and compensate them as you deem appropriate."

Alone and with his office door closed, Rashid poured the tea into the plant by his desk. He withdrew a half-filled bottle of The Macallan from his desk drawer and refilled the tea cup, taking a sip as he leaned back in his plush chair. *"The infidels know how to make scotch taste like heaven,"* he thought.

As he sipped the dark amber liquid, he imagined the news headlines featuring his crusade to save the masses from the oppression of the Great Satan. He could visualize a throng of raggedly dressed peasants exalting him as their leader—no, as their savior.

As Rashid popped a stick of gum into his mouth, he glanced around the hotel's meeting room at the men gathered around the expansive walnut conference table. He had taken the precaution of renting a nearby facility rather than risk hosting the group at his own offices. The portable radio he had brought along played classical music loud enough to frustrate anyone attempting to use listening devices. One could never be too careful, he maintained, not wishing to fall victim to the very same techniques employed by his own "consultant."

The brilliant and cunning Akmed, whose religious zeal made his motives pure, was Rashid's most trusted man. Though he also trusted Talib, Rashid doubted that his allegiance ran as deep as Akmed's. Omar's deviant nature and propensity to use religion to suit his own dark purposes oftentimes proved useful, even though Omar's loyalty was not a given.

All of them had witnessed firsthand people begging in the streets for food and water, and all were united in placing the blame at the feet of the United States and its allies. "Is it not said that a man's stature is measured by the size of his enemies?" Rashid often said. "And what greater enemy than the West?" Regardless of the tenuous chain of logic used to defend his assertion, the men before him were believers. But Rashid alone saw himself as his people's savior, who would one day fill their bellies. The man who would give all of them shoes so families would not have to share. The man who would give them what they needed, according to his definition, of course.

"Thank you for coming on short notice," Rashid began, knowing the men would never have considered doing otherwise. "The special project I mentioned at our last meeting has borne fruit. Gentlemen, we are gathered here to develop a plan to recover a nuclear bomb." Rashid smiled at the shocked response to his own "bombshell."

"Recover?" Akmed asked. Though a man of modest size and strength, on numerous occasions Akmed had saved Rashid with his suspicious nature.

"Yes. I have information regarding a nuclear bomb already in the United States. My sources have confirmed its existence and have provided the bomb's general location. The challenge will be locating and retrieving it without raising undue attention. But once we do, we are free of the issue of how to get it into the country—it's already here." He went on to outline the historical context and details he had been provided about the bomb.

"Splendid," Akmed replied. "Our success is ordained. We will find it." His face clouded. "But after all of these years, will the bomb still work?"

"I have been led to believe that it is constructed of the highest grade materials and, therefore, should still be operational. But even if it's not, the nuclear core, combined with conventional explosives, would prove valuable as a dirty bomb to spread nuclear filth over a wide area, panicking the infidels."

"I'm confused. Is this in lieu of our other efforts already under way?" Talib asked. Akmed's opposite in many ways, Talib was an enormous man whom Rashid often pictured astride a white stallion, dressed in a turban and, baggy silk pants, a wicked scimitar secured to his ornate belt. Rashid liked the fact that Talib was a devout Muslim who strictly practiced Sharia Law. Though he did not share Omar's reputation as an established sexual deviant, Talib believed that if an infidel was not to be killed, then he or she should at the very least suffer humiliation.

Rashid also valued Talib's fanatical loyalty and the fact that he was a savage killer when provoked. It was rumored that in one instance he thrust his hand inside a man's chest and ripped out his still beating heart, gnawing on it before tossing it to the ground. Rashid thought this fanciful but found the fear invoked by Talib's very name quite useful.

"Certainly not," Rashid replied, shaking his head emphatically. "We will temporarily put our other efforts on hold. The bomb will serve as our opening volley," he smiled, as he considered the full extent of his brilliant master plan.

"I thought your Chinese 'death by a thousand cuts' strategy was to concentrate on smaller targets to avoid the attention that led to Osama's downfall," Talib continued. "Detonating a nuclear weapon is hardly a *minor cut*," Talib continued in his direct manner—always expressing himself without sugar coating.

"This will be more of a *deep gash*, but it will serve us well," Rashid replied. When the prospect of having a nuclear weapon arose, Rashid intended for his wave of terror to reach a crescendo before employing it. But with the chance to possess the weapon close at hand, the prospect of detonating a nuclear bomb was irresistible.

Talib continued to press the issue. "Do you not fear the use of the bomb as an opening card rather than the grand finale will unleash the fury of the United States much as the Japanese did by attacking Pearl Harbor?" Rashid was visibly irritated at having his plans questioned and toyed with the gum wrapper while bending a paper clip into different shapes.

"Talib is right," Akmed said. "While the 9/11 debacle gained Osama untold fame, with a little finesse he could have whittled away at the U.S.'s might for years, accomplishing far more than that single grandstanding play. U.S. special forces gutted his organization while he hid in caves to evade capture. So while Osama successfully awakened the sleeping giant, it responded by kicking his ass before killing him."

"Thank you for the history lesson," Rashid replied sarcastically. "Obviously, we must exercise great care not to be caught. I plan to offer several martyrs as sacrificial lambs for the media's feast while we resume our slow and steady approach," Rashid said, frustrated to sound like he was rationalizing his change in plans.

"Merely possessing the bomb will put us at great risk of being caught, so it is best to quickly detonate it. Besides, a nuclear event will magnify the effect of our further efforts, making the public wonder each time whether a small event is the prelude to another colossal one. Do not forget this is my plan, my decision. I am in charge."

"Assuming we are successful in finding the bomb, what is our... I mean *your* plan for using it?" Akmed asked, unabashed.

"Excellent question," Rashid replied, pleased to change the subject from justifying his plans. "We will load it aboard a fishing boat and move it up the east coast where we will detonate it near the World Trade Center site. Imagine the effect of killing scores of infidels in this location a second time. If for whatever reason that is not possible, we will divert to an alternate target. Perhaps we'll head up the Potomac and detonate it near the White House.

"Should things go awry shortly after we have the bomb in our possession, we must be ready to detonate it quickly. Maybe we could target New Orleans and *really* send the Saints marching home."

CHAPTER 7

Quint had not slept well. As he headed to the FBO he recalled the dream that had awakened him throughout the night. Actually more of a memory, it was about his father's recovering from a drunken binge. In the middle of making a cup of coffee, he stormed out of the kitchen in a rage, an unopened can of evaporated milk still in his hand.

Quint could never recall what had angered his father. Nor could he recall what his mother yelled next. But what he could vividly recall was his father's turning around, his face contorted in anger. He could still see the image of his father winding up like a baseball pitcher and firing the can down the hallway. The can nailed his mother in the forehead, her blood spraying Quint and the kitchen cabinets as he clutched her leg, sobbing. He could still recall the fear he felt as she tried to comfort him, ignoring her own real pain. It had been a while since the dream had haunted him, and he hoped it was not back to stay. In fact, when he and Evie had gotten together, the dreams had receded. If it was not a coincidence, it gave him one more reason to get back with her.

Dawson joined Quint mid-morning at the FBO, where once again they boarded Rogers' jet for the flight to Miami. Quint felt obliged to wear a navy sport coat but refused to wear a tie. "If that's what it takes to do business with Rogers, oh well," he told Dawson, after being forced to wear one at their initial meeting with Rogers. Dawson had gone a step further, refusing to wear even a sport coat.

Quint glanced down at his freshly laundered khaki slacks and noticed a dark coffee stain near the cuff. *It's going to be one of those days,* he thought, before his mind returned to Evie.

He hated being single and missed their little weekend getaways to nowhere special. He longed for someone to rush home to at the end of each day for a shared glass of wine that made cooking dinner an event, not a chore.

He liked the fact that she was not a picture-perfect model-type but more the wholesome girl-next-door. A smile crossed Quint's face at the memory of her broken nails and bandaged hands from weekends they shared doing fix-it projects on the old house she had inherited from her mother. It was one of the many things that made what they shared seem genuine.

Since the moment he had told her of his abusive childhood, and she reciprocated by confiding the mystery of the tree behind her house, they had developed a special bond. That was, until their tiff that evening, after which he briefly lost sight of what he had with her. Now that they were no longer a couple, their former closeness seemed all the more precious.

Though not certain Evie was *the one*, she was certainly the leading contender, and he cursed himself for letting their relationship fizzle out. By the time they had landed and climbed into Rogers' gleaming 12-cylinder BMW sedan to be whisked away to Monty's Conch, he had renewed his resolve to find some way to gain her forgiveness for his foolish behavior.

After answering their questions over lunch, Rogers added, "I was also going to give you a copy of the 1958 incident file, but I seem to have misplaced it. When we get to my office to sign the agreement I'll see if I can get another copy, though when I scanned through it, I found little of value."

Quint and Dawson waited patiently in the conference room, until a large-boned but well-built and exceptionally beautiful blonde entered the room, dressed in a form-hugging sapphire skirt and matching silk blouse. "Hi, I'm Rachel. I work in accounting for Mr. Rogers," she said in a whiskey voice as she offered her hand to Quint before locking eyes with Dawson. "I believe we've had the pleasure," she said suggestively.

"Here's the agreement his secretary prepared for your review. I'll be the one taking care of you," she added in a sultry voice, causing Quint to wonder if Dawson, who was nearly slobbering on the polished conference table, could control himself. "We'll review the invoicing procedures to make sure you get paid promptly." By the time she exited with a mighty swish of her hips, Quint had completely taken over the conversation, answering for both, as Dawson became tongue-tied every time she asked a question.

When she was out of earshot, Dawson's power of speech returned. "Boy, is she hot!"

"Yeah, I noticed the drool." While Quint wanted him to find that right someone, it saddened him to see his buddy still struggling to fill the emotional void in his life with a string of one-night stands.

"Was I that obvious?"

"Duh, you don't do subtle well."

"Good thing I wasn't negotiating the deal with her. I probably would've agreed to do it for free."

Quint's landlord, Eddie, was waiting when he and Dawson pulled up in front of his house in Key West. "I'll go get us a six pack while you talk to him," Dawson said, leaving Quint to greet Eddie.

"Hey, 'tenant mon,'" the wannabe Rastafarian said in greeting. Dressed in a garish t-shirt bearing the green, black, and gold colors of the Jamaican flag, his impressive red dreadlocks were splayed across his shoulders. Eddie's transformation had occurred during a trip to Jamaica, where a "ganja" experience evidently made quite an impression. Although born with pale white skin, what Eddie lacked in skin color, he made up for with his commitment to the role, punctuating nearly every sentence with "mon."

"Hello 'landlord mon,' what's up?"

Eddie took a seat on Quint's sofa, flinching as it groaned beneath his weight, threatening to finally collapse after years of service. He sat fidgeting for a minute before blurting out, "I'm selling my place."

"I didn't know it was for sale."

"It wasn't, but this mainlander came along and flashed so much money I couldn't refuse. I'm sorry to spring this on you, especially since one of his conditions was to take possession by the end of the month."

"Oh," Quint replied, realizing that wouldn't give him much time. "Where you moving?"

"Umm... I'm staying with a friend," Eddie replied evasively. Quint was sure Eddie was gay, but he maintained a low profile and, in deference to Eddie's privacy, Quint never broached the subject. He suspected Eddie's pending relocation had played a major role in the sale of his house, rather than the other way around. As Eddie rose to leave, he paused, "If you can't find a place, I'll talk to my friend about renting *our* I mean *his* spare bedroom for a couple of weeks."

"I'll figure something out."

Eddie excused himself when Dawson returned. "So what did Eddie want?" he asked, popping open a beer.

"He's selling this place; I've got to move. Finding another place on short notice will be tough."

"You can crash with me until you find something," Dawson offered, handing Quint a beer.

"Thanks, but I'd prefer to stay in Key West, what with Evie and all."

"Why not stay with her?"

Quint shook his head, "Yeah, right. She won't even take my calls. But Eddie offered me his spare room for a few days."

"*That* would be interesting for your reputation."

"Cut it out! He's in a relationship, and his offer was sincere."

"Whatever you have to tell yourself."

Quint thought for another minute. *Maybe I could replace Mojito and live aboard the boat. It's not a great long-term solution, but it'll buy me time to find another place.*

"I sold most of my stuff in a garage sale. Everything I have left is loaded in the back of my truck. Okay if I park in your garage for the time being?" Quint asked, as Eddie met him beside the garage.

"No problem. Leave it as long as you need to."

"I'm out of the apartment. Here's the keys."

"How's the boat search going?" Eddie asked.

"It's taking a lot longer than I expected."

"Well, the guest bedroom offer still stands."

Quint hesitated for a minute and replied, "If you're sure it's okay, I'll take you up on that." It turned out not to be a great idea. The next morning, Quint called Dawson the minute it was late enough to wake him without feeling too guilty.

"Yeah," Dawson's sleepy voice answered on the third ring.

"I'm taking you up on the offer to crash at your place."

"What, you and Eddie have a spat?"

"Ha, ha. I was exhausted from moving so I hit the sack early last night. The noises coming from Eddie's bedroom woke me just after midnight, and I spent the rest of the night with a pillow over my head trying to get back to sleep. I don't know what the two of them were doing in there, but this isn't going to work."

"Come on over."

"I'll be there as soon as I can make the drive." Quint hung up and as quietly as possible packed his bag. He wrote a brief note expressing his heartfelt thanks and slipped out to avoid an awkward conversation when his host couple awoke.

CHAPTER 8

Evie studied her image in the mirror while putting on her makeup and for an instant imagined Quint approaching to take her into his arms and softly kiss her head. Seeing him as she passed by in her car the day before brought back memories she had worked hard to bury deep.

At first, she took Quint for one of the common macho types who viewed himself as God's gift to women. But she quickly learned that he did not take himself seriously and was charmed by his ever-present mischievous grin. She liked his blunt manner and his insistence on living life on his own terms—never seeking anyone's permission or approval. He still believed in the American ideal of rugged individualism.

An image flashed into her mind of his entering the restaurant that day with a bottle-blonde dripping with jewelry, wearing a body-hugging dress and clinging to his arm. Evie looked self-consciously at her broken finger nails and hands covered with fresh cuts from her latest house project, and the anger she had felt welled up inside her once again.

Fine. If all he wants is arm candy, let him have those whores, she had thought. *There are plenty of men looking for a real woman capable of actual thoughts beyond what shade of makeup to wear— a woman who knows how to do something besides shop for the latest fashion, bat her eyes, and thrust out her chest.* Then she had gone home to cry her eyes out.

Though Evie felt something special between them, she sensed Quint was not ready to get serious, despite his earlier claims to the contrary. She liked him just like he was and cursed the prosperity that seemed to pull him away from her.

But it's over, so you just have to get on with it, she told herself, though the recent onslaught of fresh flowers and gifts made it difficult to take her own advice.

Quint's date had not appreciated his cancelling at the last minute the night of Rogers' party, and she was refusing to take his calls. Perhaps she sensed that his heart was somewhere else. So he sat alone while Dawson left for the evening.

He longed to be free of singles bars and disastrous first dates. He longed for the warm feeling of knowing he was special to at least one person. He longed for the security of having someone to share his nights and weekends.

The flowers and gifts seemed to have had no effect on Evie. At first when she failed to answer his calls, he tried to convince himself that she had turned the ringer off while working and had forgotten to turn it back on, which she often did. It was a constant source of frustration for him when they were dating. But eventually he had to admit she was refusing to take his calls. Of course, even if she did answer, he doubted it would be a pleasant conversation. Nonetheless, he summoned his courage and dialed her again.

"Quint? Oh, I do believe my knees are so weak I don't know if I can remain standing," Evie answered in a thick, sarcastic Southern belle accent, which Quint hoped was masking her excitement. "Imagine little ole' me getting to talk to the most handsome, charming, witty, brilliant, strong, virile, popular…"

With no end in sight to the string of false compliments, Quint finally interrupted: "Okay, okay, enough, I get it." It was then that he realized he was no longer sure what to say. "It was good to see you when you passed by the clinic the other day," Quint said, cursing himself for such a lame lead in.

"Oh, I didn't notice you," she lied.

"Look, I'm calling to apologize for being a jerk. I was overwhelmed by everything and lost sight of what was really important. But I'm over all that."

"Are you now? That's just peachy. The problem is—I'm not," she replied coldly.

"Do you even remember what caused our silly fight?"

"No, but I do recall you with that bleached blonde with gold digger written all over her huge fake tits."

"Evie, please. You didn't deserve the way I treated you. I was wrong, horribly wrong. Sometimes thick-headed people like me have to lose something to appreciate its true value. I know I don't deserve it, but please give me a chance to make it up to you."

"What happened, your whores left you?" Quint's silence made it clear she had scored a verbal body blow, and she faltered for a moment. "Quint, what do you want?"

"You. I just want you and me, back together again. Like it was. More than anything that's what I want." He sensed she wanted that too, but he also knew her pride would not let her go easy on him.

"Perhaps you should have thought of that earlier."

"Evie, I can't undo what's done. If I could, I would. But it's just not possible. Just give me a second chance," Quint replied, holding his breath as he awaited a reply, her pause giving him hope.

"Remember how you had to grovel last time you were gone for a long time, with the flimsy excuse of having your boat sunk and getting stranded in the jungle? Well, that was nothing compared to what you're facing if you want us to get past this."

"I already have dinner plans laid out."

"Dinner? We're way past dinner here. We're talking serious ass kissing."

"Can we at least discuss it over dinner? We can celebrate 'National Daiquiri Day.'"

"National Daiquiri Day?... Never mind. Pick me up at seven tomorrow night. Be on time or lose my number," she finished, making it clear she was calling the shots.

The next night Quint rang the doorbell at 6:50 p.m. "Be with you in a bit," Evie's voice came from within, leaving him to stand outside. With no chair on the porch and not wanting to dirty his pants on the steps, Quint stood waiting patiently. He recalled the nights and weekends spent remodeling the house with Evie, sharing laughs and growing close in the process.

Twenty minutes later, after making it clear Quint was being punished, the door opened, and Evie appeared radiant in a breezy white skirt and peach-colored top. The highlights recently added to her otherwise dark brown hair fairly glowed. Turning her head, she accepted his kiss on the cheek rather than the lips. As she turned back, the flower-filled garbage can caught her eye long enough for Quint to notice.

"I see you got my flowers," he said with a sad smile.

Evie hesitated for an instant, and then responded with only a quick nod before proceeding on to the car. Pausing for him to open the door, she slipped into the passenger's seat. Her single-word responses foiled Quint's repeated efforts to break the cool silence while they drove.

"So what's National Daiquiri Day?" she finally queried.

"Glad you asked. While looking for a way to boost the Cuban miners' morale during the hot summer months of 1898, a man named Jennings Stockton Cox developed a concoction made from three parts rum, one part lime juice, and one-half part sugar combined in a shaker filled with cracked ice. He called it a Daiquiri, and July 19th has been designated to commemorate his contribution to mankind. In my humble opinion, it's right up there with the discovery of penicillin."

He finished his anecdote just as they arrived at the restaurant. Once seated, they ordered daiquiris while perusing the menu. Quint's efforts to be engaging and witty were lost on Evie, distracted by a busboy scurrying about lighting alcohol table lamps. The heavy smell of sulfur hung thick in the air as he struck a wooden match at the next table.

The slender teen-aged boy reminded Evie of her brother. She missed him so much and thought of him and the banyan tree beneath which he lay.

Quint abruptly ended his latest animated tale in frustration, noting that Evie seemed preoccupied. Desperate to put her in a better frame of mind, he asked the returning waiter, "Perhaps you could settle our debate: Do fish sneeze?"

The ridiculous question struck the poor waiter speechless, forcing Evie to study the menu more closely to conceal her wide grin. After recovering from his bafflement, the waiter recited the specials. "With the start of our own lobster season still a few weeks away, tonight we have some excellent fresh Australian lobster. The 12-ounce grilled tails are paired with asparagus and served over the chef's special scampi pasta."

Despite the frightful expense, Quint pushed the special, hoping to impress Evie. "Grilled lobster—God's perfect food against which he intended all others to be judged."

"Might I take that as your recommendation?" Evie asked.

"Indeed, but choose whatever suits you," Quint replied.

"I intend to," she quipped while nodding to the waiter. "I'll go with the lobster." Quint took her acceptance of his suggestion as a small step in the right direction.

Evie's icy disposition gradually thawed as the meal progressed. By the time their entrees were finished, things seemed almost back to normal. When Evie declined dessert, Quint suggested an after-dinner cordial. "How about some Ke Ke?"

"Ke Ke? That sounds like a child's name for a nasty the dog did on the floor."

Quint laughed. "I call it key lime pie in a glass. I doubt you'll find it nasty," he said, while discreetly positioning his water glass over a butter stain on the otherwise pristine tablecloth. A minute later the waiter returned with two glasses half-filled with a green liqueur.

Evie took a tentative sip. "Mmm, that is good. Who makes it?"

"The Dutch. Now how do you suppose they, of all people, invented this liqueur? I doubt the Dutch even have key lime trees. It should have been invented by the Conchs."

After a brief pause in the conversation, Quint looked Evie in the eye. "Evie, I'm truly sorry. I guess with the sudden prosperity and all the media attention, I lost my bearings. While I'm certainly not proud of it, over the past few weeks, a number of women have come and gone."

"Yeah, sometimes literally," Evie interjected with a smirk.

Ignoring her barb, Quint continued. "But not one could hold a candle to you—on their best day and your worst. I'm not trying to make excuses, only to explain."

Evie sat brushing a stray bread crumb from the linen table cloth, remaining silent for so long Quint became uneasy. "Quint, you really hurt me. I was... still am... in love with you," she looked off with her eyes reddening and fumbled through her purse for a tissue to blot the forming tears.

"And I am with you."

"Then how could you cast me aside for those cheap skanks?"

"Evie, I was monumentally stupid. I never made a choice intentionally. We had that fight and... well... things just came between us. But in my defense, and Lord knows I need one, when I earlier broached the subject of making things more formal, you put me off."

"Wait a minute. I merely said I was hesitant because of my parents' experience. I told you I wasn't seeing anyone else and that I didn't want to, which is more than I can say for you," Evie said, her voice trembling.

"You're right. But that mistake helped me see what you mean to me. I can't change the past few months, but I'll work hard making it up to you—starting with this," Quint said, as he removed a man's gold wedding band from his pocket. "You remember this?"

"How could I forget? You gave it to me the night you celebrated your 40th birthday and your divorce. I slipped it back into your top dresser drawer after managing to get you to your place before you passed out drunk."

"I know you're not ready for anything too serious, but I want you to have this as a symbol of how much I care."

"Does this mean we're going steady—kinda' like giving a girl your class ring?" Evie asked.

"No, smart ass, it means I love you." She made no effort to wipe away the single tear that ran down her left cheek.

"Can't we get the team together any quicker than that?" Quint asked Dawson.

"I tried, and two weeks is the soonest most of them can break free, unless you want to proceed with those who can meet sooner."

"No, I want everyone there, but Rogers is on my ass for us to get started."

"Look, the bomb's been lost for 50 years. I don't think another couple of weeks is going to matter."

"Maybe, but there haven't been a bunch of lunatic terrorists looking for it either."

"If it makes you feel better, it's not completely wasted time. I've got each of them planning their individual responsibilities so when we do meet, they'll be well along."

"You didn't tell them about the project yet, did you?" Quint asked.

"No, all they know is that we're doing another exploration job on *Searcher*."

Quint nodded. "Well, I need to work on finding a boat before we leave so that I won't still need to bunk with you when I get back."

"I hate that *Mojito* sank in that storm off the coast of Venezuela.

She was a good boat. Any luck finding a replacement?"

"I found lots of trawlers and motoryachts, but my heart's set on another sportfish. I found an older one with an enclosed bridge and a tower. It'd give me more living space, and I'd still have the option to charter."

As Quint arrived for his appointment with the listing broker, he noticed weeds growing high along the borders of the boatyard, dotted with piles of junk and debris. Out of the corner of his eye, Quint spotted a familiar outline, and his heart skipped a beat. He stood admiring the boat's lines then walked down the finger pier to meet the broker, whom he found friendly but uninformed.

"What kind of engines does she have?" Quint asked about the engine manufacturer.

"Oh, big ones, really big ones."

Quint glanced at him with a grin before realizing the man was serious. "How much fuel does she hold?" he asked, trying again for useful information.

"A lot, a whole lot."

"*What a dufus,*" Quint thought, as he found a spec sheet in the salon that provided the *real* answers to his questions.

"Want to take her for a sea trial?" the broker asked, surprising Quint since they had not yet discussed the customary contract and earnest money.

"Like her?" the broker asked, as soon as they were back from a quick run down Hawk Channel. Quint nodded. "You know I probably shouldn't tell you this, but the owner can no longer afford the boat and with his recent health problems, is *really* motivated to sell. He dropped the price $15,000 last month, but I'm guessing he'd go down another 10 or so."

Glad he's not my broker, Quint thought. While not one to make snap purchasing decisions, Quint did not have much time; he had a bomb to find. So he made an on-the-spot offer well below the broker's suggestion. "That's contingent on its passing a survey, and all major problems are to be fixed at the seller's expense prior to sale."

"It may take me a few days to get back with you," the broker replied.

"Well if it does, you won't have a sale. I need to close by the end of the week. I have to do... I have a business trip and need it done by then."

"I'll let you know by tomorrow," the broker said but left without bothering with a contract.

Quint's ringing cellphone woke him early the next morning. It was the broker. "We've got a deal."

"Found me a boat," Quint said as he followed Evie into her kitchen. He saw that she had stripped the finish from the cabinets but had not begun refinishing them. *Not a half bad job,* he noted.

"That's great, tell me about it while I make coffee." Quint filled her in while she built a pot of the coffee Quint so loved, with fresh ground, vanilla-flavored beans and real cream. He excused himself to use her bathroom and took a wrong turn, ending up in her spare bedroom. A minute later, his voice exploded from the far side of the house.

"What the... Holy shit!... Evie, there's a lizard in here the size of a canoe!"

"That's Fred, my iguana," Evie replied with a laugh.

"When did you get that?"

"You weren't around, and I needed company."

"So you replaced me with a giant lizard?"

"At the time, it seemed like a trade up," she teased. "I started with a Crested Gecko when I was a kid."

"But of course," Quint replied. "Call me crazy, but if you wanted a pet, why not a cat or a dog?"

"I figured with his teeth and claws, coupled with his sharp dorsal spines and killer tail, perhaps I could train him to be an attack iguana," she said with a straight face. Following her back into the room, Quint was pretty sure she was kidding, but knowing how some people are with their pets, decided not to press the issue. "Actually, he belonged to a friend of mine. She's got cancer and couldn't care for him any longer. I took him in rather than see him put down. Supposedly, I'm just looking after him until she is able once again, but it's pretty clear that won't happen. I hate it too; she's a fine woman and a good friend."

Quint reached down to pat the enormous green animal then

withdrew his hand quickly as the animal lunged at him. "Try it from the side. Coming from above, he sees as a threat and talk to him."

"Huh?"

"Do it in a low, gentle voice. Keep your movements slow and easy. Let him get to know you, and use his name, he recognizes it."

"So Fred, what did you think of the Superbowl this year? Seen any good movies, Fred? Fred, you seem kinda' quiet today." After Quint demonstrated that he wasn't a threat, Fred seemed to enjoy being stroked along the side of his head. "He really is laid back, once he gets to know you."

"Yeah, she did a terrific job of taming him by spending lots of time handling him over the years. Hand feeding him instead of using a bowl helped a lot too."

"How old is he?"

"She said he's pushing 17 years old, so considering that they rarely live past 20, he's an old timer. He used to get ornery every year during breeding season. Imagine a 15-pound iguana coming at you with love on his mind."

"I'd rather not," Quint laughed. "Well, I suppose I'll get used to him."

"Hey, love me, love Fred. We're a package deal now. Next time, you can try picking him up."

"That'll give me a reason to go on living," Quint replied dryly.

"Just avoid grabbing him by the tail as it'll probably break off, and at his age, probably wouldn't grow back."

"Oh, the horror," Quint quipped, cringing as Evie punched him.

CHAPTER
9

Dawson entered the Smirkin' Shark in Ft. Lauderdale and spied Quint seated at the back of the bar. At the near end of the bar, he noticed Leo making time with two attractive women. One wore a t-shirt with *I wish these were brains* printed across her ample chest.

"Hey Leo, how's the wife and kids?" Dawson asked loudly, as he strode by.

After a shocked silence, Leo, who was single, protested, "He's just screwing with me. I swear I'm not married, and I sure don't have kids. Ask anybody." The women replied with withering looks before exiting in a huff, leaving Leo proclaiming his innocence. As soon as they cleared the door, he charged to the back of the bar where Dawson now sat drinking beer and enjoying a laugh at Leo's expense.

"You bastard, you know I'm single! They believed you."

"Relax, Leo. You would have spent a bunch of time and money and still not gotten lucky. I figure you owe me one," Dawson replied with a grin.

"Yeah, I owe you one right up the—," he stopped when he noticed Kira and Mimi sitting nearby. "What goes around, comes around!" he said, storming out of the bar in pursuit of his love interests.

"It appears Leo will not be joining us tonight after all," Dawson commented to Kira and the rest of the team who had gathered.

"Thanks to your perverse sense of humor," Kira replied.

"Oh well, he'll either get over it, or he won't," Dawson replied, unfazed.

Kira shook her head. Like most of the team members, she had invested half her share from the *Almiranta* treasure to buy into the LLC. She was a stunning woman who could pass for a somewhat older college cheerleader. Her model-like face was framed by a head of thick blonde hair, and her dark tan appeared natural, though it could have come from a bottle. She was a brilliant and dedicated professional whose only downside was that she brought too much drama to the party in her on-again, off-again relationship with Colin.

Quint studied the team members seated around the room, busy

catching up after being apart for several months. The group was well versed in various disciplines. Those not already experienced in the art of special ops and related skills had undergone extensive, on-the-job training during their first assignment. Despite their various quirks and eccentricities, each was a key part of an effective team.

He saw Colin arrive and anxiously scan the room. Quint guessed he was looking for Kira. After a bumpy romance before joining the team, they were a couple once again—at least they had been until their spat the previous week. Colin spotted Kira, only to have her turn away without acknowledging him, so he opted to join Quint and Dawson at the bar.

Barely in his 40s and in good physical condition, Colin was a Brit hired by Dawson to oversee operations. Standing roughly six feet tall and weighing in at 200 pounds, Colin had piercing grey-blue eyes and a square jaw that looked like it could crush nails. These assets set off an otherwise ordinary appearance. He wore his prematurely gray hair in a brush cut.

"How'd you piss off Leo?" Colin asked. "He nearly ran me over as he burst out of here cussing your ancestors. I've never seen him so hot."

"Shit if I know. I just greeted him when I came in," Dawson replied innocently, though the others' grins and a snort from Mimi indicated otherwise.

Mimi was short and more than a few pounds overweight. Her short black hair did little to complement her plain facial features. From a poor family in which higher education was a fanciful dream, she had nonetheless proven to be a quick study. Kira had taken her under her wing, grooming her to be a critical part of the technical team.

Mimi insisted that joining the team was the highlight of her entire life, despite losing her left index finger to pirates and nearly dying from a gunshot wound a short time later in the Venezuelan jungles. The distinctive snort she made when she laughed was the source of constant ribbing.

"What'll it be?" the bartender asked.

Though tempted by the smell of frozen bushwackers and seeing the moisture dripping down the side of Mimi's chocolate-streaked glass, Colin replied, "I'll have a beer on my buddy's tab." Quint nodded at the bartender in resignation, motioning for another drink as well.

"Enjoying your signature Mojito?"

Quint nodded. "Yep, this was one of Hemingway's favorites. Given the quantity of alcohol he consumed, I believe in following the lead of a professional."

Armed with a beer, Colin again considered approaching Kira, but her cutting look sent him retreating. Dawson took a swig of beer and noticed a man midway down the bar with the words "Cold Beer" tattooed on his arm. "How important you reckon beer is to that guy?" Dawson said in awe.

The group laughed, and Colin piped up, "Quint, you called this meeting, so what say we get started?"

"Yeah, now that *you've* finally arrived," Quint answered, noting his tardiness. "We'll recap things for Leo tomorrow after he's cooled down. Grab your drinks and let's adjourn to the back room. If you haven't already ordered a burger, you might want to do so now," Quint said, rising from the bar.

Dawson, who had been surreptitiously admiring Kira, rose to follow. It was not the fact that her figure was worthy of a *Playboy* spread, he found himself attracted to her down-to-earth manner and the fact that she never flaunted her good looks. Nor did she seem to feel any special entitlement because of them, unlike so many of the attractive women who had passed through his life.

As he walked toward the rear of the bar, his hand brushed against Kira's arm. Both recoiled as if from an electric shock. Kira blushed and quickly looked around for Colin—finding him in the midst of a political debate with one of the team.

In order to create background noise in hopes that no one could overhear their conversation, Quint pumped several dollars into the bar's jukebox before following behind the team. The back room was festooned with authentic old street signs and a number of humorous posters. A dart board hung on one wall covered with tiny holes, and a broken pinball machine laden with dust sat jammed into the far corner. A haphazard collection of rickety tables filled the room, matching only in that they had seen decades of use.

When the team was reseated, Quint closed the door and began the meeting by passing out copies of a document. "Though everyone has an e-mailed copy of this LLC charter, I'll pass around these hard copies—edited to include your comments—for purposes of our discussion today. We don't need these floating around the bar, so I want them back when we're finished.

"The three purposes of the LLC are the pursuit and acquisition of objects with intrinsic, historical, or other value; the neutralization of special threats for which conventional remedies are inappropriate or otherwise impractical; and missions involving the rescue of key personnel assets or execution of other programs deemed worthy for humanitarian, scientific, or other such reasons.

"The Company will be operated as a for-profit business entity under the control of the board, comprised of all shareholders. Unless otherwise agreed, the LLC's board will select projects with an acceptable risk-reward ratio, preferably those offering significant economic upside. Projects may have multiple objectives, with some deemed to have a higher purpose than financial gain. A separate set of rules of engagement will be developed, outlining how and when the use of force is authorized by the organization.

"Initially, the LLC will be U.S. based. However, our ultimate intent is to be headquartered offshore, where we can operate independent of government oversight and be unconstrained by political forces, media, etc. We will, of course, follow the basic tenets of U.S. law."

After they had time to finish their review Quint continued. "The charter is broad and open to interpretation, but I believe it expresses the basic interests we share and outlines the principles for which we would be willing to place our own lives and fortunes at risk. I will now entertain a motion to adopt the revised charter."

Willy reviewed the document with keen interest. An enormous black man, standing nearly seven feet tall and weighing well in excess of 300 pounds, Willy had heavily muscled arms that were larger than most men's thighs. He relished toying with those who mistakenly assumed him to be a "dumb jock" because of his size.

Though top in his class, Willy struggled through the Merchant Marine Academy working two jobs to support his mother and siblings. After attending class he would report to work as a security guard where he would study whenever he could. Sometimes he would then spend most of the night finishing his homework and grab a couple of hours of sleep before rising at 4 a.m. to stock groceries at his second job. He was hired as ship's engineer during the team's quest to find the Spanish treasure galleon, the *Almiranta*.

After he reviewed the document, he spoke up, "So moved." Kira gave a second.

"Any discussion?" Quint asked.

"I think this sums up my understanding. It looks fine," Colin said. The rest of the group agreed and accepted the charter, after which they voted Quint chairman of the board by acclamation.

A knock signaled the arrival of their food. Dakota rose to open the door, giving Quint a glimpse of his latest t-shirt bearing a quote from Capt. Tony, the owner of the original Sloppy Joe's bar: *All you need in life is a tremendous sex drive and a great ego – brains don't mean shit.* Quint enjoyed Dakota's seemingly never-ending supply of t-shirts emblazoned with obnoxious slogans.

Dakota was an authentic American Indian with the broad shoulders, powerful physique, and complexion to match. He sported a shaved head except for a round spot in the back from the center of which sprang a long braided pigtail. This, paired with a half-inch wide moustache and beard, made for a true ethnic fashion statement. A Medal of Honor recipient, both he and Willy had demonstrated their ability to handle boats and to stand tough when the situation called for it.

Though everyone called him Dakota, his legal name was Jimmy Dakattopadhyay. He joked that it was spelled just like it sounded. Before joining the team, he ran oil field supply boats for years as well as crew boats, tugs, you name it. He claimed that if it had propellers and floated, he could run it.

The team took a quick break while the food was served. Then, with everyone busy working on their burgers, Quint wiped a glob of mustard from the corner of his mouth and continued. "Okay team, with the LLC business behind us, let's talk about the mission details that couldn't be discussed over the phone or Internet," he said, opening the file folder containing his notes.

"On Feb 5, 1958, an F-86 fighter jet engaged in a nighttime training mission failed to spot a nearby B-47 bomber and collided with it. The impact ripped off the fighter's left wing, forcing the pilot to eject from the plane before it exploded and plunged into the water below. The fighter pilot did not survive.

"The bomber sustained heavy damage but remained flyable. The B-47 was carrying a 7,600-pound, 12-foot-long Mark 15 hydrogen thermonuclear bomb SN 47782 with an explosive power equal to 3.8 million pounds of TNT. Concerned that the bomb might detonate or rupture during a possible crash landing, the crew was granted permission to jettison it.

"After descending to an altitude of 7,200 feet, they believed they were still over deep water when they jettisoned the bomb and observed no resultant explosion. They then landed safely at Belle Chasse Naval Air Station near New Orleans, Louisiana. It was later determined that they were not over open ocean but had dropped the bomb in the area between the Chandeleur Islands and the Mississippi Sound.

"At the time the Air Force publicly stated that two planes had collided during a training mission off the Louisiana coast without bothering to mention the little matter of the lost nuclear weapon. The bomb was never found and eventually forgotten."

When Quint finished, the team sat stunned. Finally Kira broke the silence, "You mean to tell me there's a live nuclear warhead off the U.S. Gulf Coast?"

"Yep. Of course, I have come to learn that this is only one of some 50 lost bombs scattered around the world."

"They must have tried to find it," Colin said.

"Sure. They sent in a team posing as fishermen and attempted to locate it using radiation detection equipment. But after a fruitless two-month covert search, on April 16, 1958, the Navy confidentially declared it to be irretrievably lost and called off the search. Then in 1959 a shrimper snagged his net and dove down to try to cut it free. He claimed it was caught on a bomb, though he was unable to later relocate it.

"At the time, the bomb was alleged not to have the plutonium trigger needed for a nuclear explosion and, therefore, was judged 'probably harmless' where it was. The Air Force assumed that it landed nose first and was buried in mud beneath 20 feet of water. They postulated that recovery of the bomb could take up to five years and cost millions of dollars.

"You may remember the 1966 Palomares, Spain, episode in which four hydrogen bombs were released when a KC-135 tanker and the B-52 bomber it was refueling collided. Two of the bombs were destroyed on impact, showering the area with radioactive material. A third bomb was quickly recovered largely intact, but the fourth was found only after the U.S. spent some $182 million on the recovery effort—back when $182 million was serious money."

Mimi started to raise her hand but remembering her disfigurement, began speaking instead. "Well, seeing as how the bomb has remained lost for all this time, what brought this up now?"

"It was forgotten until 2004 when a retired Air Force Lt. Colonel, unconvinced that the bomb was harmless, towed a Geiger counter behind his boat and detected radiation levels 10 times the normal level in the surrounding 12-foot-deep waters south of Pass Christian. Without divulging the bomb story, he went public with his find, fearing the radiation might poison marine life in the area.

"Shortly thereafter, the government concluded that his radiation readings were 'normal for the naturally occurring minerals in the area.' Problem was, not many people bought that—including at least one group of terrorists we believe have been nosing around the area to find out why someone would tow a Geiger counter around the Sound."

"So how do we fit in?" asked Leo, who had finally cooled off and returned.

"Welcome back," Dawson piped up, earning him a cool glare from Leo.

Ignoring their interplay, Quint continued, "The government doesn't want to revisit the incident or give the rumor of a lost nuclear device additional credibility, lest they end up with Greenpeace and every other activist group protesting. But neither do they want to sit back and risk having terrorists stumble upon it."

"Why not let the terrorists find and retrieve the bomb, then simply seize it?" Colin asked.

"They feel the risk is too great that the terrorists might abscond with it before being caught."

"So, that's where we come in?" Willy asked.

"You got it. Our cover story is that we're looking for a treasure ship. We got lots of press coverage about our recovery efforts with the *Almiranta,* so we can credibly distance ourselves from any hoopla about nuclear weapons. The Navy can provide us with detection technology several times more sensitive than today's commercial equipment and probably a thousand times better than the stuff available in the '50s. The only drawback is that it doesn't have a great range, which means it'll take quite a while to cover the target area."

"What's the pay?" Leo asked skeptically.

"We may get paid two ways. First of all we'll get paid our actual expenses up to $15 million, plus a $10 million fee. Once we find the bomb, the Navy will remove it without fanfare." A murmur of approval rose from the team.

"What if we don't find it?" Kira asked.

"We will," Quint replied firmly.

"You said we might get paid two ways. What's the second?"

Colin asked.

"We are going to search for an actual treasure ship—on our own nickel, of course. We can do it at the same time, provided it doesn't interfere with our search for the bomb. The information Rogers provided is pretty vague; so finding it will be a long shot. Leo, since you're our resident shipwreck expert, please familiarize yourself with Rogers' package," he said, handing him a thick folder.

"I am honored to be entrusted with this assignment," Leo replied, with mock formality.

"Evidently, Jean Lafitte and Henry Morgan traveled that area, and a few artifacts, including some doubloons, washed up on nearby beaches after storms. There are sketchy accounts by survivors, but it's not even clear what the name of the wreck is. Rogers claims it could be the *El Cazador*.

"Leo, your job is to familiarize yourself with Rogers' information and provide a detailed briefing to the team so we all understand our cover story. If we do find the wreck, we'll have the right to work it with both federal and state claims waived, as well as any taxes."

"How sweet it is," Colin said, his smile fading as he caught one of Kira's withering glares. A few minutes later the group approved the project and began talking excitedly about plans for moving forward.

Mimi caught Kira's eye and pulled her off to the side. "I think you should know that before all this came up, I made plans to visit Everett's family in England in two months. We may have completed this project by then, but if not, I thought you should know. I don't expect to be gone more than a week or 10 days."

Mimi had become involved with Everett for a brief period before his death during their Venezuela adventure. Since he was one of the few men to enter her life, she had arranged to visit his family to pay her respects.

"I understand," Kira said, having shared Mimi's grief over Everett's death. "Don't worry; I'll hire someone to fill in," Kira said. Noticing the look of concern on her face continued, "Of course, there's no way we could find anyone to adequately fill your shoes. Or maybe I'll just cover for you myself. Either way, just plan on going and have a great time." They rejoined the group as Quint resumed speaking.

"One more thing, in the interests of transparency, it is reputed that an April 1966 letter written by the assistant secretary of defense for atomic energy claimed it was a complete weapon. In other words, it was armed.

"In 1961, two nuclear weapons lost in a plane crash in Goldsboro, NC, were similarly armed with their safeguards engaged. One bomb is believed to have fallen in a marsh and was never found. The other one was recovered from a cotton field after the crash at which time they discovered that five of its six failsafe gates were active—only one prevented it from detonating. So there is a wee bit of danger associated with this, though we should be long gone by the time they set about recovering it.

"We'll use the *Searcher* for both the bomb and the treasure ship search. It's still in the Bahamas, right where we left it after our last adventure. We'll have to do some re-rigging, but the main modification will be to add a large davit capable of hoisting the bomb on deck, should the need arise."

"I thought the plan was for the Navy to take care of that little chore for us?" Kira asked.

"That is the plan. Rogers wanted this just in case," Quint replied, though Kira still seemed concerned.

"Willy, you and Dakota inspect the ship and oversee the modifications and any needed repairs." Willy looked up from answering a text and nodded. "Rogers is in a bit of a hurry, so we'll need to charter two more boats when we get to Mississippi and outfit them with survey gear.

"Colin, I'd like for you to review Dawson's equipment list; add anything else you think we'll need and send Rogers the modified list as soon as possible. Then I'll need you to take care of provisioning. Mimi, help Kira develop the search operations plan.

"Now that this project is a go, Dawson and I will depart for Pass Christian, or the Pass, as the locals call it, to reconnoiter the area and prepare for the team's arrival. We'll charter the additional boats, arrange for a place to dock *Searcher* when we bring her in, find living accommodations, and get a handle on the local area. I don't anticipate any problems, so we should be back in a couple of days."

Willy, the first to leave, emerged from the bar anxiously scanning the street. On the opposite corner he spotted a man lurking in the shadows. After glancing over his shoulder, Willy briskly crossed the street. The two men stepped into a nearby alley. A moment later Willy emerged palming a small package and nervously glancing back at the bar and walking quickly away.

CHAPTER 10

"You need to ease off on that stuff; it'll kill you," Dawson said pointing to the airport coffee Quint had purchased on the way to the gate.

"I'll have plenty of company. Did you know that Americans drink over a quarter of a billion cups each day, enough to fill 35 Olympic-sized swimming pools? Besides, I need my brain juice. I just wish that after charging me four bucks, they had vanilla creamer."

At the gate area stood an older man. His pot belly overhung his belt, and the front of his wrinkled shirt was festooned with mementos of several past meals. When the gate agent announced preboarding for their flight, he launched himself from the wall to walk past a line of people already waiting to board. After the preoccupied gate agent scanned his boarding pass, he waddled down the jetway. Several passengers glanced at one another with raised eyebrows.

"Guess he fancies himself more important than the rest of us," one person commented.

Determined to get his full 40 dollars' worth for the business-class upgrade he had purchased, the man started giving orders the minute he sat down. A few minutes later, he began registering complaints, acting like he owned the airline. The liquor wasn't the right brand; the snacks were not to his liking; the service was not quick enough, and on and on.

Dawson bumped the flight attendant's arm causing her to dump a tray of soft drinks in the man's lap. Though it could have been an accident, Dawson did little to conceal his mirth despite the angry glare from across the aisle.

"Poetic justice, I love it."

"What's that?" the man challenged.

"Oh, nothing. Just enjoying the flight," Dawson said, with a direct stare and a "don't-screw-with-me" grin.

Shortly after takeoff, Quint set his watch back an hour, always preferring to operate on local time. He figured it really didn't matter what time it was at home; he preferred to know what time it was where he was.

During the flight, Quint was considering his living arrangements when he had an idea. "Dawson, I think I'll bring *Mojito* up to Mississippi to live aboard and use as our headquarters. If we get in a pinch, we can use her, though I'd prefer sticking with our plan to use smaller and cheaper search boats." Dawson nodded in agreement.

Their flight arrived in Gulfport, Mississippi, mid-afternoon. Quint winced at the wave of steamy air that accosted him upon exiting the terminal to find their rental car. With no reason for caution, they failed to notice the men who waited in front of the airport and followed them to their hotel in a plain black sedan.

After changing into t-shirts, shorts, and deck shoes the two spent the afternoon cruising the coast, stopping at several marinas before arriving in Pass Christian. "Here's a little local history I bet you never knew. Upon her death in 1799, Ms. Julia de la Brosse, who owned this area, bequeathed it to her freed slave. His heirs chartered the town in 1848. See, it paid you to get out of bed; you learned something today," Quint said. Dawson just rolled his eyes.

"Okay, Mr. Smart-Man-Know-it-all, where did it get its name?" Dawson asked.

"Ha, an easy one. They named The Pass after the deep water channel and in honor of Cat Island resident Nicholas Christian L'Adnier."

It was nearly dark by the time Quint pushed aside his half-eaten shrimp poboy and platter of baked oysters, with only the shells remaining. From the outside deck at Shaggy's in Pass Christian Harbor, he gazed at the chocolate-colored water of the Mississippi Sound below and thought about old times—chasing speckled trout in the marshes to the south. The salty ocean smell and local shrimp and oysters perfected the meal, reminding Quint he was home.

"Man, I'm too stuffed to eat another bite. Let's waddle down to the marina and check out the local boats for hire."

Quint and Dawson strolled casually down the main pier scrutinizing the charter boats. As they headed back to their car, unaware of the dark sedan parked near the seawall, two men stood waiting in the shadows. "We can dock *Searcher* at the end of that transient pier," Quint said. "Those charter boats could possibly serve our purpose, but maybe we can locate something more suitable."

"I agree. Gulfport marina has... " Dawson stopped in mid-sentence as the two men emerged from the shadows. One pressed a gun barrel to the back of his neck while plucking the rental car keys from his hand. Three more armed men stepped from the sedan, one a nearly seven-foot-tall giant, making it clear that this was not the time to pick a fight.

"Get in the car," the one behind Quint spoke quietly in a thick Middle Eastern accent pointing toward the sedan. As they neared, the men standing beside the sedan slipped plastic-tie handcuffs on the duo and shoved them into the back seat. "The rest of you follow in their rental car," one said to the man behind Dawson without using his name.

"Yes, Akmed," he replied and immediately saw Akmed's face change to a mask of anger at the mention of his name in front of their prisoners. "Oh, sorry."

"Just do it... Omar," Akmed said, returning the favor of having his name disclosed, as he slid into the passenger's seat.

"Howdy, Akmed. I'm Dawson, and this here's Quint. I don't believe I caught your partner's name," Dawson said to the giant stone-faced driver. Neither responded as the giant drove, and Akmed sat sideways, his gun pointed in their direction.

"Not big talkers, are they?" Quint said to Dawson.

"Nope. They're probably the can't-walk-and-chew-gum-at-the-same-time types," Dawson replied sarcastically, eliciting no response. "Might I ask where we're headed? Hope it's a hot party. Quint and I were looking for some action."

"You'll be getting that all right. Now shut up or I'll start using this gun instead of just pointing it."

Dawson shut up and watched where they were being taken. He knew that their chances of escaping would quickly diminish when they reached their kidnappers' destination.

A minute later Dawson piped up again, "You know this reminds me of our stay in Syria," referring to a similar situation in which he created a diversion while Quint escaped. Akmed's glare suggested he best not reply.

Lacking a better idea, as they rode Quint worked on his plastic cuffs to be ready when Dawson acted. By the time they arrived, he had worked his right hand loose to the point he was sure he could free it with a hard jerk.

The cars stopped in front of a modest stucco house on a street lined with similar dwellings all backed by a bayou. A red convertible with the top down sat in the driveway.

Akmed, the giant, and one of the others proceeded into the house while Omar prodded Dawson forward, and the remaining man accompanied Quint. As soon as Dawson stepped inside, he dove forward, knocking Omar into the foyer wall while screaming, "Get in here, he's getting away," in hopes that the man outside would instinctively react to his words and not his voice.

Without pause, Quint's guard ran into the house assuming his prisoner couldn't get far. Seizing the opportunity, Quint bolted for the front yard of the house to his right and then ducked toward the canal in back. He jerked his right hand free, leaving the plastic cuffs dangling from his left hand while formulating a plan on the run. Behind the neighboring house he spotted a Jet Ski perched on a floating dock and headed for it, praying it would not have a fancy keyed-starter—luck was with him.

Though the kill switch clip was missing, he whipped out his pocket knife and cut off part of one shoe lace to improvise a fix. Pulling out the kill switch with one hand, he wrapped the lace around it with the other, jamming it tightly.

Yes! he whispered with a smile as the kill switch remained extended when he released it. Confirming that the fuel switch was on, he pulled out the choke and pressed the green starter button. The starter spun for several seconds, the motor coughing and sputtering while the battery weakened.

Come on, come on, please start, he pled, knowing that his captors were searching for him and would be drawn by the sound of the motor cranking. Finally the engine caught with a roar. He gunned the throttle and engaged the reverse lever to back off the floating dock. Once free, he gave it full throttle and disappeared into the moonless night, leaving Omar, who had just reached the dock, cursing in his wake while rubbing his bloodied nose.

Rounding the corner into the main canal at full speed, Quint ignored the no-wake zone. He flew down the narrow canal, bent on increasing the distance between him and the kidnappers, noting his route so he could return later. After a few minutes, he backed off the throttle to avoid smashing into a pier in the dark and pondered the question, *What now?*

Quint considered calling the police, but having stolen the Jet Ski, he was afraid that by the time the wheels of justice turned, Dawson would be dead. Also, due to the sensitive nature of their mission, unwanted publicity could force the end of their search, thus making it easier for the bomb to fall into the wrong hands. Then there was the issue of oily defense attorneys whom Quint could imagine lined up— eager to free the scum who had kidnapped them for the right size pile of greenbacks.

No, Quint knew he had no choice but to go it alone, though it might well be his death sentence. Dawson would do the same if their roles were reversed. By the time he pulled the Jet Ski to the canal bank, he had formulated a plan to free his buddy.

With the watercraft hidden in the shadows, he headed for the lights of a convenience store across the street. Rummaging through the dumpster beside the store, he found three empty water bottles and used his knife to slice off a several-foot-long section of hose from the pay air station. *Sorry,* he thought, picturing the angry owner discovering his act of vandalism. *It's for the team.*

Quint hugged the shadows as he walked down the empty street toward a used-car lot. Each time headlights approached, he slid behind a bush or tree to avoid patrolling policemen. Near the back of the lot, he found an older truck without a locking gas cap. With one end of the hose in the gas tank, he placed the other end in his mouth to begin the siphoning action.

"Damn!" Quint cursed, as he spat out a tablespoon of gasoline, gagging at the foul taste from being a second late in his reaction time. He wiped his mouth on his sleeve and spit several more times. Finished filling the three bottles, he tossed the hose beneath the truck.

With the bottles stashed behind a dumpster, Quint ducked into the convenience store. A bag lady was on her way to the counter to buy a Miller High Life beer. *Guess everybody's got to have a dream*, Quint thought to himself. Grabbing two beers from the cooler by the cash register and a butane lighter, he also paid the clerk for the bag lady's beer, only to watch her wander out without bothering to thank him.

Hurrying back to the Jet Ski with the gasoline-filled bottles, he drained a beer to slake his thirst and wash the taste of gasoline from his mouth. Using an old towel and some dock lines, he chocked the three gasoline-filled bottles and the remaining bottle of beer in the Jet Ski's front compartment and carefully secured the compartment lid. Climbing aboard the Jet Ski, he headed back intent on paying back his "new friends."

Akmed ran a hand through his greasy black hair as he set a yellow plastic case on the floor and took a seat on a bar stool in front of the chair to which Dawson was tied.

"You've screwed up and captured the wrong guys," Dawson said firmly.

Akmed smiled, "No, we have the right guys, or guy, I should say," looking at Omar, who was fuming over Quint's escape. "We've confirmed the information on your driver's license, and you're our guy, all right. You're here to charter a boat to search for something."

"Yeah, a wreck, which we probably won't find. And, even if we do, probably won't have much on it."

"Please, do not take me for a fool. Tell me what really interests you enough to bring you here."

"I already told you."

"You lying infidel; you'll never get the bomb before we do," Omar said, unable to contain his frustration. He punched Dawson hard in the head, knocking over him and the chair.

"Shut up, you fool," Akmed said, slapping Omar hard across the face. "Thanks to your ineptness we don't have much time, but he will tell me what I wish to know before we leave. Now pick him up." Omar lifted the chair upright while Dawson's eyes remained riveted on the yellow case, blood pouring from a cut on his cheek.

"Talib," he said to the giant man. "Take Omar and ditch their rental car. Make sure to wipe it down before you leave it." Talib nodded, motioning for Omar to follow him. Akmed then turned to the fourth man, "Go outside and perform a security patrol in case Quint returns before I'm finished. Make sure the boat out back is ready if we need to escape that way." Akmed knelt on the floor and opened the plastic case. Inside was an electronics box with two large paddles connected by electrical cords.

Uh-oh, things are about to get a whole lot more unpleasant, Dawson thought to himself, unsure what Akmed's equipment was but confident it was intended to cause him pain. Akmed plugged the device into the wall outlet and turned the unit on, confident he had Dawson's attention as he made some adjustments.

"Mr. Dawson, we would appreciate your giving us the details

of your plans."

"I'm not telling you shit."

"I was hoping you'd say that," Akmed said, a sadistic grin spread across his face as he ripped Dawson's shirt open and placed the paddles on his chest.

"A defibrillator?"

"Right you are," Akmed replied, as he keyed the unit. Dawson's body stiffened, and he screamed at the pain from the electric charge surging through his body. "On this modified model, that was merely half power. As I increase the charge, the pain will become much worse, possibly damaging your heart. Now let's try again; what is your group up to?"

Quint approached the house where Dawson was being held captive, pausing to consider his next move. Though at this hour it wasn't likely he would run into anyone, noisy dogs were a concern as he idled up the canal. Spying a walkway with a clear shot to the street, he killed the engine and cleated-off the Jet Ski beside a large motoryacht.

He retrieved the three gasoline-filled bottles, cutting a hole in the center of each lid with his knife. He ripped several strips off the bottom of his t-shirt, stuffing one into the hole of each lid to form fuses and screwing the lids back onto the bottles. *Now I can serve my new friends a cocktail—Molotov, that is,* he thought with a grin.

Quint hopped onto the dock and eased up the path to the tree-covered walk beside the street. Pausing beside a spreading live oak, he studied the house two doors down. The black sedan was gone, leaving only the red convertible in the driveway; his rental car was nowhere to be seen.

A light in a room at the end of the house revealed shadowy figures moving about inside. He just hoped Dawson was still there and alive.

Quint duck-walked to within 50 feet of the house; where he stashed the three bottles. Loud voices punctuated by the lights dimming and Dawson's screams removed any doubt about what Quint planned next.

As he prepared to make his move, a metal click and the creaking hinges of a gate opening beside the house caught his attention. The orange glow of a cigarette lit the face of a swarthy man holding a gun, engaged in a perimeter check.

With no time to study the situation, Quint chose to even the odds. While the man moved toward the front of the house, Quint chose two stones from the landscaping bed where he knelt. When the man passed, Quint rose, and taking two long steps, launched the first rock like a shot put. Sensing, rather than hearing Quint, the man turned, and the stone struck him full in the face.

As he collapsed with a grunt, Quint sent his emergency back-up rock crashing into the side of the man's head for good measure, then snatched the gun from his motionless hand. A dark stream poured from the man's temple, staining his shirt collar. A pulse-check indicated Quint need not worry about restraining him—he would no longer be causing anyone problems. A quick search yielded an extra ammo clip, which Quint slid into his pocket along with the gun.

I don't know how long before the feces hits the fan, but the clock's running, Quint thought as he retrieved the three bottles and crept past the still-open gate between the two houses. Setting two of the bottles beside the walk, Quint removed the gun from his pocket and, carrying the third bottle, quietly made his way around to the front of the house.

Removing the cap-fuse from the bottle, he poured the contents over the seats of the convertible and tossed the lit t-shirt-fuse into the car. By the time the flames flared, he was in the back yard with the fuse lit on the second bottle. Tossing it into the cockpit of the go-fast boat docked behind the house, he crouched behind the bushes to wait—it did not take long.

The Molotov cocktail exploded with an impressive boom, engulfing the boat in flames. When Quint saw a man open the back door, he threw the last lit bomb at the house. "What the—!" the man exclaimed as he began to catch fire—along with the back porch and the inside of the house. Quint then headed to the front of the house once again.

Drawn by the flames from the car, Akmed had gone out front but quickly returned inside when he heard the sound of the explosion from the rear of the house. He was busy with a small fire extinguisher trying to save his flaming comrade when Quint barreled through the front door. Before he could react, Quint let go with two rounds, dropping him to the floor, unconscious but still breathing.

Quint maintained his momentum running down the hall, pausing only to kick in the bedroom door. He shoulder rolled and came up ready to fire, but Dawson was alone, tied to a chair, the defibrillator lying on the floor beside him.

"I'm having a really crappy night, so I'd consider it a personal favor if you didn't shoot me," Dawson quipped.

Eying his bloodied face and torn shirt, Quint replied, "Don't you look nice?"

"Yeah, well you should see the other guy's knuckles." Dawson replied wryly, one eye swollen and blood from his battered face covering his chest.

"I promise you, his knuckles are the least of their problems right now," Quint said with a smile. He withdrew his knife and sliced the plastic ties on Dawson's hands and legs then helped him to his shaky legs. Quint steadied him as they headed for the back door.

Dawson spotted Akmed lying on the floor and paused to deliver a kick to his side. "Wish I had the time to revive you with your little toy in there but maybe I'll get lucky, and you'll die without my help."

Quint guided Dawson over the smoldering body and out the back of the house to the Jet Ski. "Up for a moonlight cruise?"

"Yep, my evening plans just cleared. You got beer?"

"As it turns out, I do," he said retrieving the second beer from the Jet Ski compartment.

Dawson popped the top and took a long pull. "A little warm."

Quint rolled his eyes. "You're freakin' never happy. Shut up and drink while I get us the hell out of here." With the sound of sirens approaching, Quint jumped on the Jet Ski, and after a quick check of his homemade kill switch, fired it up.

The neighbors on the front side of the house were staring at the automobile bonfire, cringing as the fuel tank exploded in a spectacular display. Those across the canal were similarly engaged watching the burning boat erupt in a massive fireball when the "cocktail" ignited the fumes from its fuel tank.

Dawson raised his beer to toast the open-mouthed people gathered across from him and yelled, "We're going to get marshmallows. Get some coat hangers; we'll be back in a jiffy." Quint gunned the Jet Ski, and they roared down the canal.

"Let's see about getting some more wheels," Quint said, ditching the Jet Ski back near the convenience store. He felt guilty about not returning it to its rightful owner but made a mental note to anonymously report it to the police.

While they waited for the cab Quint had called, Dawson said, "They knew."

"Knew what?"

"They knew why we were here."

"How?"

"That, my friend, is the question," Dawson replied in a low voice, as he dialed the rental car company using Quint's cell phone. "Hello, I'd like to report our rental car stolen," he said, hoping to keep things low key. "Yes, it was parked right outside our hotel, and when we went to get it, by gosh, it just wasn't there." He provided the requested information, after which he was advised that the police would contact him for a complete report. They also promised to have a replacement car brought to the hotel.

"What happens if Akmed's boys leave the keys in the car? How are you going to explain that one?" Dawson simply shrugged, implying he would cross that bridge later.

The sun was rising by the time they returned to their room. While Dawson headed for the shower, Quint checked in with the team. "We were worried about you. You guys all right?" Kira asked.

"Dawson is somewhat less beautiful, but we're otherwise intact. We probably won't be having any more trouble in the near term from these particular bad guys. Two of them were gone, but two of the rest are dead and, if the third isn't, he probably wishes he was. By the way, these guys knew why we were here. Figure out how they found out."

"Okay. You headed back?"

"Not until we finish here. I'll call again tomorrow."

After Quint hung up, Dawson said, "Let's get breakfast. Being taken hostage, beaten, defibrillated, and rescued always makes me hungry." Quint followed him to the hotel restaurant, stopping at the front desk to leave word where to direct the police.

By the time they had eaten breakfast, the police were finished taking their statements, and the replacement rental car had arrived. Stepping from the hotel, Dawson turned to Quint, "Okay. Let's try this again."

Rashid was rapidly clicking through his e-mail in preparation for beginning his work day when his assistant buzzed him. "Akmed is here to see you."

He had not heard from Akmed since the previous week when he failed to interrogate and kill Quint and Dawson. "Tell him I'll be with him in a while. Keep him waiting for 30 minutes," Rashid replied. He did not accept failure graciously and decided to let Akmed stew in his own juices.

"Quint's team is ruining your plans," Akmed said, after squirming for a half hour waiting to see Rashid.

"Really? I thought it was *your* failure to carry out *your* mission," Rashid said, the venom thick in his voice. The two men sat in silence with Akmed's eyes darting about to avoid the angry, laser-like beams of Rashid's stare. "And how is it that *both* of them escaped?" Rashid asked Akmed, plainly furious over the failure.

"Please forgive me. Two of my men were killed; only I survived along with Omar and Talib, whom I had tasked to ditch Quint's rental car. Although I was taken to the hospital and questioned at length, I was careful not to permit the unfortunate situation to become even worse. I claimed I was shot by a crack addict and did not contact you to shield you from any unwanted attention."

Unlike Osama, Rashid always maintained a low profile. In fact, he was fanatical about remaining anonymous. As his right-hand man, Akmed had failed in his mission. Now with a bowed head he quietly explained the events after Quint and Dawson's capture.

"You were right, maintaining my cover was the highest priority. I am disappointed with the way things turned out, but we can overcome this setback." After considering the situation, Rashid decided to grant Akmed another chance, not out of mercy or compassion, but to avoid the inconvenience of finding a replacement. "You ready to work?"

"I stand ready to serve you however you desire," he replied. Though barely able to function from his gunshot wounds, Akmed would never succumb to weakness and was eager to redeem himself for his failure.

"Hire some more men and get back there. Find the bomb before they do."

CHAPTER 11

Quint was pleased to find Evie waiting for him at the Key West airport upon his return from Mississippi. She looked fit in her hot pink t-shirt and snug shorts, her shiny brown hair gathered in a simple pony tail. They made small talk as they headed for the Conch Republic restaurant, where Evie ordered an Island Salad and Quint went for the appetizer-sized tuna tataki and an order of cracked conch.

"So what were you doing at the clinic the other day when I passed by?"

"Oh, so you did see me?" Quint asked with a broad smile as Evie blushed.

"Uh... yes. So was it an STD scare?"

"Ha ha. I was scheduling my hysterectomy," Quint replied.

"Very funny. Seriously, what was that about?"

Preferring not to get into the Lefty thing but unwilling to raise her suspicions over an innocent matter when they were just getting back on track, Quint honestly replied, "Taking a friend to dialysis."

"Who?" Evie asked with raised eyebrows.

"Lefty, doubt you know him."

"Not that one-armed guy who hangs around the harbor?"

"The very one."

"He's strange."

"That he is, but a good man. While fighting in Vietnam, Lefty was engaged in a fierce firefight when his lieutenant was hit by sniper fire. As Lefty carried him to cover, a mortar round claimed his left arm above the elbow and scrambled his brains. The two of them lay there for nearly two days amidst the pieces of the rest of his squad before the medics found and evacuated him.

"Lefty credited the lieutenant with saving his life by applying a tourniquet to stem the bleeding from the stub of his arm and offering words of encouragement. Problem was, the medics confirmed the lieutenant died instantly from the sniper fire.

"Though Bob is his real name, his buddies took to calling him Lefty until he eventually adopted the name himself. On bad days, he sits astride his perch right outside the restaurant and sheds silent tears most of the day. On good days he's a regular chatterbox, talking in sort of a rap-style."

"I hear he disappears at night then pops back up in the morning to reclaim his station. I've seen a lot of the locals and even a few tourists give him spare change or an occasional sandwich. I even recall seeing you slip him a couple of bucks."

"Guess I'm not as subtle as I think."

"Hardly, but then there's no reason to be. That's really sweet, I mean looking after him like that. Who subs for you when you're not around to take him to dialysis?"

"Since I started, it hasn't been a problem. I've always been able to find someone."

"Count me in as a sub anytime. He gave his arm, and I guess his mind, to some extent, for the country. Least I can do is help you help him," Evie said as she polished off the last of her salad.

After lunch, Quint rode with Evie to her house, where they launched into a project to replace the dining room ceiling fan. It had been a long time since they had worked together like this, and it felt good. *Maybe we're going to be a couple again,* Quint thought to himself.

I don't think I'm up to it today, Kira thought to herself, tossing her sneakers beside the chair, deciding to postpone her morning workout until after the meeting with the team. Though she always tried to run once a day, after waking this morning she still felt tired and out of sorts. For an instant, the image of her mother lying in the hospital bed dying of cancer, her gray skin cold and clammy, flashed through Kira's mind.

Though Kira was a black belt in karate and an experienced marksman capable of handling virtually any weapon, including field stripping an M16 in 35 seconds, the thought of cancer left her weak in the knees. She gave up smoking when her mother died— determined not to meet the same fate. Unwilling to entertain even the possibility of the cancer that took her mother and her grandmother before that, she forced it from her mind.

But why am I so tired? she wondered. After calling Mimi to tell her she might not make the meeting, she went back to bed hoping to sleep off the nausea.

"Where's Kira?" Quint asked, as he entered the suite they had rented for their meeting at the Galleon in Key West. Most of the team were already gathered, eager to discuss plans for proceeding with the project.

"Mimi said she's under the weather," Colin replied, appearing more concerned than he intended.

Quint noticed Dawson pressing his fingers to his lower right jaw, apparently in pain. "Problem?" Quint asked.

"Tooth ache. It acts up occasionally, but a couple of aspirin usually fixes it."

Quint nodded and turned to Colin. "While we're waiting for the others to show up, why don't you get started." Colin explained what they had learned about how the terrorists had found Quint and Dawson.

"So you think someone in Rogers' office or further up the chain leaked our plans?" Dawson asked.

"It appears so, unless it was one of us, which I doubt," Colin replied.

"Though we didn't have the luxury of interrogating the guys in Mississippi, it's clear they're linked to the terrorists looking for the bomb," Quint added.

"We may have a lead," Dawson said. "After they finished using me for a human punching bag but before they started with the electro-shock therapy, one of them, assuming I was unconscious, speculated about how someone named 'Rashid' would take it when he learned of your escape."

"Did they mention where he might be?" Dawson shook his head. "At least it's a lead of sorts. I'll pass it on to Rogers."

"Rogers?" Dawson asked, surprised. "The leak might have come from his office."

"You can't seriously think it was from him?" Quint replied, unconvinced. "He has to know about the leak so we can help him plug it. Tell you what, since you're skeptical of Rogers, you go meet with him face-to-face about the leak so you can judge his response first hand."

"No problem," Dawson answered enthusiastically.

Quint smiled, "I figured you'd jump at another chance to see Rachel."

"Who wouldn't? There's definite chemistry there. You saw the way she looked at me."

"I'm going to Miami tomorrow; you can hitch a ride with me," Leo interrupted, appearing to have forgiven Dawson for his earlier prank.

"Go along to the meeting too so you can hose down lover boy if he gets too hot and bothered. And take a leash," Quint added.

"Not a bad idea," Leo laughed.

"You better bring one—for restraining her," Dawson said cockily.

"Okay Leo, where do we stand on our treasure-wreck cover story?" Quint asked.

Leo, a free spirit with ceaseless enthusiasm and energy, brought a different dimension to the team with his unorthodox approach to problem solving. As a young boy growing up in the Keys, Leo would scrape together money to travel the Keys by bus. Once, he embarked on a two-day adventure to Miami, much to the chagrin of his worried mother. Upon his return, Leo found sitting down an adventure after his mother finished working over his backside.

"Rogers' information suggests our wreck might be the *El Cazador*, which was loaded with treasure. In the late 1760s, Spain's holdings in the New World were teetering on the brink of collapse. Counterfeiting in the U.S. colonies, coupled with Spain's devalued paper currency, was making it impossible for them to finance trade.

"To save his New World empire, the King of Spain decided to redeem the worthless paper currency for fresh silver coinage from Mexico. So on April 20, 1783, he sent his most highly regarded captain, Gabriel de Campos y Pineda, to sail the *El Cazador* to their mint in Veracruz, Mexico. A few months later, they set sail from Veracruz headed for New Orleans loaded with 450,000 freshly minted 1783 Spanish silver reales.

"Whether this Spanish Brig of War fell victim to pirates or a storm is unknown, but she never reached New Orleans. King Charles IV of Spain was forced to cede Louisiana back to France, setting the stage for the Louisiana purchase which, as you know, doubled the size of the United States at the bargain basement price of three cents per acre. All because the *El Cazador* failed to reach port."

Dawson woke the next morning feeling the familiar symptoms of a hangover, except that he had not been drinking the night before. Instead, dreams about the beautiful wife and daughter he had lost in a fiery automobile mishap had awakened him, and it took nearly an hour to get back to sleep, only to have a second nightmare. This one involved the French doctor, Margaux, for whom he had developed strong feelings. Sadly, she was killed during their Venezuelan adventure. All night long he alternated between the two horrific nightmares with long, lonely sleepless hours in between.

Dawson desperately longed for a serious relationship to fill the aching void. Not so much for the sex, seldom a problem, but rather to give his life meaning. In the Keys it was hard to find an unattached woman who was not a tourist looking for a fling, a barfly living out of a bottle, or just plain weird.

When Leo arrived in an Excalibur replica, Dawson hesitantly climbed in, and they headed for Miami. "Like my new wheels?"

"Nice," Dawson lied, wondering if the creaking rattletrap would make the trip.

"I wish I could have found one of the originals built in the late 1960s, but they're expensive and rare. Few people would appreciate the difference anyhow, and I practically stole this one."

Dawson looked forward to their trip to Miami. One of his favorite parts of living in the Keys was the occasional drive on the overseas highway. No matter how he felt at the start of the trip, driving up the Keys, surrounded by the full palette of the ocean's blues and greens, always improved his mood.

As they rode along, Leo regaled Dawson with stories about himself, the authenticity of which Dawson questioned. Leo claimed that during his more prosperous times, a stream of attractive ladies found their way to his door, providing him with an endless supply of sex for the taking. While he attributed this to his good looks and sexual prowess, Dawson suspected the real attraction was his generosity with cash and drugs.

Leo was a boom-or-bust kind of guy. During his latest bust, oil prices sent his multi-million-dollar oil drilling business down the tubes. Leo struggled with conventional jobs, becoming predictably stir crazy before joining the team. A free spirit, he claimed to have Gypsy blood flowing through his veins. Dawson believed him.

They arrived in Miami in time for lunch. Without bothering to include Dawson in his lunch venue planning, Leo parked on a congested downtown side street and announced, "Lunch time." Scurrying from the driver's seat, Leo headed toward the corner at a brisk pace with Dawson in his wake wearing a worried look.

Leo's taste for pricey old Añejo rum was fully developed as was his affinity for Cuban cigars smuggled into the country by some of his Key West buddies. But his best known and least understood passion was eating weird foods, which he insisted on calling "exotic." At one time or other, he had managed to gross out the entire team.

Rounding the corner into a narrow alleyway, Leo made his way halfway down the block before stopping before a tiny restaurant called "Akihiro's," the faded paint on the window barely visible through what appeared to be decades of grime. "It means 'large glory,'" Leo said, pointing at the sign, "and you, my friend, are in for a treat." Leo burst through the door without waiting for a reply while Dawson eyed the place warily, torn between his concern about getting mugged if he remained outside and dying of food poisoning if he entered.

Leo spied the only empty table in the dwarf-sized restaurant and plopped down. "Timing is everything," he said a minute later, nodding at the line of people already forming outside the door.

Dawson's heart sank as he scanned the battered menu Leo handed him—it was in Japanese. "Okay, Leo, I'm all too familiar with your penchant for weird food..."

"Exotic, not weird," Leo interrupted.

"Okay, exotic food. But as I was saying, since I don't read Japanese, I'm at your mercy. Unless you have grown tired of living, you had best not take advantage of the situation."

"Don't worry, I'm not one to hold grudges over little things like your ruining my love life." Leo replied, the memory of the Smirkin' Shark episode still fresh in his mind. "I'll take *real* good care of you. A minute later, a brusque waiter arrived.

"Order?" the waiter spat like a command more than a question.

"Let's see, we'll take the sakuraniku, and a sampler including nankotsu, kinkan, warabimochi, and natto."

"Drink?"

"Hot green tea and we'll both have a Kirin beer," Leo replied, excited at the prospect of their dining experience. The waiter nodded without replying and disappeared toward the back of the restaurant, reappearing seconds later with a pot of tea, two greasy cups, and two cans of beer then vanished once again.

"Okay, what did we just order?"

"Wait until the food arrives; otherwise, you'll just have to ask again. But trust me, you'll like it." Dawson was not convinced.

"For me, eating is a pleasure not a necessity," Leo said.

"No shit. With that gut of yours, I'd never have guessed."

A few minutes later, the waiter reappeared with chopsticks and a small plate, which he set down between them. Dawson eyed the plate filled with what appeared to be carpaccio.

"This is sakuraniku, which the Japanese call 'cherry blossom meat.' It's thinly sliced frozen steak served on a bed of rice. You can dip it in soy sauce or this minced garlic dipping sauce." After several tries, Dawson tentatively picked up a piece with his chopsticks and bravely dipped it into the garlic sauce before popping it in his mouth with closed eyes. To his surprise, the taste was quite mild, and it literally melted in his mouth.

"Not bad," he commented, while he fumbled over another piece with his chopsticks. Had he known that Leo neglected to mention it was horse steak, Dawson would have shown much less gusto. By the time he had downed his third tiny piece, Leo, much more adept with chopsticks, had cleaned the plate. It was clear that Dawson would need to eat fast whenever he found something he liked.

Leo had no sooner taken the last bite when the waiter whisked the empty plate away to replace it with a larger tray. "I ordered several things so you can try whatever strikes your fancy. This is nankotsu, deep-fried cartilage from chicken breast, and this is kinkan, basically, grilled chicken livers," except that they were chicken ovaries rather than livers, a fact that Leo also neglected to mention.

Dawson examined a piece of the cartilage and nibbled it. He found it was crunchy but otherwise had little taste and decided one piece was plenty. The kinkan wasn't too bad, and he went for seconds on that before Leo polished off the rest.

"This is warabimochi," Leo said, pointing with his chopstick at a pile of balls on the far side of the platter. "They boil these flour balls in water before coating them with syrup and more soy flour. This," he said, pointing to a glob beside the warabimochi, "is natto—which is made from soy beans that we would consider rancid. I've been told you have to eat them seven times before starting to like them. This is my third time, and I've still not found them tasty, so you might want to pass on them."

Dawson agreed and after downing one of the flour balls saw nothing remaining of interest. Putting down his chopsticks, he concentrated on a second Kirin. From the way Leo was relishing his meal, Dawson suspected he had not been completely honest but decided ignorance probably was bliss in this case.

Leo was still raving about the lunch when the two men entered Rogers' office and began their meeting. Leo noticed whenever Dawson commented on Rachel, his accountant heart throb, Rogers smiled. When Dawson caught a glimpse of Rachel passing by in the hallway, he excused himself to go to the restroom. Once he was gone, Rogers leaned over to Leo and confided, "You need to tell your partner that Rachel is not what she seems."

"Huh?" Leo replied, puzzled.

"Three years ago Rachel was Ralph."

"You're shitting me; she's a transvestite?"

"At least, though by now he may have had a full sex change—it's not something I feel comfortable asking about. I subscribe to the philosophy of tolerance, accepting people as they are, provided their ability to do 'their thing' doesn't impact the rights of others or interfere with the performance of their job.

"Ralph, I mean Rachel, is a good employee and took pains not to make this an issue more than I suppose it had to be. Initially, the bathroom situation was a bit of a challenge, but we eventually worked it out. I should have mentioned this sooner, but it was somewhat awkward."

Leo started to blurt out, *Oh, this is too good*, but quickly feigned an air of genuine concern. "It'll be hard on the poor man, but I'll try to handle it without embarrassing him," Leo said, struggling to suppress a smile.

"As you wish," Rogers replied, changing the subject as Dawson returned. He related the kidnapping episode in Mississippi, culminating in his conclusion that there was a leak.

"Guys, I'm truly sorry. I have no idea how this happened, but it must be up the chain on the government side. Not many people in my office know about 'our deal' and those who do have been with me for years. I'll do everything I can to find the leak and plug it. In the interim, we'll increase security to keep this from happening again. I'll also have some folks research this 'Rashid' guy and let Botz know we have a leak."

As they left the office, Dawson stopped to finish his conversation with Rachel. Afraid he couldn't keep a straight face, Leo walked ahead.

A minute later, Dawson caught up with Leo. "Victory! I got a date with her for this weekend."

While Evie was getting ready, Quint decided to offer Fred, the iguana, his surprise gift. A minute later, Evie entered behind him and yelled, "What are you doing?"

"Giving Fred a treat," Quint replied, holding up one of the crickets.

"No! Don't give him those."

"Why? The pet store told me iguanas love them."

"But what those idiots didn't tell you is that iguanas can't digest insect protein, and it's not good for them. They eat only fruits and vegetables. Bananas, green beans, and strawberries. Dandelions are nice."

"Sorry," Quint said, looking dejected as he handed her the rest of the bag, which she accepted with two fingers and held at arm's length. She immediately felt bad for yelling at him when he had intended to do something nice.

"Here, try giving him some of these sea grapes I brought back from Sugarloaf last week." Quint fed him three and left him still munching away as they headed out for drinks and appetizers at Louie's Backyard.

"I hate that you have to go again just as we were getting things back on track." Evie said, after downing one of their famous flaming ouzo shrimp.

"Remember when you told me that getting back in your good graces would take serious effort?" Quint asked, changing the subject.

"Yes," Evie replied with a laugh. Quint removed a velvet-covered box from his pocket and handed it to her.

"Ohhh," Evie responded, as she slowly opened the box to find an exquisite tennis bracelet. "Quint, I wasn't serious about making you grovel to square things with me."

"I know," he answered.

CHAPTER 12

Kira awoke dreaming of her mother crying silently in her hospital bed during one of her rare lucid periods when she had enough morphine in her system to numb the cancer pain but not enough to dull her mind. As Kira's stomach cramped, she launched herself from the bed to the bathroom. Still wiping bile from her chin, she began to get dressed, determined to make the team meeting.

Kira entered the meeting room and made a beeline for the bathroom, where she proceeded to lose the light breakfast she had forced down. Her stomach convulsed again as the image of her mother lying cancer stricken flashed before her. After the heaving subsided, she rinsed her mouth then discreetly re-entered the conference room.

The team, gathered to finalize the plan to search for the nuclear bomb, gasped when LaRue, an authentic south Louisiana Cajun, walked in. Both of his eyes were bruised, his broken nose covered in a large bandage, and he was missing a front tooth. "What the hell happened to you?" Quint asked, while hunting for the vanilla creamer to add to his coffee.

"Done fell off my tricycle," LaRue replied with a laugh. "No, had a car wreck. But I be good as new, Hoss." Quint, refusing to believe the flippant explanation, wondered about the *real* story.

During their recent *Almiranta* venture, LaRue proved to be one of the best divers Quint had ever known. LaRue was also skilled in the kitchen, for those with a cast iron stomach able to deal with his spicy Cajun fare. Sensing it was pointless to press the issue, Quint continued toward the front of the room.

He noticed that Kira, who normally looked ruggedly fit, appeared fragile, maybe even ill, though not nearly as bad off as LaRue. "Kira, you sure you're up for this?"

"Why wouldn't I be? Of course I am!" she replied defensively, cutting Quint off before he could dig deeper. Turning her attention toward the rest of the group, she heard Dawson boasting over his weekend date with Rachel.

"Leo saw the way she looked at me. I'm telling you, she's hot."

"Is he being straight with us?" Mimi asked Leo.

Leo laughed at her phrasing. "He is. Believe me, they have a *lot* in common." Though puzzled by the comment, Dawson ignored Leo as he continued, "Yeah, Dawson and Ralph, I mean Rachel, will make quite a couple."

Dawson bristled at Leo's mistake. Seeing the annoyed confusion in Dawson's eyes, Leo could not resist spilling the beans. "I'm sorry, Dawson. I didn't mean to use her former name."

"What in the hell are you talking about?" Dawson challenged.

"You know, I didn't mean to use the name she used before *he* became a *she*."

Quint, seeing the drama unfold, saw Dawson preparing to launch himself at Leo and intervened. "Leo, you better stop trying to piss off Dawson and explain yourself."

"Better to be pissed off than pissed on," Leo said defiantly. "During our meeting with Rogers, Dawson took a bathroom break, the one where he lined up his 'hot date.' While he was gone, Rogers confided that before Dawson's romance progressed much further, he needed to know that up until two years ago," Leo paused for dramatic effect, "Rachel was Ralph."

"You're full of shit," Dawson said, as the color drained from his face.

"No, I'm honest, unlike you claiming I was married and gumming up the works for me at the Smirkin' Shark. Payback's a bitch, isn't it?" Dawson started toward Leo, then caught himself and stormed out of the room without replying.

"Okay, let's get started," Quint announced to the rest of the team, ending the awkward episode. "Kira you go first." Kira overcame her dizziness to stand on shaky legs.

"As you know, I've been working with Rachel in Rogers' office," Leo's face broke into a wide smile, earning him muffled laughter from the team and a withering look from Kira, who appeared concerned over Dawson's pain. "We have all the necessary permits and authorizations for our treasure ship salvage cover. The bomb search electronics have been staged in Gulfport, ready to be installed when *Searcher* arrives.

"By the way, it might be best if we avoid the term 'bomb.' We don't need anyone overhearing it mentioned in conversation or on the radio. Might I suggest that we refer to the bomb by the code name 'Big Bertha,'" Quint nodded his consent.

"We've issued a press release announcing our expedition cover. Assuming we find Big Bertha, we'll turn her over to the Navy to handle the recovery and then devote our energies to actually searching for the wreck. Or if we're really lucky and find the wreck while searching for Big Bertha, we can begin salvage operations concurrent with our further bomb search efforts."

"Oh, so we should just plan on staying another week to find the wreck and recover the treasure," Colin replied sarcastically, as Kira gave him a sour look.

"It's lagniappe, Mr. Smartypants," she replied. "I've acquired charts for the entire area and laid out search grids using the same approach we employed with the *Almiranta* in Cay Sal. Dakota and Willy have *Searcher* ready for operations and can give her status."

Willy deferred to Dakota who rose to speak next. "*Searcher* is ready to depart once we return to the Bahamas. Since most of the work was labor, we readied the ship there as the cheaper alternative. It was simple to set up *Searcher* to pose as a legitimate treasure hunter, since that was her previous use. We eliminated our former disguise as a seismic exploration ship including removal of the streamer reel, damaged during the Cubans' attack.

"Unlike our last expedition to Cay Sal, this time we want the treasure hunting equipment prominently displayed. So, we've added a 'mailbox,' a large metal structure that may be lowered to deflect the prop wash and scour away the sand over the wreck site, should we find it. We also repaired the airlift, which we can use to vacuum sand and silt with more finesse if needed.

"As Kira indicated," he paused, noticing her hurriedly heading for the bathroom once again, and continued, "we'll install the high accuracy radiation detector, basically a sophisticated Geiger counter, on *Searcher* the day after we arrive. As we work a grid with it, we'll also deploy our magnetometers and side scan sonars. It'll appear that we're simply searching for a treasure wreck, which we actually will be doing at the same time," Dakota finished, nodding to Quint.

"Dawson and I have arranged docking space for *Searcher* and lined up two charter boats so we can cover ground more quickly while searching for the bomb, excuse me, Big Bertha," Quint said. "The other two radiation detection systems are not as sensitive and won't cover as wide a swath as *Searcher*, but they'll still speed things up. Well, if there are no further questions or comments, that wraps things up. See you in Mississippi."

By the time he finished, Kira reappeared looking pale, but Quint elected not to comment. "Quint, Mimi is planning on visiting Everett's family in England."

"I'm not surprised. They were quite close before his untimely death in Venezuela. She's a good hand, so we'll just make do while she's gone."

"Well, that's just it. She could be gone quite a while, perhaps even permanently," Kira said, exaggerating the length of Mimi's absence to cover the possibility of her own. "I plan to hire someone else. We need more depth even if she does come back."

"I trust your judgment. But after our recent experience in Mississippi, if we're going to hire someone else, I suggest we go for someone who adds more muscle to the team."

"So, you want me to hire a man?"

"Not necessarily a man, just someone who can handle themselves if things get dicey. It's a lot easier to teach them the rest of the stuff they need to know," Quint said.

Quint was headed to his car and spotted Mimi in the parking lot. "Good luck."

"On what?" Mimi asked.

"I hear you're leaving for England to visit Everett's family."

"Not for long."

"Oh, Kira was under the impression you might be gone a while and wanted to hire a replace... somebody... never mind, I probably misunderstood her," Quint said, continuing to his car.

"Two-faced bitch," he overheard Mimi mutter while getting into her car.

It was early morning when Quint and Dawson rose to move *Mojito* up to Mississippi, but the leaden sky made it appear even earlier. Already, thunderheads loomed over the Keys to the west, and there was sure to be rain later. The normally aquamarine waters looked dull, reflecting the graphite skies. Quint felt the gloom to the bone.

Dawson did an engine room check after they had been under way for just over an hour and, smelling of diesel fuel from his trip below, joined Quint in the enclosed bridge. After Quint declined his offer to take the helm, he climbed into the second helm seat.

"Man, my stomach is still screwed up, not sure why. Didn't get much sleep."

"I'm sure that fifth of Jack wasn't to blame," Quint replied.

"I didn't kill the whole fifth; plus I had help."

Quint laughed. "True, I had two drinks, and Evie had one, so technically, you're right. Go sack out on the couch in the salon. If I need you I'll slow down or maybe sound the horn."

Dawson nodded slowly, in deference to his head, and disappeared down the spiral staircase to the salon where he spent most of the day.

Quint looked forward to spending time back on the Mississippi Gulf Coast until his ex-wife Becky's face popped into his mind. It would be awkward if he ran into her.

It had been well over a year since Quint abruptly departed the Coast leaving behind the job he hated and a cheating wife. With no plan or forethought, he had finally decided that it was time to begin a new life. Following his gut, he headed for the Keys, where he ran a charter fishing boat until a fishing trip to Venezuela launched him on the adventure of his life.

His mind wandered as monotony set in and his thoughts turned to Evie. She had agreed to take over the responsibility of getting Lefty to his dialysis appointments during Quint's absence. Like a rock, she was there, eager to help. A feeling of relief washed over him at the realization that he had her back after nearly losing her—he vowed not to make that mistake again.

As they ran north from Key West, the skies cleared, as did Quint's dispostion. It was late by the time they docked near the St. Petersburg Yacht Club, where they refueled and grabbed a burger before catching a few hours of sleep.

Under way before sunup, Quint drove until noon then headed for the salon couch to take a snooze when Dawson, feeling much better, took his turn at the helm. With the gulf showing only a light chop and the boat running perfectly, he looked forward to crossing the bend.

As they headed west, a school of porpoises frantically swam to catch up and take turns riding the bow wave. He wished Quint were back on the bridge so that he could leave the helm and go to the foredeck to watch them riding the bow wave, but he had seen it many times.

Two hours later, the building seas were now running 3-5 feet. Dawson checked their course heading on the autopilot and noted their position in the logbook. Before leaving the bridge to climb down to the cockpit and relieve himself over the side, he created a waypoint on the chart plotter, as Quint insisted he do periodically. He hated to think what Quint would say about his leaving the bridge unmanned with the boat under way.

Dawson was nearly finished when he glanced to port in time to see a large wave breaking beside the boat. He clutched at the gunnel, his wet hands slipping on the slick fiberglass as he felt the boat heel sharply and his feet rise off the deck as the boat plunged down the wave. For an instant, he remained suspended in air, still grasping for something to cling to before toppling over the stern and plunging into the wake.

His head burst from the water, and he yelled at Quint knowing his voice would never carry over the sound of the engines. Help-lessly, he watched as the boat rapidly grew smaller continuing to the northwest on autopilot.

"Damn it all!" he cursed his own stupidity. "Why didn't I stop or wake Quint to take over? I'm screwed now," he said to himself as he tread water fully aware that the odds of seeing another boat out here were slim. Chances were, his rescuers would be recovering a body.

Quint loved to nap while they cruised offshore. When he finally awoke, he stretched and checked his watch. Grabbing a soft drink from the step box cooler, he meandered up to the bridge to relieve Dawson, only to find the helm deserted.

He probably ran down to check on the engines or to get some-thing from his stateroom, Quint thought. Even so, he was somewhat surprised that Dawson would venture from the bridge, leaving the unmanned boat on autopilot—he knew better. Quint eased the throt-tles back to keep from pounding in the building seas.

After a few minutes, it became clear that something was wrong. Quint pulled the throttles back to idle before heading below. A quick search of the staterooms and engine room confirmed his suspicion— Dawson was not on board.

"Shit," Quint yelled, as he scrambled back to the bridge. He had no idea how long it had been since Dawson had fallen over but he must be miles back. Reversing course, Quint steered the boat back along their previous track, following the dotted line on the chart plotter while scanning the seas in front of him. Ignoring the pounding of the hull, he pushed the throttles all the way forward.

The logbook, Quint thought out loud as he snatched it off the small chart table. Noting the last location Dawson had recorded in the book an hour earlier, he set the autopilot to navigate to that waypoint. *He has to be somewhere between here and that last log entry.*

Even though he knew they were likely out of range, he picked up the VHF radio mic to hail the Coast Guard. "Mayday, mayday, mayday, this is the motor vessel *Mojito*. We have a man overboard." He gave his position and repeated the message twice more, but got no response. This far off the normal shipping lanes and over fifty miles off shore, he was not surprised. He wished now he had installed a single side band radio for greater range like the one on his old boat.

Tossing the mic aside, Quint left the bridge and climbed to the tuna tower, taking great care in the building seas. If he were to fall, it would be a death sentence for both of them. Quint clung tightly to the metal tower leg while constantly scanning the sea surface. From this higher position, he could see farther and would have a better chance of spotting Dawson in the frothing seas.

At the top of the tower, the effect of the seas, now building to 4-6 feet right on his beam, was magnified, and he struggled to hold on. Under way for nearly half an hour, he spotted something that looked like a man's head. He felt a burst of adrenalin as he punched off the autopilot and swung the boat toward the object. But the excitement was short lived as he closed the distance, and the "head" sprouted wings and flew away. "Damn, seagull."

Coming back on course, Quint re-engaged the autopilot and began searching once again. Slowly scanning the endless seas, he strained his eyes, praying to catch a glimpse of his buddy, but the minutes ticked by until an hour had elapsed with no sign. *Must have missed him.*

After getting a few mouthfuls of water as he struggled against the heavy seas, Dawson finally fell into a rhythm in which he would raise his head for a quick breath each time the crest of a wave passed. Having had lifesaving training, Dawson knew about drown-proofing techniques for remaining afloat with the absolute minimum effort. He had no idea how long it might be before he would be rescued, if at all.

Fighting an initial wave of panic, he quickly realized he was over fifty miles off shore—there would be no swimming to safety. Despite his strong survival instinct, after examining his options he realized he had only one, and finally accepted the likelihood of dying. A strange sense of peace came over him as he lay face down in the water, occasionally lifting his head to snatch a breath.

Dawson realized that once the sun sank below the horizon, the threat of sharks would become more serious. His only chance was that Quint was searching for him by now and would somehow spot him before sunset. If not, he was finished.

Onboard *Mojito,* Quint felt nauseated as he disengaged the autopilot to run downwind a few hundred yards before reversing course and heading back in their original direction. He planned to make a second pass downwind keeping a hundred yards or so off their original track. He resolved to continue back and forth until sunset after which... well, he really did not want to think about that.

Quint's arms ached from his death grip on the tower leg, and his eyes were blurring from staring at the ocean for over an hour and a half. The salt stung his eyes, and he wished he had goggles, not so much to relieve the pain but to see clearly. He was reaching the point of despair when motion downwind to starboard caught his eye. Whatever it was had disappeared behind a wave, but he pointed at the spot with his right arm to avoid losing his bearing.

Quint knew that if Dawson was nearby, he would hear the throaty growl of the big diesels engines and respond by signaling. Quint stared without blinking, determined not to miss this chance. As *Mojito* rose on the next wave, he thought he spotted an arm waving. With his eyes riveted to the position, Quint punched off the autopilot and spun the wheel to bring the boat around. He had idled for about two hundred feet when he caught another glimpse of an arm atop a wave—he had found Dawson!

Quint maneuvered the boat downwind and put the engines in

neutral before dashing down to the cockpit to open the transom
door. Afraid to take his eyes off his buddy to go find a throwable
cushion, Quint watched helplessly as Dawson swam the last fifty feet
toward the stern. Dawson grabbed the line Quint tossed and held on
as he was pulled to the back of the boat and jerked inside.

"Next time you decide to take a swim, I suggest that you either
wake me or at least take the boat out of gear, dumbass." Dawson
nodded, too tired to comment.

The rest of their trip proved uneventful, and they arrived in the
Pass just as the sun was setting below the horizon. Quint eased between the harbor walls and took a lay-along slip at the end of the farthest dock, as prearranged with the dockmaster.

As the rest of the team arrived in Mississippi, they busied
themselves with the various odds and ends necessary to prepare
the ship. The installation of the radiation detection electronics on
Searcher progressed quickly. All that remained was to finish
loading provisions, install a new side scan sonar, repair one head,
and fix a steering problem that had surfaced on the trip over from
the Bahamas.

The former oilfield supply vessel, purchased from their friend
Tex, who was happy to unload it, was not a thing of beauty. Sturdy,
affordable, and reliable, its high, bright blue bow wrapped around a
spacious bridge and painted white superstructure before falling to
the enormous flat deck below. Chosen largely for this reason, the
deck spanned nearly two thirds of the ship's length. This facilitated
the addition of six functional doghouses—portable modules that
could easily be lashed in place, thereby simplifying rigging and out-
fitting the ship.

Toward the forward end of the huge deck, two doghouses were
stacked atop one another. The lower one housed a lab and electronics workshop while the upper module contained an additional crew
bunk area. Behind these sat another stack with the lower one filled
with a vast array of sophisticated electronics dedicated to search operations. This module was where the radiation detection electronics
were now being installed.

The last two modules held the dive locker with an empty doghouse above which, hopefully, would later be filled with treasure and

artifacts. It contained rows of bins for sorting items and large plastic tubs for soaking artifacts. Workbenches at either end held secure storage for an array of chemicals to be used in cleaning and preserving treasure and artifacts. The upper module also had a hidden storage area, now empty but which earlier held Dawson's considerable array of firepower.

Since they did not anticipate needing such firepower on this project, it had been decided to leave all of their weapons securely stored in the Bahamas to avoid a run-in with U.S. Customs. One of Dawson's jobs was to re-arm the ship, and he was waiting on Rogers to provide the replacements he had requested.

Kira was running end-to-end system checks on the search electronics and needed a hand. She found Mimi doing busy work, labeling and organizing operations manuals and documentation. All day, Mimi had been curt with Kira. Nothing she could make an issue over, but enough to make it clear there was a problem—and it was getting to Kira.

"Mimi, could you give me a hand?" Kira asked.

"I'm busy," Mimi replied, not bothering to look up.

Shocked by the rude response from someone who was always polite and helpful, Kira felt her anger rise. "Look Mimi, I'm your boss. I need a hand on something important, and that stuff can wait."

"Okay, *Boss*," Mimi replied, slamming down the stack of manuals in her hand and heading for the doorway where Kira stood.

"Mimi, I've had enough of this bullshit. Something is obviously bothering you, so out with it."

"It's nothing," Mimi replied defiantly.

Kira fixed her with an unblinking stare. After a minute Mimi continued. "Okay, I'll tell you what the problem is; you're a two-faced bitch."

"Might I remind you that you work for me?"

"You certainly don't need to do that, I'm *very* aware. If you want to fire me, be my guest," Mimi said, angrily folding her arms, wincing when they touched her chest, still tender from the gunshot wound she sustained in Venezuela.

This was not at all like Mimi. Kira took a deep breath, determined to keep the situation from spiraling out of control. "Okay, why do you think I'm a two-faced bitch?"

"You know."

"Mimi, if I knew I wouldn't waste time asking. Now, tell me before I lose my patience!"

"When I confided in you that I was going to visit Everett's family, I made it quite clear that I wouldn't be gone long. You said it wouldn't be a big deal. You said you'd cover for me. But then you told Quint that I'd be gone quite a while and might not be coming back, so you're looking to replace me."

"Damn it, the new hire I'm looking for isn't to replace you!"

Surprised, Mimi replied, "Then... then who are they replacing?"

Kira looked away for a moment before raising her face, eyes filled with tears. "They're to replace me!"

"You? I don't understand."

"I'm dying." Mimi's mouth dropped open in surprise before she could catch herself. "I mean, I've been really sick—just like my mother and grandmother. Both died of cancer."

"What type of cancer is it?"

Kira paused for a moment. "Well, I haven't actually been to the doctor but I'm going to make an appointment for as soon as they can see me." She went on to describe her lack of energy, nausea, and muscle aches.

"You don't think you're pregnant?"

"Hardly, my periods have been regular as always. In fact, I just finished one last week. The symptoms have persisted for some time just like my mother's. I don't want to die like her. I'm so scared," Kira sobbed. Mimi put her arms around her, sorry for her childish behavior.

"Mimi, I watched my mother fade away until nothing was left. I can't go that way; I won't go that way."

"Look, you don't know that you have cancer and won't know until you see the doctor."

"I know. I... well... kept hoping all of this would just go away. I'll call and set up an appointment. Should I tell Colin?" Kira asked. She and Colin had not spoken in several days, their most recent spat brought about mostly by her gnawing worry over her health problems. They would have to make up first, and she was not sure if she was up to the challenge.

"I would," Mimi replied.

"Isn't that your fancy sportfish down at the harbor? Why don't you use it?" Doug asked in reply to Quint's proposal to lease his boat for a few days.

Quint had just learned that one of the two boats they had agreed to charter was down with engine problems. "Aside from the fact that it sucks fuel like a pig and is not well suited for a work boat?" Quint answered.

Doug scratched his chin, "I don't normally let anyone take *Reel Eazy*. I'm funny that way."

"I understand. I feel the same way about my own boat."

"Yeah, but we've been handling boats for years. We've already chartered *Blaize,* and we need the two boats only for a few days. I promise you'll get her back without a scratch," Dawson added.

Though Quint worried about Dawson's sweeping statement jinxing them, he peeled off ten bills from a roll of hundreds. This seemed to ease Doug's concern somewhat, but he still appeared hesitant until Quint peeled off five more.

"She's full of fuel. Take good care of her and bring her back full when you're finished," Doug instructed, snatching the money from Quint's hand. "Call if you have any questions," he added over his shoulder as he headed down the dock.

Dawson smiled, "It appears the color green is very persuasive."

"Think so? I thought it was my honest face."

CHAPTER 13

"See, I got it here in one piece just as promised," Leo said, tossing the keys to Quint's prized vintage Plymouth Road Runner he had driven up from the Keys. "What's the big fuss about an old car?" Leo asked.

"I'll tell you what the fuss is. This is the fourth hemi manual four speed ever built in 1969. Look it up, and you'll find that only three are known to exist. This is the missing fourth, and it's worth a bundle."

"Then what the hell you doing driving it?"

"I figure it ain't worth much sitting in a garage," Quint replied while performing a detailed inspection. "Now Dawson and I can visit our old haunts in style while the team finishes up," Quint said, as he cranked up the big block. He felt a little foolish when he accidentally spun tires in his excitement at being behind the wheel again.

"It's good to be back home," he said to Dawson, as he swung the powerful muscle car onto the beach road. The hard south wind had blown the powder-like sand off the beaches, nearly burying the road. Though cleanup crews were hard at work clearing dump trucks loads of sand, Quint was forced to drive slow.

"I agree. We've been to the far corners of the earth, but the Mississippi Gulf Coast is a special place. In less than an hour, we can be fishing the Louisiana marshes. In a couple of hours, we can reach the offshore oil rigs to catch snapper and grouper or bluewater fish for billfish, tuna, wahoo, or dolphin. Doesn't get much better than this."

Being home brought back memories—some good, others not—like Quint's divorce from Becky. Already feeling sentimental, he was vulnerable when they ran into her at The Half Shell Oyster House. Dawson was busy trying to catch the bartender's eye to order a beer when Becky approached. Quint's first inkling of the pending encounter came when he heard a woman's soft voice behind him.

"Hello Quint; it's been a while."

A long pause ensued as Quint recovered from the shock of the unexpected encounter. "Uh... hey... Becky."

"Hello, Dawson," Becky said, with far less enthusiasm. Quint knew the two had never really cared for each other, but when Dawson learned she was cheating on Quint, he made it clear his indifference had turned to loathing.

Dawson cancelled his beer and in a low voice said, "I need to go sort my socks so I'll leave you two *lovebirds*. Maybe I'll give Evie a call." Quint shot back daggers as Dawson left to call a taxi.

"Heard you were back on the coast; news travels fast here. How you doing?" Becky asked, easing onto the bar stool beside him.

"Uh... I guess okay. And you?" Quint said, struggling to collect his thoughts.

"Been getting by. Got a make over. Like my new blonde hair?"

"It looks great. Never imagined you as a blonde. Becky, I'm sorry about leaving you with the message on the answering machine. I guess I just didn't know how to—"

"Yeah, wasn't one of your classier moves. But we all make mistakes. I haven't heard a peep about you until you showed up back here. How you paying the bills these days?"

"Well, I was running a charter boat until it sank," Quint replied. "How about you?"

"Casino, marketing department."

"You know, many times I thought about running into you and imagined a range of scenarios. Us having a pleasant conversation wasn't one of them."

"Quint, what happened with us?"

He took a deep breath. "Well, as you know things weren't going well between us. But what tore it was when I hacked into your e-mail and found out about your affair," Quint replied, and was surprised when Becky laughed. "You find that funny?"

"I didn't have a 'real' affair. Before the divorce, I entered into a 'virtual affair' with Brad. Had you gone back further in my e-mail, you would have found us chatting about handling our frustrations that way. I know it wasn't right; it definitely wasn't a great idea. But nothing ever really happened."

Quint sat silent. "Gosh, I'm sorry, Becky. I mean, we had other problems but—"

"What's done is done," Becky said, glancing at her watch. "Wow, it's late. I was due at a party a half hour ago. It was good seeing you. Maybe we can..." Becky paused and looked off for a moment. "Look, if you aren't busy, join me. Just because we're not married any longer doesn't mean we can't be friends. I'll introduce you to some of my new friends, and you might see some of our old ones there too."

Torn between his loyalty to Evie and the past he had shared with Becky, Quint debated the seemingly innocent offer. Though his gut screamed *bad idea*, he heard himself reply, "Sure. Why not?"

"You drive. After the party, you can drop me off at home, and I'll worry about getting my car tomorrow." Quint nodded, worried about what else she might have in mind.

"Remember Mrs. Evers?" Becky asked as Quint drove.

Quint thought for a moment. "Oh yeah, that old woman who lived next door to your mom."

"Good memory. I hear she still talks about how you used to cut her grass after her husband, Henry, passed on. She's not doing well; I think she's got Alzheimer's. If you can find the time while you're back, you ought to pay her a visit. I know it'd mean a lot to the family."

"She was a kind woman, and I thought a lot of her. Shame about the Alzheimer's. I'll make it a point to go and see her."

When they arrived, the party was well under way with music blaring and people spilled out onto the front lawn of the large beach-front home. Quint spotted a half dozen old friends before making it to the bar inside. Becky insisted that they dance, to fast songs at first, then slow ones later in the night. As the alcohol flowed, Quint found it difficult to focus on why they were no longer a couple.

"So, finding that Spanish galleon must have been exciting."

"That it was. Nearly got us killed too," Quint replied, launching into one of his favorite stories about their adventure. Only later would he wonder how Becky knew about the *Almiranta* if she "hadn't heard a peep about him" since they parted ways.

By the time they left, it felt natural when Becky took his hand on the way to the car. He drove her home with her hand on his leg, reminiscing about the good times. Entering the driveway of their old house, he turned to her, "Becky, it was great to see you. And thanks for the invite—" his last words lost as she leaned over and placed her lips on his. The goodnight kiss quickly unleashed their old passion, and he found himself standing on the edge of a precipice, struggling to regain his balance.

Mustering his self-control, he broke the kiss, stepping from the car to walk her to the house. After unlocking the door, she invited him inside. Alarm bells clanged inside his head, warning him not to head back down the old road and risk screwing up things with Evie—again.

"Thanks for the evening. I'll call you," he said, turning quickly away before he could be further tempted.

The next morning, Dawson and Quint met for breakfast. "So, how'd it go last night, Romeo?"

"Went to a party and had a good time. Wish you'd stayed and gone with us."

Dawson shook his head, "I'm not going to be standing in deep shit alongside you when Evie finds out. Have you forgotten why you divorced Becky?"

"No, but maybe I was too quick to judge her on the Brad thing," Quint said, trying to explain the "virtual affair," as Becky had called it. Dawson listened patiently before replying.

"Quint, that's virtual bullshit. I ran into some of our old buddies last night too. She had been doing the deed with Brad for a long time before your divorce, and there was nothing 'virtual' about it. Once again she's lying, and worse, you're falling for it. I can't believe you'd blow your second chance with Evie to get jerked around again by that unfaithful bitch. Furthermore, she's been asking everyone she sees about how you're doing. Quint, you did yourself a favor leaving that gold-digging whore."

They rode in silence to the restaurant where Quint found he lacked an appetite. After finishing his second cup of coffee, he looked at Dawson. "As much as it pains me, I admit you're right. I'm an idiot to even consider risking things with Evie again. I got thinking about last night. Becky told me she hadn't heard a word about me, but later asked about the *Almiranta*. I'm just glad I cut things off before they went any further."

While Dawson worked on his omelet, Quint stepped outside to call Evie. He tried three times before finally giving up, and was about to step inside when his phone rang—it was her.

"Hey, Babe. Things okay back in paradise?"

"Yeah, sorry, I had my ringer turned off. I miss you," Evie replied. Quint breathed a sigh of relief to hear her voice and confirm that things were still okay between them. "What exactly are you doing there? When will you come back home?" Quint had managed to avoid telling Evie about their real mission. While he hated to deceive her, he had to tell her something and that something had to be the treasure wreck cover story.

"Remember the *Almiranta* we dove on last year? Well, we're working another wreck. Could be even bigger."

"Sounds exciting. I want to be there."

Quint desperately missed her and wished she could join him, but it was far too dangerous. "I'd love for you to be here too, but I'm too busy for us to spend much time together. Plus, I'm offshore most of the time. You wouldn't enjoy it. I'll be back as soon as we finish, and we'll go some place fun. Think about where you'd like to go."

"Okay," Evie replied, the disappointment evident in her voice. "Miss me?"

"What can I say? I'm hopelessly in lust, err, I mean love," he said with a chuckle. "Gotta go. I'll call again soon."

After Evie hung up the phone, she sat thinking for only a minute when her face lit up. With a grin, she opened her laptop.

CHAPTER 14

"He should have named her *Reel Lazy*," Dawson said to Quint, as he cranked up Doug's boat. Though she would serve their needs, *Reel Eazy* was the exact opposite of *Blaize*. Whereas the latter boat was meticulously maintained, *Reel Eazy* looked as if Doug couldn't be bothered with mundane tasks such as cleaning and polishing. She was not a pretty boat. Too short for her cabin and bridge and with a bow rail perched too high above the foredeck, she had a dull finish that contrasted with the highly polished *Blaize*.

Quint leaped onto *Searcher* as soon as they were tied up alongside and headed to the galley for a team meeting. The heavy smell of bacon hung in the air and made his stomach growl.

"The plan is for *Searcher* to conduct operations around the clock while the two charter boats return to the Pass in the evening, ferrying crew and supplies as needed," Quint began. "Any 'hits' that *Searcher* marks at night will be checked out the next day.

"As we earlier discussed, I'll retain overall project responsibility and will remain offshore for the first couple of days until the operation becomes routine. Kira will have first shift and will also oversee *Searcher's* operations as well as coordinate 'fleet' search activities. Colin, you'll run operations on *Blaize*." Kira caught his eye and smiled at him.

"That will leave Dawson to run our second leased charter boat, *Reel Eazy*. Leo, you'll run *Searcher's* second shift, and Tom will run third." Tom was another holdover from their previous expedition in search of the *Almiranta*.

"LaRue will head up dive operations," Quint said, noticing Dawson flinch. Quint knew LaRue had gained Dawson's trust while diving on the *Almiranta*. But while Dawson agreed that it made more sense for LaRue to handle the diving while he ran *Reel Eazy*, he hated to relinquish a job he so loved.

"Whenever we get a hit on the magnetometer, side scan sonar, or the radiation detection system, we'll deploy a numbered buoy to mark the spot. LaRue or one of the other dive team members will then check it out. Okay, that's about it. Let's get started," Quint concluded, as the team exited the room.

"I saw Kira smile at you during the meeting," Quint commented as he approached Colin in the passageway.

"Yeah, but we're still not speaking. I did see her chatting with Dawson yesterday, and they seemed flustered when I noticed," Colin said, seeming a little jealous.

Quint shook his head. "I wouldn't worry. Dawson couldn't handle her."

Colin smiled. "You're probably right. Instead of avoiding her, maybe I need to work at getting back in her good graces." Colin continued, "Something's bothering her. She's not herself." Unsure what to say, Quint just nodded as he left for *Searcher's* operations center and Colin headed for *Blaize*.

Following the procedures established during their search for the *Almiranta,* 30 minutes later, Kira's voice erupted over the ship's PA and the VHF radio. "Search operations commencing."

Over the next two days, the hits they encountered were junk ranging from washing machines to automobile bodies to sunken barges. Having learned from experience, the team took the false hits in stride.

At the end of the third day, Quint headed back to shore aboard *Reel Eazy* along with Dawson. They waved at the crew of a shrimp boat working the waters nearby. A flock of sea gulls hovered over the boat but oddly did not appear to be diving for scraps. Quint noticed a sleek racing-hulled boat alongside.

That's odd, he thought, noting the lone shrimp boat. *Why was this one working alone? I thought they usually worked an area together once the shrimp are located. And what in the world would a go-fast boat be doing pulled up alongside?* Since he saw no one in the boat, they didn't appear to be simply customers buying shrimp. And he doubted it belonged to the shrimper. *What shrimper could afford or, for that matter, want a go-fast boat?* he wondered.

His further thoughts were interrupted as they reached the dock, where a dark-skinned, raven-haired woman waited, tapping her foot while puffing impatiently on a cigarette. "You Quint?" she asked.

"Could be; why do you want to know?" Quint said, noting that the woman reeked of money, if not class. While her skin-tight black top with its plunging neckline accomplished her apparent goal of showcasing her massive chest, it also highlighted some less flattering bulges around her mid-section, only partially concealed by a wide belt.

"I'm looking for Dakota. I understand he's working for you," she said, her eyes hidden behind an enormous pair of designer sunglasses.

"And you are?"

"His previous employer. He captained my boat."

Uh oh, Quint thought. *It's the owner of Squatopee. This can't be good.* Quint's mind raced as he decided how to handle the situation. "He's doing offshore survey work for us looking for a wreck."

"When's he coming in?"

"Don't know. He stays out on the boat along with most of the crew."

"Well, tell him I'm here," she instructed, passing him a card with her phone number and the address where she was staying written on the back.

Though Quint was dreading it, he headed off to pay a visit to see Mrs. Evers. "Hello, my name is Quint," he said when a woman opened the door. "I used to know Mrs. Evers; she lived next to my ex-wife's mother. Since I was back in town, I thought I'd drop by to see her, if it's okay."

"Quint, yes, I've heard both her and her son, Gordon, mention your name. Please come in."

Quint followed Lucy, Mrs. Evers' caretaker, into the next room where an old woman lay propped up in bed. "Mrs. Evers, Quint is here to see you." The old woman turned her head slightly but showed no sign of recognition as Lucy left the room to give him privacy.

Unsure what to say to someone who obviously was not comprehending, Quint began babbling. Finally, when he could think of nothing else to say, he became quiet; the only sound was Lucy in the next room washing dishes. He took Mrs. Evers' hand in his own as he sat beside her. For a moment, he thought he saw a fleeting expression of recognition. It was sad to see the lady who had shown him such kindness reduced to this.

Having stayed long enough to avoid feeling too guilty, he made his excuses and left. A sadness hung over him for the rest of the day.

Billy was a simple man. He never wanted much; he never tried for much; and he never got much. But he was happy. It was his nature. All he ever wanted was to enjoy his life working just hard enough to afford the essentials and maybe a modest luxury or two, like a bottle of whiskey once in a while and a nice new shirt and pants on occasion. Since he spent most of his free time either out on the ocean or working on his boat, his life was about as uncomplicated as life could be.

After retiring from his job with a local banking products manufacturer, Billy took a part-time job running the local fuel dock, more out of boredom and his love of the water than the money. It was mid-morning when Billy looked up at the sound of a pelican diving into the water just outside the harbor and noticed a dark-complectioned man idling up to the dock in a rented fishing boat. Billy tossed him a line as the man cut the engine.

"Need fuel?" Billy asked.

"Yes sir. Give me 10 gallons," Omar said.

"Where you headed?"

"To explore the north side of Cat Island."

"I envy you. I'm stuck running this fuel dock. But at least I'm on the water."

"You a pleasure boater or fisherman?"

"Both, but fishing is my first love. I used to oyster, but my back played out years ago, and I had to get a real job with that ATM manufacturing company over in the industrial park. What you doing in town?"

"I'm from the University of Florida doing research in your town library for a class project about life in small towns during the late '50s. Mainly going through old newspapers."

"Sounds boring."

"That's why I'm taking a break to go exploring. The work's not too exciting, but occasionally, I run into something interesting. Like yesterday I was poring through old papers from 1958 when I stumbled on an article about a plane collision. It was fascinating, but the article really didn't develop the story. A shame."

Billy continued pumping fuel for a minute before replying. "That... that... was about me. I'm... uh... the one who saw the plane."

"Oh sure. You kid around all the time?"

"No, I'm serious." Billy launched off into a description of the events that evening, dulled only slightly by the passage of time.

"Wow," the man whistled, "that's some story! What a coincidence running into you after just reading that article. I guess that's the neat thing about small towns. Anyone ever come looking for it?"

"Not that they would admit to. Some government landlubbers claimed they were fishing and hung around for a few weeks. But I know it had to do with my sighting."

"You ever go back looking for it?"

"Sort of. A few days later I was oystering in the same area and pulled up the remains of the pilot. Scuba diving was in its infancy back then, but with the murky water, there wouldn't have been much chance of finding anything. I know right where it happened, maybe a couple hundred yards off the old Pass Marianne light. Tell you what, I made a little map at the time. I'll look for it tonight and bring it here tomorrow if you're interested."

"That would be quite a coup for my research. I've got a small budget, so I can pay you for it, or make a copy if you don't want to part with it."

"Stop by tomorrow. Anything else I can do for you?"

The man handed him cash for the fuel and replied, "No. Think I'll go cruising now," he added, idling away from the dock.

What a remarkable coincidence! Billy thought to himself. By late afternoon, he had only two more customers and decided to call it quits for the day. He made his way down the rickety docks, picking up a used oil container and a dirty rag lying beside it. He tossed the items in the trash barrel at the end of the dock and saw the owner of the concession stand wave, "Slow day for you too?" Billy asked.

"Was it ever. Hey, did that guy find you?"

"What guy?"

"Said he was a student, looked middle-eastern, asked where to find you, didn't say why. He knew you were at the harbor, though."

"Yeah, he found me," Billy said as he headed for his car. Their meeting was not chance after all. *Why would he come looking for me but pretend it was a coincidence? If he comes by tomorrow for the map, I'll ask him,* Billy thought, feeling more troubled than the simple incident warranted.

CHAPTER 15

"You remember that big, fancy yacht you used to work on? *Squa-topee*, wasn't it?" Quint asked Dakota as he stepped inside *Searcher's* bridge the next day. "I believe you were captaining her when you tired of starched uniforms and left to run our rusty work boat." Dakota nodded.

"Well, the owner's in town and wants to see you." Dakota's face turned white. "Wasn't she the one whose husband caught you servicing more than her boating needs?"

Dakota ignored the last question. "Well... you tell her... you tell her... nothing. And I'm sure not calling that crazy woman."

"Okay, but she struck me as the determined type. I doubt she'll leave until she sees you." Quint said, handing him her contact information.

"She's gonna have a long wait. Was her pissed-off husband with her?"

"Nope, and she didn't mention him. Maybe she's free now and wants to make you an honest man," Quint said, laughing at Dakota's rude response.

"Dammit all!" Kira yelled, tripping over a hatch coaming as she burst out on the port side of the ship, showering Quint with her load of small boxes and packages. Slamming down the remaining armload, she began plucking items off the deck and slinging them overboard as Quint looked on in amazement.

"What's going on?" Quint asked, concerned.

"What's going on? I'll tell you what's going on. I've had an ass-full of Leo and his weird-ass food. That's what's going on."

"Why do you care what Leo eats?"

"I don't. He can eat monkey brains, snail poop, or whatever else his deranged mind pleases. But when he tricks people who aren't out of their freakin' minds, I draw the line," she said while tossing the remaining items overboard.

"I thought you were wise to Leo's tricks."

"I was. But I didn't know Leo cooked breakfast."

Quint decided it was best to leave her alone. As he eased past her to duck into the hatch, Kira spoke up again. "Deal with Leo and put an end to this bullshit, because when I finish throwing his nasty shit overboard I intend to make a eunuch out of him."

Spotting Willy in the galley taking a huge bite out of a hamburger, Quint walked over and asked, "What set Kira off?"

"Leo cooked up a bunch of sesos—tacos made with cow brains. She's chowing down when she realizes it isn't sausage on her taco and goes ballistic."

"I better find Leo before she does. Any idea where he is?"

"Check his stateroom," Willy replied.

"If she finds Leo before I do, be the adult." Willy chuckled.

Quint found Leo sprawled on his bunk, reading. Boxes of his personal food filled nearly the entire stateroom.

"What can I do you for?"

"Nobody cares what you eat. If weird food is your thing, so be it."

Leo rolled his eyes. "Exotic food, I like exotic food."

"Well, one man's, or woman's in this case, weird food is another man's exotic treats. But this has to stop."

"You the food police telling us what we can and can't eat?"

"Maybe you didn't hear me. I plainly said, I don't care what you eat, but most of the crew doesn't share your taste—Kira in particular."

"Look Quint, I don't make anyone eat anything. I—"

"Don't bullshit me. We both know you love nothing more than for folks to try your epicurean delights—but it's not right when they don't know what they're eating. either keep your shit to yourself or put up a big sign labeling your strange food du jour. No more repeats of this."

"Yes, your royal führer," he replied sarcastically, as Quint turned to leave.

"Oh, by the way, Kira is busy throwing all your weird—excuse me: 'exotic'—food overboard." Leo reacted as if he had been hit with a cattle prod, leaping out of bed to run out the door.

Quint saw Dakota shaking his head as he headed for the bridge. "This weather report doesn't look good. Tropical Depression Ten was just about to peter out when a second tropical wave combined with it. They've renamed it Tropical Depression Twelve, which is unusual. Normally, it would retain its old name. Anyhow, it's a more advanced system, and I have a bad feeling about it; call it Indian intuition. We'll know more in a day or so."

"That reminds me; we haven't discussed what to do with the ship if a storm threatens. Let's have a look at the charts and discuss our options," Quint said. As they entered the bridge, he noticed an unfamiliar boat come alongside the ship.

"Most of the hurricane holes I'm familiar with won't handle a ship this size. We could head over to Mobile Bay and go up the Tombigbee until we find a safe place to tie up."

Dakota nodded, "Or go up the Mississippi River and do the same... " he stopped as a woman burst onto the bridge—it was the owner of *Squatopee*. She was not happy and targeted Quint first.

"Didn't you give him my message?" she asked, with eyes blazing.

"Yes, ma'am, as soon as I got back on board," Quint replied as Dakota gave him a "thanks-for-throwing-me-under-the-bus" look.

"Then why the hell didn't you call me?" she snapped, whipping her head back to face Dakota. Seizing the opportunity, Quint eased from the bridge to escape the crossfire.

"Baby, I was going to but... I... ," was the last Quint heard.

He noticed the boat that had pulled alongside was now headed back to shore. *This should be interesting,* Quint thought, wondering how this reunion would play out now that her ride had left.

After a heated argument, much of which was overheard by the crew, Dakota and the owner of the *Squatopee* retired to his stateroom while Guillermo, the ship's mate, ran *Searcher*. Except for a late-night foray to the galley, the two were not seen until the next evening at dinner when Dakota appeared with the woman in tow. They looked happy and relaxed after spending time in his stateroom "resolving their issues."

"Guys, meet Lolo, an Apache Indian. Her real name is Lolotea, which means 'gift from God.'" She smiled at the crew, who nodded back and focused on their meals, uncertain how to react to the bizarre situation. Needing little encouragement, Lolo grabbed a plate and made herself at home. By the end of the meal, she had made quite an impression, regaling the crew with a string of tales about the rich and famous friends she entertained aboard her yacht.

After dinner, Quint managed to get Dakota aside while Lolo entertained the crew.

"Dakota, she's got to go."

"Fine, you tell her."

"I'm not telling her."

"Well, neither am I. Look, what about Kira and Colin? Or how about Mimi and Everett when we were searching for the *Almiranta*? And Dawson and Margaux, what about them? You cut them slack; why not me? You're not discriminating against minorities, now are you?" Dakota asked, a twinkle in his eye. Unsure what else to say, Quint stormed off in frustration and ran right into Dawson.

"What do you think we should do?" Quint asked, after explaining the situation.

"I know he was joking about the discrimination thing, but he had a point about Kira, Mimi, and me as well. Give it time to work itself out."

It was a peaceful afternoon at the fuel docks. A powerful "go-fast" boat, still tied to the docks, shattered the quiet when the operator over-revved its engines in a seemingly meaningless expression of power.

Inside the tiny fuel shack, Billy didn't notice the sound. He was leaned back in his chair snoozing, his head against the wall and a half-eaten candy bar in his hand when a bullet pierced his forehead. He made only a slight grunt and slumped to one side when the second bullet tore through his chest and into his heart.

Omar stuck the pistol in the waistband of his shorts, covering it with his shirt tail, eyes darting around the room. On the side of the desk, beneath an empty soda can, lay the folded piece of yellowed paper he had come for.

Omar re-emerged a minute later, carrying the paper, and walked briskly down the dock as the noise of the "go-fast" boat terminated abruptly. The man in the go-fast boat leapt onto the dock and strode down the opposite side to join Omar in the parking lot where they left in a nondescript sedan. Omar anxiously studied the yellowed paper map. He was not the college student he had led Billy to believe.

Several hours later, a boater fueled his own boat after failing to raise Billy with his shouts. When he stepped impatiently into the fuel shack to demand service. "You going to take my money or...," his voice trailed off. Flies buzzed around the foil-wrapped remains of Billy's chocolate bar and clustered around the neat round bullet hole in the middle of his forehead. More flies were gathered on Billy's blood-soaked shirt decorated with bits of chocolate and on the splatters of bright red mixed with grey on the wall behind his lifeless body.

CHAPTER 16

The orange ball of the sun had just cleared the horizon when Quint and Dawson eased *Reel Eazy* out of Pass Christian harbor headed out to *Searcher*. Just outside the harbor wall lurked the same low, sleek, go-fast boat Quint had earlier spotted beside the shrimper. "Wonder what those boys are doing up at this hour? I don't see any bikini-clad girls around to impress," Quint said. Dawson shrugged in reply.

They were four miles offshore when the boat came roaring up behind them, the driver waving frantically. Thinking there must be an emergency, Dawson throttled back—only to have the men in the boat raise sinister-looking machine pistols and begin firing. In a cloud of fiberglass splinters, he and Quint dove to the front of the bridge, where they crouched behind the steering console while the three men continued to squeeze off rounds whenever they thought they had a shot.

"Quint, we have someone who wants to meet you. You and your friend Dylan need to come with us," a man yelled in a middle-eastern accent.

"I'm pretty sure I don't want to meet him," Quint yelled back.

"And it's Dawson, not Dylan," Dawson chimed in.

"Look, Dylan, we're supposed to bring you both with us for a friendly chat, after which I'm sure you'll be free to go."

"Right," Dawson said sarcastically.

"But we can settle for taking only one of you alive or, in a pinch, both of you dead."

"And you still expect us to believe you'll let us go—when you just admitted it's okay to bring us in dead? Where is your boss, on that shrimp boat you guys were visiting yesterday?"

"As if he would be out on that piece of shit," he replied as another burst of automatic weapons fire sent a stream of lead ripping through the side of the boat.

"You okay?" Quint whispered.

"Yeah. You think this is the same group who welcomed us on our last visit to the Coast?" Dawson asked.

"Good question; let's ask," Quint replied.

"And you think he'll just tell you?"

"Depends how you ask," Quint replied, and yelled, "Where's Akmed? Rashid decide to send in the second string?"

The shorter man squeezed off a burst from his weapon and smiled as he replied, "No, Akmed couldn't make it, but he told me to give you this," he said, holding his crotch.

"Shut up, you idiot," the large man in the back yelled, firing into *Reel Eazy's* cockpit.

"There's your answer. Same boss, different thugs." Quint whispered to Dawson, who nodded in reply.

"This is getting old, not to mention the boat is quickly becoming Swiss cheese. Eventually they're going to get bored and risk boarding us. We need to put an end to this shit."

"I agree."

"If we try to run, they'll simply follow and continue firing at us. Without weapons, it appears we're out of options. Any bright ideas?"

"No bright ones but I do have an idea," Quint replied, retrieving a life jacket from the starboard compartment and tossing it to Dawson. "When I yell, hold that up to create a diversion; then hang on."

Crouching low, Quint eased from the front of the bridge. He could see three men biding their time waiting for a clear shot. With their quarry cornered, they seemed to be in no hurry.

Without hesitation, Quint yelled, "Now!" Dawson raised the life jacket, and the gunfire response was immediate, shredding the orange vest. Bits of orange material flew as Quint jerked the starboard throttle forward. The big sportsfish immediately leapt ahead, arcing to the left. When he was out of the line of fire, Quint scampered around the console, swung the wheel hard to the left, and slammed the port engine throttle forward. The boat quickly accelerated in a tight turn, creating an enormous wake.

Reel Eazy's mountainous wake nearly capsized the gun men's boat, throwing them off their feet, and making it impossible to reach their helm. On his third lap, Quint swung wide and immediately doubled back, drawing a bead on the boat.

Using the brief respite, the men were attempting to stand as Quint bore down on the small craft. The men gaped in wide-eyed horror to suddenly find themselves the prey rather than the hunter. That moment's hesitation proved costly as the huge hull tore through the small boat with a piercing shriek.

The dark painted hull's bottom crashed through the side of the smaller boat, slicing one man in half. His scream ended abruptly as blood gushed onto the deck.

As *Real Eazy* continued forward, crushing the smaller boat's hull, the remaining two men tried to dive over the side. But one's head was struck and instantly split open by the huge spinning prop, while a blow to the other's back severed his spine. The impact flung Quint into the port helm seat, striking him hard in the chest as he fell to the deck.

Dawson reached over and pulled the throttles back. "Damn, you were right! It may not have been a bright idea, but it sure as hell was effective," Dawson said as the boat coasted to a halt. Seeing Quint lying in pain, he helped him up.

"I think I busted some ribs," Quint said with a grimace, holding his side. "Don't think we need to worry about survivors. Check the bilge to see if we're taking on water." All three men were floating face down, their boat sunk except for the forward section of the bow.

"Aye, aye Captain, "Dawson said, and headed down the ladder from the bridge. A minute later he reappeared. "The shaft seals are leaking, and two of the three bilge pumps are clogged or burned out. If we don't get back to shore quick, the *Reel Eazy* will become the *Reel Sunk*." Quint throttled up and headed to the marina.

"Judging from the vibration, I don't think the props fared too well either."

Dawson nodded, "They can fix the wheels when they haul the boat to deal with the fiberglass damage and fix the leaks. Boy, you're sure hard on a boat."

"Bitch, bitch, bitch," Quint muttered, shaking his head.

"You'll hear *real* bitching when Doug sees what you've done to his boat!"

"Hey, you're the one who promised he'd have her back without a scratch." When they reached shore, Quint reported the incident with the go-fast boat to Rogers. "They have to be connected to the terrorists."

"Any survivors we can question?" Rogers asked.

"Unfortunately not, but I did notice the same boat tied up alongside that shrimp boat we'd spotted lingering on the edge of

Searcher's radar range. Maybe they're working for Rashid and using the shrimper as cover to search for the bomb."

"I'll arrange to have Col. Botz check it out."

"By the way, this little episode brought up the need for us to be better armed. What about the weapons you were supposed to be getting us?"

"Hey, I'm working on it. But ever since that Fast and Furious debacle, this sort of thing gets a lot of scrutiny. Last I heard, we should have them in a few more days."

"I thought Quint was still hard-nosed about his no smoking aboard ship policy," Mimi said.

"Yeah, he sure reamed me out for it a while back," Kira replied, as they entered the mess hall and noticed the familiar odor of burning tobacco. On the far side of the ship, she saw Lolo belching clouds of smoke and shooting tequila from a nearly empty bottle while spinning yarns with the crew. Kira did an about face and headed for the bridge.

"Where's Quint?" she demanded, as she entered.

Dakota looked up from the chartplotter, "He's been on shore tending to his broken ribs, but I just saw *Blaize* pull alongside, so I imagine he's about to come aboard."

Sporting a large elastic bandage around his torso, partially visible through his open shirt, Quint gingerly boarded *Searcher* to find Kira waiting. "How nice, a welcoming committee," he said, as she launched off.

"Look, you busted my chops for smoking inside the ship while we were searching for the *Almiranta*. Now Lolo's doing it in the mess hall for cripe's sakes. I expect you'll be having one of your Dutch uncle talks with her."

Quint sighed. "I'll deal with her." He entered the galley wishing he could avoid the unpleasant task that lay before him. "Lolo, we need to talk." She followed Quint outside where he looked her in the eye. "You are here as our guest. Like everyone else on board, you must obey our rules, or I'm sending you back to shore. No smoking inside the ship and no drinking period."

"Aye, aye, Captain," Lolo replied, with a toothy grin.

"Dakota's the Captain, as you well know. I'm the boss. And I'm serious; don't let it happen again."

"Or else?"

"I'll make you walk the plank."

"Oooo, that sounds interesting," she laughed, but seeing Quint's face added, "I promise to mend my outlaw ways."

"Is that Botz headed out sporting flashing blue lights?" Quint asked Rogers, referring to the fast-moving orange inflatable Coast Guard boat off their port quarter.

"Yep. Because of our leak, I waited to contact you until the intercept team was under way. As you surmised, we think the shrimper is a cover for the terrorists to search for 'our package.' Can you help Botz comb their vessel for useful information?"

"Absolutely. We'll divert there right now," Quint said. "By the way, we call 'our package' Big Bertha." Quint hung up and quickly briefed Dawson while they swung *Reel Eazy* toward the shrimp boat.

"Guess who's heading up the intercept team? Your old buddy, Colonel Botz." Dawson grimaced and shook his head. Dawson had found Botz to be professional during their meeting in Venezuela, but a little too taken with himself at times. Their last meeting in Venezuela had not ended all that well. "Let's try to be civil, okay?" Dawson nodded, but Quint was unconvinced.

"Maybe I need to rethink my opinion of him," Dawson said, "but I doubt it."

By the time they arrived, Colonel Botz had secured the shrimp boat, and the entire crew stood handcuffed on the rear deck. Dawson maneuvered *Reel Eazy* alongside in the calm waters. "Didn't take you long to deal with these guys," Quint commented as he stepped aboard, hoping to start things off on the right foot.

"Nope. None of them seemed eager to meet Allah," Botz replied, seemingly bearing no real malice, though somewhat cool. "One look at our boys holding M-16s and that big-assed .50 caliber on the front deck, and they were fighting each other to surrender. That is—except for the chief there, who we caught trying to destroy this," he said, handing Quint a partially torn folder filled with papers.

"Sorry, it got sort of wrinkled in the scuffle. Rogers wants you to look around, so help yourself, though I doubt you'll find anything—

my boys have already gone over it. Try not to waste too much time," Botz said, clearly meaning his time, not theirs. "When you're done we're going to take these boys back for a little chat." Quint bit his tongue, vowing not to respond to his suggestion that Quint's search effort was pointless.

Quint thumbed through the file, which held a yellowed, hand-drawn map and a chart of the area—marked with search lanes the terrorists had been working. He folded both items and replaced them inside the tattered folder. The two men then spent a half-hour poking around the shrimp boat but found nothing further.

"By the way, Botz, any chance you could spare us a couple of those M-16s?"

"You kidding? They'd have my ass."

Back aboard *Reel Eazy*, Quint called Rogers. "You were right on target. We recovered some information, including a chart showing the area where they believed Big Bertha might be. Botz may have saved us a whole lot of looking in the wrong place," Quint said, trying to appear like a team player, and hung up.

"Thankfully, Omar and I were not aboard when the go-fast boat sunk and the shrimper was captured," Akmed said over the static-filled cell link. The men we hired know nothing that could cause us difficulty. It will be tough to charter another boat and resume our efforts after this episode. What do we do now?"

Rashid was not pleased by Akmed's being bested by Quint and Dawson yet again. But in fairness to him, it had been a stupid error on his men's part when Quint and Dawson escaped the last time, and just plain bad luck that the crew had been apprehended. For a moment he contemplated whether Akmed's usefulness might be in question but decided once again to spare him, at least for now.

"I agree; it would be foolish to go back out there now. As you say, it's fortunate that you weren't captured," Rashid said. "Hang back and let them do the hard work for us. Charter another boat and crew, not to search for the bomb, but to take it from them when they find it." He suggested a strategy for positioning a boat in one of three possible locations to avoid suspicion yet close enough to swoop in and steal the bomb. "Akmed, I don't have to tell you how important your success is this time. We, that is you, can't afford to screw up again."

"Yes, honored one."

Rashid's words were intended to sting, and he wanted Akmed to realize how he would deal with another failure. "Get some insurance by capturing one of the team leaders or a loved one. It might provide a useful bargaining chip should we need it."

Akmed spent the next week recruiting three teams and searching for other boats to charter, far away from prying local eyes. He planned to position boats in all three of Rashid's suggested locations to steal the bomb should Quint's team find it. When the time was right, he would launch all three in hopes that at least one would succeed.

Finding local people who were experienced was difficult without drawing attention. He was forced to settle for much less experienced men than he would have preferred, hoping that their fanatical dedication and clean backgrounds would compensate.

He assigned one team to watch Quint's team, study their habits, learn where they were staying, and identify potential kidnap victims. One of the principals—Quint or Dawson—would be best, but their women would rank a close second. He would lease another fast boat for them to use if the opportunity presented itself.

"Kira, why don't you go over the new search plan?" Quint said when the team was gathered in *Searcher's* mess hall.

Kira rose slowly, obviously not feeling well. "Based on the new information acquired from the shrimp boat terrorists, it seems prudent to shift our efforts to the northeast—near Pass Marianne, where the terrorists believed Big Bertha would most likely be found. It's in our original search area, but it would have been several days before we worked our way there. Worst case, if we don't find it, we can revert to our original plan," she said. Referring to a large chart posted on the wall, she identified the areas each of the teams would begin working the next day.

CHAPTER 17

"Pleased to meet you. You have quite a reputation. Nice suit," Rashid said, the sarcasm poorly concealed yet apparently undetected.

"Thank you. What can I do for you?" Berto asked, smoothing his freshly laundered white suit and straightening his gold chains.

Rashid glanced around the expansive living room filled with a throng of hulking bodyguards strutting about wearing dark suits with turtlenecks and sunglasses, though it was night. Enormous bulges beneath their jackets betrayed the serious pistol each packed.

"Could we dispense with some of the ears? I value privacy in my business dealings," Rashid said. Talib stood beside him unflinching, arms folded.

"Pauli, you and Lanny stay; the rest of you get dinner," Berto replied.

When the room had emptied of all but Talib and Berto with two remaining goons, Rashid continued. "I wish to purchase a piece of property you own."

"Oh, and which one might that be? I own a number."

"Your hunting lodge with some 1,500 acres."

"Ah, the jewel of my real estate holdings," Berto lied. He hated hunting and seldom went there, having acquired it from one of his loan shark "clients" who failed to control his gambling urges. "Its remoteness and the fact that the structures are not visible from the road and nearly invisible from the air offers... certain advantages."

"Precisely. That's what interests me about it. As I said, I value my privacy."

"I'm afraid I could never sell it. The family is far too fond of it," Berto replied though, his family had never seen it, refusing to set foot on the property.

"Come now, Berto, everything is for sale. Name your price."

"I'm a reasonable man. Make me an offer."

Rashid reached into his suit pocket. "Here's a check for 50 percent over the appraised value. Since you're a busy man, and I prefer not to waste time haggling, I thought we might quickly complete our transaction."

Berto eyes bulged as he struggled to maintain a poker face. "While I appreciate your forthrightness, I would need at least twice this amount to consider parting with my family's legacy."

Rashid made a subtle motion with his outstretched palm. Immediately, Talib leaped forward and drove the fingers of his left hand into the throat of Berto's closest man. He pirouetted while raising a long steel needle, concealed in his sleeve, and plunged it into the temple of the second man. Without pause, he whirled back around and thrust the needle into Berto's eyeball just below the pupil, where he held it in place. Berto screamed but remained frozen as Talib held his head firmly in one hand and the needle in the other.

Rashid moved a chair beside and in front of Berto and took a seat. He calmly crossed his legs and began picking at lint on his pants while preparing to speak.

"Now Berto, as we were saying, you must understand that my offer is more than generous, well over what you expected it might bring. Would you care to reconsider? Or do you need further persuasion?" It was clear Berto was ready to part with his prized retreat.

"Oh, and by the way, I would be quite disappointed if anyone else were to learn of our little transaction. So much so that Talib here would be forced to return. Understand?" Berto nodded. Ten minutes later, their business concluded, Rashid got into his Mercedes and drove away, bearing a signed contract for the lodge. It would be another hour before Berto's men discovered him and cut the plastic ties that secured him to his chair.

CHAPTER 18

Quint smelled LaRue's famous crawfish etouffee as he entered the galley and realized it was noon. He prepared a plate and had just sat down when Tom came looking for him. "I thought you had a talk with Lolo."

Quint looked up from his lunch. "I did, and she promised to obey the rules."

"Well, that psycho bitch straightened up Search Control."

"So?" Quint replied, looking baffled.

"She put away all of the charts, removed my sticky notes, and erased the whiteboard on which we had laid out our search lanes. It'll take the rest of the day to reconstruct everything."

Tom stormed out only to be replaced by Leo, who asked, "You doing some redecorating?"

"Huh?"

"Lolo's in the salon with piles of wallpaper samples and has a guy painting the women's toilet pink." Quint sighed. Once again he would have to deal with Lolo.

"Where is that nutjob, Lolo?" Quint asked, as he entered the salon.

Willy looked up from the book he was reading. "She and Dakota headed to his stateroom at the end of his shift. I'm guessing by now they're—."

"Never mind. I'll find her tomorrow," Quint replied, as he saw Colin enter.

"The main winch failed, and we're operating off our backup. I'm heading in early on *Blaize* to find a welding shop to make repairs. With *Reel Eazy* in the yard, if you want to catch a ride to shore, this is your last chance." Quint nodded and followed him down to the boat, secretly happy to have a legitimate excuse to escape.

Colin eased *Blaize* into the slip and killed the engines while Quint tied her up. "I'm going to check out the boiled shrimp at Lil' Rays after I'm done at the welding shop. Care to join me?"

"I appreciate it, but I feel like just holing up on *Mojito* and spending a quiet night eating the leftover etouffee I snuck off *Searcher*. I'll meet you back here tomorrow morning." Quint said, heading down the dock.

Deep in thought about their search operations and his "Lolo problem" as he stepped into the salon, Quint nearly fell backwards into the cockpit when he heard a woman's voice. "Hey, handsome. Care to get lucky?"

Dressed in a sheer black lace negligee, Evie stood in the galley beside a fruit and cheese tray accompanying an unopened bottle of wine. "Evie!" The familiar scent of her perfume filled the salon.

"Well, at least you haven't forgotten me."

"What are you doing here?"

"I'd think that would be obvious to a smart guy like you."

"But—"

"I heard everything you said when we talked about this; I just didn't agree. Since you're going to be gone for a while, I decided to come anyhow. As you know, I have a big backlog with my software development business but, since I can work wherever I choose—"

"You chose here."

"Very good. I figured even if you're gone a lot of the time, I'm no worse off, and at least we can be together whenever you're back on shore. I'll have plenty of time to get my work done and get to enjoy the change of scenery. So, glad to see me?"

"Of course I am. It's just that I—"

"You aren't happy to see me."

"Yes, I mean... that's not the point," Quint said, struggling with how to tell her she was in danger without divulging the true reason for his being here.

"Look, I'm here. End of discussion."

"Damn it! No it's not. Evie, it's not safe here. I really can't tell you everything. I'd like to, but I just can't. Trust me, there are people who don't want us here. It could get nasty."

"You're telling me that there are people opposed to your team looking for a treasure wreck?"

Quint paused, frustrated with her bull-headedness. "It's compli-cated. There are men who might go after the team's loved ones to gain information. Please believe me, I'm thrilled you're here, but I don't want you to get hurt."

Evie didn't buy the cover story, but chose to respect his privacy and the apparent sensitive nature of his work. Besides, she figured that eventually she would get everything out of him. "Okay, you win, I'll stay only a few days. You can give me a gun so I can protect myself. Now, to the matter at hand," Evie said, striking a pose. "The baked brie is divine; care to uncork the wine?" Quint accepted the partial win, hoping to get her on her way before anything happened, and retrieved his corkscrew to open the wine.

"Oh, by the way, I lined up Eddie to look after Lefty and get him to dialysis, so you needn't worry about that." Quint nodded.

"What about Fr—" Quint jumped as Fred came sliding up the stairs into the salon. "I see Eddie is not looking after Fred."

"I just couldn't leave Fred behind. He just got over being depressed from the owner change." Quint rolled his eyes. "Bringing him on the plane did prove to be somewhat more of a challenge than I had imagined, though."

"Well, if I find any iguana poop on my boat, I will hold you both responsible."

Quint had to admit his evening had turned out much better than he had imagined when he left *Searcher* the day before. As he entered the salon preparing to deal with Lolo, he noticed that Leo was barefoot. While this was not particularly notable since he seldom wore shoes, a holdover habit from being raised in the Florida Keys, Quint noticed that neither Willy nor LaRue were wearing shoes which *was* unusual.

"Did someone fail to inform me of a new dress code?"

"Evidently," Leo said, looking up. "Lolo is insisting everyone take off their shoes in the salon. You best do the same or she'll be on your butt next."

"I doubt that," Quint said indignantly, storming from the salon to find Lolo and have the talk he had avoided the previous day.

"Lolo, do you not recall our little talk?" Quint asked when he found her lounging in the salon reading a magazine.

"Why, of course. Have I broken any rules?"

"You cleaned up the Search Operations before unilaterally deciding to redecorate the ship."

"You have a rule against that?"

"No, but it caused problems."

"I got with Tom and showed him where I had placed all his precious notes and gave him a copy of the photo I had taken of the white board, so he has all the information. As to the charge of criminal decorating, you have a rule against colors in the ladies' head other than puke green and baby poop tan?"

"No, but I do with everyone having to disrobe to enter the salon."

"Please! Willy was tearing down the hydraulics on one of the winches, and the crew was tracking grime all over the salon. I simply... suggested... that they remove their shoes when entering the salon until he finished."

"Look Lolo, this is not your private yacht. This is my ship. If you want to do anything other than play with Dakota, ask me first." Dakota's voice booming from the PA interrupted his further tirade.

"Quint, you've got a call on the bridge." Quint shook his finger at Lolo and headed for the bridge to take the call. It was Rogers.

"By the way," Rogers said after Quint briefed him on their progress, "we've confirmed the guys Botz captured were working with Rashid."

"So?" Quint replied, already convinced of that fact.

"I understand you had Evie join you."

"No, I didn't. She came without an invitation, against my explicit instructions to the contrary."

"Well, these guys indicated that they're not only big on jihad against their enemies, but their families as well. Having Evie there puts her at risk and is a distraction for you."

"I realize that and tried to discourage her. She's already agreed to leave in a couple of days."

"Be careful. These guys are fanatics."

Great, Quint muttered to himself as he hung up the phone.

During the day Quint oversaw operations and at night would catch a ride back with the boat delivering the evening shift crew to spend some time with Evie. While Quint was busy offshore, she would work on her software development projects, stopping when he returned to cook dinner with him in the evening or go out for a bite. While the two spent time alone on *Mojito,* the feelings they had for each other blossomed. Quint thought he was in love before, but he *knew* he was now.

The couple was returning to their car after dinner at Back Bay when they spotted Willy. Quint was about to wave and yell when he saw a small man motion for Willy to join him in the alleyway. Quint caught a glimpse of the two men exchanging money and a small package in the shadows—Willy was up to something.

Quint eased out of bed and left Evie sleeping. By the time he slipped into his threadbare gym shorts and well-worn sneakers, the first orange arc of the sun was edging over the horizon. The naturally cola-colored waters appeared a vivid blue as he stepped off *Mojito* to begin his morning walk in lieu of a run, in deference to his mending ribs.

He walked up the gentle rise from the harbor to Scenic Drive and headed east. On the south side of the harbor sat the yacht club. Rebuilt several times after hurricanes, most recently Hurricane Camille, it was the descendant of the first yacht club in the South and the second in the entire country. On the north side of Scenic was the old theater built in the 1930s, now turned into offices. The people of Pass Christian slept peacefully in their beds, blissfully unaware that a few miles away lay a nuclear bomb that could end their pleasant existence.

Evie was still sleeping when Quint returned to the boat, and he noticed a note she had left him. She asked him not to wake her, as she had stayed up working long after he had gone to sleep the night before. In return she promised to make her famous shrimp pasta for dinner. After a quick shower, he grabbed a cup of coffee and left to take care of business and order supplies. Meanwhile, Dawson was preparing to handle the unpleasant task of meeting with Doug to discuss repairing *Reel Eazy.*

CHAPTER 19

"What the hell happened to, 'You'll get her back without a scratch?'" Doug yelled. He had just laid eyes on his damaged boat for the first time since it arrived at the yard for repairs. Because of his earlier bold statement, Quint insisted that Dawson be the one to handle the dreaded task of dealing with Doug about *Reel Eazy*.

"Look Doug, I'm really sorry, but in our defense, those guys were trying to kill us. I've instructed the yard to fix her as good as new—regardless of the cost. You'll be getting new electronics and a brand new paint job once we finish our project."

"Finish your project?"

This is the part Dawson was *really* dreading. "Yeah, they're fixing her running gear and the essential mechanical stuff so we can get back to work. Then we'll return her to have the fiberglass and paint job completed."

"What? I didn't agree to that! Find another boat to trash. Mine stays in the yard until the repairs are complete." This was going even worse than Dawson feared. They needed the boat, and he had to somehow convince Doug to let them finish.

"Our search gear is already installed, and as much as I hate to admit this, no one else is interested in renting us a boat after our little incident."

"No surprise there." Dawson started to point out that the boat was in poor shape to start with. But instead, he withdrew a wad of $100 bills from his pocket, using Quint's technique again.

"Tell you what, I'll pay you for next month and two month's loss of use. We'll be finished, and they should have her repairs completed by then," Dawson said, counting out five thousand dollars.

Doug became noticeably more calm after Dawson thrust the money into his hand. His disposition changed immediately, and he launched off telling tales of Pass Christian's local history. Dawson perked up when Doug related a story reported in the local paper about a man named Billy who had witnessed a plane crash in the '50s.

Before Dawson could question Doug further, the boatyard owner strode up and immediately began speaking, without bothering to wait for Doug to take a breather. "We've got everything you wanted done, and we're ready to put her back in the water as soon as we mount the propellers, but there's a problem."

"What now?" Dawson asked.

"The threads on this damned propeller lock nut are buggered up, and we can't get it started. I tried to order a replacement but, as you might imagine, they don't stock this size, and it will take two to four weeks to make one. I figured you wouldn't want to wait, so we gave it one last try this morning. Sorry, it didn't work."

"Isn't there anyone locally who could make one?" Dawson asked.

"Nope, it takes specialized tooling, and nobody around here can do it—well, nobody except for Crazy George. But I don't use him."

"Why not?"

The man rolled his eyes, shook his head and said, "Crazy George. Does that name tell you anything? He's a pain in the ass, and last time I had dealings with him I swore never again."

Dawson thought for a moment. "Suppose you tell me what we need, and I deal with him?"

He shrugged and handed him the prop nut. "You can find George on the *Tiburon* at the end of Pier 3 down at the harbor," the man said, and headed for the far side of the yard.

When they were alone again, Doug spoke up. "Okay, this'll square things between us, but I'll expect her to be repaired to my satisfaction," he said, sliding the cash into his pants pocket.

"You have my word," Dawson replied solemnly. "By the way, that Billy you mentioned. Where can I find him?"

"Ask George. They're big friends; he should know."

Dawson nodded and headed to the harbor to find *Tiburon*—a beat up older trawler. The salon door stood open, and the sound of loud cursing emanated from below. Knocking on the side of the cabin, Dawson yelled, "Hello?"

In response, a badly weathered and grizzled man appeared. Though it was hard to say for sure, Dawson put his age at somewhere between 68 and 108. His disheveled gray hair blew in the breeze as the sweat streamed down his neck and back. "It ain't like we don't have a sign plainly saying *No white mice in toilet*. But those women just can't resist throwing their damned tampons in the head. Then who gets to do surgery on the plumbing system? Why me, of course. Pisses me off."

As soon as the old man paused, Dawson seized the break. "Are you George?"

"No," he replied, slowly wiping his hands on a dirty rag. Turning to face Dawson, his eyes tightly squinted, he continued, "I'm *Crazy* George."

"Sorry. By the way, what does *Tiburon* mean?"

"It's Spanish for shark. You here for a Spanish lesson?"

"No sir," Dawson replied, handing him the old propeller lock nut and explaining what he needed.

"Yep, I can do it. Cost you 80 bucks and a six pack—any brand. But can't have it 'till tomorrow. If that ain't good enough, find somebody else."

"That'll do fine. I'll check back with you tomorrow. You know where I can find Billy?

"Go see Rudy at the Tarpon Beacon," the old man shouted, disappearing into the salon as Dawson headed down the dock to find the local newspaper office to learn more about Billy.

"Yeah, I know Billy. I'm the very one who took the picture in that article about him," Rudy said with pride. "The Chief wouldn't let me photograph that pilot's remains. Could've sold those photos to the tabloids for a bundle, but Chief Buck, Mr. High N. Mighty, wouldn't let me get my shots. I think that's censorship of the press," Rudy said. "What you want to know?"

"I was hoping you could tell me where I might find Billy to ask him a few questions."

"I'm afraid that's not going to happen."

"Why not?" Dawson challenged.

"He's dead," Rudy replied. "Murdered two days ago." He eagerly shared everything he knew about Billy's being found dead at the fuel dock. "But if there's anything else I can do for you, let me know," he said as Dawson turned to leave. "You know, you might talk to Jacques. He was great friends with Billy back in the old days when that dead pilot popped up. Jacques lives out on Cat Island but comes in pretty often. Check with Stella down at the harbor restaurant."

Dawson shook his head, beginning to feel like he was on a scavenger hunt. *Interesting coincidence, Billy's getting shot so recently,* Dawson thought. *And I don't believe in coincidences.*

CHAPTER 20

Finished with her day's work by late afternoon, Evie grabbed her grocery list and headed to pick up the ingredients for Quint's favorite dinner. She smiled at the other shoppers and hummed as she strolled amongst the aisles, loading her basket with fresh fruits and vegetables.

Daydreaming about drinking wine on *Mojito* with Quint as the sun slid over the horizon, Evie stood lost in thought until she noticed a woman openly staring at her and realized she had been examining the same tomato for quite a while. She placed it in her basket as she thought to herself, *Things are not as I imagined—they're far better.*

As Evie checked out, she spotted a man from the seafood market. *Hey, it's a small town,* she thought to herself to ease the nagging feeling that she was being followed. She headed for the car, anxious to return to the boat to start dinner. After unloading her groceries from the cart, she was about to slide behind the wheel when she spotted the same man—heading toward her at a run.

Quint paid the bill at the marine supply store and grabbed the bag with the items Dakota had requested for *Searcher*. With evening nearing, he was looking forward to Evie's famous shrimp pasta dinner when her ringtone on his cell phone interrupted his musing.

"I was just thinking about dinner, what kind of wine..." he stopped when he heard Evie's panicked voice.

"Quint, help! Somebody's after me."

"Who's after you?"

"I don't know. Quint, I'm so scared. At the store, I noticed this guy seemed to be following me. I wasn't too worried until he tried to get into the car. If I hadn't already locked the doors, he would have had me. As I drove off he pulled a gun. He may have shot at me."

"Didn't you have your gun?"

"Yes, but I couldn't think that fast."

"Did he follow you?"

"I don't think so. I kept looking but didn't see him."

"Where are you?"

"Back at *Mojito*," she replied.

"You're not safe there. Grab a suitcase and pack what you can. I'll be there in a few minutes. Be ready to leave," Quint said.

As Quint neared the harbor parking lot, he dialed Evie on his cell phone. She reached the end of the dock as he pulled up. By the time Quint stopped the car, she had opened the passenger door and thrown her suitcase into the back seat. As she closed the door, Quint spotted the lights of a black SUV pulling in behind him.

"Uh-oh, they've figured out where we're staying. Buckle up," Quint barked as he swung the wheel and shot through the parking lot with the SUV in hot pursuit, sending his cell phone skidding onto the floor. The bright orange paint job Quint had elected to keep on his restored 1969 Plymouth Road Runner was definitely not an asset now.

"Did you bring your gun?"

"No, I was so upset I forgot it in the rental car."

"Shit!"

"Quint, what's happening? Why are they after me?"

"Remember the part about 'it's dangerous, and things could get nasty?'"

"Look, this isn't the time for 'I told you so's.'"

"You're right."

"Let's just call the police."

"No, we can't do that. Rogers warned us that some terrorists aren't happy about us messing up their plans. I really can't tell you more than that." Quint tore through the side streets and made a hard turn back onto the beach road. "Now we'll get a chance to see what a 426 hemi engine can really do," Quint said, pressing the pedal to the floor.

"See if you can find my cell phone on the floor and dial Dawson," he said while fighting to keep the powerful car on the road. Evie punched the speed dial button for Dawson, got him on the phone and passed the cell to Quint.

"Dawson, we've got problems," Quint said, quickly filling him in. "I'm headed for the old Discovery Bay Marina to try to lose these guys. If I can't shake them, I'll find a place to hide until you arrive with the cavalry."

"I'll be there as soon as I can. How many are there?" Dawson asked.

"Don't know, but I'd guess at least two or three. And Dawson, come armed."

Quint thundered down the beach road, weaving in and out of traffic to gain a lead. He turned north onto Henderson hoping to gain enough of a lead to keep them from spotting his change in direction, but no such luck. Blasting down the narrow two-lane road, the car became airborne as he crossed a bridge over a small bayou. By the time he spotted the marina sign, the headlights of the pursuing car had faded well behind. It was spooky driving through the ill-fated subdivision. Dormant since the late '60s when Pat Boone, the project's spokesperson, tried to sell the public on building in the area, the place had its fate sealed by Hurricane Camille's flood waters.

"Get ready, the marina is just ahead. We don't have much of a lead, so we need to be quick," Quint said, jamming his phone back in his pocket. He wheeled the car around the next corner by forcing it into a slide, then accelerating to make a 90-degree turn, grunting from the force on his cracked ribs.

The road dead-ended into the parking lot of a small marina desperately in need of repair. "Move your buns, we've only a few minutes' lead," Quint yelled, throwing open the door and grabbing Evie's small suitcase from the rear seat.

"I'm moving, I'm moving. I'm just not sure where to." Seeing Quint retrieve her suitcase, Evie said, "I appreciate that, but right now my luggage isn't a priority."

"I agree," Quint said, dumping the contents onto the back seat.

"Quint!"

"We're going snorkeling."

"Huh?"

"You'll see," Quint replied, slamming the door. With the empty suitcase in one hand, he grabbed her with his other and sprinted toward the docks. At the end of the main dock, Quint turned onto a finger pier and squatted behind a large trawler. Opening his pocketknife, he used the saw blade to quickly cut through both aluminum tubes of the pop-up suitcase handle and hung the suitcase on a bolt beneath the dock.

Using the screwdriver blade on his knife, he removed one leg of the U-shaped assembly. "Ma'am, your snorkel," Quint said handing her the tube with the plastic handle still attached. "You get the deluxe 'J' model. I'll use the simpler straight version." Over her shoulder he saw the lights of their pursuers' car pull into the parking lot.

"Time to go swimming."

"Why can't we hide in one of these boats?"

"They'll expect that. Besides, there are only two candidates, and if they spotted us we'd be cornered. I like this plan a *whole* lot better," Quint replied, dropping down onto the trawler's swim platform. After ensuring that his cell phone was turned off, Quint reached over the transom and slid it beneath a coil of rope on the cockpit floor.

They slid into the water, and Quint pulled Evie beneath the platform where they could pop the ends of their homemade snorkels above the water's surface without being seen. He placed her hand on the middle bracket of the swim platform where it joined the hull so she could steady herself.

Quint peeked down the dock and saw two shadowy figures headed directly toward him, playing flashlight beams about the finger piers and boats. Soundlessly, the couple submerged, breathing through the tubes. For a moment Evie couldn't catch her breath and fought the instinct to rip the improvised snorkel from her mouth. But forcing herself to relax, she found she could get plenty of air.

"Anything over there?" the larger man queried.

"Nope. No sign in the trawler either. What you think?"

"They aren't in their car. I doubt they're in that marshgrass. They must have taken a boat. There's only one way out, so let's borrow that triple-engine go-fast boat over there and run their ass down. They can't be far."

While one of the men hotwired the ignition, the other undid the lines. A few minutes later, the engines roared to life, and the boat shot out of the marina at full throttle.

Quint had heard their exchange, and when the boat exited the marina, he pulled himself onto the platform of the violently rocking boat and helped Evie out. "Stay quiet; there may be more of them still here. We need to be gone before those two return."

Quint retrieved his cell phone and headed stealthily up the dock. With the serious blade on his pocketknife in position, Quint slid along the edge of the parking lot, hugging the shadows until he neared a dark SUV. He saw a man searching the buildings on the far side of the marina. Crouching with the knife in one hand and a large rock in the other, Quint duck-walked toward the car.

He paused for a moment beneath the side window, making certain the driver's head was turned away before crashing the rock through the window. The glass disintegrated as the rock maintained its momentum until stopped by the driver's head.

Though bleeding from cuts by the glass and stunned from the impact of the rock on his temple, the man raised a silenced .45 caliber pistol in his right hand. Without hesitating, Quint stabbed his knife into the man's throat as he brought his other fist down on the man's nose with a sickening crunching sound.

The man made a gurgling moan as Quint pushed his body sideways to keep him from slumping forward and sounding the horn. Quint grabbed the pistol, then cut the valve stems on both driver's-side tires for good measure.

Chapter
21

Quint joined Evie at their car as she climbed into the back seat with her suitcase, minus the long extension handle. "I know, I know, it's screwed up, but I can at least repack my stuff you tossed all over the back of the car like a wild man."

"I'm impressed you remembered it. You can repack while I get us going. I think I spotted a fourth guy, and he's bound to have heard the sound of the breaking car window." A minute later they were headed back out of the marina. Quint could hear the roar of the go-fast boat in the distance as the two men continued searching in vain. Water from the bayou dripped annoyingly from his hair down his neck.

"Here, wipe off your face," Evie said, handing Quint a blouse.

"Thanks," he said, noticing the designer logo on the front. "Expensive towel!"

"You saved my ass—you're worth it."

He wiped his face and handed the damp clothing back. He pushed the Plymouth hard into a turn, the tires squealing in protest as the car slid around the corner. Steering into the slide, Quint managed to keep all four wheels on the ground, while pinning Evie against the rear door.

"Richard Petty. I've got Richard Petty for a driver," Evie said, as the car straightened out, and she finally managed to sit back up.

"Hey, I'm not that old! Let's at least go with Kyle—Kyle Petty, that is."

"How long you think they'll keep searching for us before they give up?"

"Beats me, and I don't care once we make it out of here," Quint replied, as he steered the speeding car over the bumpy road, struggling to keep it aimed down the center. She winced as the spine-cracking force of a deep pothole sent her crashing back into the seat after smacking her head on the roof.

"Sorry, but we ain't out of the woods until we make the bridge," Quint said, motioning ahead. Approaching the next turn, he slowed and turned off the headlights. When he saw the upper structure of the bridge ahead he pulled into a small clearing far enough to be hidden from the road.

"What are we... "

"Ssshhhhh. Listen. You hear the boat?"

"No. Maybe they gave up."

"Either that or figured out we tricked them. Since this is the only other way out, they may be waiting for us. Take the wheel," Quint said. As he stepped from the car, he heard a vehicle drive slowly past them on the main road making an odd sound—he imagined it was a fourth man driving on flattened tires. "Damn!"

"What?"

"I forgot to take their keys. Too late now. I'm going to finish getting our butt out of a sling but, I hope to take along at least one of those guys to have a little chat with afterwards." Without questioning him further, Evie slid gracefully over the console into the driver's seat. Quint jammed into his waistband the pistol he had taken from the deceased SUV driver.

"Give me two minutes. Then turn on the lights and start the engine. Drive slowly toward the bridge, but don't stop until you reach the other side. If all goes well, I'll wave you back shortly. If I don't, you keep on going. Use my cell phone to call Dawson if he doesn't arrive in the next few minutes."

Quint crept down the road along the grassy shoulder, one hand on his complaining cracked ribs. The heavy rotten-egg smell of the marsh filled the air as he neared the bridge and edged toward the water, hugging the shadows of the pine trees and bushes. There beneath the bridge he saw two men jump off the bow of the go-fast boat resting on the muddy banks and saw them walk to the near end of the bridge. He then saw the orange glow of a cigarette and heard the sound of the two men talking low. There was no sign of the SUV he had heard passing by.

"So you think they tricked us, huh?"

"Maybe, but they haven't given us the slip yet. If they didn't take a boat, then the only other way out is across this bridge. So we should have them bottled up. I wonder why we can't reach Talib?"

"Probably the crappy cell coverage here. Either that or he's asleep in the car with the air conditioner running while we're mosquito bait."

"Ssshhhhh... you hear that?"

The crunch of gravel and the noise of an engine signaled the approach of the Road Runner as the headlights illuminated the end of the bridge.

"Here they come."

"What's the plan? We flag 'em down?"

"Hell no! I'm not getting my ass shot or run over. Once they get too close to miss, we start firing. Concentrate on wounding the driver. A dead hostage isn't worth much."

"What if it's not them?"

"Well then, that's tough shit for somebody, now isn't it? Shut up and shoot."

Quint crept close enough to have a clear line of fire before lying prone in the shadows. Holding the gun with both hands, he rested his arms on a log to steady his aim at the larger man.

As the two men prepared to fire at the approaching car, Quint slowly squeezed the trigger and... nothing. The gun had jammed. Quint leapt to his feet and jogged toward them. He saw the gun hand of the larger man raise, and without breaking stride, Quint dove forward, knocking the gun from the big man's hand. He continued forward to land on the second man, knocking the wind from both of them as they hit the ground hard, the gun sliding into the high grass.

Struggling to regain his senses, Quint reached for the gun just as the large man took a giant stride and landed a hard kick to Quint's ribs. The man reached down and jerked Quint to his feet like a rag doll, as the smaller man made it to back to his feet. Before Quint could land a punch, the smaller man struck him hard in the kidneys. When Quint doubled over, the large man punched him hard in the face, knocking him to the ground where he lay unmoving.

Evie stopped once she reached the far side of the bridge to wait as instructed. She looked back to see the men beating Quint. Before she could react, Talib emerged from the bushes and stood directly in front of the car, his gun aimed at her face.

While searching the far side of the marina, Talib had heard the sound of breaking glass. He returned to their vehicle a minute later to find the driver dead and Quint's car gone. Shoving the body over to the passenger's side, Talib drove slowly down the road on the flattened tires. Spotting the boat stopping below the bridge, he positioned himself as backup in case Quint escaped from his partners. It proved to be a good move.

"Please don't hurt me," Evie pled, the trembling in her voice betraying the effects of her fear-induced adrenaline rush. Without replying, Talib pulled her from the car and ordered her to open the trunk when she heard him grunt and saw blood pouring from his shoulder—Dawson had arrived.

When Talib raised his gun to return fire, Evie seized the chance to jump back in the car. She slammed it in reverse to head back across the bridge, ducking low in the seat. Talib jumped aside and fired, exploding the windshield and showering Evie's with glass. After emptying his gun at Dawson, Talib cursed and ran for the cover of nearby bushes.

Evie continued past the two men beating Quint and tried to draw their attention, while Dawson ran behind her over the bridge. The surprised men tried to locate their weapons while Dawson fired as he approached, hitting both men.

After confirming that Quint was alive, Dawson kicked the men's weapons farther into the marsh grass and kneeled to check the men for a pulse. Both were bleeding heavily from wounds in their arms and legs, but assuming they didn't lose too much blood, none of their injuries were life-threatening. He gave each a blow to the head with the butt of the .45 to stifle their further resistance.

Evie helped Quint struggle to his feet. Though dazed, he was not badly injured aside from his already broken ribs, which now sent pain shooting through his upper body. On the far side of the bridge, they heard the sound of a car engine starting followed by the sound of gravel crunching as it drove away.

"The one that tried to kidnap Evie just got away. I guess he had a car hidden in the bushes. I doubt we'll catch him, so we need to have a chat with the two goons we bagged," Dawson said while securing the wounded men's hands. Then declining Quint's offer of assistance, he dragged both of the semi-conscious men to the back of Quint's car, where he unceremoniously dumped them inside the trunk before slamming the lid closed.

Dawson then headed for the place the team was renting, with Evie following close behind and Quint fighting waves of pain from his ribs. Safely inside the garage, they quickly closed the doors, and Evie went to shower.

"Pop the trunk," Quint said to Dawson, who stood behind the car. "Dawson, we really need to get a handle on the situation, and that means getting these knuckleheads to talk. This is the third time we've been lucky enough to escape, and while they didn't get Evie this time, I don't want there to be a next time. If we just turn them over to the law, they'll lawyer up and be out in a couple of hours. Next thing, they'll be after us once again. I don't intend to let that happen."

"Look Quint, I know how you feel—believe me. When that idiot with the fuel truck killed my wife and daughter, all I could think about was getting even. But the difference here is that Evie's still alive. This is not about vengeance, at least not at this point. You can't objectively interrogate these guys. Let me do this."

"Like you're objective after your little torture session with the defibrillator?"

"Good point. I admit I'm a little perturbed over that, but I promise to be thorough."

"Dawson, I'm as objective as you are. I want to learn from these guys so we can avoid a repeat performance. We'll do it together. Now, pop the trunk."

"Okay," Dawson said. "You're in no shape to hoist these boys out of the trunk. So while I deal with them, could you gather a few things we'll be needing?" Quint nodded and listened as Dawson ticked off a list of items they would need.

When Quint went inside, Dawson turned to deal with the two bloodied men lying in the bottom of the trunk, who were alternating between complaining, whimpering, begging, and threatening. "If you don't shut the hell up, I'm going to finish what you guys started right now." The effect was immediate; both men went silent. He helped the men out one at a time, only half-heartedly trying to avoid causing them any unnecessary pain in the process.

"Here's the first aid kit," Quint said, setting the item on the table. Dawson performed first aid on the two men to stop their bleeding and stabilize them.

"Guys, Dawson got to have all the fun shooting you, but since he's a lousy shot, and my ribs are a tad sore, I've decided to give him another turn." Assuming he was serious, the two men looked worried. "Of course, we can dispense with all of the unpleasantness if you want to go ahead and fill us in on who you're working for and where we might find him."

"You're wasting your time. We'll tell you nothing," the smaller dark complexioned man said defiantly.

"Really?" Dawson replied jumping into the conversation. "We'll

see about that. Quint took your aborted kidnapping attempt personally, and I've got a score to settle after your buddy Akmed tried to fry
my heart. Since he's not here, you guys get to be his surrogates.

"I have a little present for you," he said as he screwed a gadget
onto the end of a garden hose while whistling as if he were without a
care in the world. "Wasn't it that Japanese guy in the *Bridge Over
the River Kwai* or was it Chairman Mao, who said, 'Be happy in your
work?' I'm not sure, but I think it was one of those two. Good advice,
don't you agree?"

The larger of the two men watched without speaking until he
could stand it no longer. "What's that?"

"This? This is called a 'Drain Czar.' You just hook it up to a hose,
stick it in a drain, or other orifice in your case, and turn on the water.
This big black cucumber-looking part expands to fit the orifice, locking it in place. Then the small hole at the end allows water to pass
through, pressure builds up, and bam! The drain obstruction pops
free. Of course, in your case I'm not quite sure what's going to pop
loose. So if I were you, I'd seriously reconsider your vow of silence."

Dawson continued whistling as he applied a liberal coating of
petroleum jelly to the large black object. "Now you may experience a
little discomfort. Nothing compared to when I turn on the water—
but nonetheless." Dawson flipped the man over and bent him across
the table with his pants around his ankles. The man grunted as Dawson inserted the device into place.

"Now that I've had my way with you, so to speak, it's show time.
Anything you want to chat about?"

"Eff you. I got rights."

"That you do. You have the right to an enema, which I'm going to
administer right now," Dawson said with a grin. "Here we go," he
said turning on the faucet. The hose stiffened as did the man. Dawson continued humming as the man's eyes widened. A low groan
started, rapidly increasing in volume and pitch.

"Turn it off! Turn it off!"

"Beg pardon, did you say something?" he asked calmly.

"Turn it off! Turn it off! Pleeease."

"Oh, so you have something you want to chat about now?"

"Yes, yes, turn it off!"

"Okay let me make sure now; you say you want the water off?"

By now the man could barely speak, "Yes," he croaked.

"You got it, boss," Dawson said, closing the faucet to allow the pressure to slowly subside.

As the hose deflated, the man did likewise, water streaming out of him onto the floor near the drain. Dawson pulled a chair over and sat down, straddling it backwards resting his head on his arms. "So, whatcha' wanna' chat about? How about we talk about where your scumbag buddy was going to take Evie." The man sat gasping as water continued to pour out, but said nothing.

"Give him one more chance, and then if he has nothing to say, flip the water back on and let's go get a burger," Quint said.

Dawson nodded. "You heard him. Talk."

The man hesitated until Dawson reached for the water valve, "I'll tell you anything you want to know. Just ask me a question, any question—I'll tell you the truth, I swear I will. Just ask me," he said, then finally paused after his machine gun verbal barrage.

"Shut up, you idiot," the smaller man yelled at him.

"You'll get your turn, but if you open your mouth one more time before we tell you, we're going to assume you want it right now. Got it, knucklehead?" Quint said. The smaller man went silent and insolently turned his head away as Quint put a set of earphones over his head. Quint tuned the portable radio to a rap station and cranked up the volume so the man could not hear what his partner had to say.

"Let's see now, what are your names? Why are you here? Who do you work for? And oh, by the way, when we finish, we're turning you over to our buddy, who will be holding you for a while. If I find out you've lied to us, we'll have another session only I won't be asking any more questions, nor will I be turning off the water." The man began talking nonstop for the next 30 minutes requiring only occasional prompting from Dawson while Quint took notes.

"Now that wasn't so hard was it? Let's just see if your little friend agrees." Swapping the men, he repeated the process with the same result.

"Gentlemen, I want to thank you for your cooperation. Now, who wants to climb back in the trunk, and who wants another round with Mr. Drain Czar?"

Once they were finished, Quint called Rogers to brief him.

"The good news is I think we learned everything these guys had to offer, though it appears they don't know much about the big picture. They are working for Rashid, the same guy who hired thugs to kidnap Dawson and me, but they have no idea where we might find him. The only time they met with him was at some deer camp when they were briefed on this job."

"I'll have someone pick them up and give our guys a shot," Rogers replied. "Maybe we can squeeze a little more out of them. Oh, by the way, you didn't violate any of their rights or use undue force in interrogating them, did you?"

"Us?" Quint replied, as he hung up the phone.

CHAPTER 22

"Quint, I doubt they'll try to kidnap me again. Please let me stay a couple more days. I'll stay on the boat and keep the gun with me." Quint was a basket case over nearly losing Evie and refused to discuss it.

"We got lucky last time, and I'm not about to give them a second shot. You're not safe on shore. You're going back to Key West, and that's final." Though Evie was not accustomed to having someone give her orders, she appreciated Quint's concern.

"Okay, even though I'm unconvinced that I'm in danger, you win," Evie said. "But look, I probably can't get a flight out for a day or two," she said, knowing full well she could most likely book one that same day, "so if you don't want me staying on *Mojito*, why not let me stay out on *Searcher* with you for a day or so until I can work things out? Then I'll go quietly. I can ride out with you this morning and use the ship's sat phone to change my return flight." Though obviously not happy with her proposed compromise, Quint begrudgingly agreed.

Evie smiled, threw her arms around his neck, and then hurried to pack her things before he changed his mind.

Quint arranged to have the doghouse above the dive locker "iguana-proofed." Leo gathered a wide array of food in accordance with Evie's list of strict dietary restrictions and placed it in a cabinet for Fred, who seemed to take to Leo. "Looks like you became buddies with him a lot easier than me," Quint noted.

"Yes," Leo replied pompously. "I hear iguanas are excellent judges of character." Quint chuckled as he closed the locker door and headed for *Searcher's* salon. As he entered, Quint spotted Lolo and introduced her to Evie.

For three days, *Searcher* methodically swept the Sound, looking for the bomb, while Kira directed the remaining support boat into a new search area each time they completed their assigned one. She made a point to compliment Colin's efforts and chat a little longer than necessary whenever she hailed *Blaize*.

Each day, they reviewed their results and planned the search effort for the next day. It was monotonous work, but the considerable stakes kept them focused. Quint enjoyed having Evie on board. While not as pleasant as being together on *Mojito*, at least he was not worried about her.

For the most part, the crew had taken to Fred, adopting him as the ship's mascot. The attention lavished upon him seemed to offset any stress about his relocation. Lolo was one of his few non-supporters, referring to him as "that damned lime lizard" and avoiding him at all costs. Evie was more than a little offended by Lolo's *very* vocal opposition whenever one of the crew allowed Fred entry to the ship's living quarters.

The crew took turns spending time on shore to break things up. Although it was not Willy's turn, he had swapped with Leo, to head ashore for the evening. He hitched a ride on *Blaize* with Dawson and Quint, who planned to pick up *Reel Eazy* the following morning now that her repairs were complete. Quint wondered about the urgent nature of Willy's business but elected not to make an issue of it.

Jacques liked living on Cat Island. The Spanish explorers who discovered the island named it for the island's raccoons, which they mistook for cats. Jacques was proud to be descended from the original Cuevas who, as the old lighthouse keeper, was granted ownership of the island. It was his reward for delaying the British attack on New Orleans, thereby giving General Andrew Jackson time to successfully prepare an army. Nearly 10 years ago much of the island had been sold to become part of the Gulf Islands National Seashore, but Jacques still held onto his small piece on one of the manmade canals.

Jacques heard the sound of his son arriving at the dock in their bay boat as he continuously stirred the darkening roux to keep it from sticking in the worn cast-iron skillet. This was the base for the gumbo they would enjoy for supper. On the counter, a Mason jar full of oysters stood beside a heaping bowl of crabmeat picked the evening before from a hamper of crabs he had pulled from the bayou.

Jacques preferred to live like his ancestors, spending much of his time securing daily sustenance.

The battered screened door slammed as his son entered and set his bucket of shrimp on the counter, along with a bag of andouille sausage from the freezer in the shed. "Saw Miss Stella in town this afternoon after school."

"Really? What wuz she up to?"

"Said some folks wuz askin' about Billy and you—probably more smart-assed know-it-all reporters."

"Watch your language; you know your mother, God rest her soul, wouldn't stand for you having a foul mouth," he said, lost in thought. The slamming screen door signaled that his son was headed for the tire swing beneath the stilted house to enjoy the cool shade after completing his chores.

Once the roux had darkened to the proper copper hue, Jacques removed it from the heat. Returning the seafood to the rusty refrigerator, he grabbed his keys and strode out of the kitchen, across the porch, its weathered boards creaking in protest, to climb into the bay boat. "Be back in a little while," he hollered to his son and cranked up the antique Evinrude. He had traded up from his old skiff after it nearly sank while he tried to make it to shore in a northern blow. He liked the new boat but had kept his faithful old motor.

Jacques pulled into the Pass Christian marina and tied off the boat. Though his vintage Dodge pickup truck sat waiting with the new battery he had installed the previous week, he opted to walk the short distance to the small café. He slipped inside the restaurant, choosing a seat at the bar. The smell of cheeseburgers cooking on the grill tempted him, but he decided to resist and stick to his plan to have gumbo with his son later.

Stella saw him and slipped around the corner to undo her top button and tug at the bottom of her blouse to accent her cleavage before grabbing a mug and the carafe of coffee. "Heard you had some folks asking about Billy and me," Jacques said.

"Well hello, Stella, so glad to see you. My, but you're looking pretty today," she said sarcastically, while pouring his coffee. "Yeah, a couple of guys with that group that's been looking for the shipwreck. Seemed like all right fellas, 'specially the one with the dark hair, Dawson. Rudy sent him my way."

"Reporters?"

"Nope. Said they were just asking about that night Billy saw that plane or whatever it was. Rudy told them Billy and you used to be friends. I didn't say nothing, but I think they want to talk to you."

"I appreciate your not saying nothing. Where they staying?"

"Most of 'em are over at the Magnolia. Been there for the past week or so." Jacques nodded and tossed a five-dollar bill on the counter. The waitress's eyebrows arched, and she flashed him a broad smile as she slipped the money into her apron. "Come back soon; don't be such a stranger," she said, toying with her hair.

Jacques crossed back to his truck and reached through the open passenger side window to remove a small revolver from the glove box. He checked the load before walking behind the hotel and climbing the back stairs, where he waited just inside the door. He knew out-of-towners were always charged a premium, but given second-floor rooms with a view as consolation.

He slapped his forearm, smashing an engorged mosquito that had been feeding off him, and wiped the insect remains from his arm and fingers with a crumpled paper towel that he then thrust back into his pocket. A minute later, he forgot and used the same paper towel to blow his nose, leaving a red smear of insect remains on the side of his nose.

Before long, he heard footsteps coming up the stairs from the lobby and pressed himself into the shadows. The men were talking as they turned away at the top of the front stairs to head down the corridor away from him. Quint was joining Dawson in his room for a beer before heading back to *Mojito*. Once they closed the door, Jacques waited only a minute before following them.

"Bellman, you have a message," Jacques announced with a loud knock.

Unsure how he could possibly have a message but having no reason to be suspicious, Dawson opened the door. As soon as he did, Jacques pushed the door open hard with his gun drawn. "Step back!" he commanded quietly but sternly, kicking the door closed behind him. "Who might you be?" Jacques asked.

"Well, seeing as how this is my room, I have the same question. Why don't you go first?" Dawson calmly replied.

"It may be your room, but I got the gun."

"Good point. I'm Dawson, and my buddy here is Quint. Now, once again, who the hell are you?" he asked, trying to ignore the gun.

"You reporters or lawmen?" Jacques asked, ignoring Dawson's question.

"Neither," Dawson replied.

"Then what you doing here?"

At this point Quint interrupted, "Look, unless you tell us your name is Jacques, the same Jacques who was Billy's friend, then you can stick that gun right up your ass 'cause we've got nothing else to say to you."

Jacques stared at them for a moment. "You sure got balls. Yeah, I'm Jacques. Why you looking for me?"

"First, put down the gun. It makes me nervous, and we're not here to cause you any trouble. All we want is to talk to you about Billy and that article they printed in the paper about his story back in the '50s," Quint said.

"You kill Billy?"

"No," Dawson replied.

Jacques eyed him for a moment and lowered the gun but didn't put it away. "You say you aren't with the law?"

"Scout's honor," Dawson replied, raising his hand in a scout salute. "By the way, you've got red shit all over the side of your nose."

While pausing to wipe his nose, Jacques decided to trust that they were being straight with him. "Sorry, but with what happened to Billy, I guess I'm a little jumpy. Yeah, I knew Billy; we grew up together. He was a Ladner; claimed he was a descendant of L'Adnier, who named Pass Marianne after his wife. Billy always maintained that his folks lived on Cat Island before mine, so we were squatters.

"We played football together, but Billy started drinking as he got older and got strange ideas in his head. Claimed he saw UFOs. I always figured it was his liquor-fueled imagination.

"I guess I'm supposed to believe that you're really hunting for the galleon," Jacques said eyeing Quint carefully. "But that ain't why you're here. And it ain't why I'm here. And it ain't what got Billy killed, now is it?"

Realizing the importance of keeping the lid on the bomb, Quint hesitated. But Dawson, trusting his gut, barged ahead, ignoring Quint's dirty look. "No, it's not."

"Good thing you're honest, or this conversation would be over. Just before Billy died, a guy, supposedly a middle eastern student, was doing some research at our little town library. He was keenly interested in that 1958 article about Billy claiming to see a plane crash or whatever. That's what got Billy dead, and that's why I'm here—I don't plan on ending up the same way."

"What can you tell us about Billy?" Quint asked.

"Nobody would ever believe him, but Billy did see something that night. I know because I did too. I was floundering down at Smuggler's Cove and saw a plane explode in the distance. Billy and I talked, and he told me everything. He was fishing that night..."

CHAPTER
23

Billy loved night fishing while sipping whiskey in his ancient wooden skiff. He was peacefully drifting across the inky, still waters of the Mississippi Sound, enjoying the last of his nearly empty bottle when he heard the labored sound of aircraft engines approaching and saw the shadow of a large plane above.

From his front-row seat, he saw an orange explosion and an object detach from the plane. Trailing a long white streamer, it plummeted into the water, barely a mile away. "*What the...,*" he said to himself as his alcohol-dulled mind tried to process what he had just witnessed. A short time later, he saw another object fall a few miles away.

He sat stunned, an eerie cold washing over him, his interest in fishing suddenly gone. He cranked up the motor and ran west of the Pass Marianne light, where he thought he had seen the first object land. Of course, in the blackness of night he could see nothing. *With this murky water it wouldn't help even if it was daylight,* he thought, as he headed for home.

The next day he told the unbelievable story to his fellow oystermen. They were quite familiar with Billy's drinking and the wild tales he told about seeing UFOs whenever he got into the bottle.

"I'm telling you, there was this explosion. Then something with a long white tail fell into the water. A minute later, I saw something crash into the ocean a couple of miles away."

"On the sauce again last night, huh Billy? You didn't see any UFOs filled with little pink aliens, now did you?" they laughed. Frustrated, he walked off in a huff and climbed into his beat-up skiff to begin another day of oystering.

A few days later, the placid waters mirrored the clear blue sky as the sun gradually burned off the morning chill. A flotilla of ancient oyster skiffs hovered on Pass Marianne reef, where men harvested the shellfish with long wooden-handled tongs as had their fathers before them. Billy scoffed at those so-called oystermen who had forsaken tongs for dredges pulled by boats. That was not the way oysters should be taken, and he had no use for the dredge operators.

Several "true" oystermen chatted while taking a smoke break from the backbreaking work. Once their harvest was culled and bagged, they would chug back to shore. There most would sell their bags of oysters at the dock, though some preferred to load their haul into the back of rusted pickup trucks and head down the beach in search of a better price.

Each day the cycle repeated itself as it had for decades. The harvest was particularly bad this year. Maybe it was all that rain the previous year. Or maybe it was simply a quirk of fate.

Billy was working well to the west of his normal area, near where he had seen the falling object that no one seemed to believe existed. He massaged his aching shoulders and lowered the tongs for what felt like the millionth time. As he raised the tongs they felt unusually heavy. *Probably hooked some debris*, he thought as he continued raising the tongs.

One time he had brought up an old rusted bicycle. Other times he had hauled up tires and other automotive parts. It was hard to imagine how these things came to be in the middle of the Mississippi Sound, but at least they broke the boredom.

Billy gasped, nearly dropping his tongs as they broached the surface. Inside the rakes was a human head—still wearing a pilot's helmet—attached to a partial torso that included one arm. A long section of white mud-stained fabric, which appeared to be torn from a parachute, was attached to the torso remains. A shark, following behind his meal, lunged and scored a chunk of the torso just as Billy plucked the remains from the water.

Billy stood frozen as his weak mind struggled to accept what his eyes beheld. In a daze, he fired up the one-cylinder engine and headed to shore, the rest of the oystermen just staring. At the dock he threw a ratty line around one piling of his slip and ran in search of the police chief.

An impressive collection of flies greeted Billy when he returned with the police chief, Buck. While not yet overpowering, the stench was strong enough to make the Chief queasy. Reaching in his hip pocket for a handkerchief, he held it over his mouth and nose as he examined Billy's odiferous find. "So tell me Billy, where did you find this?"

"Shit Buck, I've already told you five times, Pass Marianne reef," Billy responded.

"I know *that*. I mean where specifically."

"How the hell do I know? I was a few hundred yards west and a little ways south of the old Pass Marianne marker. That's the best I can do," Billy replied, his voice filled with frustration.

"Look, Billy, you got your job and I got mine. Folks are gonna' want to go out there and search for the rest of the body. So somebody's gonna' be asking me where to go."

"Well, damn. I don't know what they're expectin' to find. We got the head still wearing a pilot helmet and the torso with one arm still attached and part of a parachute. Either they can figure out who it is or they can't. Finding the guy's other limbs, kidneys, or whatever ain't gonna' help too much—you reck'n? Besides, the sharks probably ate the rest. They were hard at work on the remains when I found 'em."

Buck replied calmly, "I know, but that ain't our problem. No one else reported hearing a plane having difficulty. Sure you weren't hitting the white lightening?"

"Not you too. No, I didn't have any last night," he lied, "but I wish I did now. Besides how do you explain him wearing that pilot's helmet?"

Buck ignored his question and handed Billy a pad of paper. "Sketch me a map of where you think you found the remains." Billy began sketching and was almost done when he tore off the sheet, stuck it in his pocket and started on a neater version. Later, when he came across the first version, he threw it into his top dresser drawer and saved it.

While he was sketching, Rudy, a reporter from the local newspaper, showed up and got in an argument with Chief Buck over taking photos of the remains. They were still arguing when Billy finished his second sketch and handed it to Buck. Then, eager to exploit his shot at fame, interjected, "Well, I guess I found me some really unfortunate soul." Rudy dutifully snapped several photos of Billy, one of which made the front page the next morning, along with the headline: "Local Oysterman Finds Airman's Remains."

The paper's circulation was tiny and the brief story never gained much exposure. But the article gave Billy publicity he would later regret.

The man the Air Force sent down to claim the remains gave Rudy a brief press release referring to a training flight crashing the night before. Then shortly after Billy's story ran, a group of three particularly unlucky fishermen showed up and hung around for two weeks without catching a thing. Each day they would leave in a boat they had rented from Barney's Bait Shop loaded with their rods and shiny cases too big to be tackle boxes. Barney offered to be their guide for a couple of bucks, but they politely refused. After offering a couple of times, he finally gave up, figuring as long as they paid the boat rental fee and brought his boat back in one piece, what they did was their business.

"Another beer," Dawson said offering Jacques a bottle dripping icy wet from the cooler. Jacques eyed it for a moment before nodding.

"Anyhow, nobody came asking Billy questions until that student claimed he found the fifty year old news article at the town's library."

Quint could tell Jacques was getting antsy and would want to leave soon. "So Billy saw the explosion. Then the pilot, whose chute didn't open, landed near Billy over by Pass Marianne. But Billy, drunk as usual, got confused and thought the plane crashed a while later. But it couldn't have happened that way, now could it?" Jacques asked.

"Why not?" Quint asked.

"Because even without his chute fully opened, the pilot couldn't have fallen that much faster than the plane. I think the plane had already crashed before the pilot hit the water. A minute or so after the explosion, I heard a second plane laboring; then its engine pitch changed like it had dropped a heavy load before flying off. I don't know what it was, but I'm guessing you boys do. I think that's what Billy witnessed after the pilot landed."

"But why didn't he mark that on the map ?" Dawson asked.

"Because he drew that so the police chief could find the rest of the pilot's remains. Plus with his alcohol-addled mind, Billy had no idea exactly where the second impact occurred, other than a couple of miles to the southwest, he told me."

"But you didn't see what Billy saw or anything else actually hit the ocean?" Dawson asked.

"No, I didn't," Jacques replied, appearing irritated that Dawson was questioning his conclusions. He paused for a minute, considering the offer he was tempted to make, but decided to wait. "I'm guessing Billy's map was important enough for someone to kill him over. Anyhow, that's all I know. I don't want nobody showing up on my porch looking to put bullet holes in me, so keep your mouths shut."

"You have our word."

"Well, I got a gumbo waiting on me at home. Pleasure chattin' with you boys." With that, Jacques opened the door and headed for his truck.

"You think he's right? If Billy's full of crap, maybe we ought to pull off the Pass Marianne area and go back to working our original plan."

"I don't know. The terrorists obviously bought Billy's story, and Jacques admitted he didn't see what hit the water," Quint replied. "Let's keep on going for now and either find Big Bertha or eliminate Billy's area before we change our game plan."

Quint spent the night on *Mojito* but slept with a loaded gun. When he joined Dawson for breakfast the next morning, the waitress brought coffee and vanilla creamer—he had trained her well the few mornings he had stopped here for breakfast. Once they finished their meal, the two men headed to settle up with the boat yard and get *Reel Eazy*.

"*Reel Eazy* is back in the water and ready to go. But repairing the cosmetic damage will take weeks. We'll get on it as soon as you bring her back," the boatyard supervisor said, handing Dawson a clipboard to sign paperwork accepting delivery and authorizing payment via wire draft from the team's bank account.

CHAPTER 24

"You here for the morning team meeting?" Mimi said as she hurried down *Searcher*'s companionway to catch Colin.

"Yeah, Quint asked us to stop by before we get started on *Blaize* with today's search operations.

"How are things with you and Kira?"

"Good question. She seems like she's over being pissed, but I'm not up for another round of drama," Colin replied.

Mimi hesitated, struggling with whether to tell him about Kira's cancer concern. "You guys have been together for a long time; it'd be a shame to lose all that. Give it another shot; I think you'll find her receptive."

Colin stopped and looked her in the eye. "You know something you're not saying?"

Unable to meet his gaze, Mimi continued walking. "Just friendly advice," she said over her shoulder.

"We've been having a number of hits during the night that need to be checked out more quickly. LaRue's divers need to report here first thing each day," Leo reported at their morning meeting. They continued to discuss a few more details before Quint adjourned the meeting.

Colin approached Kira once the others had left. "Are you okay? It looked like you weren't feeling well."

Kira smiled, "I appreciate your concern. Just tired, haven't been getting much sleep."

"You're not..." Colin's voice trailed off as Kira jerked like she had been jabbed with a pin.

"No!" she blurted before continuing more calmly. "No, Colin, I'm not using drugs again. I'll be okay, and thanks for caring." After a car wreck a few years before joining the team, Kira had become hooked on prescription pain killers and had struggled to break her dependence.

"How about I buy you a cup of coffee?" Colin asked hesitantly, halfway expecting rejection.

"Something a bit stronger would be better, but coffee's what I need." As the two emerged from the meeting room holding hands, Mimi smiled then scurried away.

Kira finally made a doctor's appointment when it became obvious that her weakness and nausea were persisting far too long. Using the trumped-up excuse of a sick relative to cover her absence, Kira left the next day for the dreaded return trip home to keep her doctor's appointment. Since she hoped to know something soon, she opted not to tell Colin for fear he would insist on accompanying her on a trip she felt was better made alone. Evie's offer to help take up the slack while she was gone lessened her guilt.

The 30-minute wait seemed more like hours before she was called to the back. After taking her vitals, the nurse handed Kira a gown and promised the doctor would be in soon. As she waited once again, she stared at a poster on the wall depicting the human body with its skin removed and each of the major muscles and organs labeled.

After completing his exam, the doctor offered his preliminary diagnosis, qualifying it by adding that he could not be certain until all the tests were completed. Kira dressed then resumed staring at the poster. When the doctor returned he informed her that the tests did confirm his earlier diagnosis, then he discussed her options. After he left, she felt numb, lacking the energy to leave until the returning nurse finally urged her out the door.

The team had covered over half of the new search area off Pass Marianne by the time she was back aboard *Searcher*. She thanked Mimi and Evie for covering for her while she was gone but chose to say only that they would have to run more tests. While it wasn't true, it bought her time to decide how to handle her situation.

Quint entered the bridge and picked up the satphone to take the waiting call. He spotted an uneaten sandwich. Though sometimes Dakota would eat to be polite, when he was working he could be like a machine, seldom breaking to drink or even use the bathroom, much less eat. Quint smiled as he read Dakota's t-shirt of the day: *"I'd agree with you, but then we'd both be wrong."*

"Quint."

"Sorry I missed you when you called earlier. How are things going?" Rogers asked.

"We've moved our search area near Pass Marianne based on the map we found on the terrorist's shrimp boat but so far no luck. How about the terrorists Botz arrested and the ones who tried to kidnap me and Evie? Anything come from their interrogation?"

"As we assumed, their operation is compartmentalized, and they are only one of several groups in the area. However, with the proper encouragement, we learned where a couple of the other cells are."

"If you know where they are, why not arrest them right now? I'll be happy to join you."

"Quint, we have good people working this. They're tapping the terrorist's communications to get the guys pulling the strings so we can cut off the head."

"Okay, keep me posted," Quint replied. "Any word on our weapons request?"

"I checked again right before I called you. It was hung up in the system, so I chewed on a few asses and got it back on track. Give me another day or two."

"Maybe we just ought to go buy a few pistols and a rifle or two," Quint replied.

"Doing that is likely to raise a lot of questions we don't want to answer about why a treasure hunting operation needs to be armed during the search phase. I'd really prefer that you give me a little longer."

"Got another weather update," Dakota said when Quint was off the phone. "That storm's hurricane-force winds are pounding hell out of the south Florida coastline. It's jogged to the south but is expected to cross the tip of Florida and enter the Gulf, perhaps as a Category 1 hurricane predicted to strengthen."

"Keep an eye on it," Quint said then called a second number. "Hey Eddie. I know you're busy with the storm headed your way, but

I just wanted to check on Lefty."

"I figured you'd be calling. After I took him to dialysis yesterday, I finally convinced him to hunker down with us. The winds are not predicted to go much above 75 miles per hour, and the storm surge is not predicted to be very bad, so we shouldn't have any problem. But I promise to keep him safe and call you after it passes."

"I'll count on it," Quint said as he hung up, feeling relieved.

CHAPTER 25

Dawson elected to stay on *Searcher,* while Colin, who needed to attend to business on shore the next day, headed into shore for the night. When Dawson entered the galley to grab dinner, the only open seat was at the table with Kira, Leo and Mimi. Both Kira and Dawson tried to ignore the tension whenever they neared each other. Like a charge in the air, the slightest accidental touch electric, they found themselves making nervous conversation, trying a little too hard to compensate.

He tried hard but continuously struggled to suppress his feelings for her. She was spoken for, with his good friend Colin, for goodness' sake. So why did he feel like an awkward teenager whenever she was around? His heart beat a little faster, and he became tongue-tied around her. No matter how many times he vowed not to let it happen, she always made him feel giddy, oftentimes feeling like an awkward teenager deep in puppy love.

While Leo launched off on one of his roguish tales, Dawson's mind drifted to that lunch a few months before in Ft. Lauderdale. Quint and Leo had been forced to bail at the last moment. By unspoken mutual consent, Dawson and Kira continued with their plans for a platonic meeting.

The view from the restaurant – a series of squalls marching across the ocean—was spectacular, as was the lunch. The two of them seemed to click that afternoon, laughing and telling amusing tales of their younger years. After settling the check, Dawson offered to give Kira a lift to avoid a taxi as they left the restaurant.

Upon entering the elevator, she turned abruptly just as he reached to push the first-floor button. As he straightened up, and the doors closed, his lips were scant inches from hers. Their eyes locked.

The elevator's abrupt stop and the rapid opening of the doors sent them scrambling to move to a "safe" distance. Embarrassed at the knowing smiles of the waiting passengers, they exited quickly, eyes cast down from their crimson faces.

As they emerged from the building, rain was pouring, and lightning danced in the clouds. They paused for a moment while considering what to do. "I don't think this is going to let up any time soon. We can either head back and have a couple of drinks or make a break for it."

"Let's go for it," Kira said then darted out into the rain, headed for Dawson's car on the far side of the parking lot. By the time they reached the car, they were both drenched, Kira's thin blouse hugged her ample breasts, prominently displaying her nipples. Fumbling to unlock the car, Dawson tried to keep his eyes from being drawn to her chest. His face flushed red with embarrassment, Dawson was relieved she appeared not to notice.

Shaking the water from their hair, Dawson reached into the back seat for a spare t-shirt to use as a towel, and once again, his lips were scant inches from hers. Alone in the car, the charged air finally prevailed, and their lips touched for the first time. Softly at first, then firmer, with a passion long denied as his tongue eased between her willing lips. The pent-up frustration of fighting natural forces for so long poured out as he held her tightly in his arms. Her fingers ran softly through his hair as she pressed her body against him, surrendering to the moment's passion.

As if on autopilot, they found themselves at a hotel lobby desk checking into a room where they spent the afternoon and evening. He marveled at how natural it felt at the time. The next morning, as they left the room and walked by the remnants of the previous evenings' room service, the world was a different place—Cupid's arrow had found yet another target. Dawson had a new spring in his step, and where there had been numbness and loneliness, passion now resided. At least for another week, a month, or year, he hoped to know the peace of new lovers. But it was not to be.

Though he suspected that she shared his interest, for reasons Dawson never understood, things went no further. He didn't push, and she failed to encourage. With a start, Dawson re-entered the present.

Kira, who seemed preoccupied during dinner, was the first to leave, her dinner half uneaten. With Leo's latest tale finally ending, she seized the chance to leave the galley headed for *Searcher's* stern where the world was defined by the edges of the pool of light cast by ship's floodlights. The night was absent a moon, with the inky dark making the stars seem much brighter.

The soft night breeze washed over Kira's upturned face, pushing her hair back from her forehead. How she wished she had a cigarette, though she was determined not to yield to the urge again. Instead, with eyes closed, she took a deep breath of the salty air and sighed, soaking up the peacefulness. Realizing she had to get some sleep, she was headed to her stateroom when she bumped into Dawson.

They stood face to face, inches away for seconds that seemed an eternity. Then slowly, like a gravitational attraction, their faces came together, and they kissed. Their lips pressed together hard, almost brutally, and her tongue darted inside his mouth, then his in hers. Both felt the electric jolt of passion, repressed since their previous afternoon fling.

Kira made a slight moaning sound. Both knew what they wanted, what they needed. But at the same instant, both pulled away. Staring into each other's eyes, Dawson shook his head slightly. Kira replied with half-closed eyes, then lifted her hand to his face and softly touched his cheek before turning away. In that moment both acknowledged the unspoken agreement that *they* could never be.

Both knew it could not happen. They could not let it. It was about Colin; it was about honor; it was about a passion they both knew was better left denied.

But at the moment of this single kiss, something had changed, and each would now be special to the other through an emotional attachment. Though not love, neither was sure what it was.

CHAPTER 26

With the volume turned up on the television inside and the door open, Jacques sat on the wooden porch watching a blue heron standing frozen in the shallow bayou behind his fish camp on Cat Island. With blinding swiftness, it speared a small fish that had unwittingly approached too close. After swallowing its prize, it unfolded its giant wings and took to the air like a pterodactyl from prehistoric times.

Jacques swallowed a mouthful of thick, chicory coffee while listening to the Weather Channel's tropical update. As expected, it was not good. Tropical Depression Twelve was now hurricane Katrina. *Hurricanes! Unpredictable as a woman and mean as one scorned*, he thought to himself.

"Hurry up. We don't want to miss your plane," Jacques yelled, suspecting that his son was playing video games instead of packing. His son normally went to visit his grandparents this time of year, when there was the first hint of an impending hurricane. Katrina had triggered his departure.

That afternoon, with his son safely aboard the plane, Jacques was heading back to Cat Island in the slick calm water when, on a lark, he changed direction to visit Quint aboard *Searcher*, which was now working to the northwest of Cat.

"How things going?" Jacques asked once aboard and seated in the expansive salon.

"Slow," Quint replied wondering why Jacques had come.

"Yeah, there's a whole lot of bottom out there to search in the Gulf of Texas." Jacques refused to use the accepted name for the Gulf of Mexico. He hesitated for a minute then continued. "You know you're wasting your time searching around Pass Marianne. As I told you, Billy saw the pilot's body fall there but, despite what he may have thought, there's nothing else," Quint halfway nodded, not wishing to disclose anything confidential.

Jacques seemed lost in thought as the two men sat in silence. Finally, as Quint was about to break the quiet, Jacques spoke. "I've got a shrimper's snag log we can use."

He continued to remain silent while Quint pondered his reply. "That's great," uncertain what a "snag log" might be but reluctant to offend Jacques by asking. The silence continued until Jacques broke it once again.

"You have no idea what I'm offering, do you?"

"Sorry Jacques, but honestly, I don't. Care to enlighten me?"

"The thing shrimpers hate most is snagging their nets on the bottom. So they carefully note the location each time it happens then share the locations amongst themselves. Billy was friends with several and willed me his snag log. Good fishing on a lot of those snags. As you said, there's a lot of ocean out there and no guarantee that one of the snags is what you're looking for, but it might speed things up." Quint considered the possibilities.

"You could keep your main boat, *Searcher*, and one of the other charter boats working like they are. If you want to hire me, I'll take the other charter boat and go to work where I think the odds are highest, a couple of miles to the southwest where Billy saw the second impact. We'll just work from one snag to another. Of course, it would help if I knew what we're looking for—I'm guessing a bomb." Quint could not conceal his surprise.

"Yep, I figured something sensitive like a bomb that nobody would want to talk much about."

Quint considered the offer then spoke. "I'll have to run it by my partners, but I'm pretty sure they'll go for it. If so, we'll pay you the standard charter boat captain rate," Quint said. Jacques paused for a moment, obviously uneasy. "Something else?" Quint asked.

"A few nights ago, I was in Flatfish Bar and met one of your crew—LaRue. He has problems. You should watch out," Jacques said as he rose to depart. Quint made a mental note to probe into the situation with LaRue. "One more thing: you probably don't watch the weather as close as me, but that's a bad storm brewing in South Florida. Best keep an eye on it too."

Quint rounded the middle doghouse headed for *Searcher's* salon to brief the team on Jacques' offer during their morning meeting when he nearly ran into Colonel Botz coming from *Searcher's* stern.

"Stopped by to pass on the latest intelligence, but since you weren't here, I found Dakota back in your operations shack." Botz said, looking somewhat uncomfortable, perhaps even guilty, Quint thought.

"You can get with him if you like; I don't have time to go over it all again. Impressive amateur operation you've got here. Well, got to run," Botz said as his boat approached, and he stepped aboard.

Quint watched as they roared off while considering Botz's response before heading to his meeting. "Everyone's here except Dakota. He asked that we call him on the bridge when you arrived," Kira said as she rose to hail him over the ship's intercom.

"That's okay, I'll go get him," Quint replied.

"Hey big man," Dakota greeted Quint as he stepped onto the bridge.

"Things going okay?"

"Yeah, other than that we haven't found the bomb."

"How about Operations, things going smoothly down there?"

"You'd have to ask Kira."

"But you were just down there."

Dakota looked up puzzled. "No I wasn't. Haven't been there in the past couple of days."

"You didn't just speak with Botz?"

"Yeah, but he was standing right where you are."

Hmmm, Quint thought.

Kira, who was not feeling well, went to Search Control to see if Tom and Colin could run things without her, but when she arrived, she found only Mimi. "Where are Tom and Colin?"

"Beats me. Leo came by a little while ago. After a bunch of whispering and giggling, they left together."

"I'll be back." Kira checked the salon and galley, and after failing to find them, continued on to the bridge. As she opened the door, Tom, Leo, Willy, and Colin were standing at the front of the bridge beside Dakota and Guillermo engrossed in something on the foredeck below. They failed to notice Kira enter. Easing beside Colin, she looked below to see Lolo sunbathing nude.

"Sonofabitch! I can't believe it. Mimi is running search operations by herself while you immature morons are gawking at Lolo's boobs. I guess she was right; tits and tan is all it takes to get your attention,"

Kira said and stormed out of the bridge in search of Quint.

"Damn it all! This is insane," Quint said as he arrived on the bridge, steam practically coming out of his ears after hearing Kira's report. "What did you say Lolo means in Apache?"

"Gift of God," Dakota replied.

"Well it should be Chaos. That woman has singlehandedly turned our entire operation upside down with her smoking and shooting tequila in the mess hall, redecorating the ship, and now topless sunbathing." Quint angrily plucked the PA mic from its holder. "Lolo, clear the foredeck, now," he yelled before turning back to Dakota.

"But she is kinda' cute; the crew likes her, and she's got great tits," Dakota replied. Quint answered with a glare. "Besides, you've let Evie join us onboard."

"Don't even go there. I've cut you plenty of slack. Much more so than with either Kira, Mimi, or Dawson, none of whom disrupted our operations. Lolo has to go."

Dakota nodded, amazed that it had taken this long for Quint to draw the line. "Okay, I'm just not sure how to do it. You've seen how difficult she can be."

"I don't give a shit if you throw her overboard, but you are just going to have to find..." Quint stopped in mid-sentence as the sound of a helicopter hovering above the ship caught his attention. The radio crackled to life, "*Searcher* this is Amerigo Chopper Service requesting permission to land on your helipad, over."

"Permission granted," Dakota replied. The helipad over the doghouses on the aft end of the ship had never been used until now. Quint left the bridge to see what this was all about. As he arrived on the back deck, the chopper touched down, and a figure emerged wearing two holstered pistols.

"Shit," Dawson said running for the armory.

"Can I help you?" Quint asked.

"Yeah, you can give me back my wife before I start kicking folks' asses."

"You're Lolo's husband?"

"I am, and I intend to remain so. Where the hell do you have her?"

"*We* don't have her anywhere. She's—"

"What do you want?" Lolo said appearing behind Quint and wearing only a swimsuit coverup.

"Sweetie, are you okay? They haven't hurt you or anything?"

"I'm fine," Lolo replied as Dakota appeared from the bridge.

"There's that Indian sonofabitch! I'm going to skin your hide and make a teepee out of it, you wife-stealing, red-skinned, low life, piece of shit," he said, drawing both pistols. Dakota ducked back into the hatch while Dawson popped up from below on the port side carrying an M4A1 and spotting Lolo's husband brandishing his pistols. His mind raced to find a way to avoid shooting him when Quint solved the problem.

Furious over the way Lolo, and now her husband, had turned *Searcher* into a floating circus, Quint strode across the deck, determination written on his face. Without breaking stride, he stepped up to Lolo's husband, jerked the pistols from his hands, and slung them over the side. Before he could speak, Lolo intervened to defuse the situation.

"I don't know why you're here, but you've wasted your time."

"I was worried about you being here with that storm coming," her husband replied.

"That's sweet and all, but we're done. It was over for us when you hit me. You had one chance, and that was it. So, you can climb right back in your fancy helicopter and fly back to wherever the hell you came from," she said, finishing by walking away, her eyes searching the deck before locking on to Dakota's, who had re-emerged from the bridge. Her soon-to-be ex started to follow when he heard Dawson.

"Stop right there. Turn around and get your ass back on that chopper. You're done here." The man hesitated for a moment, watching Lolo walk away before returning to the chopper. She turned back for one last look and held his stare for a moment, a sad look passing across his face as he entered the chopper's cabin. He situated himself beside the pilot, and the helicopter lifted from the deck.

Though Quint had wondered whether Lolo was playing games with Dakota or had real feelings, it now appeared that she was serious. Worried about what other problems she would bring to the ship, he wished she were aboard the chopper headed out of his life.

With the incident concluded, Quint assembled the team, which unanimously agreed to accept Jacques' proposal and hire him. They decided to let Jacques direct both of the charter boats, leaving *Searcher* to continue the original systematic survey approach. Quint contacted Jacques and arranged for him to start on *Blaize* the next day.

Colin continued to captain *Blaize* while Dawson ran *Reel Eazy*. Once they were south of Cat Island, Jacques directed the two boats to their first waypoints. Each time they found a "snag" they would make a pass directly over it with the radiation detector, and each time failed to get a reading.

This continued the entire day, and by dusk, Jacques was headed back to his home on Cat Island. As he idled his boat down the canal, an osprey flew by with a fish nearly as big as the bird itself, clutched in its razor-like talons. After a quick reconnaissance circle, it settled on a branch high in a pine tree to enjoy its supper. Jacques studied the bird for a while. With Katrina headed their way, he knew all this might not be around much longer.

CHAPTER 27

For a while, it seemed like Jacques' snag log was a waste of time. Then at mid-day Dawson radioed Kira from *Reel Eazy*. "We've got something on one of Jacques' snags. We're picking up a much higher level of background readings." He avoided referring to the fact that he was speaking of radiation readings for fear someone might be listening. "Head *Searcher* over here and send Colin too," he said, giving her the coordinates in a previously arranged code to avoid publicly disclosing the location.

Before she could call *Blaize*, Colin, who had heard the exchange, radioed Kira. "We just got a big hit on the magnetometer here too."

"What about the background readings?"

"Nothing."

"Nothing?" she asked as she took a sip of soda.

"Nope, but LaRue wants to check it out. It's in the area of highest probability for target two," he said avoiding mentioning *El Cazador* over the open radio, "and based on the magnetometer hit, he thinks it's a possible. He said he'll have one of his other divers check out Dawson's hit."

"No, you're closest, and I prefer to have LaRue do it anyhow."

"He says this'll only take a few minutes."

Kira hesitated. "Put him on. LaRue, we've got a highly probable target to check out, and this is the bazillionth time you've thought you found target two. You can have five minutes, then I want you joining us. Understand?"

"You 'da boss, hoss," he said, and finished suiting up. He gave Colin a high five then rolled off the back of the boat.

Searcher joined Dawson on *Reel Eazy,* and they began working the new search lanes Kira had assigned. Thirty minutes later, she announced over the ship's PA that they had the target located, then she hailed Dawson. "We've pinpointed your target. Based on the readings, this could be Big Bertha. We're going to put a buoy dead on top of it and then anchor *Searcher* once we check it out."

"Is LaRue standing by to make a dive?" Dawson asked having heard the earlier radio exchange.

"No, but he will be shortly," Kira bristled at the realization that Colin had not yet joined them. She snatched up the ship's phone to take Dakota's call from *Searcher's* wheelhouse. After providing the anchoring location to Dakota, Kira radioed LaRue. "*Blaize,* this is *Searcher.*"

"Go ah—," Colin started before Kira interrupted.

"What in the hell were you thinking? Damn it all, you agreed to take five minutes. Not 10, not 15 and certainly not 30," Kira launched off.

"Wait a minute, LaRue's still down, and I can't communicate with him."

"What? Have him contact me as soon as he gets up."

"Roger."

The visibility had worsened with the building seas, but as he sank through the murky water, LaRue's sixth sense told him that this was the Spanish wreck. The shadowy darkness below indicated he was on the bottom, and he thumbed his inflator to add air to his vest for neutral buoyancy. The occasional flash of a fish darting away, spooked by his presence, was all that broke the cloudy curtain of water.

Reaching out, he expected to feel his gloved hand sink into the silty bottom muck, but it struck something hard. He pressed his face closer and saw a piece of timber exposed by wave action. He swam along the bottom, feeling more bumps and pieces of debris but nothing recognizable. It was definitely some sort of wreck—but was it *the* wreck? His five minutes elapsed quickly, and he decided to risk continuing.

After 20 minutes, LaRue knew he was in big trouble with Kira. His eyes, now fully adjusted to the dim light at the bottom, were picking up shapes farther away. Ahead he saw a mound of debris appearing to have been recently uncovered. He saw an even larger shadowy mound beyond.

He held his breath and kicked harder, closing the distance, a pulse pounding in his head. As he approached, the larger mound resolved itself into a pile of objects with a large shape transiting the middle. His pulse skipped a beat as his hand came to rest on a long cylindrical metal object. "A cannon!" he thought to himself—his hunch had paid off.

"It's da wreck—with cannons!" LaRue's yelled as his head broke the surface.

"You're going to need them—Kira's pissed. She's expecting a call as soon as you're back on the boat."

"I done got my sorry butt in some kinda' crack with her," LaRue said dumping his dive gear on the deck of the boat. Colin nodded his agreement, handing the mic over with a grin, glad to not be in LaRue's shoes—or flippers in this case.

Before LaRue could key the mic, the radio erupted, "LaRue? I want to speak with LaRue," Kira's voice boomed.

LaRue took a deep breath then keyed the microphone, "Kira, I think I found her, Hoss. Do Dawson want me to check her out?"

"It doesn't matter what Dawson wants. You work for me when we're in search mode. We don't have time for treasure ships now," she spoke over the open channel, realizing too late what she had said. "We think we've found Big Bertha, and I need you back here doing your *real* job. Head to *Searcher* immediately. Do you understand the definition of immediately better than five minutes?"

"We're on da way, Hoss," LaRue replied. Colin struggled to suppress a grin. "We be there as fast as da boat'll go."

"Do that then come see me as soon as you get here," Kira said, breaking the link.

Thirty minutes later LaRue entered search operations looking for Kira. She glanced at the others in the doghouse and announced, "Would you please excuse us?" The sound of sliding chairs was her response as the other team members scrambled to escape Kira's wrath.

Once the room was empty, Kira began. "You're a good diver, and I like you. But if you ever pull a stunt like that again, you'll be off the team," Kira said, deciding the occasion called for short and sweet. As she stormed off, she nodded to the others that it was okay to return while LaRue followed behind her like a scolded puppy.

Arriving in dive operations, LaRue suited back up then, along with two other divers, plunged over the side to check out the target and report back. A few long minutes later, LaRue emerged with a broad smile on his face. "Hoss, one of dem fins be sticking right out of dat mud. We got us a bom'."

For the past day, every time Dawson took a sip of a cold liquid, a pain shot through his jaw. His tooth had bothered him off and on for years but never when he had the time and opportunity to deal with it. Now was not a convenient time for it to act up. He would have to tough it until he could get to a dentist in a day or two.

Quint eyed the heavy clouds scudding before the approaching storm, now predicted to hit them directly. After LaRue's confirmation that they had found the bomb, Quint released both charter boats to return to the dock. He had then left Rogers a message and awaited his return call—now long overdue. He was glad they would be leaving after the Navy relieved them.

Leo was sprawled in *Searcher's* salon watching television, and Quint plopped down on the sofa to join him. When the show returned from a commercial break, Quint realized it was golf. "Any other channels, where we can watch grass grow?" Quint ignored Leo's reply and headed for the mess hall to grab a cup of coffee.

"Where's the vanilla creamer?" Quint asked Kira, who had just entered.

"We must have used up the last of it this morning; the empty container's in the trash," Kira replied. Quint cursed then poured himself a cup, uncertain how the nearly new container was already gone when he thought he was the only one normally using it.

"I think I chipped a tooth on that coffee of yours. You reckon you can make it any stronger?" Quint said to Leo, who seemed to find his comment more humorous than warranted. Dawson's entry into the salon interrupted Quint's train of thought.

"See, that *was* a piece of cake. We found Big Bertha; called Rogers; he'll call the Navy to retrieve it; soon we'll get our fat check and go home. What could be easier?" Quint said.

"Hope your gloating doesn't jinx us, but you were right. I got to hand it to you; it ended up being a lot easier than I imagined," Dawson agreed before changing the subject. "Dakota is ready to hightail it for shelter ahead of this storm as soon as the Navy relieves us. I pity those poor bastards having to remain on station with that big mother headed our way. I'll be happy to have my butt planted on shore watching it on television."

"You and me both. As soon as the Navy gets here, *Searcher* will head up the Mississippi with me following in *Mojito*. We'll go as far north as we need to in order to escape Katrina's wrath."

Rogers leaned back in his plush leather desk chair. Beside the window sat a side chair, a green palm embroidered on the white material of its round back framed in dark walnut. He loved palms, the mere sight of one transported him to a white beach with gin-clear turquoise water. Unfortunately, today his thoughts were drawn elsewhere as the trio of royal palms outside his window bowed before the storm's raging winds.

Although the storm model was only updated every few hours, he checked its progress on his computer for the millionth time. No matter how hard he tried to avoid falling into the trap, each time a big storm threatened, he was sucked into his vigil of watching the computer model and listening to the repetitious drone of the Weather Channel. It was as if by being well informed he could somehow change the storm's course through sheer will power. Though he had tuned out the drone of the newscaster on the television, it now caught his attention.

"This time of year, waves of turbulence roll off of Africa to form hurricane embryos which, like defenseless young animals in the wild, are vulnerable," the news caster said in a dramatic voice. "Upper atmosphere shear, high pressure waves that force them north to a premature death, or a number of other factors kill these fledgling storms before they can realize their full potential for evil.

"But particularly hot summers such as this year's, offer perfect conditions for the creation of a true killer Category 5, so rare that only three such storms have had the distinction of making landfall in the United States. These were Hurricane Camille, Hurricane Andrew, and the hurricane of 1935, which occurred before the convention of naming storms.

"Few people in recorded history have experienced and lived to tell about such storms with wind gusts reaching 200-miles-per-hour and yielding the destructive power of a nuclear explosion. Predictions now have Katrina on track to make most storms look like a Sunday afternoon shower.

"Already, she's crossed Florida, and is in the Gulf, where the high pressure area is no longer predicted to move south in time to deflect Katrina to the east. This slight change in its path will take her toward a warm water eddy southeast of the mouth of the Mississippi river. If this happens, the eddy's heat energy will enable her to grow from the vicious storm she already is into a Category 5 beast."

Headed right for Quint's team, Rogers thought. This change in the forecasted path also meant that the Navy could not arrive before the storm hit. While he hated to ask Quint's team to hang around with such a storm bearing down on them, he had no choice. Now that it had been found, the bomb could not be left unguarded. If it ended up in Rashid's hands, Lord help them—Katrina would be the least of their worries.

It was midnight when Dakota picked up the ship's phone, "Quint we've got traffic for you on the bridge. Sounds like trouble."

"Uh-oh. Maybe you spoke too soon," Dawson said as Quint rose to leave. Quint entered the bridge, and Dakota gave him the handset. "Quint here."

"We got a problem," Rogers said flatly.

"I take it that you're referring to my half of the *we*," Quint commented.

"Sort of. First of all, the latest update on the hurricane has it changing direction and heading your way. She's predicted to be one of the worst in history.

"Secondly, the reason it took me a while to get back to you is that I've been on the horn with the Navy. We had hoped they could skirt the far side of the storm, pluck up the bomb, and slip back out. But the storm is now headed down the path they intended to follow. They're still trying to get to you, at risk of losing men and assets, but they've been forced to slow and change heading. The reality is they can't get there until late Monday, assuming they're still floating."

"This sucks."

"Well, it gets better. We've kept close tabs on the charter boats in your end of the Mississippi Sound in an attempt to make the terrorists' life tougher. However, we have reason to believe that we may have simply forced them to charter farther away.

"We've been watching five targets, at least one of which we believe is under the control of the terrorists. All five boats are now under way ahead of the storm. Two of them are moving in a direction which removes them as a threat, but any one of the remaining three in Pascagoula, Grand Isle, or Lake Borgne could be our boys."

"Why not send out a chopper full of SEALs to check each one out?" Quint asked.

"And what, ask each boat if they're bad guys? Look, with this storm's sudden change in direction, everyone is scrambling. The weather has already degraded too far to launch a chopper interdiction. And on top of that, three other unrelated threats have arisen."

"So bottom line is the terrorists are headed for us to recover the bomb; you can't intercept them, and the Navy can't get here to relieve us. Any other bad news?"

"I'm afraid there is," Rogers replied. "We have to assume that they have your position either from our mole or by using satellite imagery to spot you anchored and know where the bomb is located. So if you leave and they find it, they may be desperate enough to detonate it right there. The approaching storm would spread the fallout, making a horrible situation unthinkable.

"The chatter we're picking up indicates a near certainty that the terrorists are going after the bomb. Since they're prepared to die anyhow, the storm is the perfect cover for them to snatch it."

"What, you want us to remain here and defend the bomb?"

"No, you don't have the resources to stay and match up with these guys. We need you to recover it." The line went silent as Quint absorbed the shocking statement.

"Recover it? What about the concerns you voiced at our first meeting that the Navy needed to handle the recovery because of the bomb's possible instability after all those years on the bottom?" Another long silence hung in the air before Rogers answered.

"Quint, I know it's asking a lot to put your team and your ship at risk, and it kills me to ask it."

"Kills you?"

"Given the stakes, I have no choice," Rogers replied, ignoring Quint's comment.

"Rogers, why can't you guys call down the Coast Guard on the three targets and at least get them off our asses?"

"I tried. With the approaching hurricane, they have their hands full, and I don't think we could get approval in time. Secondly, we have to keep this as low profile as we can," Rogers replied.

"Well if this thing blows up in our face, pun intended, it damn sure won't remain low profile." Quint thought for a minute. It was a long shot that they could recover the bomb and an even longer one that if they did, they could stave off the terrorists. But the prospect of a bomb's being detonated in Washington D.C. or New York, as Rogers had suggested, made the request impossible to refuse.

"Okay, Rogers, I don't see that we have any choice. Assuming my people agree, which I believe they will, we'll give it a try. But you're asking them to risk their lives and their assets, since they're all now shareholders in the ship. This wasn't our deal, to say nothing of the suicidal aspect."

"No problem, the pay goes up twofold with the same tax-exempt status for all parties."

"It's not about the money. Dead men don't spend much."

"I know. But all the same, you'll earn it. We'll also agree to re-place your ship should you lose it in the process, and we'll do every-thing within our power to get support to you as soon as we can. And yes, you'll have it in writing, I'll fax it after we finish."

"What about the weapons you keep promising us? I think we're about to need them."

"I've also been working on an angle to get you reinforcements. We're about to launch a C130 to airdrop your load of weapons and some gear you may need. I've also got approval to send a SEAL team along, if they can get here before the plane takes off. Wish I could fill it up with a whole division of paratroopers, but air traffic into or out of the area is shut down. This plane is coming in from the west and after their airdrop will head right back. They wanted to cancel the flight, but I talked them out of it. A number of people, including me, have their butts on the line over this.

"I'll fax a list of the equipment we're sending. Get your folks to review it and add anything else you can think of. But you'll need to do it quick—the plane has to take off before the weather window closes. Once the SEALs arrive at your site, they'll take over security, help recover Big Bertha, and organize your folks to deal with the terrorists."

"We'll get on it."

"Quint... Evie needs to be off that ship and headed back to the Keys."

"She was planning on flying out tomorrow anyhow. I'll have Doug run out on *Reel Eazy* first thing in the morning," Quint replied, impressed with Rogers' concern.

"Good luck," Rogers finished then broke the connection.

Quint gave the handset back to Dakota and briefed him on the situation. Quint thought his t-shirt of the day was particularly appropriate, *Please! Let me just drop everything and work on your problem.*

"Like your t-shirt," Quint said.

"Thanks, but after your conversation with Rogers, I think I need my, *Boy, are we screwed now* one," Dakota replied.

As Quint left the bridge, the oppressive reality of the situation sank in. Not only were they being asked to remain in harm's way during one of the worst storms to hit the United States in over a century, they were being asked to recover an ancient, unstable nuclear weapon and then tote it around in heavy seas while being chased by terrorists. He picked up the ship's phone to summon the crew to the mess hall.

CHAPTER
28

Dawson sat in the salon hoping the coffee would perk him up. His tooth was killing him, and he had not slept much the night before. Though he was tired and nauseated from the pain, he would tough it out. Long ago he had learned to block out pain, thoughts, desires, and emotions to focus on his mission. And he would do so now, at least until the situation with the bomb was resolved.

Kira entered the room and chose a chair beside Colin. Things were better now, but she knew he sensed something was worrying her that she had not shared with him. *Should I tell him?* she asked herself. *Perhaps, but it's hard to predict how he'll react. I don't want to screw things up just when it looks like they're about to get better. And, I don't want everybody treating me like an invalid.* Finally, she decided that whatever she might choose to do she wasn't going to choose it now.

Seeing no one in the galley, once again Leo dumped out Quint's vanilla creamer into the sink and returned the empty container to the counter by the coffee maker. He was still washing the remains of the powder from the sink when Quint entered to get a cup of coffee. Leo nodded then left Quint cussing as he prepared his coffee.

"Damn, out of vanilla creamer again." Leo smiled surreptitiously, appearing proud of his ongoing prank.

"Dawson was right—I spoke too soon about this being a piece of cake," Quint went on to brief the crew gathered in the mess hall on the details of the situation. "We've finished the job we signed up for. They can't force us to stay here or try to recover Big Bertha; that was never part of our deal. It's up to us, but I can't overemphasize the danger. What do you want to do?"

The group was silent for a minute as they struggled to grasp the dire situation. Then, before Dawson could speak, Willy stood. "Though I'm normally not one to go first, I feel this is the time. The situation sucks, but sometimes you have to play the cards you're dealt. I don't want to risk dying any more than the rest of you. But neither do I want to sit in some quiet harbor riding out the storm only to hear on the news next week that terrorists blew up the Capitol when we might have stopped it.

"You're right, they can't force us to do this—but they shouldn't have to. We're Americans and, though we're not military, it's our time to stand tall. To do anything less is something I don't think any of us could live with—I know I can't."

Dawson spoke next, "While I couldn't have stated it as eloquently as Willy, I agree with every word. But let's not kid ourselves; this has all the earmarking of a suicide mission."

"Yeah, for one thing," Dakota interrupted, "don't forget that we bought *Searcher* cheap because she's far past her prime. Though she may not survive this storm, I too say we go for it. Without the SEALs Rogers has on the way, I might be a little queasy, but with the Navy's finest at our side we can handle a ragtag group of fanatical terrorists."

The somber group nodded their consent, fully appreciating the grave danger they faced. "As the Navajos would say, 'There is nothing as eloquent as a rattlesnake's tail,'" Dakota finished quietly.

"What the hell does that mean?" Dawson asked.

"Beats me, just thought I'd throw it in to lighten things up." Mimi's snort led their laughter.

"Okay, let's work up a plan to be out of here before Katrina arrives," Quint said.

Guillermo handed Quint a copy of an e-mail, which he scanned before speaking. "Here's our written agreement with Rogers and a list of the equipment they're sending. Dawson, you and Colin review this list and send back any additions.

"Willy, figure out how to hoist Big Bertha off the bottom and secure it on deck. LaRue, what's your opinion about recovering the bomb?"

"Hoss, don't think it's dat big a deal. With one of da fins sticking up all we got to do is blast a hole in da mud with da mailbox deep enough to get a sling 'roun her. Best pray she ain't so rotten she breaks up. We be screwed den, Hoss," LaRue said, shaking his head.

The conversation in which Jacques expressed his concerns about LaRue flashed through Quint's mind. *Now's not the right time to pursue that, plus I'm not exactly sure what I'd do right now even if Jacques is correct,* Quint thought to himself.

"Okay, have the divers ready to go down at first light. Dakota, anchor *Searcher* over Big Bertha then start blasting away with the mailbox. Colin, you and the rest get the ship battened down. Dawson and I will figure out what to do after we get the bomb on board. Rogers is sending us the positions of the three possible terrorist vessels, which we'll need to avoid until he figures out which of those 'possibles' is the 'probable' terrorist boat.

"One more thing, I called Doug, and he'll have *Reel Eazy* out here right at daybreak to take the women and all non-essential crew to shore. Evie is already packing. And Dakota, Lolo better be on the boat to shore too." Dakota nodded with a wide grin.

Kira looked at Mimi before speaking. "We're not going anywhere. We're as much a part of this team as the rest of you. Evie's not, and I agree she should go back with Lolo."

Quint nodded, accepting the position he knew she would take. "What about you Jacques? This isn't your fight. You don't have to stay and risk your life."

"True, but I'll stick around. You might need another hand, and I'm guessing I best not be in my house when the storm hits. If it's as bad as they say, I really don't have anywhere else to go."

Quint nodded. "Okay, let's do it."

Thirty minutes later, Dawson joined Quint. "Colin and I reviewed the equipment list and sent a couple of additions to Rogers. His guys did a good job of getting us most everything we need plus some things I wouldn't have thought to include like a couple of the Navy's latest Smart Underwater Bombs they call micro SUBs. You just throw them over then control them like an autonomous ROV, remote-operated vehicle. They might just give us the edge we need," Dawson finished, then turned to Quint.

"What about *Mojito*? As bad as this storm is, I don't think she'll fare too well in the harbor."

"Well, I guess that's what insurance is for. We've got our hands full, and keeping the bomb out of terrorist hands takes precedence over attending to my sea mistress," Quint replied glumly.

By sunrise, frigatebirds soared above, confirming that a bad storm was coming. Dakota had *Searcher* positioned over the bomb with both anchors set in place and ordered the mailbox swung down into position. With the engines engaged in forward, the mailbox deflected the prop wash toward the bottom and began stirring up the mud— hopefully exposing the bomb in the process. After 15 minutes, Dakota backed off the engines. "Okay LaRue, go see how we're doing."

LaRue plunged over the side with a second diver and followed the buoy line to the bottom. The poor visibility, made worse by the silt stirred up by the prop wash, was near zero. LaRue groped along the bottom to gain a feel for how much progress had been made in uncovering the bomb. A minute later he surfaced.

"It ain't workin', Hoss."

"What do you mean?" asked Dakota, who had come back to talk to him directly.

"For starters, it stirred things up so much I can't see my nose. Only a couple more inches of Big Bertha is exposed. Da boat be movin' roun' too much, and you be blowin' da hell out of dat bottom. We need us a four-point moorin' to keep da boat centered over da bomb, but even den, with us rollin' in these seas, I'm not sure it'll work."

"Well, we don't have two more anchors since we weren't supposed to be raising the damn bomb in the first place, especially in seas like this." Dakota turned to Quint and Dawson, "What you want to do?"

"Willy, rig the airlift. We'll have to do it the old-fashioned way. LaRue, take a couple of divers and get started while I suit up," Dawson replied.

"I damn sure try, Hoss. But it'd be best with just one man on each of da airlifts until dat water clear up, den we can use more folks." Dawson nodded.

Quint spotted a boat approaching and went below to help Evie with her bags. "You sure you're going to be all right? Maybe I should go with you."

"Look, we've been over that a million times. You need to stay here and find that... I mean do whatever it is you're doing," Evie said, nearly admitting that she knew what they were up to. "Don't worry about me; you worry about Fred."

Despite her best persuasive tactics, Evie had been unsuccessful in getting a spot for Fred on the plane headed back. Evidently, the local airport staff was not quite as understanding as the ones in South Florida about shipping large lizards. Of course, it had provided her with a valid excuse for delaying her departure until Quint finally

called her hand, insisting that Fred would do fine with the crew looking after him until they could get him back home.

"Doug will go with me to *Mojito* to get the rest of my things, then
I'll take a taxi to the airport like we discussed."

"Look, a taxi will be tough to find—there aren't many, and
those few still working will be busy. Take the team's rental car,"
he said handing her the keys. His stomach cramped as he remembered his Road Runner in the repair shop and pictured it floating
about in the coming flood waters.

"I'll try to keep in touch but with the storm coming, it may
be tough."

"Keep trying to call so I won't worry. I'll see you as soon as we
get this resolved," Quint said. With the non-essential crew already
off the ship, he was headed to help her board *Reel Eazy* when Colin
caught his eye.

"You deal with him. I'll call you when I can. Love you," Evie said
with a quick kiss and squeeze of his hand. Her eyes remained locked
on his, telegraphing her concern as Quint waved and disappeared
around the corner.

In the confusion, Quint forgot to confirm that Lolo was on the
boat to shore.

"Colin, launch the inflatable tender before we get divers in the
water. We'll need it to pick up the airdrop package," Quint ordered.

"Okay, but with this wind building, we may not get it back aboard."

"That's a chance we'll just have to take. Under the circumstances,
it'll be a cheap loss," Quint said with Colin nodding his agreement.
"You'll need a second person with you. Take Kira," Quint said, walking off before Colin could respond.

He picked Kira partly because it was long past time for them
to finish mending fences. The tension was affecting their performance and affecting the crew. Unaware of Kira's health issues,
he also felt that with everything else going on, she was the most
qualified of the crew available to assist Colin since her search operations were now complete.

"Mimi, grab the lifting harness and give me a hand launching the
tender," Colin shouted over the raging wind. A minute later, they had

the harness in place and were hoisting the tender over the side. Several times the wind threatened to snatch it away, but finally the tender was in the water.

"Okay, let's get dat bomb so we can skeddadle out of here," LaRue yelled over the whipping wind. He jumped into the water with a splash, his airhose and communications line trailing behind. A second diver entered behind, following the safety line marking the bomb's location. The ship was not rocking too wildly yet, but with the wind increasing, the seas would build swiftly.

LaRue quickly located the airlift lying on the bottom and swam it over to where the bomb's fin protruded from the mud. Placing the end of the metal nozzle beside it, he switched it on and began cutting a swath through the mud while the second diver manned an airlift on the opposite side.

On *Searcher's* bridge, Dakota grabbed the satphone on the first ring—it was Rogers. The conversation was brief, but it was clear Dakota was upset as he hung up to page Quint.

"Uh, Quint, this is Dakota."

"Yeah, go ahead."

"Rogers called, and we've got good and bad news. The good news is Rogers has figured out which of those three possible targets are terrorists."

"Great! Which one?"

"All of them—that was the bad news," Dakota replied causing Quint to exhale as if he had been gut punched.

"How much time do we have?" Quint asked.

"I'd say about an hour, with the other two 30 minutes to an hour later, depending on which way we run," Dakota replied. "One more thing, Rogers had something else he needs to talk directly to you about."

"Once we get this big-assed bomb up, I'll call him back. Start working on what we do next."

"I'll do what I can but honestly, we don't have much to work with. Good thing that C130 is bringing reinforcements and serious weapons—we're going to need them," Dakota replied.

"Any word on when we can expect the plane?"

"Nope, he said they'd radio us once they're in range. And the worse news is, just like Rogers said, Katrina is now predicted to reach Cat 5 status with winds of 175 miles per hour by tonight," Dakota replied as Quint broke the connection with a groan.

Donning his dive gear, Dawson gave a worried look at the wall of bruised clouds marching across the sound, the strong wind blowing the tops off the sloppy waves. Quint found him ready to step over the side of the ship, now rolling badly in the building seas. "Dakota just spoke with Rogers. All three of those targets are bad guys, so you need to hustle. Things are going to get ugly, and we need every minute we can get." Dawson nodded somberly before splashing over the side. Fingers of lightning flashed amidst the howling wind, and booming thunder hailed Dawson's entry into the frothing waters.

Below, LaRue and the second diver manning the airlifts had made little progress cutting a tunnel through the heavy muck beneath the bomb to attach lifting harnesses. While the tail of the bomb protruded from the bottom, the main body remained deeply buried.

Beneath the surface, the sound of the screaming wind was replaced by the hollow sound of air flowing through Dawson's regulator each time he breathed. Dawson oriented himself then followed the marker buoy line, eager to reach the bottom, pausing only once to clear a stubborn ear.

The mountainous waves churning up the already murky waters made it so tough to see that he nearly landed on LaRue. After reaching the bottom, one glance told Dawson the awful truth—they weren't going to make it.

A bolt of lightning lit the sky as the radio's speaker on the bridge crackled, "*Searcher,* this is Angel One, you copy?"

"This is *Searcher,* go ahead," Dakota replied.

"Our ETA at your location is 10 minutes. You still good for the drop?"

"Roger that. It's nasty but we're ready."

"We'll drop a flare before the package, but with these winds we can't fly below this low ceiling, so we'll be working blind. We'll make the drop just to the west of your coordinates—keep your eyes peeled. I'll hail you just before we dr—" static from another lightening flash masked the end of his transmission.

Dakota picked up the ship's phone, "Colin, the C130 will be here in less than 10 minutes. They plan to drop the equipment load west of us and need us in position and waiting. Then they'll swing back to drop the SEALs." Colin and Kira headed to the aft deck to board the tender.

With the crew holding the tender steady on the starboard side, Colin waited as it rode up the crest of a wave then jumped just before it headed back down. Landing in the middle, he dropped to his knees and caught the handhold on top of the inflatable's hull, then scurried to the stern. Kira tossed down two life jackets and prepared to jump next.

Repeating Colin's maneuver, she waited until the tender was on the wave top. But as she jumped, her left foot caught a line whipped by the wind, sending her sprawling forward. She belly-flopped onto the far side of the inflatable, her momentum carrying her into the seething sea.

Kira swam frantically for the surface, sucking in a lungful of air once her head broke free. Colin dropped to the tender's floor, and stretching as far as he could, snagged a handful of hair to jerk her toward him. Once she was alongside, he grabbed her arms and snatched her into the boat.

"Sorry," he said removing several thick strands of Kira's hair wrapped around his fingers. "Hope I didn't hurt you," he said, his eyes meeting hers. In that instant, Kira knew she would have to tell him.

While donning her life jacket and trying to catch her breath, Kira replied, "You can hurt me that way anytime it saves my life. Thanks," she said, unconsciously rubbing her head where the hair plugs had been yanked free.Without replying, Colin fired up the motor and moved away from the ship before it crushed the tender. The two held on while they plowed across the mountainous waves headed west.

CHAPTER 29

By the time Evie reached the marina, most of the boats in the harbor were gone or had been tied between the ends of opposing slips to ride out the storm in the waterway. Doug pulled his boat into a slip near *Mojito*. After quickly tying a breast line, he helped Evie onto the pier. While she disappeared to gather a few of her things off Quint's boat, he loaded her suitcase into the rental car, and a minute later she reappeared.

"Sorry it took me so long. I knocked my stupid purse off the back of the sofa in the salon. You sure you don't need a hand taking the boat around to the hurricane hole?" Evie asked.

"No thanks. I've been running up the bayou from storms for as long as I can remember. You best get to the airport and out of here before the storm gets any closer." She nodded and headed for the team's rental car. He watched as she drove off then, having confirmed that she was under way as he had promised Quint, returned to his boat and cast off.

Evie was halfway to the airport when she decided to call Quint one last time. She reached into her purse for her phone but could not seem to find it. After pulling to the side of the road and thoroughly searching her purse, she realized it must have fallen out. Cursing, she turned around and headed back to the boat through the torrential rain.

Back aboard *Mojito,* she shook the water from her hair and ran below to find a towel. After drying off, she was headed to the salon to search for her phone when a deep voice startled her, and a familiar face loomed above her—it was the man who had shot at her and shattered the windshield in Quint's car.

"Hi, we meet again. Permit me to introduce myself this time. I'm Talib."

Her thoughts of escape were cut short when his fist shot out, knocking her to the floor unconscious.

Evie awoke lying in the black confines of a car's trunk with her head pounding from Talib's blow. The car's stiff suspension telegraphed each bump to Evie's body, bouncing her about the trunk. By the time the car finally stopped, her entire body was shaken and numb. The lights of a warehouse blinded her when the trunk opened.

"Where are we? Who are you?" she said blinking her eyes. Talib's massive hand jerked her from the trunk, and ignoring her questions, he struck her hard once again with his fist. Stars filled her vision as she collapsed and was dragged into a small room.

"You must be punished for escaping the last time we met," he whispered to her through her half-conscious haze. "I enjoy mixing business with pleasure when it involves punishing an enemy of Islam."

Evie drifted in and out of consciousness as her clothes were ripped from her body but awoke when she felt his heavy body on top of her. Enraged, she pounded on his back with her fists, screaming loudly. Blood from her crushed nose and cheek filled her eyes and blinded her. She felt his weight ease from her chest before his fist struck again, knocking her out for the third time.

Evie was not sure how long she had been unconscious when she awoke to the sound of men's voices and a television in the background. Her head throbbed, and her chest and pelvis were sore from being taken by Talib. Tears softened the dried blood in her eyes and on her broken nose. *What will they do to me?* she wondered with little hope of escape.

She lay there for hours, alternating between crying and sleeping. The only breaks occurred when one of the men appeared to rape her again or when they led her to the bathroom to keep from soiling the already filthy mattress where she lay. Though no food had been offered, she had little appetite. The discomfort caused by her thirst was also lost in the pain emanating from her entire body. *Quint, where are you?"*

"Boy, that Lolo makes the best Panini I've ever had. With the rest of the crew gone, she's working her tail off down in the galley. Any luck getting Evie?" Leo asked, his mouth filled with an enormous bite of his sandwich.

Quint whipped around to stare angrily. "Lolo? She's supposed to be back on shore."

Leo replied with a deer-in-the-headlights expression. "Uh... I think she missed the boat to shore. Thought you knew."

"I damned sure didn't. I'm going to rip Dakota another one."

"You shouldn't be that hard on her; we need somebody to cook and..."

"I don't give a shit what she's doing. We can eat peanut butter sandwiches," Quint replied, then realized it wasn't Leo's fault. "Anyhow, in answer to your question, no, I haven't gotten hold of Evie." Quint had tried to reach Evie several times but figured she was probably still flying back to the Keys.

"You've got your hands full. Why don't I try and let you know if I raise her," Leo offered, partially to get back on Quint's good side.

"Thanks, I'd appreciate that. I'll try one last time," he said as he walked away in hopes of having a private conversation should he actually reach her. Once again, he tried with no luck. *Knowing her, she probably forgot to turn her phone back on as usual,* he thought trying to convince himself not to worry.

Several miles away, the display on Evie's phone glowed beneath the couch in *Mojito's* salon where it dutifully recorded another of Quint's increasingly frantic voice messages.

CHAPTER 30

Rather than jump into the frenzy along with LaRue and the other divers working the airlifts, Dawson hung back to study the situation while trying hard to ignore the throb of his abscessed tooth. *How do we get Big Bertha loaded in less than an hour,* he asked himself. *Looking at those fins, that sucker is probably lying at a 45-degree angle, which puts the bomb's nose several feet down.* Then it struck him.

"Quint, send down a cutting torch and lower the lifting harness," Dawson shouted through the microphone in his dive mask.

"Why, what do you—?"

"No time to explain. Just do it." A minute later, the torch popped into view followed by the harness, the fast-building seas violently jerking both as they descended.

"LaRue, kill the airlifts," Dawson said over the facemask's intercom, then swam to the tail end of the bomb to fire up the torch. A few minutes later, he had a hole cut in each of the four fins and turned off the torch. LaRue, having second-guessed him, already had the lifting harness in position.

"Thanks, LaRue. Now continue working the top of Big Bertha with the airlift. Get as much silt off of as you can." Meanwhile, Dawson and the other diver shackled one end of the harness cables to each fin of the bomb. The slings, intended to go beneath the bomb, lay cast aside.

"Okay, Quint, I've got the harness cables shackled to holes I cut in Big Bertha's fins. The plan is to slide her out of the bottom like we did that cannon off the *Almiranta*. Point *Searcher's* bow at 260 degrees, but tell Dakota to go easy—these fins are corroded badly. I don't want to find out what happens if we split Big Bertha open."

Dakota slowly eased *Searcher's* bow around to the correct heading. With Quint coaching from the back deck, he crabbed the boat until they were nearly over the bomb.

"Dawson, we're ready."

"Go!" he replied. Dakota eased the throttles forward in response.

"I hope this works," Quint said, the concern thick in his voice.

"Me too. While I don't want the terrorists getting this bomb, I also don't want a front-row seat to see this four-ton baby detonate," Dawson said.

Dakota heard the radio bark again. "*Searcher,* this is Angel One, you copy?"

"Angel One, this is *Searcher,* go ahead," he replied, still working the ship's wheel and throttles.

"We're as low as we can get and still keep the wings on in this weather. We'll drop on our initial approach. You on location and ready?"

"Roger that, proceed with the drop."

"We're releasing a flare and—second just before—make the drop," the pilot responded amidst the static from the nearly continuous lightning strikes.

The bright orange glow of a flare appeared beneath the low ceiling nearly a mile away. Dakota could see Kira pointing as Colin turned the tender. "Angel One, we've spotted your flare."

"Roger that, we're just about to drop—" a loud burst of static blared from the speaker, which went silent. A moment later an enormous fireball erupted in the sky.

"Once we deploy the supply pallet, I'll swing farther away from this thunderhead. Be ready to jump," the pilot aboard the C130 said to the SEAL team, struggling to hang on while being buffeted mercilessly. "Things are quickly going to shit, and we need to get this big mother out of here while the wings are still attached."

"Roger," the loadmaster replied. "Okay, boys, it's showtime." The team had just unstrapped and were preparing for their jump when an explosion burst the crew's eardrums. The massive bolt of lightning sent a tendril snaking up the open loading ramp, killing the loadmaster and his two crew men. An instant later, the wing tank exploded, launching five of the SEALs through the plane's open tail while the plane, along with the rest of the SEALs and their weapons load, plummeted toward the wild sea.

On the seabed below, the cables drew taut from the increasing strain. LaRue and the diver on the second airlift continued to suck mud away from the bomb, desperately trying to help free it. "LaRue, it's time for you guys to get the hell away from there!" Both men ignored Dawson's orders while continuing to work away at the muck.

The tightening steel cable worked the tail of the bomb back and forth as the waves slammed against the ship. The crew on the back deck sought refuge behind the *Searcher's* steel structure for protection in case one of the banjo-string-tight cables broke. "Dawson, talk to us. What's happening?"

"Nothing. Absolutely nothing. It's wiggling a little from the wave action on the cable, but it isn't budging. How far off are the bad boys?"

"Not far. Probably 30 minutes. Look, we need only one pair of eyes down there, and if this doesn't work, we're screwed anyhow. Why don't you send the rest of the guys topside?"

"Because these crazy bastards are still jetting away the muck to try to get Big Bertha out. Have Dakota increase throttle."

"You sure?"

"No—but do it anyway," Dawson knew it was risky, but with no option, it was a risk they would have to take.

Dakota held his breath while easing the throttles on *Searcher's* big diesels ahead yet further, cringing at the force they were placing on the cables and hoping they were not about to rip the bomb apart. LaRue's airlifts had exposed nearly half the bomb's back and most of either side of the bomb's tail. Dawson was just about to tell Quint to back off when the bomb lurched.

"Dakota back off! We just got slack on one of the harness cables," Quint yelled. "Dawson, what happened? Talk to me!"

It took a few seconds for the silt to drift away so that Dawson could see. "It looks like one of the shackles pulled through the metal on the top fin. But wait... Big Bertha slid nearly a foot before the cable end broke loose. Have Dakota ease forward again and keep shifting the heading 20 degrees to either side. Maybe we can wiggle her free."

Dakota worked the wheel back and forth, slowly easing the bomb forward. "It's working." Dawson's voice erupted from the intercom. A minute later, the bomb was free of the mud and sliding across the bottom. "Halt. She's free!" Dawson yelled. "Start winching her up. Oh, and jettison the airlifts—we're done with them."

Willy leapt across the heaving deck to engage the winches. "Dakota, ease *Searcher* back until we're over it," Willy said while watching the angle of the cable change. He continued to take up slack until the bomb was beneath them. "Okay, maintain position."

Dakota struggled to keep the ship in position as the mounting waves crashed against them. On the back deck, the groaning winches hefted the 7,600-pound bomb off the bottom. Cautiously, the divers approached to inspect the bomb for severe damage and corrosion, finding it remarkably unscathed after having been buried in the mud for 50 years.

"Quint, Big Bertha looks to be in pretty good shape. Guess they don't build 'em like this anymore," Dawson said.

"I hope they're not building them period. Get up here so we can be ready to run once she's on board," Quint ordered.

Colin and Kira looked on in open-mouthed horror as the enormous one-winged plane broke through the clouds in flames before the sudden realization hit Colin—it was headed right at them. Hoping to gain a few extra yards, he swung the motor to the left then gunned the throttle. The tender leapt around to head north through the pitching waves running down sea. Kira stared fixedly over his shoulder as the plane seemed to be locked onto them, the remaining wing slicing toward them like an enormous knife. Colin coaxed the tender to move faster.

As the plane plummeted, the fuselage rotated and was now sideways, so close that Kira could see the slit in the belly where the landing gear was stowed and the windshield behind which the helpless pilot still sat harnessed. She closed her eyes and prayed as Colin braced himself.

By the time the divers surfaced, wind-blown spray poured over the ship. The seas had increased and were now breaking hard against the far side of *Searcher*. Getting back aboard was not going to be fun. "Dawson, gather the divers on the leeward side. We're lowering a scaffold to hoist you up two at a time. But hustle, things are getting worse quick," Quint yelled over the roar of the wind.

Dawson saw the scaffold hit the water and then jerk back into the air as the boat rolled. The first two divers waited for it to descend again then climbed onto the scaffold. The rolling boat rocketed them out of the water to be dragged aboard by the crew stationed along the side.

As Dawson waited for his turn, he was shocked to see the hulk of the burning C130 falling a mile from the boat. "*Damn*," he said to himself in awe from his front-row seat.

The scaffold's reappearance forced Dawson to shift his attention back to escaping the angry seas. As the ship rolled, he sailed out of the water but was jerked backwards off the scaffolding when his tether and air hose snagged on one of the ship's through-hull fittings. Realizing what was happening, he yielded to the pull on his tether and rolled off the scaffold, striking the water hard.

Reaching for his chest harness straps, he found the emergency knife in its inverted sheath while swimming frantically away before the ship could come crashing down on him. A downward pull freed the blade, and he slashed at the tangled tether, communications, and air hose lines, the latter torn and no longer delivering air.

Dropping the knife, he ripped the full face mask from his head and burst through the surface to suck in air. An orange life ring nearly struck him on the head, and he worked both arms through it as the crew retrieved the line, drawing him toward the boat. While they lifted him from the churning waters, he struggled to remain facing the boat, cushioning himself with his feet each time the boat rolled to avoid being bashed senseless. A minute later, he lay on the deck, too weak to stand.

"Now that wasn't so bad, was it?" Quint smiled down at him. Dawson lacked both the energy and the will to respond. With the divers back aboard, the crew resumed winching up the bomb. With the bomb's full weight now suspended on the cables, Willy timed the winch operation to take advantage of the ship's pitch, thereby reducing the strain on the lifting cables.

The C130 continued to tumble as it fell, striking the ocean tail first, the ragged stub of the missing wing landing just behind Colin. With the tail below the surface, the plane pitchpoled, landing upside down, the spray nearly filling the tender. The force ripped off the remaining wing, freeing its load of fuel to pour onto the ocean's surface, where it was instantly set ablaze by flames from the burning fuselage.

Kira opened her eyes to realize the tender was sitting where the first wing would have been had it not already been torn off. Her relief was short-lived as an orange explosion from the fresh load of fuel erupted, so close she could feel the heat on her face singeing the rear of the inflatable's tubes.

With the throttle wide open, Colin moved away from the burning wreckage. They rode to the top of a giant wave then surfed down the far side, gaining enough distance to escape being burned alive. Free of the falling plane and burning fuel, Colin took stock of their situation. They were over a mile from *Searcher* and out of sight of the ship except when they topped the larger waves. The tender was filled with water, and the fuel tank bobbed about at their feet.

"Kira, grab the fuel tank. If we get water in it, we're done," Colin said.

Kira wedged her feet between the inflatable's tubes and the deck to keep from being flung from the boat. Then holding the fuel tank with one hand she bailed with the other using a plastic cup.

"We're still headed down wind, away from the ship. We've got to get turned around, so stop bailing and hang on," Colin said. He knew that if he turned sideways and broached, the next wave would capsize the tiny boat, drowning them in the wind-whipped seas.

Kira yelled something.

"What?" Colin replied unable to hear over the howling wind.

Her head whipped around to face him and, in a moment that would be forever frozen in his memory, yelled, "I'm pregnant. You're going to be a father." She then turned back around and grabbed hold of the tender while Colin saw his chance and went for it.

He had nearly turned the boat when the raging wind lifted the bow off the top of the wave. Reacting instinctively, Kira threw herself to the front of the boat, teetering on the edge of overturning. With her added weight the bow was forced down, and the boat eased over the wave's crest to surf down the far side.

Colin continued toward *Searcher,* his mind replaying the scene over and over of Kira's announcing her pregnancy. As they slugged their way through the waves, he caught a glimpse of red just off their port bow and altered course. "Kira, there's something floating up ahead from the wreckage of the plane. Take this stern line and see if you can secure it. Maybe we can tow it back to *Searcher.*"

Colin eased toward the slender red plastic container. He could make only one attempt, unable to risk another try if they missed. As he came alongside, Kira grabbed the large handle protruding from the red object's side and slid the line through quickly tying two half hitches. "Got it," she said releasing the line to let it follow in their wake. As it passed he read the large stenciled letters on the side of the case: *Smart Underwater Bomb (SUB).*

After a lengthy struggle, they reached the ship where the crew threw a line. Kira quickly tied off the tender as Colin eased alongside. "How do we get back aboard?" he yelled while maintaining position.

"Jump overboard. LaRue's lowering the diver scaffolding, and we'll hoist you up. It's the only way." Kira looked at Colin. While neither seemed enthusiastic about Quint's solution, they had nothing better to offer, and after cinching their lifevests tight, eased over the side of the tender opposite the ship. Once they were in the water, Quint pulled the tender toward the back of the ship where he tied it off clear of the crane lifting the bomb.

A minute later, Colin and Kira appeared, climbing over the side of the ship from the scaffold. With eager hands, Leo and Jacques helped them onto the heaving deck, where Colin looked up and yelled, "Guys, I'm going to be a daddy!"

Leo and Jacques stared back, certain that Colin had struck his head.

By the time the bomb was nearly to the surface, Colin had recovered and joined the crew on the back deck. "What are you doing with our tender?" he asked pointing at the tender lying sideways just out of the water on the ship's sloping aft deck, the red SUB case secured on the deck to one side.

"It's no longer our tender. That's the ship's inflatable nuclear bomb cradle. We decided we needed to prevent the bomb from being detonated worse than we needed a tender," Quint replied. Colin nodded his hearty consent then lugged the SUB forward out of the way and tied it off to a cleat amidships.

"Dakota, we're ready to bring Big Bertha on deck. Ease us forward and keep us steady as you can in this slop," Willy radioed the bridge while he manned the winch.

"Will do. Good luck. And Willy... be gentle," Dakota replied.

"Okay, guys. Let's do it. I'll bring her up slowly," Willy said after he had gained a feel for the seas. "Position the tender to cushion Big Bertha as best you can. Here comes the harness end. Quint, yell when you see her."

Peering over the stern Quint yelled, "She's up," as soon as the bomb broke the surface.

Searcher plunged down the next wave, and the bomb swung forward over the tender. Quint reached out for the handling line attached to the harness to help control it while Willy raised the arm of the crane swinging the bomb onto the ship. The crew slid the inflatable beneath the bomb, which now hung less than a foot off the deck.

As *Searcher* climbed the next wave, Dakota's voice screamed over the ship's PA, "Rogue wave! Hang on!" An instant later the ship slammed into a massive wave, the deck shuddering in response. The force slammed the crane arm forward, and a loud crack accompanied the snap of one of the lifting cables. The crew on the back deck looked on in horror as the nose of the bomb fell to the deck, crushing the inflatable while all held their breath, praying it would not explode.

With only two lifting cables and the handling line holding it, the bomb lay with its nose on the crushed inflatable, which had cushioned the blow. The bomb's tail teetered between falling into the ship and backwards into the sea. Willy eased the winch in gear, and the bomb slowly swung forward as he took up the slack. A minute later, the 12-foot-long, 7,600-pound bomb lay atop the ruined tender.

Willy killed power to the winches and ordered the crew to lash the bomb in place before it could roll or swing about. He stood catching his breath and drenched, partly from the windblown spray but mostly from his own perspiration caused by the tense ordeal of hoisting the bomb aboard.

The first tiedowns were nearly in place when the ship took another huge wave on the beam and heeled over on her port side. The bomb, not yet restrained, rolled across the deck. A horrified crewman, who saw it coming but could not move out of the way fast enough, was crushed between the bomb and the side of the ship, blood spraying across the deck. As the ship righted itself, the bomb rolled back toward the center, freeing the crewman's body to slide off the back of the ship and quickly disappear in their wake.

"Don't let that sonofabitchin' bomb slide overboard too. We can't lose it now," Willy yelled into the howling wind. Immediately, Jacques leapt across the bomb and resecured the tiedowns. Finally, the bomb was under control, too late for the unfortunate crewman whose body drifted away in the towering seas. The crew would mourn the loss of one of their own, but they would do it later—now they had other problems.

CHAPTER
31

Quint changed clothes and headed for the bridge. Against long odds they had recovered the bomb but still had to elude the terrorists in hot pursuit. "Explain to me why Lolo is still aboard. I thought I made myself clear that she was to leave," he said to Dakota upon entering the bridge.

"You did, and I thought she had. I intended to see her aboard the boat to shore, but you may have noticed, things got a little crazy. I knew you'd be pissed so I sent her to the galley to make sandwiches for the crew. Sorry." Before Quint could reply, the phone rang, and Dakota, grateful for the diversion, quickly answered. "It's Rogers," he said handing over the receiver.

After throwing on dry clothes and bandaging the larger of the cuts from his dive-scaffold encounter, Dawson entered the bridge and spotted Quint on the satphone. "Who's he talking to?"

"Rogers."

"More cheery news?"

"Sounds like it," Dakota answered as Colin and Kira entered the bridge.

"Congratulations—mom and dad," Quint said to the pair as he hung up the phone.

"Huh?" Dawson asked puzzled.

"I guess you were getting patched up when we heard the news— Kira is expecting. These two are parents-to-be."

Dawson's half smile poorly concealed his disappointment—any chance with Kira was now history for sure. Colin seemed to notice the odd expression on his face but said nothing.

"I hate to spoil the party," Dawson continued, "but our SEAL reinforcements just went down in flames along with our planeload of weapons. If the terrorists get the bomb we just worked so hard to recover, they'll probably blow up the ship and us along with it. So my thought, and it's just a thought, is that if you want to live long enough to see that baby, we get the hell out of here while we're all still in one piece," Dawson said, making his sense of urgency clear.

His hand shot to his jaw as he grimaced in pain.

"Tooth again? Quint asked. Dawson nodded somberly.

"With the storm, we won't be getting any more visible-band satellite imagery," Quint continued. "Rogers will see if he can find anything of use in the other bands. One more thing, he thinks we may have our own mole on board."

"What!" Dawson yelled.

"Rogers' group picked up burst mode transmissions from *Searcher* as well as chatter from the terrorists—they know precisely where we are. The only way that's possible is if they have a mole onboard who's sending information or a radio beacon automatically transmitting our position."

"Now *that* pisses me off," Dawson replied angrily.

For an instant, Quint recalled the day he had found Botz on board the ship and wondered if he could be involved before quickly dismissing the thought as absurd. "Dakota, how long do we have before the closest terrorist boat reaches us?" Quint asked.

"About 20 minutes, maybe a little longer; these seas should slow them down. Plus, now that we're moving, their rate of closure has fallen off further. The problem is they're still closing.

"This will help you visualize our situation," Dakota said, motioning for Colin to take the helm as he walked to the starboard side of the bridge, where a chart lay unrolled on the table. "This is Chandeleur Sound," Dakota said, withdrawing some change from his pocket. "These quarters represent our three targets, which are located here, here, and here," he said, placing the quarters onto the chart.

"This brass weight is us, and we're right here. The storm is coming from the southeast, forcing the Navy farther south to ride out the storm. They won't be any help to us until after the storm passes. The boat headed from the west from Grand Isle faces a head sea and will get pounded. Unless we get lucky and they give up, they'll be a while getting here.

"The Lake Borgne boat is headed at us from the northwest, while the Pascagoula boys are headed down our throat from the northeast end of the Mississippi Sound. Rogers' last satellite update showed them hugging the lee side of the barrier islands headed for Ship Island Channel. They probably aren't far away, but without updated satellite imagery we don't know for sure. Oh, and Rogers suspects they may also have a team in Venice, Louisiana, but can't confirm.

"So in summary, unless we head southeast into the storm, any way we turn we'll face one of them. So the question is, 'What do we do?'" Dakota finished as the men studied the chart, and Dawson tapped his finger on the table.

Quint finally spoke: "Without satellite data we're blind, but so are they. Unfortunately, with a beacon operating on our ship, they know exactly where we are and where we're headed. And their chartered boats are most likely faster than *Searcher*. Unless we can find a place to hide, they'll eventually catch us.

"At this point, they'll need frequent position updates, which means transmitting more often. Kira, you and Mimi use the 'sniffer' to see if you can locate the source. If we can't stop the position updates, we're dead!" Kira nodded then left the bridge.

"The worst part is, they won't necessarily just kill us and take Big Bertha. As Dawson mentioned, it's entirely possible they'll detonate the bomb rather than risk getting caught while moving it to a more 'desirable' location. That might not achieve the collateral damage they'd prefer, but it'll still be plenty nasty, especially with this wind dispersing the fallout. What do you guys think?" Quint concluded.

"We could run for open water and either try to elude them or jettison the bomb in deep water before they catch us. They would play hell retrieving it even if they could relocate it. That, of course, puts things back exactly where we started, which I don't like but at least they might not get the weapon," Colin said.

"Or we can fight them, which is going to be tough, especially if all three of their boats make it into the Sound. Without the SEALs and the weapons package Rogers tried to airdrop, we're down to a couple of guns or maybe throwing canned goods," Dawson added.

"Or we can try to outrun them up Baptiste Collette bayou to the Mississippi river and hide out in Venice," Dakota said.

Kira's call on the ships' phone interrupted their debate. "Quint, we found the mole's transmitter. Meet me in Search."

Quint turned to Dakota. "Keep running toward Baptiste Collette while I deal with our mole problem."

"You got it," Dakota said, steel in his voice.

Quint stopped as he noticed Leo entering the bridge munching on yet another sandwich. "Any word from Evie?"

"No, with this storm coming, the circuits are slammed. I'll

keep trying. I wouldn't worry too much; she's probably trying too but can't get through." Quint nodded and eased the door closed behind him. Maybe Leo was right, but until he heard Evie's voice, he would worry.

"Where did you find the transmitter?" Quint asked as he walked into Search Operations.

"In an overhead compartment in the doghouse on top of the dive locker where no one goes very often. It was set to transmit on auto so we disabled the antenna," Kira said.

"Now we got an edge."

"How so?" Kira asked.

"Either it's automatically transmitting our position or we do have a mole who has been updating it with a laptop. Since the terrorists don't know we're onto them, we can transmit whatever position we please." Quint picked up a ship's phone, "Dakota, talk to me about our three targets."

"Extrapolating from their previous position, and allowing for the weather, I'm guessing the boys to the northeast are still slugging it out but haven't made much headway so they're probably a several miles away. Same for the boat out of Lake Borgne. If the guys from Grand Isle are headed toward us from the south and have shallow enough draft, they could be at the mouth of the Sound in 15 to 20 minutes. Of course, they may also run up southwest pass intending to meet us in Baptiste Collette."

"I'll be right up," Quint responded. "Kira, figure out how to download position data to that thing so we can send our own message. We don't have much time, so be quick. Bring it along with a laptop to the bridge when you're ready."

"So what about the mole; who do you think it is?" Quint asked then noticed Dawson grimacing. "You okay?"

"No, this damned abscessed tooth is killing me. I'm not sure I can stand it much longer. Anyhow, in answer to your question, I have no idea," Dawson said as they sought the privacy of the small salon off the bridge. "Jacques was concerned about LaRue's gambling and money problems. And he did join us late because he had problems with raising the money to invest with the team after having just been paid his share a few weeks earlier."

"Yeah, then there's Rogers' folks, like your girlfriend, Rachel, who could have 'hooked up' with someone on board," Quint said with a smile. Dawson responded with a withering look.

"So how do we find our mole?" Kira asked after joining the two men.

"I don't see that we can. For now, we'll just have to keep our eyes open," Dawson replied.

Quint nodded, then said, "You don't think it could be Willy?"

"What could be Willy?" a voice from behind them spoke up. Quint whirled around and came face-to-face with the big man.

Damn, who invited the whole damned ship to our private mole discussion? thought Quint. They stood staring at each other for a minute before Quint broached the subject. "We were discussing who might have a motive to be our mole."

"Any you think it's me? Willy said, incredulous.

"I don't know. When you went ashore in Pass Christian, I saw you meet someone in an alleyway, and it sure looked a lot like a drug buy."

Willy looked off—it was clear Quint had struck a nerve. "Well, that's because it was."

Quint looked at Dawson in surprise. "You admit to buying drugs?" Dawson asked.

"Yeah, but not the type you think. My niece is a victim of the Wolf," Willy said in full explanation. When it was obvious the two men did not understand, he continued. "Lupus. We hoped to get her in a clinical trial, but she's too sick to be admitted into the program. There are drugs used successfully outside the U.S. but not approved for use in the States. I located a guy in New Orleans who agreed to help me smuggle a few batches into the country. That's who you saw me meet. I gave him most of the money that I could scrape together to save my niece's life. So if that makes me your 'mole,' oh well.

"Besides, if as you say one of us is a mole then why have the transmitter on auto? Why not load it manually along with other key information on our status, etc.?"

"Good point," Dawson conceded.

"Okay, we can't have the team falling apart with each of us suspecting everyone else. So we'll assume it was placed on board earlier, and we no longer have a mole onboard," Quint said. He and Kira stepped back out to the bridge to speak with Dakota, but Dawson lingered.

"Willy, I need a favor."

Willy looked surprised. "You want a favor from a mole?"

"Get over it. You *were* buying illegal drugs, just not the type we suspected. Willy, I can't stand the pain of this tooth any longer," Dawson said, and then told him what he needed.

"Okay, where do we stand?" Quint asked as he reentered the bridge.

"We just picked up a target on the radar moving fast out of the northeast. I'm guessing it's the Pascagoula team," Dakota replied. "They're about here," he said pointing to the chart.

Jacques stood beside Quint studying the chart for a few minutes. "Shouldn't we have enough water to make it across this shallows area?" Jacques asked Dakota.

"Yeah, with the water high from the storm. But we'd get slammed against the bottom every time we came off a big wave. I'm not sure how much of that *Searcher* can take."

Jacques continued, "I'm guessing the terrorists were hard pressed to find anyone crazy enough to take them out in this slop, so there's a good chance they stole the boat and are running it themselves.

"With the rising storm surge, this rock jetty near the old Gulf Outlet should be nearly submerged by now. If we send them a 'mole update,' putting our position just past the jetty, I'll bet they come directly at that position without bothering to check their charts.

"Meanwhile, we head straight for Baptiste Collette across those shallows."

"I hope you're right," Quint replied. "Because if you're not, they'll catch us."

"Trust me; they'll never see the jetty until they're on it," Jacques said.

"Dakota, what do you think?" Quint asked.

"The transmitter has been down long enough for that position to appear possible. So, provided we don't destroy our running gear, it could work."

"We'll see just how tough this mother is. Dakota, give me the coordinates for a position just south of Jacques' jetty location," Quint said. "Kira, we need to send this immediately," Quint said, handing her a scrap of paper with the coordinates he had scribbled.

Kira loaded the coordinates into the mole's transmitter with the laptop and headed below to reconnect its antenna. A minute later, she reported that the green status light indicated the data appeared to be transmitting.

"Now Jacques, let's see if our boys fall for your trap," Quint said.

"Hang on," Dakota said as *Searcher* slammed hard against the bottom of the shallows area as he had predicted. "Damn," he yelled, but *Searcher* kept plowing forward, hitting bottom on every third wave. With little choice, he throttled back to keep from shearing off their running gear.

The crew stared as Dawson emerged from the small salon carrying a partially-full bottle of whiskey. "For medicinal purposes," he said and slipped out the door with Willy. Once in his stateroom, Dawson unscrewed the cap, placed it to his lips, and emptied the bottle.

When it became obvious that the liquor had taken affect, Willy removed the pliers from his pocket. "Okay, let's deal with this tooth." Dawson obediently leaned back, opening his mouth. Kira heard his blood-curdling scream all the way in the salon and looked horrified when Willy walked through a minute later carrying a pair of pliers and wiping blood from his hands.

Beneath the churning seas, each time the keel struck bottom, a rotten section of hull plating flexed. After the fourth impact, a crack formed in the weld between two plates, and water began rushing into the hull.

"Jacques, you're a freakin' genius. They've altered course and are headed right at the jetty," Dakota reported, staring at the radar display. Quint's stomach knotted as the terrorists rapidly closed the distance.

"Come on, hit the jetty. Hit the jetty," Quint muttered under his breath until the target abruptly stopped. He studied the radar display for a minute to be certain. "It worked! They're dead in the water," he finished as the massive seas slammed *Searcher* into the bottom again.

"Okay guys, kill the mole transmitter and let's head for Baptiste Collette. Maybe the other boats won't make it this far or, if they do, will have gotten the bogus message and head for the jetty," Quint said. They continued through the sloppy seas, slamming the bottom on occasion when Dakota spoke up.

"A new target just entered the sound from the north, probably the Lake Borgne team. They may have nailed us on their radar," he added glumly.

"Shit!" Quint muttered. "Can't we catch a break?"

"You want to keep heading for Baptiste Collette?"

"Do we have a choice? Keep an eye on the other boat. Maybe they can't keep us on radar in all this slop. Or, better yet, won't figure out it's us."

A few minutes later, they were not hitting bottom as often or as hard when Dakota spoke again. "The second boat is headed our way. The first one is still dead in the water where it hit the—" a high-pitched squeal interrupted him.

"What the hell's that?" Quint asked.

Dakota glanced at the alarm panel, "High water alarm. We must have a break in the hull from all that pounding—we're sinking."

CHAPTER 32

Evie awoke with a start and brushed her face—a hulking cockroach seeking moisture had found her lips. "Eeek," she shrieked and scooted up in bed, sending several large shadows scurrying for cover like politicians under harsh scrutiny. The floor seemed virtually alive, and on the far side she saw the much larger shadow of a rat skulking along the edge of the floor. Evie spent the rest of the night leaned in the corner, balled up and periodically shooing away more moisture-seeking bugs.

By dawn, she finally dozed off in time to be awakened for her morning rape. She no longer struggled; after her repeated beatings she knew it was futile. Instead, she focused on something far away in her childhood, a pleasant memory of picking roses with her mother, to escape the brutality. Her breasts and privates ached from being raped, her hands and arms from her struggles, and her face and body from the blows which rained in against her pitiful resistance.

For the first time in her life she felt beaten—she wanted to die. *How can I ever feel clean again? Who would want to be with me now? Quint deserves better than what I've become,* she said to herself as the savagery worked on her psyche.

After her latest rapist left still buckling his trousers, she returned to the present to study the room. The barred window positioned in the solid concrete block wall far above was too small to escape through even if she could somehow find a way to reach it and remove the bars. The heavy steel door led into the room where *they* always remained—there was no escape.

For an instant, she considered how she might kill herself, but then forced the thought from her mind. *Where's Quint?* she wondered. Her thoughts were interrupted as the door opened, and she was forced into a van to take her farther south.

Akmed met Talib and the rest of his men at Rashid's marina in Venice, Louisiana. He entered the filthy makeshift cell with a photo to confirm that they had kidnapped the right woman. As he emerged, he dialed Rashid. "We've got Quint's woman. We've moved her to Venice where she's likely to be handy if needed for leverage."

Rashid leaned back in his desk chair with a broad smile. "Excellent!"

"And I have three boats in pursuit. One out of Pascagoula, another from Lake Borgne, and yet a third on its way from Grand Isle," Akmed confirmed.

"Good. With the storm approaching, things will get messy. If we're unable to seize their ship with the bomb still aboard, she may indeed give us the leverage we need to deal with them."

"And if we don't need her?"

"Then do as you please with her. Just see to it that she causes me no problems," Rashid said and hung up.

CHAPTER
33

"How bad is the leak?"

"Don't know. I'll get Willy to divert the engine raw water intakes to the bilge. Maybe between that and the bilge pumps we can remain afloat."

A few minutes later, Willy rang Dakota back on the ship's phone, "Bad news—we're still sinking. The damaged area is no longer accessible, and even with the pumps fully engaged, the water is still rising. I can secure the compartment where the water appears to be entering but, if it floods all the way, we still may sink."

"Seal the compartment," Dakota said and turned to Quint. "What you want to do?"

"Keep heading up river. If it looks like we're about to go under, we'll either run her aground or scuttle her depending on our position and how close the boys behind us are at the time." Dakota nodded, returning his focus to running the ship while Quint's mind raced.

When they entered the still waters of Baptiste Collette, *Searcher* stopped rolling. A short time later, their pursuers followed down the bayou, steadily closing the distance. Ahead, the Mississippi River emerged from the wind-driven spray. "How far behind us are they?"

Dakota glanced at the radar, "A little over two miles. At least the boys from Grand Isle didn't arrive in time to meet us," Dakota said as he emerged into the giant Mississippi River and angled south, heading for Venice on the far side. Quint glanced at the chart and noted that once they entered the channel leading to Venice, they would be out of view from the river, and the structures would block the terrorists' radar.

"Maybe we'll get lucky, and they'll think we headed up the Mississippi River," Quint said as they approached the Venice waterfront, which was filled with barges, heavy equipment, and warehouses. Ahead, Quint noticed several empty barges tied up on the left, but on the right a tug was tied to—*a fuel barge*. "I have an idea. Dakota, swing close enough to that fuel barge for me to leap on.

Where's Dawson?"

"He just finished having some dental work done by Willy," Dakota went on to explain. "It'll be a while before he's back in service."

"When he sobers up from his 'procedure,' tell him to work on what we do if my plan doesn't work. I'll take a VHF radio, listen on channel 72. Have Leo keep trying to raise Evie, I'm worried. LaRue—come with me," Quint barked as he headed out the door. He made a quick stop to stuff a few items into a small daypack and ran to starboard as Dakota brought *Searcher* in close.

Quint keyed the radio. "Dakota, come as close as you can and slow, but don't stop. Once we're off the boat, haul ass." Quint stuck the radio into his bag and stepped over the railing with LaRue beside him. He eyed the line of approaching weather and heard the rolling thunder signaling its imminent arrival. The wind had picked up, and a white sheet of rain hung midway across the river. *Just hold off for a few more minutes*, Quint prayed.

Lolo appeared from around the corner, and Quint started to light into her about ignoring his order to go ashore. "Lolo, you don't know how mad..." She interrupted him by thrusting a plastic bag filled with sandwiches into his hand. He looked at the sandwiches then, noticing that they were alongside the fuel barge, turned back to her. "Thanks. We'll talk later."

Both men leaped across the gap. Quint skidded on the slick deck and went sprawling. He landed on the bag of sandwiches while his pack slid to the rusted edge of the barge, where he watched helplessly as it teetered for a moment and then fell into the water. "Damn!"

LaRue scooped up the bag before it could drift away, too late to save the phone and radio. Ignoring the damaged electronics, Quint jumped to his feet and waved at Dakota, who yelled back from the wheelhouse, "Good luck!"

"What's da plan, Hoss?" LaRue asked.

"We're going to prepare a warm welcome for the terrorists. Hook a length of fuel hose to that discharge line. Then see if you can find some reducing fittings to jury-rig a nozzle." LaRue nodded and went to work. Quint found the fuel system control panel sealed with a large padlock. He removed a pistol from his shoulder bag.

"Cajun crowbar," LaRue said as he saw what Quint had in mind.

"Yeah, I just hope this wind is strong enough to blow away the fumes from any leaks, or we're likely to have a Cajun funeral."

Both men cringed for fear of an explosion as Quint fired a round at the lock. They breathed a sigh of relief when none followed, and the lock fell to the deck in pieces. Quint flipped open the control box door and studied the various breakers and valves.

A minute later, he looked back at LaRue, "You ready?"

"Ready, Hoss."

"Point the hose over the side and hang on," Quint yelled as he switched on the pump breaker and heard the sound of a large motor spooling up, but nothing happened. He studied the system and turned on a valve which sent a geyser of fuel erupting into the air from the aft end of the barge. Luckily, it was downwind and blew harmlessly off the barge. Quint quickly shut the valve off and turned on a second one. LaRue's hose came to life, and fuel spurted over the side until Quint shut it off.

"Let's see how far you can reach." After a brief test, Quint turned the valve back off.

"Secure your end of the hose from whipping about," Quint replied. LaRue found a length of rope and tied the hose to a cleat. "Follow me," Quint said returning to the control panel. "We'll take a position up on the bridge of that tug to get out of this weather. When we spot the terrorists coming up the river, you can dash back down," Quint said. "You'll need to turn this breaker on and open that valve to start the fuel flowing out of the hose.

"If they pass close enough, soak their boat with fuel. If they don't, hose down the river around them. In either case, I'll ignite the fuel with a flare. If we don't stop them, maybe we'll at least slow them down."

"Got it, Hoss," LaRue replied. The two men headed for the tug boat as the bottom fell out of the sky—the rain had not held off.

Beneath the *Searcher* the opening in the weakened hull had widened, worsening the leak and making the ship sluggish as she filled with water. Knowing the end was near, Dakota frantically scanned the banks of the bayou for someplace to ground the boat.

Quint and LaRue shook the water from their hair and clothing as they entered the bridge of the tug, relieved for at least a temporary respite. "Care for a smashed sandwich?" Quint asked, offering him the bag. The two men made small talk while watching the rain and eating their mangled lunch.

"I hope Rashid is with these guys. I'd love to get my hands on him," Quint said.

"Who's he, Hoss?"

Quint explained how Dawson had heard Rashid's name mentioned when he was kidnapped.

"That's interesting," LaRue replied.

"How so?"

"I heard Berto," LaRue paused, "da man who gave me des black eyes, talkin about selling land to some Rashid guy. Didn't sound like he liked him much. Can't be many Rashids around."

Quint glanced at LaRue's face, which was still bruised but healing. *Now's the perfect time to explore Jacques' concern about LaRue,* he thought. "So, you going to tell me what really happened to your face before you finally joined up with the team, or is that going to remain a big secret?"

LaRue stood silent for a moment, then spoke . "It ain't no big secret, Hoss, I just didn't want to talk about my stupidity. I got me a gamblin' problem."

"Tell me you didn't gamble away your share of the *Almiranta* treasure. That was over a half million dollars!"

"No, Hoss. Before I hook'd up with you, I borrowed $35,000 from Mr. Berto, a loan shark, to settle my gambling debts. I figured it'd grown to $100,000 or so, and I'd square things with plenty left over once the *Almiranta* loot was distributed. So I goes to see Mr. Berto.

"He located his office in a medical clinic. Nobody think to look der for sure. I climbed da stairs where there was a door with this big guy sitting in scrubs. Didn't look much like no doctor with that bulge beneath his arm I'm guessing is a gun. He sees me and puts down his magazine, but don't say nothing. I say, 'I'm LaRue, here to see Mr. Berto.' Den I members da code phrase, 'They didn't have no anchovy pizza,' I says thinking what a stupid phrase is dat.

"He nods then pushes a button beneath da desk to unlock the door. This other big guy grunts at me to hold up my arms and frisks me. As I walk in da office, I hear Mr. Berto's aide, saying, 'He's in to us for $110,000 and with our regular vig, he's up to $250,000 but that boy been running his mouth. The word on the street is he just finished a job and be holding $500,000.' I admit, I likes to talk when I get into the sauce—not too smart.

"Mr. Berto says, 'Well, you forgot our monthly service fee and accelerated interest rate.' Then he shuts up as I walk in. Mr. Berto was leaned back in his chair smokin' dat cigarette. 'LaRue, how nice to see you. How you been?' he says.

"'Fine, Mr. Berto. I be here to settle up on dat loan I owe you. I told you I was good for it.' He smiles and said, 'Excellent. I like customers who settle their accounts. How much does he owe?" His aide thumbs through this tattered notebook and says, 'Well, let's see. We got $110,000 balance, plus interest for what, six months, plus the monthly service fee, a late fee, and an accelerated interest adder. Come to $635,000.'

Boss, you could'a knocked me over with a feather. I axed him how I owe so much, and Mr. Berto shakes his head, 'LaRue, LaRue, you lost gambling, and we bailed you out. Now, this is the gratitude you show, questioning our rates?'

"I says, 'Mr. Berto, I don' got that much.' He axed me how much I got."

"I told him, 'How 'bout I pay you $300,000, and we call it even?'

Mr. Berto nods to these gangster-looking guys. One grab me by da arms while da other starts punching me. They beat me some kinda' bad, and I'm laying in a pool of blood with my nose all broken, puking on da floor.

"Mr. Berto says, 'LaRue, do you think I be stupid? How much you got?' I don't want no more beating so when I finished vomiting I says, "$500,000. I give it all to you and call it even.'

"But that wasn't good enough. Mr. Berto says, 'I'll take the $500,000 but I can't call it even. You think I can let people pay whatever they want whenever they want? Why I'd be out of business in a week. Get me da $500,000. When can I expect da balance?'

"I wasn't gonna' tell him no more, but then those two big dudes stepped toward me, and I agreed if he leave me $250,000 to buy into this deal, I could pay him da rest after we finish. Hoss, I didn't want to but was afraid dey kill LaRue."

Quint shook his head and took the last bite of his sandwich. "That's incredible. Maybe the team needs to pay Berto a visit when we get done here. What kind of criminal stuff is he into?"

"Damn near everything. If dere's money in it, you can bet he's in on it, Hoss."

The two men stood in silence lulled by the sound of the wind-driven rain on the tug's windows. As they stared down the river hoping to spot the terrorists when they rounded the bend, Quint's mind wandered. He hoped the terrorists had been suckered up river, but he doubted they would be fooled for long. He wondered why the tug had been left rather than moved to a safer location. A fax lying beside the wheel gave the answer. The engine was down, and they were waiting on parts.

"Hoss, I think I go back down and wait to make sure I be ready when they come," LaRue said, stepping back into the weather.

For a moment Quint thought about their mole. *Could it be LaRue? Maybe he didn't tell me everything. Could he be working for Berto? Is their plan to sabotage our effort to get the bomb so they can get it to sell?* Quint wondered. *I've got to stop the second guessing. Besides, maybe someone outside of our crew planted the transmitter—like Botz.*

The wind-blown rain whipped LaRue's hair about as he crouched behind the control panel to shield himself from the full brunt of the weather. A shiver ran through him as he pulled the collar tighter around his neck in a futile attempt to stop the icy fingers of water that ran down his neck and drenched his shirt. He kept his eyes riveted to the tug wheelhouse to make certain he didn't miss Quint's signal in all the wind noise.

For the fiftieth time, Quint checked the flare gun he had removed from his shoulder bag and practiced loading a spare shell. He might have time for a second shot, but he doubted there would be a third. Reaching back in his pocket for the hundredth time, he retrieved his cell phone to dial Evie's number but it went straight to voicemail. While trying to decide what to do about her, he swatted at a pesky gnat buzzing around his face and cursed as it flew into his left eye.

Quint crossed the bridge to use a shiny strip of metal as a mirror. He forced his watering eye open in search of the pest but his repeated attempts to remove the insect from his eye proved futile while taking more time than he realized. Turning to check the river, he cursed—a boat had already rounded the bend and was rapidly closing.

Quint snatched up the binoculars and peered through them with his good eye to confirm it was the terrorists and not some poor souls running from the storm. When he saw a man armed with an AK-47, Quint shouldered opened the tug's bridge door and yelled into the howling wind, "It's show time."

LaRue replied with a thumbs up and opened the valve. After flipping the breaker, he confirmed a stream of fuel was flowing from the hose then duck-walked back down the barge. As he reached the hose end, he looked in horror as the stream of fuel dwindled. "Shit," he exclaimed as he scurried back to the control panel.

On the tug, Quint waited, the delay renewing his doubts about LaRue. In a matter of seconds, the boat would be past them. LaRue noticed another valve labeled "vent" and turned it on—the stream rapidly increased, and he resumed his position once again.

With his watering left eye closed, Quint watched the boat come out of the turn heading for the narrow spot in the river between the fuel barge and the barges moored on the far side. *Please come this way*, Quint prayed as he held his breath and crossed his fingers. He exhaled with a smile—the boat was headed right at them.

"LaRue, they'll come within range so hold off until you can hit the boat with a steady stream. Then hose them down," Quint yelled over the wind's fury.

"You got it, Hoss. What if dat ain't da right boat?" LaRue yelled back.

"Then I hope they have on their fireproof underwear," Quint replied with a chuckle, masking his nervousness over just that issue. Even if the radio hadn't been ruined when it got dunked, it wasn't like he could call them and ask, *Hey you guys wouldn't happen to be terrorists looking for a nuclear bomb, would you*? The man with the AK-47 would have to be adequate confirmation—the stakes were too high to risk assuming otherwise.

LaRue raised the hose with both hands keeping it pointed down so that the stream would be barely visible as he peeked around the corner of the bulkhead at the approaching boat—it was time.

Searcher was listing badly, and Dakota knew they didn't have much longer. So far, he had been unable to bring himself to scuttle the ship in the river partly because he hated to risk losing the bomb again, partly to avoid admitting defeat, partly to avoid an environmental mess with all the fuel they were still carrying, and partly for sentimental reasons.

With Colin relieving him at the wheel, Dakota strode to the radar, but even with the "rain clutter" feature activated it was hard to make out detail far ahead. Instead, he moved to the chart table to explore his options. The banks of the river were too steep to beach the ship and offered no way to hide. Searching the chart for someplace to duck into, a mile up the river he spotted a narrow branch running off to the right. If he could make it past the first bend, they might have a chance. *But can Searcher stay afloat long enough?* he asked himself.

LaRue rose from behind the short bulkhead and swung the hose until the stream fell onto the foredeck of the approaching boat. Gallons of fuel poured onto the front of the boat, filling every nook and cranny, running down the deck beside the wheelhouse and into the open cockpit in the stern.

The man captaining the boat saw LaRue but wasn't sure what to make of this crazy man with the fire hose. He continued on the same heading while studying the situation. His face changed to a mask of horror at the realization that LaRue was standing on a fuel barge—that was no fire hose he held. Opening his mouth to scream, he saw a flare pass just in front of the wheelhouse, barely missing the boat, and he pulled hard away.

Quint's shaking hands opened the flare gun to insert another round. He swore as it slipped from his fingers and dropped to the deck, rolling beneath the console while the terrorist's boat slipped farther away. Snatching the last round from the counter in front of him, he slammed it into the breach and flipped the flare gun closed.

A man stepped from the bridge of the boat and raised a wicked-looking machine gun. Quint dove to the floor as bullets shattered the tug's windows above, raining glass down upon him. By the time the man had emptied the magazine and Quint brought the flare gun back to bear, the boat was nearly out of range. Steadying himself against the bridge railing of the tug, he carefully aimed, using his good eye, and said a prayer before squeezing the trigger.

Dakota continued downstream and swung the wheel hard over to slide *Searcher* into the narrow river branch he had spotted on the chart. With the boat listing and threatening to capsize, Dakota slowly straightened their course hoping to make the first bend. "Come on baby, just a little farther," he coaxed.

Heavy with the water they had taken on, the boat moved even slower now that they were no longer riding the river current. They approached the bend and made it past. "Thanks, baby. You did it," Dakota said, affectionately stroking the ship's console like the neck of a horse. Deciding not to press his luck further, Dakota eased back the throttles and swung the bow toward the gradually sloping bank. Just before the ship impacted, he advanced the throttles.

Searcher plowed into the muddy bank, groaning like an animal in its death throes as the props drove her hard onto the shore. The ship shuddered as she slowed then came to a stop when the engines could force the boat no farther aground. Dakota throttled back and signaled Willy to shut the engines down to avoid sucking up more mud, trying out of habit to minimize the damage, though it was unlikely the ship could be salvaged, especially once the storm hit.

An eerie silence followed the sound of the engines dying, broken only by the creaking of the hull as the stern settled beneath the surface. A few minutes later Willy popped up on deck. "We're taking on water in the engine room now. By the time the stern comes to rest on the bottom, the engine room will be totally flooded."

"At least we made it. I can't see the terrorists having the time to search every one of these branches. I guess we beat them at their own..." Dakota froze as the horrible realization struck him—he could see the river. The boat's hull was hidden, but with only marsh grass and low bushes between them and the river, the bridge was still visible from the river.

Quint's second flare made a graceful arc but fell a foot behind the boat. "Damn!" he exclaimed, furious to have missed. After shutting down the fuel pump, LaRue joined Quint to escape the stinging rain. Quint looked up from packing his shoulder bag. "Guess we better come up with a plan B."

"Maybe not, Hoss," LaRue replied.

Quint jerked his head up and through the wheelhouse window could see the stern of the boat covered in bright orange flames. The flare had fallen short but ignited the fuel streaming off the boat's stern. "All right!" Quint yelled, giving LaRue a high five, feeling guilty about his earlier suspicions.

Realizing the boat was on fire, the terrorists poured out of the cabin, apparently in no hurry to meet Allah. Emerging into the cockpit, they were quickly covered in flaming fuel before they could jump into the river, where most did not resurface. The captain and one other man on the bridge managed to jump from the wheelhouse and made it into the river where they swam toward the far bank, leaving the boat to run in circles.

Before they could reach shore, a secondary explosion sank the flaming boat. Quint kept his eyes trained on the far shore and saw the two men emerge from the oily water, each clutching what appeared to be an AK-47. Having found time to leave the boat armed, they were prepared to continue the fight. A minute later, two more men emerged from the river; one appearing to be badly hurt but the other seemingly unscathed.

"What now, Hoss?" LaRue asked.

"Good question. I'm guessing they won't call it a day," Quint replied. The terrorists headed toward the far end of the dock where, much to Quint's horror, they reappeared in a small workboat, resuming their relentless pursuit.

Dawson awoke with a hangover headache and his jaw aching but not as bad as before. He went to the galley for a bottle of water to rinse the coppery taste of blood from his mouth and headed for the bridge.

Dakota was having no luck reaching Quint on his cell phone. "Damn! I guess the cell system is down."

"Did you try the radio?" Willy asked.

"No, since we're sitting ducks, I didn't want to risk having the terrorists intercept a radio conversation."

"Maybe they won't spot us, or if they do, won't recognize the ship," Willy said, more to comfort than to convince the others.

"Maybe isn't good enough," replied Dawson as he entered the bridge. "But you may have something there. You and Colin cover Big

Bertha with a tarp so it's not just lying there out in the open. Then grab some of that netting off that old shrimp boat's deck and drape it across the bridge so we can make ourselves look like a derelict. At this point, it shouldn't be that hard."

"You okay?" Willy asked with genuine concern.

"Yes, thanks. I owe you one, Dr. Willy," Dawson replied, and continued: "Kira, you and the rest follow me to the mess hall to work up a defense plan." Dawson popped two aspirins, swallowing them with a slug of water to deal with the aftermath of Willy's dentistry.

With the bomb covered with a tarp, securely lashed down against the wind, and the bridge draped with the shrimp net, Willy and Colin joined the others. "What'd we miss?" Colin asked.

"Unfortunately, nothing. We've got two pistols and one rifle. Not exactly the equipment necessary for launching a formidable defense," Dawson replied.

"We've got surgical tubing. We could make slingshots," Kira offered with a grin.

Colin joined in, "Yeah, firing water balloons ought to fix 'em." Dawson remained stone-faced, not in the mood for sarcastic humor.

In his mind Dakota envisioned the blinding flash and mushroom cloud of the explosion he could not permit this bomb to make. If the terrorists came, he was prepared to die, better that than living knowing he might have stopped the bomb from detonating. In a way, it would give value to an otherwise empty life. *A string of bar rooms and cheap women is not much of a legacy to leave behind. But saving the world or even a small part of it, now that's heady stuff*, he thought to himself. "Dawson, take the team to shelter," he blurted out.

"What about you?"

"I'm staying. A captain never abandons his ship," he said with a sad smile. "I'll babysit Big Bertha. You get the team to safety and take Lolo," he said, a quick grimace crossing his face.

"We're not leaving you. If somebody has to stay, we all stay," Dawson replied.

Dakota shook his head. "That makes no sense. If the terrorists find us, we can't hold them off. They'll have us outgunned and will kill everyone in short order. But if they don't spot us, and that storm comes in, having the team on a half-sunk, beached ship puts everyone at risk. Take the team to shelter before it's too late. I imagine the roads out of here are already flooded, so head to high ground and find someplace sturdy to hunker down.

"Someone needs to stay here, and that person should be me. I'll keep you updated on the radio. If they come, I'll hide and see what they do with the bomb. I'll have something rigged so that if it appears they plan to detonate it, I can take them out. Maybe I'll set the ship on fire, those tanks of diesel ought to do the trick."

"And how do you propose to do that without getting killed in the process?" Dawson said.

"I don't—I will die. But that's better than losing the entire team, and if Big Bertha goes off, we all die anyhow." Dawson nodded, grimly accepting Dakota's logic. "Besides, as the Indians say, 'You haven't lived until you know what you'd die for.' I'm willing to die to keep that bomb from blowing."

Resigned, Dawson began mobilizing the team.

CHAPTER 34

Quint and LaRue left the fuel barge and sloshed through the driving rain toward the boarded-up buildings in Venice to find a vehicle. Finally, they spotted a truck parked in back of a warehouse. "You know how to hotwire this thing?"

"Yeah Hoss, but we don't have to," LaRe replied pointing to the keys lying on the floor. Quint fired up the engine and noted the fuel gauge indicated near empty. While they drove, he dialed Evie's cell phone once again but now could no longer even get a connection.

"We've only got a pistol with a few rounds. I don't think we'll fare too well against those AK-47s. Any idea how we might even the odds?"

LaRue thought for a minute, "Let's check out that supply house over there, Hoss."

Quint swung into the parking lot, and the two men found the door locked as expected. Borrowing Quint's pistol, LaRue broke the glass and opened the door. "Cajun door key," he said.

As LaRue rummaged through the storage area, Quint checked out the front office desks. "Bingo," he exclaimed upon finding a pistol with five rounds in a drawer. "This will help, but we need more bullets."

Quint noticed LaRue place $20 on the counter and retrieve a baseball bat. "Planning on taking a break for a little recreation?"

"No," LaRue said blushing. "In case we run out of bullets... and... Kira's little one will be needing some toys."

"Yeah, a baseball bat, the perfect gift for a new born," Quint said with a chuckle.

Continuing their search of the next two buildings, they found food, fresh water, and a cheap VHF radio with an extra pack of batteries but no more weapons or ammunition. Quint placed cash on the counter to pay for the things they took and switched the radio to the right frequency.

Dawson was startled to hear Quint's voice on the channel 16 hailing frequency. "Dawson... this is... you copy?" came Quint's broken transmission.

"Dawson here. Switch to the working channel," he said then heard Quint's broken confirmation.

"Quint, you on this channel?" Again he heard Quint's faint reply.

"Let me give you our situation." Realizing that it was risky, Dawson briefed Quint in hopes that he could hear but the terrorists could not. As a precaution, he declined to give their exact position and any nonessential details.

Unfortunately, the terrorists had switched the workboat's radio to scan mode, and with the storm evacuation complete, no one else was transmitting. When their radio came to the channel Dawson was using, it stopped. Quint was not the only one to hear Dawson's briefing.

Quint spread the chart he had taken from the tug's wheelhouse on a table. "I'm guessing they've ducked into one of these small canals. He didn't give a definite position, probably afraid the terrorists might be listening. We'll continue along the river checking out the feeder bayous. Then we'll raise them on the handheld again and try to home in on their position."

LaRue ducked into the break room and was working on something with his knife when Quint walked in. "Cajun raincoat, da latest in south Louisiana rainwear. Want one?" he asked while sliding on a plastic garbage bag with holes cut for his arms and head.

"Why not," Quint replied. A minute later they were back in the truck dressed in their homemade rain gear, headed to find *Searcher*.

Colin swam across the canal to a small skiff, and after failing to get the engine started, rowed back to *Searcher*. "Your water taxi is here," he called through the screeching wind, ducking his head against the bullets of rain which stung his face.

Aboard *Searcher*, Lolo slipped away to the back of the ship carrying a plate piled high with an assortment of sliced bananas and other fruit. After cautiously opening the door to confirm Fred was far enough away to risk quickly dashing in, she set down the plate of food. "Here you go. Keep an eye on Dakota," she said feeling more than a little foolish about talking to a reptile. The plate caught Fred's attention, and he came scampering across the compartment floor. Unsure whether he wanted food or attention, Lolo quickly shut the door behind her. Feeding him was one thing, touching him quite another.

As Colin returned to the ship on his last trip, he found Lolo standing beside an enormous pile of plastic containers filled with food. "At least with my world-famous Paninis, we won't go hungry. Plus, I brought a wide selection of chips and assorted junk food."

Once the rest of the team was aboard the skiff along with the food, Lolo turned to Dakota. "Take care of yourself, you big oaf," she said hugging him tightly and blinking away tears. "Don't tell Quint, but I'm glad you stayed. Real glad," Dakota said, kissing her deeply as she stepped into the skiff and Colin pulled away from the ship. Dakota stood watching her, an uneasy feeling in the pit of his stomach. This was one time he hoped his Indian intuition was wrong.

The team, gathered on the far bank, helped unload. After solemnly waving to Dakota, they followed Dawson along the narrow trail at the head of the rickety dock through the marsh to a muddy road beyond. The hoods on their rain gear were pulled tight to stave off the sheets of rain dumped on them by the raging storm. Though it was bad, the main storm remained well offshore, making it clear that there was much worse to come. For half an hour, they plodded through the thick mud before reaching the asphalt road. They had just rounded the corner out of sight when a pickup truck slowed then turned onto the muddy road they had just left behind.

Dakota stood tirelessly on the bridge, binoculars hanging ready. He felt stubble as he ran a hand over his shaved head, reminding him he was overdue for a shave, not a high priority at the moment.

With the ship's stern mostly under water, Dakota clung to the steeply slanting deck. He scanned the main river searching for the terrorists' boat, finally spotting a workboat headed downriver. Realizing it was far too small to be the boat which had chased them into the river, he nearly ignored it before glimpsing a man bearing an AK-47.

That's our boys. Wonder what happened to their other boat? he asked himself as the terrorists approached the junction between the main river and the canal where *Searcher* was beached. Silently, he prayed they would not turn.

Dakota's prayers were answered when the boat continued downstream. Though relieved, he realized this was far from over. They were certain to be back when they found nothing, so he began planning a suitable reception.

Wearing a dry t-shirt bearing the slogan, *You probably don't recognize me without my cape,* Dakota figured he would need to be Superman in order survive this. While searching for bits and pieces to make improvised weapons, he had the thought to disable the bomb's detonator. The problem was, he didn't know the first thing about detonators or bombs.

If the bomb's detonator compartment is flooded, the wiring is probably corroded, he thought, unsure whether that was a good or bad thing. *What are the chances of accidentally detonating the bomb?* Dakota wondered but pushed the possibility from his mind. He stuck the .45 pistol in his pants waist, grabbed a tool box and headed for the back deck.

Icy needles of rain made him wish he had another hooded slicker like the one he had loaned Mimi. He lifted the tarp from the front of the bomb and wiped away the remaining mud from the scarred black metal surface of its nose. Big bertha felt cool to his touch, a feeling of power emanating from within her four-ton womb.

He was hard at work on a corroded screw when he felt the boat lurch. Puzzled, he ran to the bridge and was stunned to realize—the rising water had re-floated the ship. A minute later, the ship broke free and, listing badly to port, began drifting low in the stern. The wind had shifted with the storm's approach. With the rising flood water, he was horrified to see the boat headed back down the canal toward the river.

This is nice. What the hell am I supposed to do now? Dakota asked himself. He would not abandon the ship with the bomb still aboard, but he was under no illusions about *Searcher's* seaworthiness—she was sinking, and there was nothing he could do to save her. He cursed himself for not trying to stuff blankets into the hole in the broken hull to stem the flow of water while they were aground, but he had not considered the possibility that they might be refloated.

Dakota's first instinct was to start the engines and move the ship back onto the bank before remembering the engine room was under water. The ship bumped drunkenly against the bank toward the river, driven by the force of the wind propelling *Searcher* helplessly back down the bayou. Peering through the heavy rain, he sighed in relief that the terrorists' workboat was nowhere in sight.

Finally, he resigned himself to riding the ship until she grounded again or sank and struggling to survive in hopes of passing on her location. He saw the fuel barge where he had dropped off Quint and LaRue. Near the far bank, he spotted the charred wheelhouse of a sunken boat poking above the surface. *So that's what happened to the second terrorist's main ride. Congratulations, Quint*, he thought.

Remembering Fred, he went below and let the iguana out of the compartment. "I don't know how this story is going to end, but I think you'll be better off not locked up, especially if we sink." Fred followed behind as Dakota headed back toward the bridge, becoming separated after Dakota climbed the steep stairs.

As Dakota approached the Mississippi River, its bank marked only by a line of partially submerged trees, the ship's bow slammed against the limbs. The broken branches screeched against the wheelhouse as they drifted past, the current pushing the heavy stern relentlessly through the swollen river waters.

A thought struck Dakota, and he bolted from the wheelhouse to the foredeck, cursing himself for not having the idea earlier. He worked his way up the slanted deck through the blinding rain hoping to drop the anchor and snag the bottom to keep the ship from drifting out to sea. He struggled to free the pin from the anchor's chain stopper, scraping skin off several of his knuckles, exposing raw flesh. Finally, the anchor was freed.

His elation was short-lived as his heart sank—without power for the winch, he could not deploy the anchor. He threw the pin to the deck in disgust before retreating to the bridge. Just before rounding a bend in the river, he spotted a workboat passing the fuel barge. His stomach knotted—the terrorists were headed toward him.

Quint and LaRue reached the end of the muddy road in time to see *Searcher* float past, its heavy stern nearly under water and listing badly. The two men stared open-mouthed before scrambling from the truck to watch the ship disappear around the bend. Spotting a skiff tied beside the rickety pier, Quint yelled to LaRue, "I'll grab our stuff from the truck. Try to get that boat running."

"You got it, Hoss."

As Quint tossed their gear in the bottom of the boat, LaRue had the little engine running, which had earlier stymied Colin. They cast off only to find that with the undersized engine at full throttle, they were barely keeping pace with the wind-driven *Searcher*. Quint spotted a battered workboat still tied to a section of dock floating beside it. "We need a better ride; pull over to that workboat. Maybe we can upgrade." LaRue eased them alongside the boat and quickly tied off.

In a repeat performance, LaRue worked his magic to get it running while Quint transferred their gear. Like some homeless duo dressed in their garbage-bag-rainwear, the men headed down river once again. They spotted *Searcher* entering the main river but were sickened to see a second workboat well ahead of them bearing down on the ship.

Dakota stood in the wheelhouse, the water running off him in streams. *Well, it looks like we're about to re-enact the Little Big-horn, only I get to play the hopelessly outnumbered General Custer.* With a sigh, he prepared to defend his sinking ship. Though not eager to die, Dakota would not let the terrorists take the bomb unopposed.

His search of the tool room looking for weapons yielded only a large wrench and a hammer before he finally spotted a hatchet. *This'll make a great tomahawk. It worked for my ancestors,* he thought, hoping he would not be forced to cut the bomb loose with it.

Working on the slippery bridge roof with waves crashing against the side of the ship, he cut the shrimp net camouflage loose, and piled the net atop the life raft. He laid his rifle and pistol beside the improvised cover, wedging the hatchet beneath the life raft. At least he would give the terrorists a fight.

Rain poured from his shaved head, his long pigtail whipping about in the gale-force winds. He sheltered his face with a hand to his brow, trying to catch sight of the terrorists' boat through the heavy rain. A bouncing shadow well behind *Searcher* told him all he needed to know. He squatted patiently behind the mound of net while the men in the workboat roared toward him assuming the ship was easy prey. Sighting down the rifle, he gained a feel for the ship's motion as he targeted, through the rain-obscured glass, the man captaining the workboat.

"As my ancestors believed, *'Anger ends in cruelty.'* You guys provide the anger, and I'll deal with the cruelty part." When the ship reached the end of its roll, he squeezed the trigger. A red mist sprayed the inside of the spiderweb-cracked glass, and the helmsman dropped out of sight, the workboat veering off to the right.

Aboard the workboat, a second man jerked his dead partner from the helm seat and grabbed the wheel to regain control. A second bullet pierced the window beside him and slammed into his shoulder, knocking him to the boat deck. "You idiots, throw up some covering fire before we all get picked off!" he yelled to the others as he crawled back to the helm. A moment later, the AK-47 roared to life, sweeping *Searcher's* wheelhouse and forcing Dakota to hug the roof.

Only four rounds left with at least two more terrorists remaining, Dakota said to himself, as a second burst of fire erupted from the far side of the boat. *Make that three more.*

Unable to see far through the relentless rain, he knew from the motion of the ship that they were nearing the mouth of the river. Soon, they would be out in the open ocean and pounded by the giant seas once again.

Since he had not yet been spotted, and given his poor odds made worse by his dwindling ammunition, Dakota laid low, hoping to avoid giving away his position while waiting for the right moment. As the workboat eased alongside, the wounded man ran the boat while another stood ready to tie up, leaving the third man to fire covering bursts. Dakota patiently sighted the rifle once again and squeezed off a shot just as they lassoed one of *Searcher's* cleats.

Yes! he said to himself, as the second helmsman slumped to the deck. *Down to two, unfortunately, they're better armed.* As Dakota shifted to a better position, the ship took an unexpected roll, and he lost his balance. He sprawled backwards and the rifle skidded across the wheelhouse roof, disappearing over the side. Dakota frantically grasped for something to stop his slide. As his legs swung over the ship's side, he clutched an antenna base and stopped with half of his body hanging over the edge while the ship continued its roll.

Something steel struck him in the face and he cursed to see the pistol fall into the roiling water beneath him. Gritting his teeth, he pulled with all of his might, gradually easing his body back atop the bridge roof. *Okay, the good news is I'm still on board. The bad news is I have two terrorists remaining and no guns.* He was relieved to find the hatchet still wedged beneath the life raft. He grabbed it, firmly resolving to hang on to it no matter what.

Meanwhile the two remaining terrorists had regrouped and boarded the ship. Taking turns, they squeezed off bursts from their AK-47s providing covering fire while one searched the doghouses on the deck below, and the other headed for the wheelhouse.

Dakota lay frozen, peering through the netting at the man slinking toward the bridge. When the man reached the top of the stairs leading to the wheelhouse, he was still staring in Dakota's direction.

Come on, come on, Dakota thought to himself, hoping the man would look away if even for an instant. But it appeared that Dakota was about to be forced to face the armed man with only his hatchet. As he tensed to attack, he saw a streak of green and heard the man yell. "What the hell?" It was Fred. The man turned and fired his weapon.

Dakota glimpsed the lizard's green body erupt with a red geyser and then, with the man's attention momentarily diverted, Dakota stepped off the bridge roof. Holding the hatchet raised in one hand, he let out a "war cry" and plunged below, sinking the hatchet into the man's head, nearly splitting it in two.

Dakota landed on the bridge deck with the hatchet still clutched in a death grip. Before he could grab hold, the ship's heavy list sent him over the railing. He plummeted onto the main deck below, striking his knee before landing on his back with a heavy thud. With the breath knocked out of him, he still clutched the hatchet. When he finally opened his eyes, the remaining terrorist stood over him holding an AK-47, a wicked grin on his face.

Dakota's mind raced over his options before realizing—he had none. "Look, if you shoot me, how are you going to offload the bomb?"

"I'm not. I like it right where it is," he said with a smile.

The sick realization that the maniac intended to detonate it right where it was hit Dakota. With seconds to live, Dakota felt his muscles tense. He prepared to raise up and throw the hatchet like a tomahawk and launch himself at the man, if he was still able. The man would shoot him, but perhaps he could live long enough to swing the hatchet or at least knock both of them off of the ship. Not a great plan, but the only one remaining. As his arm started forward, a crack of thunder sounded, and the man's eyes widened before he toppled onto Dakota, who was still tensed to sling the hatchet.

Dakota glanced up to see a second workboat pull alongside with Quint standing in the cockpit lowering his pistol. Focused on *Searcher*, the overconfident terrorists had failed to notice Quint's and LaRue's approach. Dakota extricated himself from beneath the man's body and struggled to his feet. "Cut it a little close there, didn't you boys?"

"We didn't want to butt in on your fun, plus you were doing fine by yourself."

Dakota shook his head. "Okay, the terrorists are dead, but we still have a sinking ship with a nuclear weapon on board."

"Big Bertha appears to be trying to head back to where she came from. Now that we're out in open water, I say we help her along, sort of," Quint said, as LaRue disappeared on the violently rolling back deck.

"Huh?"

"Look, the ship is sinking, and without power we can't offload the bomb onto another vessel, even if we could find one big enough. If the ship sinks with the bomb still on board, it could be crushed. Or the bomb could end up in deep water, making recovery more difficult. Big Bertha is going down, and our only option is to choose where. Given all we went through to find and retrieve her, I hate to do it, but we have to cut her loose. We'll mark the bomb's position, then recover it after the storm."

"And how do you suggest we mark it?" Dakota challenged, as he leaned against a bulkhead and rubbed his injured knee.

"With this," Quint said, removing a waterproof GPS from his backpack. He walked to the back deck, where LaRue stood wearing scuba gear and holding a float with a reel of line and a small transponder in a submersible housing he had retrieved from the dive locker.

"LaRue will follow her down and attach that transponder to her so it doesn't get damaged when she lands, then he'll attach this float so we can get a good position fix on her."

LaRue climbed on top of the bomb and motioned for Dakota to cut it loose. As it slid into the water, LaRue yelled, "Yahoo, I'm Slim Pickens!"

When the float popped to the surface, Quint saved the position in the handheld GPS, making a mental note to write it down as a backup and phone Rogers with the bomb coordinates as soon he could. A minute later LaRue surfaced and grabbed the line Dakota tossed him. The two men hauled LaRue back aboard the sinking ship. "The transponder is on da bom', and the float is tied to Big Bertha's fin," LaRue reported.

Before reluctantly leaving *Searcher* for the last time, the trio spent a few minutes salvaging what they could from the ship, which was nearing its death roll.

"Where's Fred?" Quint asked.

"Fred's dead."

"Dead?"

"Yep. Got shot when he lunged at one of the terrorists. Saved my butt," Dakota replied.

"Crap. Evie's not going to like that."

"Like what?" LaRue asked as he walked up.

"Fred's dead."

"Shame. But, Hoss, at the risk of sounding insensitive, I think we've got bigger problems to worry about right now." Quint nodded and resumed offloading the pile of supplies they had gathered.

Though favoring the leg he had banged when falling off the bridge, Dakota made a point to be the last one off while quietly muttering something beneath his breath. Just before stepping off *Searcher* to climb aboard the workboat, he froze with his eyes scanning through the sheets of rain to the southwest. "Boys, we got company."

"Who is it?" Quint asked, amazed that Dakota could see anything in this slop.

"Given the direction they're coming from and the fact that only an idiot or a fanatic would be out in this, I'm guessing it's the third boatload of terrorists out of Grand Isle."

"Shit, them boys don't give up," LaRue said, shaking his head.

"Nope, but that sort of perseverance is what makes for a successful terrorist," Quint quipped and frantically began to form a game plan. Glancing at the two workboats, he had an idea. "Dakota, your leg hurting too bad to climb aboard the workboat your deceased terrorist buddies left?" he asked.

"Nope," he said. Quint suspected that he would say that even if his leg were missing completely. "What you need me to do?"

"Let's give our new load of terrorists two targets to worry about. We'll lash the two workboats together. When we get under way, set your autopilot for a heading of 90 degrees. When I signal, push the throttles all the way forward and jump on our boat before we cut it free." Dakota nodded.

"Give me a minute," Quint said as he jumped back on *Searcher's* deck. He found the miniSUB that Colin had retrieved and opened the case. The guidance controls were in an aft compartment already under water. Without the controls, he wasn't certain the miniSUB would be of much use, but on a lark, he removed the safety pins to arm it before closing the bright red case and sliding it into the sea. He let out the attached lanyard and secured it to the ship to tether it nearby. Though he knew it was a long shot, he hoped the U.S. Navy lettering plastered all over the bright case might draw the terrorists' attention. He climbed back up the steep deck of the sinking ship and boarded his workboat.

After retrieving his hatchet, Dakota struggled onto the second boat. *Searcher* was settling low in the water and threatened to capsize at any minute. He slipped and fell into the workboat as *Searcher* took a heavy roll. Before he could get back on his feet, the small boat listed sharply—*Searcher* was capsizing and pulling his workboat along with her.

With seconds to react, he lunged across the deck and swung the hatchet down to sever the breast line, which had his workboat nearly submerged. The boat righted itself as Dakota set about to sever the remaining lines.

Searcher continued her slow death roll, drawing Dakota's bow and stern lines tight and pulling the workboat under water once again. Dakota swung the hatchet twice more to cut the stern line then turned toward the bow.

Seeing Dakota's predicament, LaRue lunged onto the bow of Dakota's boat, struggling to keep from falling overboard and being crushed by *Searcher's* rolling hull. Dakota tossed him the hatchet, which he caught and swung down in one motion, cutting the bow line, now stretched banjo-string tight. The cut line snapped, sending the free end shooting backwards to slice open his face. Ignoring the blood gushing from the wound, he jumped back onto Quint's boat and lashed the two workboats together.

With the two boats no longer tied to *Searcher,* Dakota ducked into the tiny cabin to start the engine while LaRue hung onto the bow rail of Quint's boat. When both boats were turned onto the right heading, Dakota engaged the autopilot, threw the throttles forward, and dove onto Quint's boat. LaRue swung the hatchet yet again, severing the bow line to cut loose the empty workboat to continue heading east. He then worked his way back to the cockpit.

"What happened to you?" Quint asked seeing LaRue's blood-covered face.

"Just a scratch, Hoss," LaRue replied.

Quint smiled. "Let's hope they follow our decoy boat instead of us," Quint said, swinging their boat toward the mouth of the river.

"Yeah, and while we're busy hoping, let's also hope *Searcher* drifts far enough so that they don't spot Big Bertha's marker buoy," Dakota added, his attention riveted to the ship's capsized hull.

The empty workboat pounded into the head seas until the autopilot linkage broke. With no one to correct the boat's course, the seas deflected her bow until she was headed down sea and began to run in circles.

The terrorists spotted the circling workboat and quickly confirmed it was unmanned before turning their attention to the capsized ship. Quint's plan had not bought them the advantage he had hoped it might.

Quint knew there was little the terrorists could do in these seas, even if the bomb were still aboard, so they would soon begin to follow the trio toward the river's mouth. "LaRue was right; these guys just don't give up," Quint grumbled. The seas had steadily worsened over the past hour as the hurricane approached landfall. Once away from the lee side of *Searcher*, Quint was barely able to keep the workboat headed down sea without being swamped or broaching. He willed the mouth of the river closer as they struggled toward the protected waters with the terrorists nearing *Searcher*.

"Well guys, if they catch us, let's stand ready to call them ugly names, stick out our tongues and flip them off. My hatchet and your two pistols won't be too effective against a fresh load of AK-47s." Quint nodded then noticed the terrorists' boat turn and slow, appearing to be about to give the *Searcher* a quick 'once over.'

"Maybe they spotted the miniSUB that I armed. Come on, go for it."

As the terrorists approached *Searcher*, they noticed the bright red container and slowed to retrieve it, perhaps thinking it had floated off the ship and might be of value. After a few clumsy attempts, they lassoed the miniSUB and began hoisting it aboard as they began their pursuit of the workboat. The miniSUB swung violently once it cleared the surface of the water. The third time it struck the boat, the nose of the miniSUB hit square, and an enormous explosion erupted.

"Yahoo!" LaRue yelled as he saw the bright orange flash followed by thick black smoke.

"It worked," Quint added, hardly believing his desperate trick had been successful. "We were due some long odds. Now let's find the rest of the team before Katrina finds us." The image of Evie popped into Quint's mind. *I sure hope she's back in the Keys by now,* he thought to himself.

CHAPTER
35

The team continued up the road with Jacques keeping an eye out for a boat large enough to transport all of them.

"If the storm hits as they predict, what about your place out on Cat Island?" Leo asked.

"It'll be gone," Jacques replied.

"Too bad you can't do something to protect it."

"Like what? I'd need a floating moving van and another day to load everything. Katrina will wipe it clean. You know, everyone wants to live on the ocean. Don't get me wrong; there's nothing wrong with that—I love being on the ocean. Some prefer boats so they can tuck tail and run when weather threatens. I guess building your house right on the water down here is like thumbing your nose at ol' Mother Nature and saying nanner-nanner. It's not real smart 'cause, it's just a matter of time before you're gonna' get your ass kicked. I guess I'm about to have my turn," Jacques said and returned his attention back to looking for a boat.

"You'll lose everything. You seem awfully calm about it."

"At one time, my family, like most, were collectors and felt life was about acquiring, ever building, ever stockpiling more, and more, and more. But in 1969, Hurricane Camille broke them of that. In just a few hours, she took everything my family had collected. Not like a fire, where it's really gone. No, just ruined, leaving the carcass for them to pick over, agonizing at the loss as they were forced to consciously throw away each ruined treasure. So long as my boy is safe, I'll be okay. I can replace the stuff."

Noticing that none of the men were within earshot Mimi eased up beside Kira. "So, you're pregnant, not dying of cancer?"

Kira smiled at her bluntness. "Thankfully, yes. The doctor said that it's possible for a woman to seem like she's having her monthly and still be pregnant. I'd never heard of it but was overjoyed with that news, I can tell you." Mimi nodded. As Kira glanced back, she thought she caught Dawson staring at her for an instant before looking off. A sad smile crossed her lips before she resumed talking to Mimi.

Leaving the group for a minute, Leo re-emerged carrying a football he had seen in a store window. After forcing open a back door, he plucked the item from the front display case, dropping some cash in its place. He eased alongside Kira and handed her the ball. "Kid might like this," he said, picking up his pace to catch back up with Jacques, who was chatting with Colin.

"So, how does it feel to be an expectant dad?" Jacques asked.

"You know, after the initial shock, I was surprised to be thrilled. I had never really thought much about it before. Me a dad. Imagine that," Colin replied.

"Trust me, it'll be great. I think everyone's scared at first, I know I was. But my boy is the most important thing in my life, especially since his mom was taken. I love watching him play football."

"Yep, my kid's gonna' be a star college quarterback," Colin boasted.

"What if it's a girl?"

"Well, then I guess she'll star as the first female one," Colin said and continued to talk nonstop about his being a father-to-be while Jacqes listened patiently.

The team continued for another mile before reaching a dilapidated metal building sheltered from the wind by a massive warehouse perched on a rise near the river. "This will probably be our best shelter. The sturdier buildings are too low to the water," Dawson said, struggling to be heard over the howling wind as he kicked in the door and entered the musty-smelling, dirt-floored building. Jacques entered close behind and immediately took advantage of the relative quiet.

"Dawson, this is a Category 5 hurricane. You can't imagine what a Category 2 or 3 would be like here, much less a 5. If it's as bad as I think, there's no place for miles around that's high enough to remain above the flood waters or sturdy enough to withstand them. Even if we could find a vehicle with enough gas, Dakota was right, the roads are already flooded, so we can't leave. The only chance we have is to make a run for the Port Eads Lighthouse. It won't be comfortable, but we can survive there."

"The forecast calls for it to be downgraded to a three or four before it makes landfall," Leo challenged, as he greedily accepted one of the sandwiches Lolo was passing around.

"Look, there's a massive warm water eddy out there that will provide enough energy for Katrina to go nuts. After she moves past that, she probably will weaken. The problem is, by then she'll be pushing a Category 5 tidal surge ahead of her. The shape of the coastline will act like a funnel, magnifying the effect as the surge approaches. That's what we have to worry about.

"You guys can do whatever you want, but I'm headed for Port Eads. I plan on seeing my son graduate from high school, hopefully college too, and that's not gonna' happen if I stay here. I'm going to the lighthouse—in a pirogue if I have to."

Dawson considered the situation in silence. While the prospect of making a 20-mile run to the end of South Pass was not appealing, neither was the idea of being drowned in rising flood waters or crushed in a collapsing building. The fact that the lighthouse had survived untold storms since its construction in 1881 was the deciding factor.

"We're going with you. Before the wind picks up further, let's get prepared." Dawson turned to Colin, "It's been over an hour, and with the satphone dead and no luck raising Dakota on the radio or cellphone, I'm worried. You and Leo, see if you can get a car running and go check on him. Take this handheld radio," Dawson said, handing one to Colin and three to the other team members, including Jacques. "Try to find Quint too. He and LaRue may be hunkered down near the fuel barge."

"Sure, be back in a jiffy," Colin replied, exiting their shelter with Leo close behind.

"Jacques, find us a boat, preferably not a pirogue, and get it fueled. Kira, you and Mimi make a list of food and basic supplies we'll need to get us through the next day or two until the flood waters recede. Willy, help them find the supplies and keep your eyes open for weapons. You'll have to break in, since no one is open for business. Leave a list of what you take and a number where they can reach us after the storm so we can pay them. We're not looters."

Dawson tried for the hundredth time to reach Quint on the radio, finally with success. "Quint, you guys okay? Where's Dakota?"

"He's with us, and we're all okay. Where are you?" Dawson described the location, and Quint headed the workboat in their direction.

Dawson looked up as Colin and Leo reappeared, followed by Kira, Mimi, Lolo, and Willy. "You guys done already?"

"No," a familiar voice said as two men entered behind the group, "but they decided to come back, with our insistence, of course. Thanks for the radio directions. Okay, folks you know the drill, hands up."

Dawson keyed his radio so Quint could hear what was happening. While the first two men stood guard, two others entered and secured the team's hands with plastic ties then frisked them for weapons, confiscating the radio in the process.

"I remember our last electrifying encounter."

"As do I," Akmed said, unconsciously rubbing the bullet wound where Quint had shot him.

Omar stroked his wispy beard while eyeing Kira. "I'm Omar. You might be eligible for special privileges," he said leeringly. "Let's go to the workshop upfront where we can be more comfortable. I can show you my 'tool,'" he said in a thick middle-eastern accent while grabbing his crotch.

"No thanks," Kira replied. "I imagine your 'tool' is too small to take on any real man's job, and I don't need my watch repaired." Omar smiled without replying before his hand shot out and struck her across the face. Despite having his hands tied, Colin flew across the room and head butted the man hard in the stomach, his momentum propelling both onto the floor. While Colin struggled to his feet to engage Omar again, Talib calmly walked over and struck him hard in the back of his head with the butt of his rifle. As Colin fell to the ground unconscious, a piece of jagged metal jutting from the building wall sliced his arm.

Omar stood and smoothed his clothes in a futile attempt to restore his dignity. "Before this is over you'll regret that, whore. I'll teach you to appreciate 'nice' when we play later," he said, demonstrating his perverse determination by stroking Mimi's hair and fondling each of the women who, helpless to protest, stood unflinching.

"Look, if we stay here, we're all going to die," Kira said, worry heavy in her voice.

"Then that is Allah's will," Talib replied.

The men herded the team into a waiting van and drove a short distance before the van stopped, and the team was led into a metal building, Dawson and Willy carrying the unconscious Colin. Formerly the marina's storage area and workshop, it was now a repository for assorted boat yard junk.

Inside, Akmed withdrew a ring of keys, unlocked a massive padlock and swung open the heavy door to an inner room, its windows covered with thick boards held in place with impressive steel bars bolted in place. After they entered, the steel door swung shut, and they heard the distinctive click of a padlock being put in place. In the corner sat Evie, hunched over and barely recognizable with her bruised face and blood-matted hair.

"Oh, my gosh," Kira yelled as she and the other two women ran to her side.

"Thank God you're here," Evie said through swollen lips. Kira pulled Evie's dress, gathered around her waist, back down to cover her naked thighs. "I know I look bad but other than the obvious damage," she said with a quick downward glance, "I think I'm okay." But Kira could plainly see she was anything but okay.

"What are you doing here? What happened?" Kira asked as the women tried to mask their horror. After Evie related the events surrounding her kidnapping, none of them could bring themselves to comment.

Dawson's anger boiled at Evie's condition but saw that Kira was doing what little could be done for her under the circumstances. "Did you find *Searcher*?" Dawson asked Leo in a low voice.

"It's gone."

"What do you mean gone?"

"I meant just what I said. The ship is not where we left it and nowhere in sight," Leo replied.

While Dawson sat deep in thought, the rest of the team surveyed their new quarters. On one side amidst the squalor were several thin pieces of filthy foam that they could rest on. Two rickety desks were the only furniture, and they threatened to collapse when the team attempted to sit on them.

A minute later, Colin regained consciousness with a loud groan. "What happened?"

"Your hero attempt was stymied by the butt of a rifle," Dawson replied.

Colin tried to sit up and noticed his arm wrapped in a sanitary napkin. "This is cute," he complained.

"Kira bandaged your arm using the only thing we had. Would you rather she let you bleed to death?"

"I'll think that over and get back to you," Colin replied. "Damn, what happened to Evie? Looks like somebody gave her the LaRue treatment," Colin lamely joked, not realizing how badly she had been mistreated. Kira shot him a dirty look, and he quieted.

"How long you think they'll keep us here?" Kira asked.

"Longer than I care to think about unless Quint can get here—or Jacques, I nearly forgot about him. But let's assume we're on our own. See what we can find in all of this junk to help us break out," Dawson said.

In the boatyard office closer to the river but on the same side of the storage building "prison," Omar watched a porn movie while the other men ate their meals. Occasionally, one of them would glance at the prison building, but as the movie progressed, the men's interest in keeping tabs waned, except for Akmed who refused to watch. From the office, they could monitor both entrances and most of the boarded-up windows. Only the window on the far side was out of view.

"What's the point?" Omar had argued against standing watch. "Nobody knows they're here, and they sure ain't going anywhere."

"You do not want to explain failure to Rashid. We will continue guard patrols." Omar nodded, only half listening as the movie reached a particularly graphic segment involving several actors and a farm animal. He and Kalil looked forward to tormenting the women prisoners and, while watching the movie, formulated plans involving their captive women.

Thinking of Evie and their new prisoners, Talib announced, "I think I'll go 'patrol,'" he said with a laugh.

Talib unlocked the heavy door and flung it open as if it were made of balsa. He barged into the room headed straight for the sleeping Evie. Dawson moved to intervene but stopped when Talib swung his automatic weapon on the team and threatened, "Don't try to be a hero. I'll shoot you and the rest." He turned back to Evie, "Wake up. It's play time, but I'm taking you out, so to speak, since I don't like per-forming for an audience," he said, grabbing Evie by the arm.

"Leave her alone, can't you see she's seriously injured by your 'play times?' Much more of it will kill her," Kira said.

"So be Allah's will."

"It's not Allah's will; it's your will."

"You volunteering to take her place?"

Kira recoiled as if she had been struck. She saw the look of resig-nation in Evie's eyes and knew she would not survive another round with Talib. Looking directly at Talib she replied, "Yes, if that's the only way. I'll take her place."

"No, you won't," Lolo said, walking over to stand between the two women and Talib. While she too knew that Evie could not survive another round, she also knew that Kira might lose her baby. Evie's face was filled with a confused mixture of gratitude and concern at Lolo's offer, while Kira looked relieved but furious.

"No, Lolo, I can't ask you to do that," Evie pleaded.

"You didn't," Lolo replied, looking both angry and disgusted over what she felt compelled to do.

"If you women are through fighting over me, let's go," Talib said as Lolo followed behind. Once again Colin lunged forward only to be driven to the ground unconscious again by a blow from Talib's massive fist. A moment later, the door closed, and they were gone.

Jacques witnessed the team's capture and followed the van the short distance on foot. He approached the marina cautiously, remaining hidden from sight as he eased into the dry storage area. He found a suitable boat and switched the ignition on. It had plenty of fuel, but he chose not to try starting it for fear that the terrorists might hear the sound. He located a forklift to lower the boat into the water. At least they had transportation to head south if they could subdue the terrorists and gather the team. As he came back around the corner, he saw figures moving and tried to raise Quint on the handheld radio.

Quint, Dakota, and LaRue docked the workboat and found a truck. Quint noticed that the VHF radio had been turned off to conserve battery life. He switched it back on and immediately heard, "Quint, this is Jacques. We've got a situation."

"LaRue, figure out how we break into the 'prison' while we do a recon," Quint said after the three men reached the marina. "Jacques, prepare to launch the boat." As he headed for the boat storage area, Jacques spotted a huge guard marching Lolo in front of him and followed them.

By the time Quint and Dakota rejoined LaRue, he was nearly

finished cutting through a metal bar over the window using a bat-
tery-powered diamond saw he had found earlier. Dakota caught the
bar before it could fall to the ground. Even though it probably would-
n't be heard over the shriek of the wind, he saw no point in taking
chances.

The men removed the boards from the window and climbed inside. After checking for guards, they made for the door to the room
where the team was being held. Dakota smashed the padlock with
the piece of window bar and knocked the hasp loose. Then, with a
flourish, Quint swung the door open. "Anybody want to head home?"

In a single motion, Dawson sprang from his grease-stained foam
pallet and was out the door, "You bet! But first, let's properly thank
the guards." LaRue withdrew a huge pocket knife and cut the plastic
ties from the team's wrists.

"I'll second that," Colin replied, following close behind.

Dakota noticed Colin's home-made bandage. "Why do you have
a woman's...?"

"Don't ask," Kira interrupted.

Quint was shocked to see Evie rush toward him and hug him
tightly. His heart hurt to see her in pain, but the look on her face told
him the worst of the damage was not visible. Kira shook her head,
making it clear he should wait to question her. Releasing her, Quint
placed his hand beneath her chin and raised her face to his. "What
happened, and which of them did this?" She quickly explained how
she had been captured.

"Afterwards, they all took turns, but the big one, Talib, was the
worst. He enjoyed himself the most," Evie replied. "Lolo volunteered
to save me from another round. You have to find her, before that animal rapes her... too." The look of rage in Quint's eyes scared her. She
clung to him until he finally peeled away her clutching arms.

"Stay here. I'll be back after we deal with Talib and his thugs,"
Quint said with a steely voice and left, clutching the heavy window
bar in his hand and with Dakota close behind, also visibly furious.

Colin looked at Kira, "Do me a favor without arguing. Stay and
protect Evie and the baby-to-be while we deal with these jerks." Sur-
prisingly, Kira agreed, her motherly instincts evidently kicking in.
Colin followed behind the others already gathered outside. The
group hugged the building while making their way toward the boat
storage facility's main office.

After stepping out to go to the bathroom, at Akmed's insistence the wispy-bearded terrorist, Omar, happened by to check on the prisoners. The open door told him there was trouble as he stepped inside and saw Kira rubbing her stomach with Evie sitting behind her.

Since his gun was back in the marina office, Omar drew a long knife, wielding it like a sword. He stood in front of Kira, waving the knife menacingly, an evil grin smeared across his face. "In my country kebobs are quite popular. Care to become one?" he said, lunging forward, eager to punish her for her insults.

Thinking of the baby in her womb, Kira became enraged. Time slowed as the man leaped through the air, the knife thrust forward. He seemed to hang in midair between her and the door.

Kira's eyes scanned the room for something to use for a weapon. Rolling to the side, she grabbed a pen from the top of the desk behind her and pirouetted as she drove the pen into the Omar's temple, collapsing him dead on the floor. "See, the pen *is* mightier than the sword," she said stepping on his body on her way out the door. "Come on. Let's join the team before any more goons arrive. Doesn't seem to be too safe here, either. I may be a mother-to-be, but this hanging back stuff isn't working for me."

Evie paused long enough to deliver several savage kicks to Omar's lifeless body. Kira watched without commenting. She appreciated the need for payback.

The team stealthily approached the front of the marina, until Willy planted his size 15 shoe in the middle of the door. With an enormous crack, it splintered open to hang by a single hinge.

Willy bounded across the room and plucked Akmed out of his chair and over the desk in one motion, smashing his massive right fist into the man's face. Meanwhile, Quint took two long steps and bounded atop the desk where a second man sat and swung the metal window bar with all his strength into the man's face even as he reached for his pistol. The force toppled the man backwards onto the concrete floor, where he landed dead.

Kira arrived and, without breaking stride, strode forward to de-

liver a brutal kick to the groin of Akmed, who was still lying on the
floor. "I guess this isn't exactly what you guys had in mind when you
promised we'd play later," Kira said.

"That wasn't me; it was Omar," Akmed protested.

"Guess you won't be re-enacting your sick video anytime soon,"
Kira said, ejecting the still playing DVD to gouge deep grooves in its
face with a letter opener off one of the desks.

"That was Omar's DVD," Akmed said, though Kira ignored him.

Colin grabbed the handful of plastic ties Dawson had found and
secured Akmed's hands behind his back. "I thought Jacques said
there were four of them."

"Omar didn't seem to respect motherhood, so your 'mother-to-
be' took care of him. He's lying dead back where we were being
held," Kira replied.

"Then where's Talib?" Dawson asked.

"Where's Jacques?" Quint replied as he stood beside Evie.

Determined to deal with the guard and rescue Lolo, Jacques
armed himself with a crowbar and skirted the building at a distance
while taking pains not to be spotted. He had just turned the corner
along the backside of the prison building when he heard a voice over
the shriek of the wind, "Looking for me?" Talib stood before the open
door of a small storage room holding Lolo by one arm. Seizing the
opportunity, Lolo lunged at Talib but he batted her like a mosquito
and shoved her inside the room, latching the door and turning to
face Jacques.

Taller, heavier, and more muscular than Jacques, Talib chose
not to draw his pistol, intending to face Jacques man-to-man.
Jacques had no illusions about how a bout of hand-to-hand combat
with Talib would end. He clutched the crowbar tightly. It might even
the odds enough to give Jacques a fighting chance. He lunged forward, but Talib, moving quickly for a man his size, kicked Jacques
hard in the stomach, knocking him to the ground. Talib landed two
head punches, knocking Jacques unconscious.

Talib dusted himself off and, seeing no one else threatening, returned to the storage room, where Lolo awaited. He opened the door
and stepped quickly back as she lunged at him with a board, too long

to make a useful weapon. Talib easily parried the move and back-handed Lolo, sending her reeling across the small room. He followed behind, unbuckling his pants. "Okay, little tiger, it's time for you to make good on your substitution offer."

CHAPTER 36

Katrina directed her fury at the Mississippi and Louisiana coasts, bashing the region for hours, touching the lives of thousands. Some she would touch through death, others by the loss of everything. But by the time the winds would finally die, nearly every family would have its own story to tell. Mrs. Evers' family would be among them.

Mrs. Evers suffered from dementia, punctuated by brief periods of lucidity. Her son, Gordon, came every day to fix her dinner. Sometimes, if he had a long day at work, he brought Chinese take-out or maybe just a pizza. But no matter, he came each day to care for the mother who once did the same for him and could no longer do so for herself.

"Hello, Lucy. I have to fly to Los Angeles on business. I'll be leaving Tuesday night and won't be back until next Wednesday," Gordon said when he called the week before. Lucy, the nurse who stayed with his mother each day, was one of those rare people who actually cared. Gordon knew that she loved the old woman and probably would have cared for his mother without pay. She loved all of those for whom she worked.

"No problem, Mr. Gordon. I got you covered," she replied, self-consciously preening as she spoke, though she felt far too old and plain for him. Still, her heart beat faster when they spoke, and the romance for which she yearned but which had always eluded her danced at the edges of her mind.

"I'll buy us some dinner," Lucy said, though hardly able to afford it.

"You'll do nothing of the kind," Gordon said, refusing her generous offer. "I left an extra two hundred dollars in the petty cash drawer for dinner and traveling money in case you need it."

"You don't worry about that storm. It's supposed to hit South Florida and will probably break up like most do. Even if it don't, we'll be okay. That old shotgun house of your mom's survived all these years. Why it didn't get a drop of water during Hurricane Camille, so I can't imagine we'll have anything to worry about.

"But if it looks like it's coming here, I'll get the van, and Bobby will help me tote her out. We'll head up to Meridian for a few days, then come back when the coast is clear. If need be, I'll get the house prepared for the storm."

"Thanks, Lucy. Don't know what I'd do without you.

"Have a good trip."

CHAPTER 37

Though the thought of being raped sickened her, Lolo would stand tough, determined not to let this animal have Evie or Kira. She stood defiant as Talib leered, "Strip." He raised his pistol. "Do it or I'll shoot you in the leg then rip your clothes off myself."

"Okay, big man, let's get this show on the road. We'll see if you can perform, or if you're all talk. Honestly, my experience with loud-mouthed assholes like you is that when it comes time to be a man, the problems start," Lolo said while unbuttoning her blouse.

Talib was enjoying the infidel's show and smiled broadly. "Trust me, there will be no problems in that department." A cautious man, he looked up in time to see Willy holding Akmed's gun. Both men raised their weapons at the same time: Willy at Talib, and Talib at Lolo.

"It would appear that we have what I believe you call a Mexican standoff. Problem is, I'm not afraid to die, but I'm betting she is. Toss your gun over here before I count to three. You shoot me, and I promise I'll kill her before you can send me to meet my 72 virgins."

Willy hesitated for a moment before tossing the gun on the ground to his left, standing ready to react. Talib paused then squeezed the trigger, shooting Lolo in the heart. With a surprised look on her face, she stumbled backwards over a box of spare parts. She lay on the ground, blood gushing from a hole above her left breast, as the life faded from her eyes.

"You bastard," Willy yelled. But as he prepared to charge, Talib coolly swung the pistol around, intending to put a round through Willy's right eye when Willy took two steps and lunged beside the shed and out of Talib's line of fire, where his gun lay. Hearing the voices of the others drawn by the sound of gunfire, Talib realized it was time to leave and melted away.

Quint rounded the corner of the building to find Lolo lying dead and Willy getting back up, holding a pistol. A moment later, he heard Talib slam the van in gear and spin tires as he sped out of the parking lot slinging gravel. Quint fired and shot out the back window, putting a second round inches from Talib's head before the van rounded the corner. "Dammit all! Talib got away," he yelled.

"Lolo! Is she dead?" Dakota asked as he rushed forward to kneel beside her.

"I'm afraid so," Quint replied.

"Where's another truck? That SOB's not getting away," Dakota screamed in frustration knowing that by the time he found another vehicle with enough gas to do him any good it would be too late.

"Dakota, we have to leave, or we'll get caught by the storm. Talib can't make it far with the flooding. The storm will deal with him, but if we don't leave right now, it'll get us too," Jacques said rubbing his jaw. Without replying, Dakota held Lolo's head in his lap while stroking her hair, dampened by drops streaming from his face.

Having questioned Akmed in the marina office, Leo and Kira joined Quint outside. "This goon isn't talking, and we don't have the time to fool with him any longer. I don't want to take him with us and have to worry about him getting loose," Kira said.

Quint nodded his agreement. "We'll leave him here. Katrina can show him the mercy he deserves. If he survives, Rogers can deal with—" a ringing phone interrupted him. It took a moment to realize it was Akmed's cell phone. "Akmed?" Rashid asked, when the ringing stopped.

"No, Akmed is indisposed," Quint replied. "I'm guessing you're Rashid."

"Who's this?"

"Quint. As to what I'm doing with Akmed's phone, we just killed the rest of your assholes, and now we're working on him. In addition to all of the other things they did on your behalf, your goons raped my girlfriend, Evie. How about you and I go a round or two; where you at?"

It took a moment for Rashid to grasp the situation. "You and I *will* go a round but not now. I'll find you—you can count on it," Rashid replied before severing the connection.

After noting the number, Quint slammed the phone to the ground just as Kira appeared, directing Akmed outside the office. She tied him to the flagpole in front of the building and pulled his pants down. "You guys seemed so proud of your tools, we're going to let you show them off to Katrina, though I doubt she'll be impressed," Kira said and delivered him a parting kick.

"That was Omar," Akmed grunted with fear in his eyes. "If you leave me here with that storm approaching, I'll die."

"As Talib was so fond of saying, 'Then that is Allah's will,'" Kira replied with a grin.

While the team regrouped, Willy retrieved a snorkel he had spotted in the storage building. "You might need this when the water begins to rise," Willy said and stuck it in Akmed's mouth, strapping it in place with duct tape. He turned to Kira, "Here's a swim mask. It's a gift for your little guy."

Kira smiled at the gesture toward her baby then got Quint aside. "Quint, Evie needs medical attention; she's bleeding from her private parts. I don't need to say why." Quint grimaced. "Until we can get her to a hospital, you need to comfort her. This is going to be tough on her—she needs your support. By the way, where's Fred?"

"Fred's dead," Quint said.

"Oh no."

"Oh no, what?" Leo said as he came walking up.

"Fred's dead."

"Fred's dead? Oh, the lizard," Leo replied.

"Iguana," Kira replied. "Does Evie know?"

"No," Quint replied.

"I'll tell her," Kira offered.

"Tell her what?" Willy asked.

"Fred's dead," Quint repeated once again.

"Fred's dead?" Willy echoed.

"Who's dead?" Mimi said as she joined the group.

"Fred's dead. The lizard is no longer living. He is expired," Quint said, exasperated, and glanced quickly around to confirm that Evie had not heard his rant.

CHAPTER 38

After Katrina crossed the tip of Florida, it headed northwest and on its new path drew energy from a massive warm water eddy in the northern Gulf. It bloomed into a Category 5 monster, pushing a huge surge before the massive killer headed to give the Mississippi and Louisiana Gulf coasts a drubbing.

Lucy called Gordon on the house phone. "It looks bad."

"Yeah, it's all over the news out here in L.A. You're leaving, right?"

"Yes, sir. Just calling to put your mind at ease."

"You need me to come back?"

"Mr. Gordon, you couldn't get here—they're closing the airports. But don't you worry, I'm already packing. I'll try to keep you posted."

"You really need a cell phone."

"I know, but I hate the things."

"I'd have bought Mom one, but she can't hear to use it anyhow. When I get back I'm getting you one."

"Okay, okay. I'm heading north. I'll call you as soon as I know where we're going to be. I'm picking up Bobby so he can get the house battened down and help me load up your mom. Just finish your business, and we'll talk once I get up north and can get an open line. You know how the phones get with everybody calling everybody."

"Yep. Drive safely. And Lucy... thanks." As Gordon hung up, he couldn't shake a feeling of apprehension. *Lucy will take care of things; she always does,* he told himself.

Lucy put her small bag and a larger one for Mrs. Evers in the back of her car and went back into the house to get her purse when she heard the phone ring again. *My goodness, aren't we popular today?* she said to herself.

"Hello?"

"Hello, this is Quint. You may recall I stopped by the other day to visit Mrs. Evers," Quint said. He had paused to take a moment to call and miraculously reached her.

"Oh yes, she was thrilled to see you. Talked more about you afterwards than anyone else I can remember ever since she's started going downhill."

"Well, with this storm coming I just called to check on her and make sure you didn't need any help," he said, unsure what he could possibly do.

"How sweet. But no, I've got it under control. In fact, I was just about to go get Bobby to help us board up. Then we'll be on the road headed north. We're not taking any chances. Thanks so much for checking on her. You be careful too," Lucy said and headed back out to pick up Bobby before loading up Mrs. Evers. Already the traffic was bad. The store where Bobby worked was closed when she arrived. With the store boarded up, the staff had already been dismissed to make their personal preparations.

We'll make do, she thought. *Boarding up probably would have been a waste of time. That ol' house ain't going nowhere anyhow.* She did worry about how she would get Mrs. Evers in the car, but somehow she would manage.

As she pulled onto the main street, a young driver, frustrated with the traffic, sped down the shoulder of the road. She caught only a glimpse as the pickup plowed into the driver's door of her compact car, crushing her. In the last moment before her life flickered out she wondered, *But what about Mrs. Evers?*

CHAPTER
39

The reunited team gathered their meager foraged supplies and joined Jacques waiting at the boat. "We need more food and water," Kira said, handing Jacques the collection of toys the men had gathered for the baby.

"We don't have time to look for more now," Jacques replied. "If it's not already too late to make it to Port Eads, it will be shortly." It had taken nearly an hour to convince Dakota that they couldn't take Lolo's body and that it didn't make sense for him to stay with her.

"We can borrow some supplies from the New Orleans Big Game Club clubhouse when we get there. By the way, I thought the little one might need one of these," Jacques said, handing Kira a plastic Frisbee he had found lying beside the boat storage building. Kira smiled and placed the gift in the growing pile of ridiculous but well intended items.

The river waters were much higher than when they had crossed over to Venice only a few short hours before, and the seas were building even in these protected waters. They continued south against head seas as fast as the boat could run without beating them senseless.

Quint noticed Evie softly crying as she turned away. He caught a look from Kira, who mouthed the word "Fred," indicating she had broken the news. After a grueling run, the towering lighthouse appeared through the driving rain.

"There she is. After a series of earlier attempts were destroyed or abandoned for various reasons, they finished her in 1881, and she's still standing tall," Jacques proudly announced.

"You sure the lighthouse keeper will be okay with us using it as a refuge?" Leo asked.

"That's not a problem. It's been automated for over 60 years," Jacques replied as they pulled up to the Port Eads dock, catching a break in the rain.

The hoist beside the river, where tons of game fish had been weighed over the decades since the club's founding, swung about crazily. The weather-worn board used to record tournament results twisted in the fierce wind. An empty wooden rocking chair sailed across the long, shaded porch of the clubhouse, which sat just above the rising waters. A scarce few feet above sea level, the clubhouse had fared remarkably well over the years through countless storms.

During normal times the more experienced captains on the frequent supply boats would idle as they passed the docks and clubhouse as a courtesy to avoid washing away the ancient dilapidated docks. Soon this would no longer be a concern—the docks would cease to exist.

"Damn, you should be wearing your 'Where the Hell is Port Eads?' t-shirt," Dawson said as he jumped onto the rickety dock to tie up. His attempt at levity failed to elicit a response from Dakota, who had been silent since Lolo's death.

Jacques was the next out and led the way toward the base of the lighthouse. Stepping from the wooden walkway, he balanced on the remaining boards and sloshed through the dark, rising river water where others had already floated away. With Quint's help, Evie hobbled after the team, taking short steps and gritting her teeth.

Jacques jumped and Kira screamed when a huge alligator spooked ahead of them and scrambled into the marsh grass. They climbed the rust-streaked steps of the lighthouse base and unlatched the heavy metal door, which blew open on squeaking hinges. Illuminated by the beam of a flashlight, more boards set on rocks led across puddles of brackish water trapped on the corroded steel floor.

Clouds of mosquitoes rose and flew nervously about the faces of the team members, despite the team's continual attempts to shoo them away. A snake, slithering to the far side to escape the beam of light, sent Kira hopping onto the steps of a circular staircase that rose into the darkness above.

"Welcome to Port Eads," Jacques said. "It may not be the end of the earth, but you can see it from here. I need a couple of you to give me a hand for a minute. The rest of you make your way up the tower. It's 117 steps to the top not counting the 10 up to the light, so take your time. We'll be right back."

Dawson turned to join him as Quint spoke in a whisper to Willy and Leo. "Evie is barely able to walk and needs to be carried up the stairs. I'm afraid I'm not up to it with these busted ribs. If you guys can help her, I'd appreciate it. I'll follow Jacques to the New Orleans Big Game clubhouse and try to give him a hand." As Quint followed Jacques, Willy helped Evie, and Leo looked after Dakota whose injured leg was causing him trouble climbing the steps, though he suffered in silence.

The porch was nearly awash in the rising river water, and legions of crabs scurried across the deck as they walked back to the clubhouse. Finding the door unlocked, Jacques gripped the dented brass knob hard against the wind as it swung open. He dispensed flashlights and continued across the creaking floor into the kitchen area while Quint and Dawson hung back, shining their lights around the clubhouse.

Faded black and white photos of anglers with their prize catches adorned the walls above an older high water mark, the lower photos lost to previous hurricane-induced floods. Smiling anglers stood proudly beside gigantic billfish and tuna hanging from the club scale, while other fishermen crouched in front of piles of billfish stacked on the dock like cordwood. Clearly, these photos preceded the onset of tag-and-release.

"Look, Dawson, it's Guy Billups," Quint said pointing to a photo taken in the '70s of a man standing beside an enormous marlin hanging from a hoist. Dawson nodded, recognizing the man who had gained a stellar reputation as a serious blue water fisherman in his younger days.

"If this storm is as bad as I suspect," Jacques interrupted to urge them on, "this place won't be around after the storm. But we'll pay them back anyhow for whatever we take. Load bottled water and canned goods into boxes you'll find in the pantry. I'll look for batteries, candles, more flashlights and maybe a lantern with fuel."

A short while later, sweat poured down Jacques' face as he hoisted an enormous box onto his shoulder, with Dawson following suit. Quint gritted his teeth and lifted a large box, fighting daggers of pain from his cracked rib before proceeding back to the lighthouse. The rising river had washed away most of the remaining boards, and they sloshed noisily through the floodwaters, hoping to scare away any animals or reptiles.

"What you guys doing?" a voice from the dark caused the men to jump.

Jacques turned in surprise. "Oh, Jimbo. We plan to ride out the storm in the lighthouse and borrowed some stuff from the New Orleans Big Game clubhouse."

"What in the hell made you guys decide to come to the end of the earth to greet Katrina?"

"It's a long story. Basically, we ran out of time and got stuck here. Tell the Big Game folks we'll square things with them after the storm, assuming we're still here to do so."

"No problem. They'll be glad someone was able to use it before the storm blew everything all to hell. I was just checking on things over here. I've got to go back to the fuel dock to finish up, then I'll join you."

"Need a hand?"

"No, me and Tony got it under control. We started two days ago, so there's not much more we can do. Be back in a while." They would be the last people to ever see him alive.

After Jimbo vanished back into the darkness, Jacques once again climbed the dozen steps to the circular platform and continued through the doorway into the structure, pausing to secure the steel door to prevent it from pounding. The empty clang of the heavy lighthouse door closing behind Jacques sounded like a slamming prison door. For an instant, he had doubts. *Was coming here the right decision? Or have I led us all to our deaths? Whichever, I suppose it's done now,* he thought to himself.

The men stepped carefully on the boards and plastic-crate stepping stones as they crossed the flooded floor of the lighthouse. They moved slowly as their eyes adjusted to the dim light from the team above while keeping an eye out for the snake.

The dank musty smell of the lighthouse complemented the peeling paint and rusty metal, and all contributed to the depressing feeling of entering into a trap. Once the water began to rise there would be no leaving—they were here for the duration.

Jacques set his box down and grabbed two boards, setting them on the steps against the handrail. "When the serious flooding begins, we'll need these boards to battle the snakes and rats that will try to join us."

The men trudged up the endless circular stairway to the platform above, pausing at the second level. They rested at each level to stand by the single window and suck in the fresh air while adjusting their loads. Jacques took pains to avoid looking down because of his debilitating fear of heights. Soaked with perspiration, they finally emerged at the top, where Colin helped set the boxes on the steps below the glass-enclosed lighthouse room.

Dawson collapsed onto the steps to catch his breath. He stuck his tongue in the hole left by Willy's tooth extraction. It was sore, but no longer ached unmercifully. He glanced across the landing and caught Kira staring at him. She smiled nervously and looked off as she thrashed at one of the huge cockroaches swarming in from the marsh.

Even dog tired and disheveled, she was beautiful. For a moment, Dawson's stomach muscles tightened, and he desperately wanted to hold her. But, as he had so many times concluded before, it could not be, especially now that she carried Colin's child. The opportunity to be with her had come and was now forever gone. He shifted positions and in minutes was enjoying his first real sleep in several days.

The rest of the team were sprawled against the steel steps and leaning against the lighthouse walls struggling to come to terms with the discomfort of their shelter. Drenched by the relentless rains, their clothing refused to dry in the nearly 100-percent humidity and the howling winds that blew spray through every opening.

Everyone battled the mosquitoes that occupied the lighthouse, hoping that once the pests were either sated or smashed, the team would no longer be tormented by them. The legions of these particular pests, which normally infested the marsh grass, would be drowned or blown far away by the storm.

Quint considered disabling the annoying light that strobed through the narrow windows but decided against it in the off chance some poor ship captain might actually still be out there relying on the lighthouse. Of course, if he thought the authorities would come and arrest him now and take them all to some far north jail, he would cut the light off in a heartbeat.

Eventually, his thoughts drifted to Venezuela, where the team had worked well together while solely focused on their mission. During the past few days, he felt they had morphed into a special group capable of handling nearly anything, and he was proud.

Hoping to find a more comfortable position on the steel stairway, Quint kept shifting about. Evie slept fitfully, periodically mumbling and lashing out at some invisible adversary. It wasn't hard to guess that she was dealing with Talib and the others in her dreams as she probably would for a very long time. He moved her torso and disrupted her enough to seemingly stop the dreams, and she breathed deeply, no longer fidgeting.

Quint stroked Evie's hair, carefully tucking each lock in place. His heart ached for what she had endured and the realization that things would never again be the same. It killed him that he was unable to protect her from that horror, and he longed to seek vengeance on her behalf.

LaRue remained awake worrying about Berto, who would never consider his debt settled. *What would he do?* He doubted that he would find Berto to be understanding. *He could run, but where and for how long?* Berto had a long reach, and the prospect of living with the fear of being found was not appealing. *Now that Quint knew, would the team help him? Could they?* For the next hour, he replayed the same thought sequence in his mind until, exhausted, sleep finally found him.

A loud sound like ripping paper followed by a foul odor woke Dakota. He looked about and linked the problem to Leo, who lay sprawled on the landing a few feet away. Dakota pulled his t-shirt over his mouth and nose until the smell abated.

The image of *Searcher* entered his mind, saddening him. He hated the loss of any ship, especially his own. This was the first time for him, and he hated the thought. He pictured the ship lying on the bottom, clouds of fish searching inside it to find a new home. He imagined a large Jewfish manning his bridge as he had seen while diving numerous wrecks. His thoughts then drifted to Lolo, and his eyes teared.

Exhausted from their ordeal, he finally rejoined the rest of the team and managed to sleep despite the screeching wind from the raging storm, the dampness, and the discomfort of lying on the hard metal stairway. During the night, the flood waters rose, and the lighthouse door swung open, forcing the team to take turns preventing animals, rodents, and reptiles from seeking shelter by ascending the stairs.

It would be a long night.

After escaping from the episode in Venice, Talib soon found the flooded roads made vehicular travel impossible. With no other option, he abandoned the truck and climbed to the second story of the tallest nearby building to wait out the storm.

Debris carried by the wind and storm surge battered the structure, and it soon disintegrated, leaving Talib floating in the churning floodwater. Struggling to remain afloat, he clung to a treetop barely protruding above the water. For hours he fought off snakes, a variety of terrified animals, and an endless array of floating debris, which battered his body and tore at his flesh while the angry water tried to pluck him away.

Quint awoke a few hours later, his body stiff and cramped from serving as Evie's pillow. It was still dark, and he checked his watch to find it nearly midnight. He began to work his way through a long list of worries. He worried about Evie's condition and how long before they could get her proper medical treatment. He worried about their relationship and how she would handle being raped. For a moment, he confronted his own concern about how he would handle it.

He worried about how long before they would be rescued, given that their boat was certain to be swept away. Twenty miles from the closest civilization, it would be impossible to walk through the marsh. *How long before someone will think to check out the lighthouse?* Quint wondered.

He thought about how he would catch Rashid. Then he worried about whether he could restrain himself from beating the man to a pulp. Finally, sleep found him once again.

When he next awoke, he carefully extricated himself from beneath Evie and stood, working the kinks out of his back and shoulders while brushing off the flecks of black paint and rust that clung to his skin and cargo shorts.

The screeching wind poured through every crack, and the entire lighthouse structure seemed to sway in the high winds. Though Quint knew it had survived countless storms, he prayed it could survive one more to still be standing when Katrina moved on.

As he looked around, he noticed several of the others remained awake despite their struggles to escape into unconsciousness. Far below, he heard Dawson muttering as he battled some foe from climbing the stairs, and Quint decided to join him.

"Having fun?" Quint said as he approached the base of the lighthouse steps.

Dawson motioned to the large stick in his hand as he replied,

"Just defending the fort from an onslaught of slithering creatures and rabid vermin, literally, rather than figuratively, as is generally the case."

Quint saw two rats the size of cats floating on the far side beside the body of a snake. "Looks like you've been busy. Want me to relieve you?"

"No, I couldn't sleep and decided to make myself useful. You can join me, though. I've been thinking."

"Uh-oh, should I be worried?"

Dawson smiled. "You know, Quint, if we're going to be serious about this LLC thing, we'll need an operations center. Given the types of things we might be getting into, it would be best if it were non-U.S. based, if you know what I mean."

"Though I haven't thought much about it, I suppose you're right. While anything we might do would likely be sanctioned by the feds, you're right, it would be more comfortable for everyone concerned if we were based elsewhere. Probably be some tax benefits as well. Got something in mind?"

"Just so happens I do. There's a neat but little-known island a ways off the coast of Cuba, which was a base used in the '60s by the Ruskies until they abandoned it after the Cold War ended. From the research I did a while back it was developed by the Germans then used near the end of WW II when they saw the handwriting on the wall, and their senior folks started fleeing to South America.

"Since it's too remote to offer much commercial appeal and doesn't offer any particular strategic advantage, it's been abandoned by the Cubans. But it's perfect for our needs." Dawson briefed Quint on what he knew about the old base.

"You're right, it does sound perfect. High elevation, deep water, an airstrip albeit an old one, and an existing base we can use as an opcenter. But what about the little problem of U.S.-Cuban relations?"

"Well, since ol' Fidel is out of the picture, things are not as cold as you might think based solely on what we hear in the news. Behind the scenes things have been warming a great deal. With all the stroke this Rogers seems to have, I was thinking maybe he could help negotiate a deal to buy it with the bonus he offered to pay us."

"Sounds too good to be true, but I guess there's no harm in asking. You don't think our previous run-in will be an issue?" Quint said, referring to an unpleasant encounter they had had earlier with the Cuban navy.

"Not so long as they don't know. With that Admiral out of the picture, only the crew and that captain would recognize us, and none of them know our names."

"Well, you're sure thinking outside of the box," Quint said. "I like the basic idea. When we get back, we'll run it by Rogers and see what he says," Quint said as he took the board from Dawson to repel another would-be attacker from the bottom stair.

CHAPTER
40

Blissfully unaware of the looming hurricane, Mrs. Evers could not sense the time of day. She lay in the middle room of her shotgun-style house, wallowing in the damp spot of her bed while waiting for her son, Gordon, to come. A spider on the window screen to her left worked on a struggling fly caught in its web.

Mrs. Evers had been bedridden since falling and breaking her hip the summer before last. Unable to make the short trip to the bathroom in the back of her modest house, she had soiled herself more than usual that day. This, along with pangs of hunger, told her that Gordon was late. The fact was, he would not be coming to pay her a visit—but Katrina would.

Mrs. Evers could no longer read the clock nor sense the time of day as she lay watching the small spider work on its unfortunate victim. It was dark now, and she was hungry.

She grasped for the last hard candy from the bedside bowl, knocking it from her bedside table to shatter on the floor. Her arthritis-wracked fingers tore at the paper until she finally popped the partially wrapped candy into her mouth. She turned it over and over her tongue as the candy dissolved, trying to remove the remaining wrapper, which she spit onto the bed beside her pillow.

"Henry, you need to board up the windows. It sounds like a bad storm. Where is Gordon? That boy should have been home hours ago. He's in for a whipping... wait, he was supposed to bring me supper. He always brings me supper. Maybe the rain is delaying him."

Rain drumming off the tin roof made her sleepy, and when she awoke, she could hear banging against the wooden siding of her house. Through the night she lay scared and lonely, occasionally speaking to Henry, her husband, who now lived only in her memories.

She dozed off again, and when she awoke, the wind was shrieking. As she lay in her bedroom, she could hear the rain drumming the tin roof and the sound of things slamming against the wooden siding of the living room in the front of her house.

On the beach, the water began to rise, slowly at first, then so fast it appeared as an amorphous wall which, coupled with the buoyant force of the rising water bulldozed everything in its path. Houses trembled then collapsed from the lethal one-two punch. Those who had stayed, lured into a sense of false security by having survived Camille in the same location, died as the 25-foot surge moved relentlessly across the beach highway and continued unabated onto the low coastal plain.

Boats and debris became battering rams, destroying entire neighborhoods. Cars bobbed in the churning water along with the roofs of houses and some entire dwellings until they were ripped into smaller pieces. Frenzied animals both domestic and wild of all shapes and sizes, struggled to escape the liquid wall of death. But when it was over, most would end up bloated corpses.

As morning broke, the wind moaned through the attic vents, and the house groaned in protest. She felt the dwelling shudder but had no clue why. It looked strange outside. "What is a fish doing at my window?" she wondered seconds before the window shattered, unleashing the flood waters into the room.

"What's happening?"

"Gordon? I want my Gordon," she cried, bewildered as water poured into her house, quickly filling the room. In seconds her mattress was floating. Windblown rain and mist off the rising water filled the air around her.

"Oh, God. Oh, God," she yelled.

Summoning every ounce of strength in her withered body she turned on her side. She fought to raise a few inches while her claw-like hands clutched at the headboard as the salty spray burned her eyes and the shriek of the wind drowned her voice. Her hand touched the metal bedframe and a fingernail hung on a rivet, ripping it, a thin trail of blood coursing from her bony finger. With all her might, she pulled herself up, desperate to get higher as the water lapped at the edge of her mattress.

"Henry, help me. Henry..." her voice was lost when her weight shifted, and she slid off the mattress, landing face down in the water. As she sank beneath the surface, a lucid moment found her.

Oh my... it feels good to float. I'm free! Finally free of that bed. I'm going to die! But it's worth dying to be free of that bed for even a moment.

God, is it time for me to go? I'm ready. I'm truly ready.

She saw Gordon waving as he boarded the bus on the first day of second grade, not wanting her to accompany him. She saw her parents gathered at the picnic table passing a platter of Sunday fried chicken. Then a bright light burst in her head and she saw...

Henry, is that you? she cried silently just before losing consciousness.

The collapsing bedroom wall freed her body to float from the house alongside the furniture that had stood at her bedside for all those years. The surge carried her into the arms of the huge live oak tree beneath which she and her husband had watched Gordon play as a child. There she spent the remainder of the storm locked in its embrace while the mattress continued to float on its journey out to sea.

CHAPTER 41

"These are all the paper cups we have, so hang on to yours," Mimi said, handing each team member a cup of water to accompany the breakfast of sorts, which Colin and Kira organized from their collection of food stuffs. The team ate in silence, listening to the vicious howl of the wind.

It was hard to judge the time of day with the heavy layer of clouds and rain blocking most of the sunlight. By mid-morning, the wind began easing slightly. When they were not dozing, the team took turns gazing through the lighthouse windows to marvel at the angry sea, which covered the marsh grass below. As expected, there was no sign of the clubhouse, the docks, or their workboat.

The flood waters receded later in the day, and Quint saw a flotilla of unmanned boats drifting by toward the open ocean. The bloated bodies of cows dotted the waters amidst a field of debris drifting past including sections of dock, roof tops, trees, plastic items of all types, a school bus, and large tanks of various descriptions.

"Hope you guys like it here, because we're trapped until somebody rescues us," Kira said. By nightfall, the entire team was numb and dreading a second night in their Spartan refuge. Their meager food supplies were nearly exhausted, and no one seemed enthusiastic about eating Spam from a can or joining Leo, who was eating the pickled pigs feet he had found back in Venice.

Dawson awoke to the sound of a helicopter early Tuesday morning and ran out onto the lighthouse platform above. In the distance, he saw a military chopper surveying the damage. He stripped off his shirt and waved it while shouting at the top of his lungs, fully aware that he could not be heard. A minute later, the rest of the team joined him, all waving to attract attention.

Finally the pilot spotted them and swung in their direction. The crew waved back before raising the team on the radio. "We'll send help." The cheers from the team nearly eclipsed the roar of the helicopters engines as it swung around to head north.

The sound of a helicopter once again drew the team's attention a few hours later. They ran out to see a large privately labeled helicopter swoop toward them. A man inside the open side door held a bull horn to his mouth. "We are rescue volunteers here to evacuate you. Do you have any injured?" he asked. Quint held up a hand with one finger. The man nodded.

"Head to the bottom of the lighthouse. We'll hover over that area to the southeast so that you can climb aboard," he said, then the chopper dropped below to hover over the waterlogged marsh grass.

The team filed down the steps and waded across the marsh where the helicopter crew plucked each of them into the helicopter. Kira smiled at Colin carrying her load of "gifts" for their baby. Things were going to be all right.

"Anyone else?" the crewman asked as he saw Quint bringing up the rear.

"There were two guys who worked at Port Eads, but they never returned to join us in the lighthouse as they had planned. I think they're gone," Quint finished. The man nodded grimly, spoke into his helmet mic, and the chopper rose to head back north. The team was rescued.

The helicopter landed at the New Orleans airport, where rescue operations were being staged. The team exited while the paramedic, still wearing his helmet and dark visor, spoke with Evie. "You need medical attention. With most of the roads blocked by debris or flooded, the only way to reach the hospital is by chopper. We'll drop you off there before we make our next rescue foray." Medics loaded the helicopter with another patient on a stretcher and some supplies requested by the hospital. Quint was stopped when he started to re-enter the helicopter.

"Sir, I'm afraid you'll have to remain here. As you might imagine, the hospital has limited facilities and are inundated with injured. No friends, family, or caregivers are allowed to accompany the injured. And even though we're nearly full, we still have another pickup.

She'll be fine and can contact you by radio. Check with the rescue dispatch office in hangar two; they'll help you two stay in touch."

Quint gave Evie a worried look, but she squeezed his hand and kissed his cheek to calm him. "I'll be okay."

A minute later, the chopper lifted off, headed for the hospital. The shot the paramedic gave Evie to calm her left her feeling relaxed for the first time since her ordeal with the terrorists, as the pain from the abuse eased. But once they had travelled out of sight of the airport, the chopper banked west.

The paramedic unlashed the stretcher beside Evie then stood and casually remarked, "Let's make more room in here." He shoved the stretcher and patient through the open side door and tossed the hospital supplies out as well before removing his helmet. With a broad smile, he introduced himself. "Evie, I'm Rashid."

"Good to hear from you. I was worried sick." Quint's first order of business had been to find a working satphone to contact Rogers.

"We recovered Big Bertha but had to jettison her once again," Quint went on to explain what had happened and gave Rogers the coordinates where the bomb was jettisoned. "While the marker buoy will probably be gone, the transponder should remain working."

"You guys up for another shot?"

"If it's all the same, I think we'll sit out Big Bertha's second recovery. On another subject, this place is a zoo; can you extract us?"

"No problem, they're sending a bunch of military choppers down there to assist. I'll see about diverting one to pick you up."

"By the way, we left one of the terrorists, Akmed, tied to a flagpole in Venice. I'm guessing that Katrina has dealt with him already, but you might want to check it out." Quint returned the satphone to the dispatcher and advised her where he would be before joining the team lounging in the FBO hanger.

Quint sprawled out and immediately fell asleep. Asleep only 20 minutes, he was awakened by the sound of the dispatcher's voice. "Sir, you have a call," she said, offering him the satphone. Quint struggled to his feet rubbing his eyes, trying to get awake before raising the phone to his ear.

"Hello, Quint. We chat again," a vaguely familiar voice said. Expecting it to be Rogers or the chopper crew, Quint was confused.

"Who is this?"

"Well we haven't yet met, though it's long overdue, but I would have thought you'd recognize my voice from our last chat. Must have caught you sleeping. It's Rashid, and I have someone here who would like to say hello," he said, handing Evie the phone.

"Quint, I'm okay," Evie said to ease Quint's mind, "but this guy has me in some building, and it's not a hospital. I'm in Louisiana, he's—"

"Okay, that's enough chatting for now, you two lovebirds," Rashid interrupted.

"Your fight is with me."

"I agree. By the way, my men were right, your woman is, or should I say was, quite attractive."

"Well, to the extent her appearance is not up to par, we can thank your goons."

"What can I say; boys will be boys," Rashid replied.

"The only saving grace is that you can rest assured that your 'boys' look far worse than her."

"I'm not surprised; you Americans are famous for being cowboys."

"And proud of it."

"Well, I suggest you don't go cowboy on *me*, unless you wish for me to go Indian on *her*."

"Rashid, if you have any thoughts about harming one more hair on her head, much less raping her, I would suggest you reconsider. Because if you do, I will hunt you down like the dog you are and make you pay far more than you can possibly imagine."

"I'm really scared, Quint, but you're not getting her back until we work out a trade. You know what I want in return."

Quint's stomach knotted—the bomb. Dawson noticed that Quint was upset as he walked up. "Rashid," Quint mouthed with his hand over the receiver's mouthpiece. "Well, I hate to disappoint you, but we don't have it. Your guys forced us to jettison it."

"Quint, please don't think me a fool. I know that. I also know you can find it, and you will do so. That is, if you want Evie back in the same, somewhat battered shape in which I found her."

Quint wanted to jump through the phone and grab Rashid by the throat to squeeze the life from his evil body. "My ship is sunk and, as you well know, the entire area is a mess. How the hell am I supposed to do that?"

"You're an enterprising guy; you'll figure out something. I would suggest that you preempt the Navy from recovering it first as they might not be quite so willing to negotiate for your fraulein. You've got two days before I start whittling away on your girl. Spend them wisely; she needs medical attention," Rashid said then hung up.

"Damn!" Quint said, kicking a soft drink can across the tarmac. He filled Dawson in. The two men discussed options, neither mentioning the looming elephant—they could not let Rashid get the bomb.

An hour later, the dispatcher informed the team that their ride had arrived. Quint asked to use the satphone again and called Rogers. "You know I thought it over. We probably do need to be involved with the recovery. It shouldn't take long, and we don't want it sitting there unguarded. It would really suck to have the terrorists end up with it after all we've been through."

Rogers was surprised by Quint's abrupt change of mind but was glad to have the help. "Great, you want me to see how soon the Navy can get a ship up there?"

"No, Jacques has a buddy who always takes his boat up the river before a storm. He's sure it survived and that we can lease it for a couple of days," Quint said, praying that Jacques could come through.

"Okay, but I'll at least have Botz join you. The military won't be happy unless some of their boys are involved."

"No problem; we can use the help," Quint replied, cursing under his breath for having to put up with Botz again. The team boarded the chopper, and Quint briefed LaRue and Dakota on his plan while they flew. By the time they landed at the Air National Guard base in Meridian, Mississippi, the chopper crew had received their orders and immediately refueled.

"Dawson, LaRue, Dakota, and I are going to join the Navy team tasked to recover the bomb. We'll join back up with the rest of you before long," Quint said, deciding not to involve the rest of the team in the Evie issue. Despite the pressure on him, Quint took the time to arrange to fly Mimi back home so that she could make her scheduled flight to visit Everett's family in England.

A couple of hours later, Jacques had arranged to lease his

buddy's boat, and the four men re-boarded the chopper. It set down several miles north of Venice on the Mississippi River, where their leased boat awaited. Rogers had arranged for Botz to pick up dive equipment and weapons then meet them in Venice.

"Quint and Dawson, we meet again," Botz said as soon as Dakota eased the boat alongside the dock. "I didn't know Rogers was reaching so far down in the barrel. I guess it must have something to do with the storm," Col. Botz said greeting the team.

"And I thought you loved us. Rogers claimed you were quite impressed with us."

"Rogers is prone to exaggeration. I was impressed, however, with your role as bait."

Quint bit his lip and continued. "We're here, nonetheless, and authorized by Rogers to take charge. Feel free to check if you like."

"No problem, I'll be right here to take over when you fall short." A few minutes later, the equipment was loaded, and they were back under way.

After reconfirming that the coordinates for the jettisoned bomb were correctly entered in the nav system, Quint studied the waters, amazed at the debris they passed. Countless rooftops and even a few entire houses, all victims of Katrina's fury, floated by along with a herd of assorted animals and even a few human corpses. He wished they could recover the corpses for a proper burial but knew they could not afford the delay. Perhaps the Coast Guard would follow up on the positions Dakota recorded each time they spotted a body.

At least with all the confusion after the hurricane, they would be able to recover the bomb without drawing attention. When they reached the general vicinity, they interrogated the transponder that LaRue had affixed to the bomb and quickly located it this time.

Dakota signaled the dive team over the PA that they were on location. Dawson and LaRue were standing ready alongside the divers from Botz's team. With Dawson's coaching, they had the crane ready and cables rigged to retrieve the bomb much as the team had done the first time. While the buoy was long gone, the underwater beacon guided them to the bomb.

This time, the bomb was recovered in less than an hour, due in large part to the team's recent experience, the calm seas, and the fact that it was not buried deep in muck. With the bomb back on board, Dawson joined Quint, and the two headed for the bridge to discuss their plan to free Evie. They met Botz on the deck outside the bridge.

"I'm afraid we can't take that risk," Botz said reacting to their plan.

"I'm afraid we'll have to," Quint replied.

"You've already lost the bomb once."

"No, a mole in your organization was responsible for the terrorists nearly getting their hands on it."

"Mole? There was no mole. It was your ineptness that lost that bomb."

Dawson stepped forward, but Quint placed a hand on his chest to hold him back. "What about the transmitter we found on *Searcher* relaying our position? Did your mole have anything to do with that?" Quint said, removing his hand from Dawson's chest.

"Who knows? As I said, you guys make great bait," Botz replied with a barely concealed grin. "And what makes you think a mole planted the transmitter in the dive locker...," he blurted out before stopping abruptly.

A long silence ensued before Quint replied, "How did you know where we found it? We never told Rogers."

Without warning, Dawson stepped forward and landed a roundhouse punch on Botz, propelling him backwards over the railing to fall hard onto the deck below where he lay unmoving. "I've wanted to do that for a very long time," Dawson said, shaking his head. One of Botz's team went below to administer first aid while Quint gathered the rest of Botz's team aside to explain.

"Rashid's thugs have already raped and beaten Evie. I need the bomb as bait to keep him from killing her. I intend to do it with or without you, but I could sure use your help."

"We'll help you get her," one said with the rest nodding in agreement. "But Quint, you know we can't let him have that bomb," Botz's team leader said directly.

"I know. I just want a chance to get her back alive. Once we have her, we'll be ready to fight him. But no matter what happens, he's not getting the bomb."

Quint dialed Rashid on the satphone. "Okay we've got the bomb. Let me speak to Evie." Rashid handed the phone over.

"Are you okay?" Quint asked.

"Yes, at least no worse off than last time you saw me."

"He didn't..."

"No, he didn't rape me," Evie said quietly, after which Rashid was back on the phone.

"Quint, let's get this thing done. Give me your position, and we'll come meet you. I have a Sikorsky Super Stallion, more than capable of lifting the bomb, rigged with lifting gear and ready to go. Once you have the bomb loaded in the lifting harness, we'll lower your princess. Be ready within an hour and no tricks unless you prefer to get Evie back in pieces—she's wearing an explosives belt I made for her. Goes well with her outfit."

Quint gave him the coordinates. "How do I know I can trust you?"

"You don't," Rashid replied, as he hung up.

"What now?" Dakota asked.

"Rashid is bringing Evie in a chopper to swap for the bomb." They developed a plan to conceal shooters around the ship, ready to take Rashid down once Evie was safe.

"Where do you reckon they got their hands on that big mother of a chopper?"

"Who knows? With all of the confusion caused by the storm, he probably stole it," Quint replied. He called Rogers to explain the situation and try to get their own chopper brought in as backup.

"Quint, what are you thinking? I understand that you want to get Evie back, but it's not worth putting hundreds, maybe thousands of innocent people's lives at risk if Rashid gets that bomb back."

"That's not going to happen. We'll get Evie and keep the bomb. You have my word."

Though unconvinced, Rogers had few options, given the post-Katrina confusion and tight timeframe. He would have to trust Quint to deliver. "Let me see what I can do. This has priority; the problem is things are sort of crazy right now and, an hour doesn't give us much time," Rogers replied.

Sick with fear over Evie and focused on saving her, Dawson realized that Quint was not using his better judgment but understood his friend's quandary and chose not to intervene. He would, however, do whatever it took to help Quint get Evie back without giving up the bomb.

It was dark by the time they heard the approaching Sea Stallion. The helicopter made a pass over the ship then swung around and dropped until it was inches off the mirror-flat water. It hovered while

Rashid reviewed the plan with Quint. Thirty yards away, the helicopter's blinding searchlight swept the ship while the lifting harness descended on a cable through the bottom of the helicopter as it rose.

Once the handling line had touched the water to discharge static electricity, the chopper eased over the back deck of the ship, where it hovered in place. The ship's crew grabbed the lifting cable and secured it to the bomb. Three heavy cables remained, securing the bomb to the ship while Quint spoke with Rashid. "Okay, the bomb is ready to be lifted. Lower Evie." A second cable appeared out the side of the chopper, and Evie slowly descended. The crew was fixated on Evie as she was lowered, ready to grab her and then engage the helicopter.

Meanwhile, four dripping wet men appeared in dive gear from the far side of the ship holding machine pistols, now free of their protective plastic wrap. They herded the ship's crew into a group at the ship's stern to act as human shields against the concealed snipers.

"What's going on, Rashid? I thought we had a deal?" Quint yelled over the satphone.

"We do, but surely you didn't think I was so foolish as not to think past what would happen once you had your girlfriend back, even with the little belt I made for her. My divers have secured limpet mines to the hull of your ship. I have a transmitter that I can use to either trigger them to explode or disarm them. If the signal is disrupted for any reason, the charges have a 30-second fuse, not nearly enough time for your divers to mobilize and remove them. As soon as we clear the area, I will transmit the 'safe' command, disabling the remote."

"And if you don't?"

"Well, then you're screwed. Now release the bomb from the ship; we don't have much time. If you refuse, my men will mow your people down and then do it anyhow. Oh, and have your snipers stand down, or I'll blow Evie's belt right now."

Within minutes the snipers had joined the crew on the back deck, and the bomb was free of the ship. Once Evie was safely on board, Quint unhooked her harness. Rashid's divers clung to the lifting harness with their guns trained on the crew as the chopper lifted away, the bomb dangling beneath. Rashid's men quickly took in the slack until the bomb hugged the chopper's belly.

"Oh, by the way, the 10-minute backup timer just started running so you might want to get your divers in the water quickly," Rashid radioed back while still in range. The helicopter then dropped down as close as they dared to the water's surface to avoid being seen on radar as they sped toward land.

While they focused on removing Evie's explosives belt, the ship's dive team dropped into the water. A minute later the charges were removed from the ship's hull and discarded below. Once the divers were back on board, the ship got under way. They had travelled only a few hundred yards when a series of closely spaced explosions marked the detonation of the limpet mines.

Quint had Evie back but, despite his avowed intentions, the bomb was in Rashid's hands.

CHAPTER 42

Botz's face was bruised, and he was livid as he entered the bridge. "You sure as hell made a mess out of that one, now didn't you? And you managed to get my ass in a crack right along with your own."

"We'll get the bomb back," Quint said, having no idea how that would happen. He called Rogers on the ship's satphone and briefed him on the events—Rogers was not happy.

"Your chopper should be there any minute," Rogers angrily replied, not bothering to mention that it was filled with marines instructed not to let Rashid anywhere near the bomb had they arrived in time.

Quint hung up and turned back to Botz. "Rogers will have a chopper here shortly to pick us up so we can go after Rashid."

"You and I have a little score to settle," Botz said to Dawson.

"Look, Botz, you got what was coming to you after putting us all at risk twice. Besides, you'll recover to be as normal as ever." Though angry, Botz appeared unwilling to tangle with Dawson again. The chopper arrived a short time later.

They landed back at the Meridian air base and arranged for Evie to get *real* medical attention. After few hours sleep, Quint gathered the team shortly after dawn. He explained the situation and turned to LaRue, "We need to find Rashid quickly, and the only approach I've come up with is to have a chat with Berto."

"Who's Berto?" Leo asked.

LaRue hesitated, embarrassed to admit his predicament to the entire team but finally, deciding he had no choice, replied, "I'm in big trouble with a loan shark." He reluctantly explained the details.

"So after borrowing $35,000 to pay off your gambling debts, you've paid him tens of thousands in interest, then another $250,000 and he still wants another $500,000?" Dawson asked incredulous. LaRue nodded.

"Gosh, that seems a wee bit steep," Dawson said. "If we're going to pay him a visit to find Rashid, perhaps we need to see about renegotiating the terms of your loan as well."

"You don't understand; he's a bad ass," LaRue replied.

"But then, so are we," Dawson replied.

With the havoc the storm had wreaked on the cell phone system, LaRue was relieved when he heard Berto's voice. "Katrina didn't have her way with you?" LaRue said, appearing relaxed despite his knotted stomach.

"Nope. Rode her out in a plush suite at the Marriott Baton Rouge."

"I've got your money."

"That's great, LaRue. I was worried. Bring it to my office here on Airline Highway."

"No."

"What do you mean, no? Did you forget our last meeting?"

"No, in fact, that's why I'm not going there. I'm not interested in no beating again. This time, we do it my way. I'll be at da Marriott Hotel at two this afternoon. I'll go to your room and, if you ain't got no more goons, my buddy will bring your money."

"That's awfully short notice. I'm a busy man."

"I'm sorry, but it has to be then."

"Okay, since you've been a good customer, we'll do it your way. You better show up."

"I be there, Hoss," LaRue replied.

Within the hour, the team was in the chopper headed for Baton Rouge. Rogers had a government van waiting when they landed. A few minutes later, they pulled up in front of a large discount store, and Dawson stepped from the van. "We've got plenty of time before our 2 o'clock meeting. Pick me up in 15 minutes. I need to buy a few items. While I'm busy, LaRue, go find the stuff on this list."

A half-hour later, they had assembled everything on Dawson's lists and were headed for the hotel. The team dropped Dawson and Quint off shortly after noon and waited in a parking garage across the street. Dawson entered the hotel lounge beside the lobby near the front desk and used the house phone to call Berto's room. When there was no answer he gestured to Quint to confirm Berto was not in his room. He then chose a seat concealed behind a large column where he could watch who came and went.

Quint took a postion in the nearby lobby bar to watch as well. Avid football fans were drinking beer and watching a preseason game on TV, cheering each time a goal was attempted—successful or otherwise. Whenever the hotel doors opened, the traffic noise announced another person's entry into the lobby over the raucous sound of the game, so Quint was not worried about missing Berto.

Quint watched a bird perched in the still bushes of the courtyard outside. The sparkling blue water of the small pool offered cool relief from the humid afternoon heat as the pool boy straightened the chairs and lounges. A beer bottle sat beside two empty piña colada glasses that had attracted a parade of ants.

Quint heard the traffic noise increase and saw a man fitting LaRue's description of Berto. With long oily black hair, a potbelly protruding past his white linen suit coat, and two burly men it tow, it had to be Berto. The three men headed for the elevator, where Dawson, who was already in position, entered the elevator. He moved to the back as one of Berto's thugs pressed the button for the sixth floor and grunted to Dawson, "Floor?"

"I'm on six too."

Quint entered next and pressed the button for the fifth floor. When the elevator stopped at the fifth floor, Quint exited and when the doors closed, sprinted for the stairs, taking them two at a time. Pausing at the next floor, he waited at the end of the corridor, where he could see the elevator reflected in the mirror across the hall. When the elevator doors opened and he saw which way Berto and his thugs were headed, Quint ducked back into the stairwell.

Berto exited the elevator and took the left hallway, with Dawson quietly lagging behind. Dawson slowed as they stopped, and one of the thugs inserted his key card. Then, as the man pushed the door open and took one step into the room, Dawson struck the closest thug on the back of the head with his pistol, and shoved him into Berto, sending both men sprawling into the room.

Dawson pointed the gun at the remaining thug and pushed hard against the man's back, forcing him into the inside wall across from the door. The thug's head struck the wall hard, cracking his nose and spraying blood on the wall. Grabbing a handful of hair, Dawson jerked his head back and slammed it into the wall a second time.

Quint entered the room behind them and closed the door. Dawson struck Berto hard as he tried to stand and then used thick plastic ties to secure the men's hands. Quint piled the two thugs in the far corner of the room. After pulling the unconscious Berto to the small desk, Dawson retrieved his knife and with single motion of the razor-sharp blade slashed Berto's belt, pants, and underwear. He used duct tape to secure each of Berto's legs to one of the desk's.

Dawson found two Heinekens in the minibar and handed one to Quint. The two men sat with their legs propped on the bed, enjoying the cold beer while waiting for Berto to come around. Ten minutes later, Berto's heavy breathing was interrupted by a snort followed by a series of groans. Dawson fetched another beer from the minibar and poured the remains of the first one on the man's bloody face. Some of the beer found Berto's mouth, and he awoke coughing and gagging.

Berto opened his eyes to see Quint perched on the desk in front of him. Glancing down at his feet he saw his ruined pants and sensed rather than saw his nakedness below his large belly, "What the..."

"It looks like Sleeping Ugly has awakened. Ready to chat?" Quint asked.

"Who are you? What are you doing here?"

"If you don't mind, I'll ask the questions," Quint said with a smile. He sat his beer on the desk and placed a large metal briefcase on his lap. "I need to find Rashid, and I don't have much time to screw around. Where should I look?" Quint absentmindedly flipped the briefcase handle back and forth while awaiting a response.

"You don't know who you're screwing with."

"Aaaannnntttttttt!" Quint mimicked the sound of a buzzer, "wrong answer," he said, releasing the briefcase to land hard on its corner a few inches from the man's crotch. Berto twitched, startled at the impact.

Quint hopped off the desk and retrieved the case. "Sorry, almost hit your little guy. This thing is really heavy, it feels more like LaRue has lead bricks in here instead of money," Quint said, regaining his perch on the desk. "Now, what say we try this again, but next time I might not miss Mr. Weenie and the Ball Brothers."

"I don't know any Rashid."

Quint waited a few seconds and lifted the case over the man's crotch, holding the handle with only one finger. "My, this case is heavy. Better hurry, I think it's slipping," at which time the case fell, striking the man fully in his abdomen as he grunted in pain.

"Ooops... a little high, but I think we've got her bracketed now. I predict a bull's-eye next time."

Tears streamed from the man's eyes, and the spittle on his lips shook as he groaned, "No stop... no."

"Glad to oblige as long as we're talking... you know, really communicating. Okay, for the last time" he repeated the question a second time. The man just sat there. "Okay, bombs away."

"No. Stop," Quint caught the case, and Berto began babbling. "A few months ago, Rashid contacted me to buy my hunting camp north of Lafayette near Opelousas. It didn't make sense because the only reason to buy it was for hunting, and clearly, he's no hunter. The only thing my place offered him was remoteness, that and a big warehouse. Since New Orleans got trashed by Katrina, that's the only place I'd know to look." He quickly went on to provide Quint with directions to the lodge.

"Thanks. As I said, I'm a little pressed for time, but let's you and I have us a quick business discussion. It seems you're a loan shark, which I understand to be a common bottom feeder profession. But I just have to say, Berto, ol' boy, you've gotten a little carried away this time."

"LaRue owes me money, and he's going to pay."

"He has paid, much more than is reasonable. Do you want this briefcase full of LaRue's money?" Quint asked holding it over his crotch once again, "or do you prefer just to call the whole thing even and forget about it?"

Realizing what would happened if he said he wanted the briefcase, Berto replied, "LaRue and I are square. I won't give him any more trouble."

"Scout's honor?" Dawson chimed in.

"Yes. Just get your psycho partner to leave me alone."

"I'm afraid we can't do that since I don't believe you," Quint said, as he set the briefcase back on the desk. "You see, it's payback time. When we're done, unless you're even stupider than you look, you're going to forget all about my buddy LaRue to avoid a rematch with us."

LaRue, who had entered the room in time to enjoy Berto's unpleasant interrogation, slipped into the bathroom and added four grams of GHB, a date rape drug, to an energy drink. "I know you must be thirsty. Drink this," he said handing Berto the bottle.

Berto took a drink and spit it out on the floor. "What is this? It's really salty."

"Don't worry your ugly little head about what it is. You have 30 seconds to down it or have another round with the brief case," Quint replied. Berto tilted the bottle up and drained it, a horrible grimace on his face all the while. Within a few minutes, the drug began to take effect.

The bag Leo tossed on the bed was filled with an assortment of illegal drugs they had scored on a nearby street corner. He then placed a number of fetish and gay porn magazines around the room. Dawson and LaRue stripped the two thugs and piled them on the bed together, replacing the plastic ties after placing the men in an "interesting" position.

Quint called the local press with the room number and told them to be at the hotel in 15 minutes for a breaking story. He then dialed room service, "Could you please send a bucket of ice up? I seem to have injured myself. Tell the server to just come on in. I'm lying down now. And, oh, a Band-Aid or two would be nice." Next, he dialed the police to tip them off about a drug bust gone bad.

The team spent a minute cleaning up and wiping prints, and prepared to leave. "Well, Mr. Berto, it's been swell. Thanks," Quint said on his way to the door.

"Hey, you can't leave me here like this," Berto slurred.

"Oh really? Watch."

Dawson tripped the fire alarm on the ceiling and left the door propped open as he followed Quint out the door. "We don't want you to be lonely."

CHAPTER 43

"We've got a lead on where Rashid may have the bomb," Quint told Rogers and proceeded to give him the location. "We're in the van headed back to the chopper. Have a team of marines meet us a couple of miles from his hunting camp in an hour."

"Glad to see you guys," Quint said a short while later after landing beside a second chopper filled with angry jarheads.

"Jacobs," the colonel said brusquely without bothering to shake hands. "Fill me in." Quint quickly briefed him while one of Jacobs' marines handed out the weapons and Kevlar vests requested by Rogers.

"We'll land first. Your team will stand off and then land once the site is secure," Jacobs said. Quint nodded and climbed back into the chopper along with the rest of his team.

The two choppers flew over a heavily wooded area until they spotted lights around a large building in the distance. As they approached, Quint's pilot hovered in place while Jacobs' chopper descended. When the lead chopper was within a few feet of the ground, the marines spilled out, half heading for the hunting lodge and the rest for the warehouse. In seconds the helicopter was lifting back up with the gunner manning a heavy machine gun in the doorway as Rashid's men opened fire.

While returning fire, two marines headed for the windowless side of the warehouse where they placed a satchel charge and scurried for cover. After the charge detonated, the two marines rushed to the hole and lobbed in flash-bang grenades. A second later, several more marines blew through the front door and cleared the room of armed terrorists. Two scientists stood shaking, arms in the air, beside a large black object—Big Bertha. While two marines remained guarding it, the rest headed for the lodge where they could hear the sound of a fierce fire-fight raging between the rest of the marines and the well-armed terrorists hunkered down inside the heavy log structure.

The colonel directed four of the approaching marines to the chopper. A minute later, it came swooping back to rake the front of the lodge with the mini-gun, sending the terrorists fleeing the windows for cover. The marines on the ground maintained pressure while advancing.

The chopper's mini-gun raked the dormers on the lodge before disgorging the four marines onto the roof to enter the upstairs bedrooms. After quickly securing the second floor, they descended the stairs. The terrorists below fought furiously, refusing to surrender, and when the gunfire finally ceased, all were dead save one—Talib.

Only Talib's near superhuman strength saved him during Katrina. When the flood finally subsided, he was bruised and beaten but still alive. With Akmed, Omar, and the others dead or captured, Rashid had placed Talib in charge. Pleased to be in the position, he vowed not to repeat the mistakes of his predecessor.

When the first helicopter approached, Talib was halfway through his security patrol and took cover in the heavily wooded area outside the lodge clearing. With his men facing overwhelming opposition, he remained hidden as the fight unfolded. When it ended, he knew what he must do and headed for the bomb.

Quint stood with the two marines just inside the warehouse when Talib burst through the hole where the marines had breached the building. He headed for the bomb with his machine gun aimed directly at its nose and squeezed the trigger, sending a stream of lead ricocheting off the top of the bomb. With his finger glued to the trigger, he continued firing as he ran forward, chunks of metal flying off the bomb as he corrected his aim. In seconds, the bullets would find their mark.

Without hesitation, Quint raised his pistol and fired. Sensing the motion, Talib shifted far enough for the bullet to miss hitting him square in the torso where Quint had aimed. Instead, it passed through the upper part of his gun arm, deflecting his aim as he fired the remaining bullets. Talib dropped the empty weapon and turned to face Quint and the others with a defiant smile.

"Well, I almost sent all of us to meet Allah."

"Almost doesn't cut it. Sorry to spoil your fun, Talib, but it's over—we have the bomb back. Your killing and raping days are finished too. Time to pay for the trouble you've caused," Quint said. He hesitated for a moment and continued, "Why did you kill Lolo? She was no threat."

"Because I chose to," Talib said smiling. "Just like I chose to take your woman." Quint stood silently, his gun still pointed at Talib's head, his finger tightened on the trigger. "Go ahead, shoot. I'm betting your John Wayne good guy ideals won't let you. Or better yet, why not settle this as one warrior against another?"

"You are not a warrior, and you're not a soldier. The innocent women and children you kill aren't collateral damage. You murder them because you lack the courage, brains, and ability to take on real American men. You're cowards afraid of your own inadequacy, killing for sick pleasure, rationalizing it under the guise of a distorted view of Islam."

"Come on, don't you want a chance to even the score with me or do you lack the balls? I defiled your woman, for God's sake."

Seeing Quint struggle not to pull the trigger, Kira chimed in. "Quint, don't do it. You're not like him. You have nothing to prove; we've won. Leave this to our legal system." A wide grin spread across Talib's face.

"Yes, leave me to your impotent legal system. They'll probably award me damages."

"No. We're going to settle this right here, right now." Quint replied firmly, handing Dawson his gun as Talib stooped to pick up a large board, ignoring his bleeding arm.

"Quint, shoot him, don't play stupid games," Dawson urged, concerned the giant might win.

"I assure you, I'm not playing. This is about justice, pure and simple. At least to a point," Quint replied, continuing in a low voice. "If the bastard wins, kill him." Dawson answered with a firm nod as Quint picked up a heavy metal bar lying on the warehouse floor to fight the much larger and stronger man.

Facing each other the two men moved sideways, circling, each waiting for the other to make a move. Talib still had partial use of the arm that the bullet had passed cleanly through and wore a grin, relishing the chance to kill at least one more infidel. "Your woman was quite nice, at least the first few times. But after the rest had finished with her, I found her less... satisfying. Too bad, you won't live long enough to see what I mean."

Quint knew Talib wanted to use his own anger against him, but his rage had grown to a stage that he could instead channel to his benefit. The two men continued their dance as Talib spoke again. "It wasn't that long ago when I faced a man, a more worthy adversary, I might add. When I was done with him, I plunged my hand inside his chest, plucked out his still beating heart, and took a bite. Nothing is quite as satisfying as the warm flesh of your dying opponent."

"I'll consider that when you're lying dead," Quint replied, and Talib laughed with a mighty roar. Quint added, "You talk big for a man who resorts to rape to have a woman." This struck a nerve, and Talib stepped forward, stopping only as Quint raised the bar and swung it in a long arc, which Talib easily parried.

Quint landed a series of punches to Talib's face and stomach that would have brought most men to their knees. He continued facing off with Talib before swinging the bar. As it passed, Talib clipped Quint in the head with the board he wielded.

"Even if your men kill me after I send you to meet Allah, Rashid will never quit pursuing them, and when he finds them, he'll avenge me." The men continued sparring, with Quint's landing several good blows while Talib scored fewer but more powerful ones. Quint swung the bar again and after ducking, Talib stepped in and hit Quint in the head with a round house blow and jabbed him hard in his broken ribs. Quint gasped in pain as Talib retreated, allowing Quint a moment to recover, not wishing to end the fight too soon. Dawson aimed his pistol at Talib.

"Nooo," Quint croaked, fighting through the pain and struggling to clear his head while raising the bar back into position. Quint knew that he could not endure many more such blows and remain standing. The two men continued to parry, with Quint shifting to keep his cracked ribs farthest from Talib who was clearly enjoying toying with him. Quint would have to end this soon and decided on a desperate gamble. Twice more he swung the bar missing as expected both times and suffering two more blows from Talib in the process.

As Quint stepped closer to launch a third swing, he anticipated that Talib would lunge at him again as the bar swung by. So, Quint feinted, halting in mid-swing. Predictably, Talib sprang forward, and Quint continued his swing, slamming the bar down on Talib's shoulder breaking the collar bone with an audible snap. Without flinching, Talib continued forward intending to grab Quint by the neck using his other arm.

Quint dropped to a squat and swang the bar once more, striking Talib in the knee and shattering his knee cap, stopping him in his tracks. With Talib struggling to stand on his good leg, Quint rose and swung the bar again, this time hitting Talib at the base of his skull, stunning him. Relentlessly continuing his assault, Quint swang the bar once more and struck Talib hard in the chest, staggering him. Talib looked confused, struggling to breathe.

"This one's for Evie. And these are for Lolo and all the others who suffered at your hand," he said as he raised the bar again and again, bringing Talib to his knees. With his little voice screaming, "Stop," Quint lowered the crowbar. He looked down to see a sneer on Talib's face, and the image of Evie with Talib on top of her appeared in his mind re-igniting his rage.

"Ready to meet your virgins? This last one's for Evie, and the pain you caused her, you cowardly bastard," Quint said as he raised the bar.

"Quint! Don't do it. You'll regret it later," Kira yelled. Quint hesitated, turning his head toward her. They stood looking at each other for a moment.

"I know you're right," he replied and brought the bar down one last time with all of his might square in the middle of Talib's head. The bar cut a deep groove in Talib's skull down through his left eye where it came to rest nearly splitting his head in two. Talib stiffened and toppled backwards to the ground like a mighty fallen oak where he remained motionless, the bar still imbedded in his head. Still consumed by rage, Quint reached to grab the bar, to continue exacting his revenge when Dawson gently grabbed his arm. "It's over," he said, looking into his friend's eyes.

Quint met his gaze. "No, it's not over. But you're right, this part is done," Quint replied, clutching his ribs while catching his breath. He didn't bother to check Talib's neck for a pulse—it wasn't necessary. Quint looked up at the Colonel. "Well, I guess now I'll be facing murder charges."

The colonel stared back for a long moment then replied. "For what? He tripped. Most bizarre damned accident I've ever seen."

One by one, the rest of his men nodded, followed by Quint's team. Quint scanned their faces, the thanks plain on his face.

"You guys take any prisoners?" the colonel asked.

"Nope," his man replied as he joined them after interrogating the scientists. "They're all dead, refused to surrender. It appears that Rashid's scientists were just getting started disassembling the bomb when we arrived. Evidently, they were hired through a third party and don't know anything about Rashid."

Quint was about to comment when he was interrupted by a ringing cell phone. He located the source on one of the scientists and retrieved it. "Kelly's pool hall. Cold beer, great burgers, and clean balls."

A long pause followed before he heard Rashid's voice, "Quint! Damn you! How did you find my place?"

"Come on out here, and I'll tell you the whole story over a beer. I like it when we talk this way over one of your dead or captured men's cell phones. We've got the bomb back."

"You may have recovered it, but you won't stop me."

"Perhaps, but you won't be using Big Bertha. We *will* find you, and when we do, we *will* stop you. But go ahead and be cocky, it will make our job all the more fun."

"I will. The time has come for your country to atone for its sins, and I intend to administer the punishment."

"Wow, a true vision of grandeur for such a pathetic dreamer with little vision."

"You haven't heard the last of me," Rashid threatened as he crushed the foil-wrapped paper clip figure he held in his hand.

"Nor you of me," Quint said, as the line went dead.

Chapter 44

Rachel opened the door, excited about the meeting. She had dreamed about completing her transition into a woman for so long, it was hard to believe it was finally at hand.

Rashid smiled as he walked in, tossing his jacket and bag on the sofa with Rachel following behind fussing over him. "Can I get you a drink? Are you hungry? Or maybe there's something else I can do for you," she said coyly, though she knew Rashid was firm about waiting until her metamorphosis into a woman was complete before getting serious about their relationship.

"No, thank you, I can't stay long. We must use what little time we have wisely. First of all, thank you for helping us. You did your part to feed us information from Rogers' office. While we weren't successful, it was through no fault of yours. Your transmitter idea was brilliant and would have worked great had I not been working with idiots," Rashid said. Rachel looked confused, like she had no idea what he was talking about. Unfortunately, there was no time to question her.

"That brings us to the next item of discussion?" Rachel said, encouraging him to continue.

"Yes, it's time to make good on my promise to fulfill your dream of becoming a woman. Close your eyes," Rashid said opening his bag.

Rachel obeyed, trembling with excitement, a shiver running up her spine. *Is the bag filled with cash? Does he have one of those Cayman Island numbered accounts for me and maybe a bottle of champagne to celebrate? Could it be a plane ticket for a prepaid visit to that California plastic surgeon I mentioned?* The questions flooded her mind as she heard him fumbling in his bag. Then she caught a whiff of an odd odor and felt him place a wet cloth over her face.

The chloroform did its work quickly, and Rashid laid Rachel on the floor. Sweeping the centerpiece, napkin holder, and placemats aside, he flipped the dining room table upside down. Rachel was a loose end that simply had to be tidied up. Leaving her free to go about wagging her tongue was far too risky.

Rachel awoke groggy and confused. Lying naked, face-up gagged and bound to the table legs of her upside down table. Something was horribly wrong. Frantically, she looked about for an explanation and saw Rashid seated beside her in a dining room chair with his bag atop a small end table beside him.

Rashid sat silently, watching her shivering. It was not from being naked in the cool room—it was from fear. He stared at her unblinking for several minutes before his face broke into a sadistic grin. He reached into the bag and withdrew a surgical scalpel, its mirrored surface gleaming in the light of the dining room chandelier.

"Though you may be an infidel, I am a man of my word and will deliver on my promise to help complete your transformation into a woman. But I see no need to waste thousands of dollars in travel costs, surgeon's fees, and hospital expenses to accomplish what we can do ourselves right here. The transformation you have looked forward to for so very long is about to happen."

He rose to stand over her with the raised scalpel. Rachel struggled against her bonds, her eyes opened wide in horror. She screamed through the gag as he squatted beside her and began.

"Sorry, there was a wreck on the freeway, and we got caught in traffic," Quint apologized for being over an hour late.

No problem," Rogers replied, dismissing the issue with a wave of his hand and changing the subject. "You guys earned your fee and then some. The funds are ready to be wired to your account just as we agreed."

"Thanks, but hold off on the bonus. Once we get a little further along, we want to throw an idea at you that we're still working on," Quint said, and changed the subject before Rogers could start asking questions about the Cuban island he wasn't quite ready to answer. "I hate that Rashid slithered away. Any word on him?" Quint asked.

"Nope. I've run his name back through our computers again and no banana. Most of his guys ended up dead, and I'm convinced that the few we managed to catch alive don't know enough to help us find him. The only real lead we had was the hunting lodge, but that was a dead end too. After working through several layers of shell corporations, we found that it's owned by a defunct company in Brazil, of all places. Rashid is like a ghost; he doesn't seem to exist. We know he's operating under an alias, but aside from Evie, no one has ever seen him."

Rogers paused for a minute, and looked at Dawson as he continued. "Rachel is dead."

"How did it happen?" Quint asked.

"She was murdered. They found her bound and gagged; she bled to death. While she never truly became a woman, she was no longer a man at the time of her death," Rogers said somberly, declining to go into further detail. "It appears that she was serving as the mole within our organization in exchange for Rashid's promise to help her complete her metamorphosis."

"And he killed her?" Dawson asked.

"Probably. But without knowing it, she was serving as Botz's double agent too," Rogers replied.

"Huh?" Dawson asked.

"Our techie folks talk to the military techie folks. Evidently, after we delivered the Internet-monitoring software, Botz arranged to keep Rashid under surveillance. From what I've pieced together, he discovered that Rachel was a mole and used her to his advantage as a conduit to feed Rashid information making certain that you played your 'bait' role well.

"He 'spoofed' her e-mail address and sent an e-mail to Rashid regarding planting a transponder aboard your ship. Botz wanted to make certain Rashid fell into his trap and placed the device so Rashid could track you. He orchestrated things to make it appear as if Rachel had arranged to have the device installed. Of course, Rashid was only too happy to be able to track *Searcher* and didn't ask questions.

"Botz intended to track you guys via satellite, using the transponder as a backup so that he could swoop in by helicopter once Rashid made his move to hijack the bomb. Of course, his plan went awry when Katrina entered the mix, screwing up his satellite surveillance and preventing him from flying out to intervene. There was no mole on your ship," Rogers said.

"That makes sense. The transmitter we found had a built-in GPS, which transmitted our position autonomously until Kira discovered and disconnected it. And Botz knew where it was planted, even though we had told no one."

"But when could Botz have hidden it?" Dawson asked.

Quint thought for a moment. "He could have planted it that day I surprised him on the ship."

"Good ol' Colonel Botz. Just like the Grail episode in Venezuela, he used us as bait, only this time the wheels *really* fell off his finely crafted plan, and once again he left us holding the bag. Care to explain why the hell you didn't tell us about Botz?"

"We were working hard to plug the leak. I suspected Botz was involved, but I honestly didn't know for sure until it was too late to do you any good. I guess the military decided that none of us had a need to know. I understand why Botz did what he did, but I'm not happy either."

"Where is he, by the way?" Dawson said with a cold look.

"I have no idea. He was supposed to come by, but after I mentioned that you guys were going to be here for an 8 a.m. meeting, he may have delayed to avoid an unpleasant encounter."

"Well, you tell him that this isn't over," Dawson said angrily and stormed out of Rogers' office with Quint trailing behind. He walked to the lobby and stabbed the elevator button nearly breaking it and his finger, continuing to vent while they waited.

"At least that dumb SOB could have let us in on what he was doing. I hate being the lamb tied to the stake as lion bait." Quint nodded.

The elevator doors opened, and Dawson started to enter, nearly colliding with a man trying to exit—Botz. Dawson froze in the elevator doorway as the two men stood face-to-face, Dawson staring daggers at the colonel.

"I t-take it you j-just finished meeting with R-Rogers. Sorry things didn't go as p-planned," Botz stuttered.

"Well that certainly squares things," Dawson replied sarcastically, as he fought the elevator doors' repeated attempts to close, ignoring its impatient dinging chime.

"Let me explain," Botz said.

"Don't try to defend the indefensible," Dawson interrupted.

Ignoring him, Botz continued, "While we wanted the bomb, we wanted Rashid and his gang nearly as much. Even if we got the bomb, it wouldn't stop him. So yes, I used you as bait to make certain that we not only found the bomb but nailed Rashid as well."

"You were planting that transmitter the day I caught you on the ship, weren't you?" Botz grinned without answering Quint.

"Well, in case you didn't notice, your stupid plan cost us our ship and damned near our entire team."

"My plan would've worked if not for that bitch Katrina," Botz replied.

"Yeah, well maybe you should have considered that beforehand."

"Take it up with my superiors."

"Your superiors? Well now, that doesn't narrow the field much, does it?" Dawson replied.

"I don't have time for this shit. Go cry me a river," Botz shot back, shouldering past Dawson.

Already enraged, Dawson saw red. He reached out and spun Botz around by the shoulder, hitting him squarely in the jaw with a solid punch, nearly lifting him off the ground. Botz staggered for a moment, and fell backwards to land hard, out cold, in the elevator lobby.

"Dawson, you're making a habit of that," Quint said, as Dawson smiled and stepped into the elevator rubbing his knuckles.

CHAPTER
45

South of the railroad tracks, miles of coiled razor wire marked the security zone along the Mississippi Gulf Coast. National Guard troops were stationed to stave off looters who swarmed like locusts once Katrina passed. As Quint approached the checkpoint manned by the National Guard, he lowered his window and felt the molten heat flood into the car. Chainsaws in the distance sounded like angry hordes of gigantic bees. The smell of rot filled the air from vegetables, food, animals, and even bloated human corpses still hidden in the debris.

"A little breeze wouldn't be so bad now," Quint said with a smile as he flashed the permit that Rogers had managed to get for him to gain entrance.

"No, the heat is brutal, and with this humidity, the sweat just sits there," the guard replied as he checked the pass. The weary man motioned for Quint to proceed while wiping the sweat from his face with a dirty rag. Quint reached into the cooler in his passenger seat and withdrew two icy-cold waters.

"Here's one for you and your buddy." The soldier nodded gratefully and had downed most of his bottle by the time he faded from sight in the rearview mirror. Quint had arrived just before dawn, and as they flew in over the coast, was amazed at the absence of any lights—the power had not yet been restored.

Down on the beach road, the devastation was overwhelming. An entire house sat blocking one lane of the road where it had come to rest. The yellow-orange ends of stumps shone in the bright sunlight, where downed trees had been cleared to permit traffic to resume on the major arteries. Quint slowly navigated around a seemingly endless array of obstacles, ranging from an enormous casino barge that blocked part of the highway, to dumpsters, sailboats, and debris of every description.

Despite the hot August sun, Quint left the windows down, awed by the scene before him. As he proceeded west, the smell of rotting chickens, disgorged by a refrigerated warehouse at the nearby port, was nearly overpowering. Quint pulled his t-shirt over his mouth and nose until he made it past the worst of it.

Everywhere he looked to the north were piles of lumber where houses and buildings once stood demolished as if by some giant's errant foot. The trees that still remained standing were devoid of leaves, their naked branches seemingly raised in despair. By the time he made it to Pass Christian, the scene had become repetitious.

Quint crossed his fingers as he approached the marina where he had left his boat. Hardly a marina any longer, the basin was filled with a jumble of debris, wrecked boats, and battered pilings. Then on the north side of the beach road, he saw *Mojito*—or what was left of her. She lay on her side just below the old Hancock Bank building, the tuna tower bent at a crazy angle and the glass salon windows broken out.

Despite the fact that he knew things would be bad, he was not prepared for the sight of her lying broken and ruined. He stood before the dead boat, unable to bring himself to enter. He felt there was little reason to do so; it did not appear much would be salvageable. Deciding there was nothing else to be done, he returned to his rental car. Tomorrow, he would call the insurance company, then figure out how to dispose of the wrecked hull if the clean up crews had not already taken care of the issue by then.

Quint stopped by Mrs. Evers' house finding nothing remaining but a slab. A few slabs down, he found an elderly couple combing through the debris in their yard looking for any personal items which might have survived the storm. They confirmed what Quint had feared, Mrs. Evers did not make it. Though it made him sad, he hoped at least now she would find peace.

Quint then turned up a side street to pay his respects to his beloved Road Runner, certain that it too had fallen victim to Katrina. He drove slowly, constantly swerving around piles of rubbish with his fingers crossed that he could avoid picking up a nail in his tires. As he neared the shop where he had left the car to have the windshield repaired, he pulled to far side and parked. He saw the owner cleaning up debris and waved.

"Wondered if you were ever coming back. Sort of hoped you weren't. I'd love to have that beauty as my own."

Quint's heart raced. "You mean it's not trashed?"

"Nope," he replied while walking toward the four bay garage. "If you notice, we're on a slight rise, evidently enough to keep us above the cresting flood waters. The end of the building got messed up when that big live oak went down, but your pride and joy was in the middle bay and escaped unscathed," he said opening the heavy metal door. There inside stood the bright orange Plymouth, gleaming except for a few leaves that had stuck to the car when it was wet.

"Sorry, didn't have time to wash her but already had the windshield replaced before the storm. She's good to go." Quint paid him for the repair and arranged for a shop worker to return the rental car. He transferred his personal items from the rental car, sat down in the driver's seat and fired up the big hemi engine. Quint would return to the Keys in style.

Three months after Katrina, Quint and the team were back on the Coast with a leased ship to continue their treasure hunt. Only this time it was not a cover—it was for real.

Quint took the small boat they had leased for a tender and headed out to Cat Island hoping to find Jacques, but not optimistic. As he idled down the bayou, the afternoon quiet was broken by the sound of his outboard engine. A prehistoric-looking alligator cruised in the bayou, only its eyes, nose, and the ridge of its tail breaching the surface. It stopped near the bank, remaining motionless before slowly submerging beneath the calm surface as Quint approached.

Ahead, he spotted Jacques sitting outside a large tent drinking a beer. "Up for some company?"

"Sure. Beer?"

"When have I ever turned it down?" Quint said, as he tied up alongside a small barge filled with construction materials. He climbed off and gratefully accepted the beer taking a long pull. "I heard you'd set up operations here again."

"Yeah, Katrina destroyed my house, but I was determined not to let her win and decided to pitch this tent while I got started rebuilding," he said, gesturing at the small barge he had started to unload. "You picked a nice time to come back. The mosquitoes aren't too bad, courtesy of this cooler weather. So, what brings you out here?"

"We're headed out tomorrow to relocate that snag where LaRue thought he had located cannons. Want to join us?"

"Shoot, try to keep me away," Jacques replied.

The team was excited by the fond memories they had shared during their successful treasure salvage of the *Almiranta* as they headed out the following day.

Quint smiled to see Kira's hand resting on her stomach, protecting the baby within, while Colin held his arm around her shoulders. The process that began in Venezuela had matured, and they were now a team tempered by experience.

"It seems like forever since we were here. I hope it'll be worth it," Dawson said, donning his dive gear. He sported a new tooth replacing the one Willy had pulled for him.

"Wait til you see dos big-assed cannons," LaRue replied with a wide grin.

A minute later the two men splashed over the side, with the team lined up along the rail eagerly awaiting news of what lay in the murky waters below. They swam down the buoy line and reached the bottom where visibility was only a few inches. Working their way south toward the main part of the wreck LaRue had marked, Dawson encountered a "cannon."

The deck of the search boat above was wrapped in silent anticipation as the divers broke the surface. Dawson swung back his mask and inflated his vest. Floating on the surface, he looked up at the team eagerly lined along the deck. Unable to stand it any longer, Leo spoke first, "You find it?"

"Oh, we found it all right. We found a whole load of LaRue's cannons. Of course, I would call them pipe. Folks, what we have here is a whole barge load of them." A chorus of exhales and more than a few expletives followed Dawson's pronouncement, as the team glared at LaRue. Kira, unable to keep from laughing, walked toward the front of the boat to avoid offending LaRue.

Embarrassed, LaRue began to rationalize, "Look, it was rough, dos seas were beating us up, da visibility was damned near zero, I was in a hurry..."

"Save it, LaRue. You screwed up, but it could have happened to any of us. Come on, let's get out of here," Quint said.

"What now?" Dawson asked drying off with a towel after ditching his gear on the back deck.

"We go home and regroup. We came prepared to salvage, not search," Quint replied.

Evie finished her meeting with the therapist she was seeing at Quint's insistence to cope with the horror wrought by Rashid's thugs and drove directly to the airport, arriving just as Quint's plane touched down.

"This is a treat, being picked up by a beautiful woman after another boring flight. Let me buy you lunch," Quint offered as he gave her a peck on the cheek. Their intimacy had suffered after the sexual abuse Evie had endured. Though Quint understood, he was worried that she seemed to be making little progress in putting the horrible episode behind her. They drove in silence to El Siboney where they entered the restaurant and chose the table that offered the most privacy.

After the waitress disappeared to place their orders, Quint looked at Evie. "You okay?"

She paused for a minute, collecting her thoughts. "No, I'm not, I don't know if I ever will be after what those beasts did..." She paused as her voice broke and her eyes teared.

"Evie, we'll get through this we..."

"No Quint, I don't believe we will. You've been wonderful and understanding, more than anyone could expect, it's just me, I..."

"Evie, you've been through hell and handled it better than most," Quint replied, stopping as the waitress delivered their lunch. They ate in silence, both deep in thought. Quint could never admit that he, too, still struggled to put the episode out of his mind. But it hung there, like storm clouds on the horizon. He was not just being understanding when he avoided placing pressure on Evie for sex. He was disinterested and hated himself for it.

Evie finished, and as she set her fork down, seemed to have reached a decision. "Quint, as I said, you've been wonderful; it's not you, it's me. Every time we're together things will be going great, and I start thinking about what we shared in the past. Then, suddenly, I'm back in that dilapidated warehouse being raped all over again."

"But Evie, I've made a point not to make you feel pressured, I—"

"And you haven't, like I said, it's me, not you. I feel dirty every time I even think of sex, and I am so filled with hate toward those animals. I've just got to work through this... on my own. I need time, and I need to do this by myself. Quint, we need to break things off. I haven't wanted to say this... I hate saying it, but I know it's true.

"Even my highly paid therapist agrees. I have to separate my feelings for us from what happened, and I can't do that together. I'm sorry."

Unsure what to say, Quint fumbled for the right words. "Evie, take all the time you need. I'll wait, no matter how long it takes. I'll wait. I love you."

Evie smiled, then abruptly stood to leave. "I've got to go. I hope you don't mind calling a cab. Thanks... thanks for understanding," she said then turned and left. Quint understood and would wait. He just wished he were certain they would have a future.

"It's been so long I figured that maybe I wouldn't have to deliver on the considerable bonus I promised after finding the bomb turned into recovering it, fighting off terrorists, jettisoning it, and then recovering it a second time," Rogers said as he answered Quint's phone call.

"I wasn't too worried about you reneging. Instead of paying us the bonus you offered, we want you to try to get the Feds to negotiate the purchase of a small island off the coast of Cuba as part of the deal and sign it over to us. We'll need complete autonomy to operate as we please with regard to the Cubans and the U.S. Government—in writing, thank you, please."

"You don't want much."

"I guess we're about to find out just how much stroke you've got. We need it, particularly if you want us involved in future projects," he said, continuing to explain their thoughts. "I know that U.S.-Cuban relations have thawed, at least behind the scenes. I also know they're very cash-starved, so we think it's doable."

"I damned well hope you're right. I'll see what I can do," Rogers replied. Quint was silent for a minute before continuing.

"You knew we wouldn't find that ship, didn't you?" Quint asked.

"Are you complaining that the deal didn't pay well enough?" Rogers asked with a smile.

"That's not the point. You threw that old wreck into the mix to close the deal."

"At the time, I would have lied to my own mother to keep that bomb from being detonated and killing thousands. Look Quint, I'll admit I knew it was a long shot that you would find the shipwreck but you *could* have. And it could have been the *El Cazador*. Despite not finding the wreck, I believe you were still handsomely rewarded for your efforts."

"That, my friend, is a matter of perspective. You aren't the one who damned near got killed in a job that ended up being a whole lot bigger than was agreed and which cost us our ship."

"Yes, and we've agreed to replace your rusted-out oilfield supply vessel with a much newer and better one when you locate what you want. And I'm going to try to make your Cuba island deal work out. But if that's not good enough, I already have a plan to make it up to you. See, we've got this other job…"

About the Author

Award-winning author, Frank J. Wilem, Jr., is an entrepreneur living in Gulfport, Mississippi, with his wife, Dee Dee, and daughter, Brittany. Frank's love for the sea blossomed during his high school years at West High in Torrance, California, when a friend persuaded him to snorkel off Lunada Bay in Palos Verdes. When it was his turn to use the mask, he took one look beneath the chilly Pacific waters, and he was hooked. After graduating from Texas A&M with a bachelor of science degree in electrical engineering, he followed the call of the ocean to the University of Miami, where he earned a master's degree in ocean engineering.

Frank worked in the R&D departments for two Fortune 500 companies before his love of the ocean led him to join Computer Sciences Corporation at NASA's Stennis Space Center. He left there to become a founder of Triton Systems, Inc., which he and his partners grew into a $100 million company and the nation's largest manufacturer of automatic teller machines.

With the sale of Triton, Frank purchased his sportfish boat, *Vixen,* and pursued his passion for bluewater fishing. Most days he and Captain Eric Gill can be found in the northern waters of the Gulf of Mexico or the Bahamas, chasing billfish, tuna, wahoo and dolphin.

The Pass is Frank's second book. His first book, *The Keys*, received a gold medal IPPY award.

Notes from the Author

The incident involving the midair collision between a B-47 and an F-86 Sabre jet in 1958, which resulted in the jettisoning of a nuclear bomb, is true. The B-47 took off from Homestead Air Force Base in Florida and landed at Hunter Army Air Field in Georgia after jettisoning its bomb. As of the writing of this book, the bomb is still missing. I should note that, unlike in my book, the fighter pilot did survive.

For the purposes of my story, I have the incident occurring off the coast of Louisiana and Mississippi. It should be noted that Barksdale Air Force Base did have a wing of B-47s flying in the 1950s and that the Naval Air Station in Belle Chasse, Louisiana, did have a wing of F-86 Saber jets flying in the late 1950s. Also, the Belle Chasse airstrip is long enough to land a B-47.

The Magnolia Hotel in Pass Christian was built on the site of the Pass Christian Hotel, which burned down after the Civil War. The Magnolia followed suit and burned down in 1915, never to be rebuilt.

The Tarpon Beacon ceased publication in the early 1990s. One and possibly two people actually did disappear at Port Eads during Hurricane Katrina and are presumed to be dead.

The wreck *El Cazador*, The Hunter, was discovered by Jerry Murphy from Pascagoula, Miss., aboard his boat, *Mistake,* 200 years later while he was commercial fishing. Research in the Brussels archives of the Indies in Seville, Spain, enabled them to identify the wreck. Five and one half tons of silver coins were recovered.

Even though a considerable amount of effort went into editing the book, I'm sure we missed some things, and I welcome any comments about problems you note in this book or suggestions you might have for Quint's future adventures. You may forward them through my web site: www.FrankWilem.com.

I hope you like the book's characters, as I plan to bring most of them back in another sequel already in the works. If you are interested, you can find an excerpt on the web site from my next book.